THE JOHN DONNE
EXPERIMENT

THE JOHN DONNE
EXPERIMENT

STUART McLEAN

TANTANOOLA

© Stuart McLean 2018

First published in 2018 by TANTANOOLA
a literary imprint of
Australian Scholarly Publishing Pty Ltd
7 Lt Lothian St Nth, North Melbourne, Vic 3051

Tel: 03 9329 6963 / Fax: 03 9329 5452
enquiry@scholarly.info / www.scholarly.info

ISBN 978-1-925801-38-5

For Magaret Ray Ritchie Murray, who taught me about faeries, flowers and the voices in the woods. And for Tam McCulloch, the shepherd of the silver light, R.I.P.

Preface

This story contains many incontestable truths:

These days, too many people spend too much time in bizarre, imaginary factories inside their heads. Technology is entirely to blame. Instead of emancipating the human race the machines have, once more, enslaved it.

Hardly anyone stops and stares at the trees anymore. Bound to city, work, or the television, reduced to interacting with the world via the artificial brains in their pockets, so many people have become estranged from the wisdom of the natural world. Their loss is the lover's gain.

Humans do make far too much noise in places that should be silent. Listen and you will hear them, shouting, leaf blowing, and building; always building. What for, I'm not sure. Nothing is permanent except change.

All things must pass.

I had and continue to have a rich dialogue with the voices inside my head. There is nothing wrong with this, so I've been informed by sources far more learned than myself. Apparently, everyone has these voices. They form our subconscious minds. I just gave mine form, name and character. In the end, they all turned out to be nutters.

Yes, I should've married The One, and, yes, I did wait for her every night down the beach, for two long, sore years. As my reflection once told me, however, I dodged a bullet. Hard as it still is to accept, I hope The One and FTC are happy.

Aye, sure thing.

I think about Jackie every day, usually at dawn when the big sky is streaked with silver, pink and amber clouds. I still hear you whistle, my lovely little black and white bird, and I keep one of your feathers in my inside jacket pocket, close to my heart. Jackie, I'm very sorry for what happened in the forest but as a wise aviator such as you knows, kindness often does kill. My love is your love, and your song is still honey to me – sweeter than the first time we whistled together.

There was a book and it was very difficult to write. The factory inside my head did collapse for a while but that was Mr Fang's fault, our fault, it can now be said in hindsight. There were so many words, millions and millions and millions of the things. They bled from my fingers, dribbled from my mouth and rained down from the black clouds that besieged the blue cottage for months on end. Things did turn a bit mad; a bit odd. But, as we learned, madness was vital to the factory and, therefore, the ultimate success or failure of The John Donne Experiment. The book mattered then because it fuelled some piston of meaning. Lunacy blazed on the horizon and I'm not ashamed to admit that I sprinted for it. They – whoever they are* – do say everyone has a novel inside of them. What they forget to mention is that it's most probably shit.

Damned book. It almost got published. One firm "loved it" but insisted that there was no market for literary fiction in Australia. Today, they said, "people didn't want to have to think when reading a book". One of the big dogs also liked it but asked me to change. I had the following strange conversation with one of their slaves, on a telephonic device:

"The start is a bit slow. It drags." This from some young, rude person that had probably never read a real book made of paper. "Can you change it?"

"Which bit?"

"The start."

"All of it?"

"Yes. The first five chapters. It's only 20,000 words."

Grimace. "But, it's literary fiction. You're not meant to get it straight

---

* The Fates? The Furies? The Muses? Or, more likely, some secret inner circle of publishers that meet in a dark basement, drink expensive wine, smoke fat cigars, worship J.K. Rowling, and sacrifice aspiring author's souls. (BTW, thanks a fucking bunch J.K. Everyone is looking for the next "you". You and your Tolkien-for-kid rip-offs about gay wizards totally ruined it for us amateurs. "Oh, I suffered when writing Harry," Queen Rowling claims. Bollocks she did! Try dying while living in a mice-infested house in a bitter jungle with nothing to eat but your toenails. That's suffering, baby).

away." Silence. "You have to work at it." More silence. "Give it time, like a renaissance painting, or an complex piece of classical music."

"A book must have P.T.Q. From page one."

"What is P.T.Q.?"

"Page turning quality. From page one. Or we won't publish it."

Was that a threat? "Rachmaninoff didn't dive in, did he? He built compositions slowly, masterfully. He lured the audience in … then, BANG!"

"I've never read any books by Rachmaninoff."

"He's not a writer. He's one of the finest composers of the twentieth century."

"Oh," he said. "Rachmaniwho?"

In the end, I'm glad that publisher and I drifted apart.

Sod it. Move on. Close, but no cigar. Let it go.

Back to it, lad. Many more mountains to climb.

Several more truths:

On the continent of man, many invisible ropes throttle many visible people. It doesn't matter if a human is fatally attached to a career, family, a soul-sucking mortgage, or to drugs, booze or exercise; whatever. Ropes are ropes. They strangle the true purpose and meaning of our short lives on the blue planet – to breathe, relax, and enjoy the moment.

The ropes are not real, though. "Our lives are nothing but dreams and images," as the venerable Jalāl ad-Dīn Muhammad Rūmī accurately noted, way back in the thirteenth century. How little has changed. Reality still has no form to it. It's nothing but a mass, common delusion. It is nothing more than a big, bad dream.

During The Experiment, I kept seeing beautiful islands. I still really don't know why they appeared (probably something to do with that shifty John Donne character). The islands were like so many dots scattered across a vast ocean. Lots and lots of dots, just as the Old People saw and painted; just as Blake, Dali and Hoffman dreamed about.

I loved those islands, and I still see the dots.

Fuck is one of the most versatile and onomatopoeic words in the English language. For people that do difficult, oppressive and underpaid work – labourers, teachers, toilet cleaners, bin men, gravediggers, and writers, for example – fuck is a very common, useful and popular word. It should be given a knighthood. As a Scotstralian man, I use the word a lot, as in "Father, I'm very fucking sorry for using the word fuck a lot."

The word cunt is even better. You will read it exactly sixty-one times in this book. It's a hard, evil word and is not employed as to be derogatory towards woman. Ninety-nine per cent of the time, this marvellous, onomatopoeic word is associated with Frederick, The Cunt. Evil men deserve evil swear words.

Is the Mother character in this story Oedipal? Not quite; more of your 1960s crooner Dean Martin type. "I say a man who loves his mother, is man enough for me," as we heard Dean sing, over and over and over again. Those, his, human sounds were dreadful aberrations. Foul, vulgar chords struck daily against the serenity of the rainforest.

Oscar speech:

Some humans deserve thanks. For wisdom, friendship and taking me places I'd only dreamed of, Micha Lerner. A real desert father, the sage surfer is everywhere in this book. I never left his company without learning something. Dhara des Fours, the princess from Murwillumbah Castle, for helping keep my nose just above water when I almost drowned. In the end, her enthusiasm, interest and humour were the most important ropes. To the reading crew, Jeff, Gav, Lou, Cat, Pat, Andy, Jana and Laura, I raise to you many flagons brimming with goon.

And, finally, Andrew McKenzie, Esquire, is a noisy, invasive, kind, gorgeous little man. I'm still not sure about the god he kept trying to ram down our throats, however. Andrew, to point out the obvious, the Almighty Being isn't very good at appearing, is He or She or whatever gender The Omnipotent One is? No one on the island ever did get that with mainstream religious people: if God is everywhere then what are they looking for? They claim that the truth will set you free.

That is a lie.

What is truth? Does it liberate or condemn a person? Does it exult or imprison the soul? And, why do billions of humans doubt, probe and push it all the time, often dangerously so? I suppose the poet Wilde got close when he wrote that that truth is "rarely pure and never simple...".

...or kind, or clean, or sometimes that easy to believe.

This story, this book, is an attempt to explain what happened during the two and half years I spent in the jungle, experimenting on a daily with pain and beauty. It is a love letter to Binjari*, our beautiful Mother. Binjari – the word still makes me feel funny. I found it very difficult to say goodbye to Her. In the end, however, when forced apart by bad things, the laws of man, or cruel people, true lovers never really mean goodbye. They really mean, thank you.

Thank you, Mother.

This book is the end of things: alcohol, addiction, madness, ego, and bachelorhood. It is an epitaph to a long youth, a tombstone to the ascetic life, to a time marked largely by suffering.

When I edit this book (and edit, and edit, and edit – old habits die hard), I see that it's partly a story about pain. I know that I hurt poor Fingal. This form of torture bothered me for a while because I am not a dark man. I do remember how to smile. Why did I keep hurting my hero? Why all the suffering? Well, pain is vital to our simple lives. It has to be embraced if beauty and love are to be experienced correctly, for it provides balance.

Pain made me mad, and madness woke me up.

In the end, The Experiment proved three things. First, the person who knows nothing is the wisest. Second, the human who owns nothing is the richest. And, third, it is not the darkness that most people are afraid of. It is the light. We thrive and suffer in the darkness, as we have done ever since the advent of fucking civilisation (an oxymoron if ever there was one). To shine, a human must burst from the darkness like a dying star. We must, as you shall read, cut the ropes between our beautiful islands and the so-called real world.

Only then can the light blaze inside us.

Only then can the light act as a beacon to others.

---

* In the old tongue, Binjari roughly translates as spring, or brook. In Scotstralian language, it means a dear, wise eagle that nests on Burleigh Hill.

I'm happy that the ascetic life is over, though. It was a tough shift and, gladly, the light is bleeding back into my life now, all be it slowly. I need a shower, a new bird (maybe), and some human, simian company (also maybe). It'll take a while to come out of the woods.

I don't care. It took a while to go in.

I love you, Jackie-bird.

All hail the Mighty Strangler Fig.

S.M.

A place,

Somewhere on planet Earth.

August 2015

PHASE I
Homo Languere – The Man Who is Tired

Chapter One
Bazza

The birdsong was everywhere yet no bird could be seen. It was an odd, haphazard song. There was no order, civility or melody to it, just random waves of loud, terrifying screeches, sinister cackles and long, bizarre peeeeee-oows. The sounds were quite foreign to the polite twittering of the wren, nightingale and blackbird the man grew up with. It was a raw, irreverent, and confident song; an Australian song.

The forest was equally curious. Oak, beech, and willow exude majesty, grace and wisdom but all that grew here seemed lost to anarchy. Most of trees were young, drab and crooked things with lithe, grey arms and jade pompoms waving inanely against the huge, pale sky. Many bore the scars of storms and bushfires past – sheared limbs or black, charred trunks – and many trees were dead; stark, white skeletons. The understory, a mess of ferns, vines and invasive lantana bushes, wasn't much better. In reality, the rainforest looked nothing like the postcards the tourists bought down the coast. Everything looked a bit scruffy.

A river swooshed overhead. The man looked up, and realised it was just the wind playing tricks on his ruined mind. Cool and brisk, the wind swirled amongst the jade foliage. It rushed through the canopy, tearing loose thousands of dead yellow leaves that fell to the cold ground, dancing and twirling one last time. The sun rode low on the horizon. More silver than gold, it hid behind the trees, its meek light casting black lacework shadows across the driveway where the man stood, stranded. "Winter," Fingal McKay noted. "Nothing grows in winter."

The doors of a removal truck slammed shut and the driver ambled across the white gravel driveway to where Fingal stood gazing at the awesome forest. "Righto, mate," he shouted (in the new world fashion the driver bellowed rather than spoke). "That's the last of the boxes. You just gotta unpack them now, mate. Bit of work, mate. Bit of nesting."

Mate, mate, mate, mate, mate. "Terrific. Thank you."

"She's a bit remote up here," the driver continued, roaring.

Why do people have to shout in temples? thought Fingal. *Sshhhhhhh.*

"Mindya, I could do with a few months in the bush. Stuck down the coast. Bills coming out me arse. Got a big, bloody mortgage and a big, cranky wife. Expecting our third kid anytime soon." The driver gathered his courage. "But, mate, I've got me shed. And a dog."

"Sounds ideal," Fingal replied, quietly.

"You married, mate?"

Weren't you meant to be leaving? "No."

"What do you do for a living?"

"It's complicated." In the last ten years of travel and study Fingal had worked as a bricky's labourer, a bar tender, a cleaner of lavatories, a shelf-stacker and, oddly, a large chicken (in George Street, with a sign for some jewellers that said "you won't believe our clucking low, low prices"). "Today, however." Fingal frowned at the trees. "I intend to turn myself into an island of a man. Not a real island," he qualified, still staring at the trees, still trying to locate the birds snickering at him. "A relative island. It is the only way to find meaning in life. As an island. Alone."

"You been on the mole, mate?"

Fingal turned to the driver, some bloke with receding ginger hair, sleeve tattoos, and a yellow, high-visibility shirt with a name badge sewn over his heart: Bazza.

"Listen, Bazza," Fingal said with a curt smile. "I don't mean to sound rude" – *but I will* – "but I'd like to be left alone now. I've work – science – to begin." By work he meant drinking beer, and by science, staring at things. The driver said and did nothing, so Fingal added. "My experiment of living *alone* in a sub-tropical Australian rainforest has actually commenced."

That got him. "Tropical," Bazza said.

"What?"

"It's a tropical forest, mate."

"Sub-tropical."

"Tropical, *mate*."

"I think you'll find, *Bazza*, that we're standing in a sub-tropical rainforest," Fingal continued, gently, trying to keep the lid on his strong, Gaelic accent, as well as his growing anger at the world of man; his world. "The tropical rainforest begins above the *Tropic* of Capricorn."

"What would you know, mate? You're a bloody Jock, aren't you?"

And, bang. There it was – a healthy dose of Australian passive aggression, topped off with the "mate" cherry, so as not to cause too much offence. Fingal wanted to ask the driver about this strange social custom, about its origins, and about whether being on a constant aggressive footing was a good or a bad thing for a person, a community and a nation? He also wanted to tell Bazza that they *were* standing in a sub-tropical rainforest. Fingal knew this because he'd read a book about the Binjari Plateau, written by an academic, an expert. And, more importantly, he wanted to ask "what's wrong with being a Jock?" Christ, on account of his aggression, red hair, and milk-bottle white skin, there was a very good chance that Bazza's forbearers were from Ireland or Scotland. And besides, the whole bloody Lucky Country was built on immigration. Even the Old People came here by boat!

Fingal was about to mention these points but, to his horror, Bazza had reached into his pocket and produced an insidious device: a Samsung XT500 min-tablet Ver. 6.2/3 smart phone, which he began stroking and touching and prodding. "Ha, see," the driver cried after a moment, waving the infernal device in Fingal's face. "Binjari is a tropical rainforest."

The Scotsman, who just wanted to be left alone, recoiled. He despised the machines. A traditionalist, a luddite, some may say, Fingal preferred books to phones. The machines, the phones especially, had trivialised the real world. They had spread great falsehoods, and taught the dangerous knowledge that life was easy, that everything could be known or done or achieved at touch of the proverbial button.

"That doesn't prove anything," he snapped, angrier still that he was getting involved.

"Phone's always right, mate."

"It's a phone, not a book."

"So?" Bazza demanded with a huge, aggressive smile.

"*So*, it's a phone and not a book."

"Don't read books, mate. No one does."

"Exactly! That's the fucking problem!"

"Settle down, *mate*."

"There is a huge problem here, *Bazza*." Fingal threw his arms in the air. "Knowledge does not equal wisdom." The driver looked confused and, once more, began tapping the screen of his phone. The machine, a flat, sleek, shiny, lying thing started beeping and binging and bonging. The noises were disgusting, an affront to the strange forest. Fingal kneaded his sore, tired brow.

Again, he wanted to talk to this man, to explain, gently, that he wasn't trying to be a smart-arse. He wanted to tell Bazza, quietly, that he'd travelled, and that he knew things about the world, particularly that knowledge did *not* equal wisdom. How could it?! He wanted to tell the driver, humbly, that he had a degree in epistemology, the philosophy of knowledge. He wanted to tell Bazza it wasn't his fault the machines had taken over, that he was genuinely scared for the future of the species and that, in the space of but ten years or so, Emperor Zuckerberg had destroyed many, beautiful human abilities that took hundreds of thousands of years to develop: communication, empathy, logic and, again, wisdom. He also wanted to tell Bazza, honestly, they were not mates, that they'd only just met, that, in Scotland, it took an age before you called a man your friend, and that, as such, Bazza's country, his huge, red, empty country where birds taunted visitors, where solitude screamed at a man, and where strangers were friends and friends, strangers, was just a bit odd.

But that would certainly hypocritical. Fingal McKay was also a bit odd. All humans, so the traveller believed, were actually islands. Despite being trapped on the continent of man, they all longed to be alone. But what was the bloody point of saying anything? Like most, Bazza wouldn't understand. Like most, Fingal would just be accused of being a smartarse, a dickhead.

And, anyway, the mad, invisible birds in the forest starting ganging up and laughing at him again. "Oooo oooo oooo, aaaaa aaaaa aaaa," they said, reminding Fingal McKay that he was not in Scotland but in Australia, in Queensland, in a *sub-tropical* rainforest (the dry sclerophyll vegetation all around them – tea trees, banksia, and so on, were a dead giveaway – they did not grow above the Tropic of Cancer, dear Bazza) having a meaningless argument with a passive-aggressive man and his artificial brain.

"Ha!" Again, Bazza waved the infernal device in Fingal's face. "You didn't say that, mate."

"What?"

"Knowledge and wisdom."

"I did not say *that*. I said knowledge does not equal wisdom. The quote is actually a para—"

"Bible said it, *mate*."

Stop calling me mate!

Again, Bazza and his smart phone were incorrect. Ironically, the quote had grown out of a statement by Isaac Asimov who, Fingal remembered, once said "the saddest aspect of life right now is that science gathers knowledge faster than society gathers wisdom."

How did he remember this quote verbatim? Because he read it in a book. Because he'd practiced remembering it. Because he wanted to be wise, something society, its machines, and the birds in the trees mocked him for.

In the end, however, the lost, tired Scotsman just looked at Bazza. Sensing victory, the driver was hopping around like some passive aggressive human-bird, jabbering to and at Fingal, and, still, tapping, swiping his phone and waving it in Fingal's sad face.

This moment encapsulated why he wanted to become an island and leave the continent for a while. Everything was a struggle, a contest; a fight.

"*Bazza*, perhaps you didn't hear me the first time," he said in his roughest Glaswegian accent. "I don't mean to sound like a fuckin' prick, but I'd like to be alone. Can you and your phone leave? Please."

7

Bazza stopped fiddling with his stupid phone. He looked as if he was debating with a voice inside his head, probably on whether to abuse, leave or punch the dickhead standing before him – the foreign dickhead, the dickhead wearing a woollen jumper, in Queensland, in a *tropical* rainforest.

Success, thought Fingal, who fished a twenty-dollar bill from his pocket, folded it lengthways and pointed it at the driver.

"Thanks, *mate*," Bazza said. He snatched the twenty bucks from Fingal and made for the truck, gibbering as he went. "Bloody smartarse, mate. *Sub-tropical* forest? Ha, and from a *Jock*. No rest for the wicked, mate. Get back down the coast, mate; back to civilisation … bills to pay, people to see, mate. Mate. Mate. Mate. Mate. Mate."

"Shush." Fingal closed his eyes and the world vanished. "Everyone just shush."

A minute later the grotesque engine of the grotesque truck coughed into life, belched a cloud of black diesel at the shrieking forest, and headed back down to the coast. For a moment, Fingal felt a bit rude. There was no need to fight with the driver. It was not only pointless but childless and futile. The wise man wasn't supposed to roll up his sleeves and jump in. The wise man was meant to walk away, to let it go.

***

Fingal McKay was not a dickhead, you have to understand. He was simply exhausted with people and their world, particularly all the noise they made. He'd tried, by their God he'd tried, to fit in but after thirty-seven years it was all just too hard.

The last two years, for example, had passed on the coast, studying (again), working random jobs and living in a dreadful apartment. The Apartment of Noise, as he christened it, took up the middle floor of a grey, three-storey house that had been converted into three flats. Angee, the granddaughter of the lady who owned the block, lived on the top floor. Angee was in her early twenties, worked irregular hours as a bar manager, wore high heels in the kitchen, and enjoyed shouting into her phone while drinking wine on the balcony. For some reason, Angee spoke in a faint, fake and very poor American accent, used the words "like" and "literally" an awful lot, and hollered "ohmigod" at anything of the least import. Fingal hated Angee, and soon began longing for the days when phones and people stayed indoors. He never once shouted or complained, however. To his credit, he suffered like a real human – inside and in silence.

A very old man named Geoffrey lived in the apartment below. He claimed to be a painter, not of landscapes or portraits but of human things – walls, garage doors, windowsills and such. Aged eighty-three, Geoffrey was determined to go down working but the jobs were beginning to dry up. This was because old Geoffrey couldn't paint for tuppence. Poor eyesight meant that he kept missing bits. He only ever painted half of a wall, so Fingal once heard.

Geoffrey was also a dreadful person to share a poorly insulated building with. A weak bladder drove him to the toilet every hour on the hour. He urinated not on the side of the pan but right in the middle, the pissing, drumming noise easily travelling up through the thin floor. He shouted to deaf friends on the phone, suffered sneezing fits, and, when night fell, experienced very bad nightmares, groaning and shouting and thumping the thin walls until they passed. This was why, Fingal supposed, Geoffrey woke every morning at 5 a.m., cleared his throat and began pissing, and humming and shouting at his friend of the phone.

It was like that every bloody day of every bloody week.

The two men spoke only once.

"What age are you?" Geoffrey demanded.

"Thirty-six," Fingal replied at the time.

"I'm eighty-three," the old man shouted. "Enjoy it, mate. It goes bloody fast." He gazed up at the clear blue sky with clouded eyes. "Know what the most important thing in life is?"

"It's not silence."

A bent finger speckled with paint jabbed Fingal in the chest. "Work, mate," the old man insisted. "Building something and leaving your mark. Your legacy." *Half-painted windowsills?* "It's all about contributing to the community. Doing your bit and being part of something bigger than yourself."

"Not for everyone," Fingal said, but Geoffrey didn't hear him.

"No man is an island," the old painter concluded with pride. "Remember that."

At the time, Fingal just smiled and walked away, mainly because he felt suddenly inclined to grab Geoffrey by his painted shirt, snarl the word "liar", and kick the old, noisy bastard down the hill. If there was one proverb Fingal despised it was that no man is an island shite. Fingal McKay was born an island.

The neighbours on each side of the grey house were also too close. To the right lived two anxious parents, three nervous children and a stupid-fucking-dog, a small, fashionable rat-dog-thing with a human name: Christina, or Tina for short. Tina didn't so much bark as yip and yap and shriek, at anything – a passing car, a voice, the wind, a falling leaf. The sound drove Fingal crazy, as did the insouciance of Tina's owners to their pet's incessant fucking shrieking. Not once did any of them tell Tina to shut its yipping, yapping mouth. There was just no justice to it. Why did he have to suffer because of someone else stupid-fucking-arsehole-dog?

Worse, still, there was a hot tub twenty feet below Fingal's balcony. This wicked contraption hummed and bubbled to life every Friday afternoon when its crass, bogan owners would plop in, sup boxed wine from disposable plastic glasses, shout and, after an hour or so and plenty "woyne", flirt with one another. It was a bestial performance to listen to:

"Best investment I ever made, love," the tall, skinny one always yelled above the noise of the hot tub.

"What 'bout me?" the short, ugly one always screeched in reply.

"Keep your pants on, love." A slurp on the tepid wine. "Or off?"

"Cheeky! More woyne?"

"You read me moind, love."

If, heaven forbid, Fingal closed his eyes he was in the hot tub with the randy scumbags, so clear was the noise of them stealing wet, dirty kisses from one another.

"I like that."

"An' this?"

"Mmmmm."

If anything, Neville's approach was direct. "Best we get a root on, love. *Biggest Loser*'s on soon."

"Neville!"

"Can't help it, love. You're a beautiful woman."

Aye, right!

"What if someone sees us?"

I see you, you dirty bastards! Me! Fingal McKay, twenty foot above you!

"I'll take me chances, love. Toeyer than a roman sandal."

"Watch me woyne, Nev! Jesus. Careful! That's better. *Oh.*"

"Yeah?"

"Yeah, there. There. *Oh, OH!* Oh, Nev, that pushes me button every toime."

At which point Fingal would stomp inside, close all the windows and turn the radio up loud. Very loud.

There was no civility to civilisation, he soon learned, only vulgarity. The continent was a dark, brutal and noisy place, and there was no peace to be found living amongst them. In time, Fingal became obsessed with the human noise. Even though it hurt him, he couldn't stop listening to it. In fact, the worse it got, the more he listened.

Fingal booked an appointment with a doctor on the coast, easily convincing the physician that he had misophonia, something that Google – lying bastard – had easily convinced Fingal of an hour before the appointment. Literally a "hatred of sound", most people suffer mild forms of misophonia. Someone eating or yawning loudly can bring on a little attack, whereas louder, more insensitive and repetitive sounds can and do drive a person crazy – a SHRIEKING DOG, for example, or two ugly people groping each other in a hot tub, or a stupid human, using a stupid leaf blower. Like most people with oversensitivity to noise, Fingal's condition came and went and, like most psychological disorders, no one had a clue how to cure it. The doctor Fingal went to see, an older gentleman with a golf-course tan, pretended to sympathise, agreed Fingal most likely had "a nascent mental health issue", and gave him a prescription for sleeping tablets he claimed "would floor a bull elephant".

None of this helped. Neither, should you care to know, did shouting at the neighbours, punching holes in the walls, and biting and tearing his nails off until his fingers bled. When sleep came, Fingal dreamt of noise – the hiss of a rocket propelled grenade flying from his balcony into another lively, impromptu party some neighbours had decided to throw, the delightful burning smell of a rat-dog-thing-called-Tina-the-SHRIEKING-WANKER kicked into a furnace, or the fading cry of "no man is an island" as Geoffrey plummeted from a cliff that knew no bottom. But, sadly, the dreams never lasted and Fingal awoke every morning draped in a blanket of anxiety, powerless to stop the dreaded orchestra of Tina shrieking, ugly people drinking and touching each other's private parts in public, and bored, retired blokes firing up all manner of gardening and D.I.Y. equipment: lawnmowers, whipper-snippers, drills, angle grinders and, his nemesis, fucking leaf blowers.

All this pain did hold some value, however. Soon a delightful but slightly intimidating realisation came to Fingal: there had to more to life than living in a small apartment while being tortured by power tools, television sets and a small dog called Tina. He knew what needed to be done. It was time to go. Time to run.

"Again," he sighed.

***

Google, the lying slut-bastard, also caused Fingal to run away. It is a dangerous thing, Google. It puts pictures in people's heads. It promises them things that aren't real. It renders the complex world around them such a trivial, bland place. It speeds up time, forcing people into taking kneejerk decisions, demanding that a man change his life. Just a click of the button, Cob, and she'll be right.

A few weeks ago, for example, when Skinny and Fatty were groping each other in the hot tub, Fingal typed "help rent house escape please" into Google. Within .23 of a second a number of real estate adverts appeared, the first of which he clicked on. This is what it said:

> "STOP! A once in a lifetime opportunity to live in your very own slice of rainforest paradise. Escape now! to this stunningly peaceful isolated, remote and very private two bedroom, cute cottage. Blue in colour. Why not enjoy morning cuppa with a parrot, or entertain your friends, al fresco style, on huge, giant, sumptuous verandah overlooking a sprawling, private garden. YOUR little gem won't last long. Hurry!"

Fingal ignored most of the poorly written advert except for three words: remote, private and hurry. Google Earth, also a lying bastard, was then swiftly consulted and, sure enough, the "little gem" appeared. On screen, it was just a yellow dot in the middle of Binjari National Park, 274,948 square kilometres of sub-tropical rainforest, waterfalls and spiders' webs an hour's drive from the coast.

"An island," Fingal said at the time and zoomed in. Apparently, the cottage sat at the top of a long, slim clearing, which had a couple of small fields on either side of it, each one dominated by a massive tree. These puzzled Fingal somewhat but, in the end, he decided the clearings had to be sheep paddocks, the result of bushfires or a storm. The blue cottage appeared to be alone. Fingal didn't really care. This Binjari place had to be better than the coast with all its adverts, traffic, heat, people, fashionable rat-dogs-things, concrete and noise.

The night after Google-the-lying-bastard had planted the seed Fingal dreamt of a lonely forest cabin with blue smoke drifting up from a stone chimney. He smelled clean, fresh air, cool rain and freshly cut grass. He heard honeyeaters whistling in the woods, red wine tumbling into a large, clear glass, and Wagner's *Tristan and Isolde* murmuring on a radio. He saw a simple man with a simple life, a man sighing with contentment and slumping into a rocking chair where, with one hand, he stroked his mighty beard and, with the other, patted a proper sized dog with a proper dog's name (Biscuits, or something).

"It's a sign, mate," Fingal said the next morning, scared to open his eyes and come back to reality. "Do it. Do it now." So, Fingal did it. Three weeks ago now, he negotiated, amended and signed a one-year lease on a blue cottage in a rainforest, all without having to talk to another human, or even physically visit or inspect his new home. Once more, he didn't care. Goodbye to the heaving, sweltering coast. Sayonara, fucking leaf blowers. Au revoir, Tina, ya wee shite!

***

John Donne made him run away too. This aspect of the story is slightly difficult to fathom … at first. John Donne was a famed intellectual, preacher, writer, celebrity, philanderer, and merchant. During his time, Donne wrote hundreds of beautiful sonnets, love poems, epigrams, elegies, songs, satires and sermons. A gifted writer from the school of metaphysical poets, Donne's talent lay in the metaphor, vibrant language, and the seamless employment of brilliant paradoxes, ironies and dislocations. Oh, and it should be mentioned that John Donne was also very dead. He died way back, in the seventeenth century, of stomach cancer on 31st March 1631.

Fingal hated the man, the ghost, with a passion.

Five of Donne's words, in particular, greatly bothered him. You will know them and agree they must be considered in context:

> "all mankind is of one author, and is one volume … As therefore the bell that rings to a sermon, calls not upon the preacher only, but upon the congregation to come … No man is an island, entire of itself; every man is a piece of the continent, a part of the main … for whom the bell tolls; it tolls for thee."

Those five, horrible words – NO MAN IS AN ISLAND – had bothered Fingal from an early age. When *Star Wars* first came out and all the children were mucking about with imaginary lightsabers in the primary school playground in Scotland, Fingal always chose to play Obi-Wan Kenobi, just so he could hide in the bushes while waiting for the popular kid (Luke Skywalker) to arrive. When the bell rang, Fingal often lingered in the bushes, preferring the smell of the leaves or the drone of a bee to pencils scribbling and children dozing. Fingal managed to hide for ages until Mr McFarlane, the janitor, discovered his beautiful, green hidey-holes, shouting "Fingal McKay! Git oot they bushes, ya wee rascal!"

"Naw, Mistur McFarlane," young Fingal always shouted back. "I don't want tae go back tae class! I prefer it in the bushes!"

"Nae man's an island," McFarlane used to say while dragging Fingal back to school by his wee, sensitive ear. "Mind that, laddie."

Scottish parents, ministers, teachers, policemen and all manner of community-minded types never missed an opportunity to lecture Fingal about the importance of continents over islands, about why it was a person's utmost duty to be part of a community of people, to belong to a "guid clan". Even back then, however, such rhetoric made no sense to Fingal. Meaning, he felt, was not to be found in the company of others. Peace, beauty and wisdom were to be found in the primary school bushes, on the banks of the clear, grey river at the bottom of his parent's garden, or, alone, deep in the forest.

Peace, he began to realise, came from being alone.

Fingal also never got why people like old Geoffrey said "no man is an island" with such pride, as if John Donne's words held some tenet of wisdom now lost to the masses. "Proud of what, John? All that capitalism and industry? All that war and violence? All that *civilisation* and *progress*? Shite, John. UTTER SHITE! There's nothing to admire about your bustling continent of corrupt capitalism!" Fingal the pretend anarchist used to shout in the Apartment of Noise, serenaded by the sound of neighbours' TVs shouting adverts at people to buy things they didn't need and couldn't afford. "You'll see, Donne, you spectral prick. You'll bloody well see. I just rented a cottage in a rainforest, John, a real, proper, wee island. ALONE! You'll see, John. You'll see my island, and it'll be totally fucking amazing!"

This process of hating noise, society and a dead preacher from 17th century England was how a misophonic Scotsman came to be standing alone in a sub-tropical Australian rainforest, outside a cottage he'd never seen before, being heckled by dozens of mad, screeching, invisible birds. They may seem like odd motivations to run away but, if anything, most humans are odd creatures.

Fingal, always one for naming stuff, christened this new chapter in life The John Donne Experiment, or The Experiment for short. Organic, and with no rules whatsoever, The Experiment had one central hypothesis: a human being did *not* need to belong to anyone or anything to derive happiness from life. To find meaning, a person first needed peace and quiet. They needed silence, in order to hear the deep voices, and to separate the wheat of life from the chaff.

Alone it had to be, as an island of a man.

Chapter Two

Islands and Hermits: Theory

Real islands are fairly cheap and easy to own. $63,042 (USD) is all it would take to own Big Tusket Island, thirty-seven acres of pine trees "with power and a lighthouse" off Nova Scotia, Canada. If Europe is preferred, $185,972 buys you Mannions Island, four acres of bog, heath and granite sitting off the west coast of Ireland. Even the Robinson Crusoe, South Pacific-type islands are within reach of most. The one-acre Tahifehifa Island in Tonga, a "beautiful, unspoiled paradise surrounded by beach, coral reef and deep blue water where turtles and whales frolic", could be yours for roughly $377,000.

If islands are so cheap and the continent of man is so busy then why don't more people swap the grind for peace, isolation and wild, raw nature? To hazard a guess, most would put off by the impracticality of island living: how am I supposed to get back and forth? A boat? Never sailed a boat in my life. What if there's a storm or a tidal wave or a gigantic octopus attacks this boat I've never sailed? Where do I buy cigarettes, bread, wine, chocolate and milk? What? Of course I've never reared or milked a goat! Will friends and family be able to come and visit? Is there internet? What if I break a leg? Where is the nearest hospital? Police? In fact, what if pirates turn up one day and defile, murder and eat my wife and children?

The best many continentals can hope for is a temporary island, a two or three-week vacation to Bali, the Maldives or the likes. For a large sum of cash they get to experience crooked palm trees swaying over white beaches lapped by warm, turquoise waters, but only for a little while. They never linger. For one, escapology costs too much. It's not cheap to hang around a five-star island resort, stuffing your sunburnt face on endless buffets, and guzzling litres of posh wine and sickly, sweet cocktails and cheap beer. More importantly, this world is not real. The island escape is but a fantasy open only to the wealthy on a permanent basis.

Islands are also commonly encountered in the pages of a book. Library shelves groan with fictional stories about islands. If the reader is after morality, butterflies and utopia it's hard to go past R. M. Ballantyne's *The Coral Island: A Tale of the Pacific Ocean* (1858), the story of three shipwrecked boys who wash up on an uninhabited Polynesian island and build an experimental society modelled on the virtues of Christianity, hierarchy and leadership. Or, if the opposite is preferred – dystopia, violence and politics – William Golding's *Lord of the Flies* (1954) is a superb critique of how boys behave in a State of Nature. There are also plenty of weird, fictional islands. *Gulliver's Travels* (1726), where Captain Lemuel Gulliver is cast to Lilliput (where he is a giant), Brobdingnag (where he is tiny and found by a farmer twenty-two metres tall), and Laputa (a floating island in the sky devoted to the arts, music and mathematics), is a good example, as is H.G. Wells' 1896 sci-fi novel *The Island of Doctor Moreau*, on which the good Doctor creates human-like beings from animals. In literary terms the island canon is voluminous, the theme well travelled. The same could be said of cinema, art or music.

Then there are some odd cases, human beings that seek islands on the continent of man. These people are among but not of the world. Hermits and wanderers, vagabonds and ascetics, they dwell in caves, abandoned factories, campervans, railway stations and rainforests. Freed from the shackles of life, unfettered by work, marriage or mortgage, they will away time by staring at stuff, suspending all judgement and just being. Some trip or drink, others might sleep a lot or roam from place to place but they all have one thing in common: they all build and inhabit elaborate places of beauty in their minds; islands, some might say. Metaphysical islands can have imaginary temples, scared shrines or divine pagodas, but form is not really that important, so long as the retreat puts the architect at immediate and complete ease, so long as the island helps them escape for a while. Fingal McKay aimed to become one of these islanders. Transformation from man to island was, in essence, the core purpose of The Experiment.

His island would serve as a place of rest. In time, it would become temple, shrine and retreat, a place to find method in the madness of life.

***

The Island of Fingal McKay (hereafter referred to, simply, as the island) was very easy to get to. All he had to do was close his eyes. Suddenly he was no longer stranded on a white gravel driveway outside of a rainforest cottage he'd never seen before. Instead, Fingal stood on a long, pebbled beach littered with driftwood, old books and empty cans of beer. The ocean, a fierce, grey and swollen thing, pounded the bleak shoreline. Rain poured from the dark, low clouds above, crashing into the pebbles around his white, bare feet. A cold wind tore at the garish tartan suit he was wearing and made his teeth chatter but, oddly, Fingal was happy. For once, his jittery mind lay at ease.

Everything felt normal and real on the fake little island.

Fingal was able to discern two further details amidst the rain and wind: a small blue castle, further up the beach, and ropes: lots and lots of ropes. All of them were of different colours and thicknesses. Some were three and four feet wide, others were normal-sized, and many were no wider than a thread. They were all tattooed in big blue letters and words, like Society, Ego, Reality, Love, S.E.X., Family, Friends, Television, Anxiety, The Concept of Time, iPhone 5GS, Internet, Fear, and so on. They were all tied around sturdy trees or huge rocks on the cold beach, running out vertical and taught across a narrow straight of water where they were anchored to a second piece of land: John Donne's reviled Continent of Man. The island remained fixed and tethered to the world of man and all its weird, perverse ways. For now.

"The ropes that bind us," said Fingal, gazing around the curious landscape. "For now," he added with a wet smile.

Like him, the ropes behaved oddly. When, for example, Fingal reached up and plucked a big, green rope about the width of his wrist it didn't twang like a rope. Instead it made a sound like a lawnmower. "Odd,"

19

noted Fingal. This rope had the words "Incidental, Annoying People One is Forced to Live Alongside" written upon it. A second, pink rope – YOU FOOL! GOOGLE EARTH LIED TO YOU! – made a noise like a telephone ringing and a third, with the word NEIGHBOURS scrawled all over it, sounded like a hoover turning itself off and on.

"Curious," said Fingal, thinking back to the stupid real estate advert, to the fuzzy image a little yellow dot on Google Earth – lying bastard – surrounded by three, long, thin clearings.

As the strange noises intensified, Fingal's heart broke a little more. "Human noises," he said to the rain and the wind. "I am not alone."

***

Back in the real world, Fingal opened his eyes. Everything appeared normal, sort of real. The sky was blue, the trees were green, and the wind was cool and brisk. He was wearing clothes, he was not in Scotland, he desperately needed a drink, and, still, he remained stranded on the white gravel driveway surrounded by bags, boxes and invisible, shrieking birds. The Little Gem, the blue cottage, was still not visible, obscured by a wobbly grey fence and a wall of overgrown garden with a little doorway and a path.

The human noises came again. Somewhere off to the left, a lawnmower puttered and shredded and clanked, the noise of its struggling engine hideous against the silent rainforest. Stones shot and pinged off its blades. A telephone rang through some bushes to the right. A woman answered it, her voice loud and clear and very Australian. Other sounds came crawling out the trees and bushes – a hoover hoovering, a drill drilling, and a television belching forth absurd, repetitive children's rhymes.

"Google!" Again, Fingal thought of that little yellow dot, blinking and lying in the middle of a forest on a computer screen in the Apartment of Noise. "Lying bastard. You promised me I'd be alone."

To confirm this awful development Fingal walked ten metres to the right. Instead of an empty sheep paddock there was a lawn, a garden and a pink house with the lights on, at midday. The house sheltered beneath an enormous fig tree, which was why Google Earth – whore – hadn't picked it up.

"Shite," he groaned on noticing a rabbit hutch, three small bicycles and a washing line festooned with small clothes. "Children. Serious noisemakers." The most curious detail about the pink house, however, was a thirty-foot sailboat moored on the front lawn. "Why the hell would you need a boat in a rainforest?"

The experimentalist trudged to the right, peered through some more bushes and, sadly, realised he had a second neighbour. This time he saw a little cottage, drab green in colour and with a funny little turret on its roof. It too was hidden from above by a colossal tree, a silver flooded gum in this case. The yard was sickeningly neat, with a freshly painted garage and potting shed, beds bursting with colour, and perfectly straight rows of vegetables broken up by stands of manicured fruit trees. Birdlike movement in the little turret caught Fingal's narrow, scowling eye. "What manner of creature are you," he whispered, peering at a small man's shadow moving a hoover back and forth in the turret.

**

That first day in the rainforest just got stranger and stranger.

"G'day," a voice said from behind. Fingal jumped and turned at the same time and was confronted by an old Aussie bloke dressed in wellington boots, blue shorts and a gold XXXX T-shirt, all of which were covered in grass clippings, which at least explained the lawnmower.

"Welcome to Binjari," the old bloke said. "Peter moved out then has he?" Fingal's mouth hung open. *Where did you appear from, old bloke?* "Good bloke, Peter. Worked for the council. Fixed up old Holdens on the weekends." *Peter? What? Who the hell is Peter?* "But he never did settle up here. Too cold in the winter, too hot in the summer." The mower of lawns chortled. "Too wet in the wet season. And he didn't like the ticks. He hated the ticks."

"Who?" said Fingal, stunned to be talking to another human being. *And, ticks? What ticks?*

"Col, by the way." The old man offered his hand. It shook with a will of its own. "From 1967. The brown house. Two doors down. Lived there all me life," Col added with a touch of pride.

"Fingal," he said and shook the shaking hand.

"G'day, Fergus."

"It's Fingal." At last his brain caught up. "What brown house? How many houses are there up here?"

Col ignored the question and nodded at some bushes, beyond which lay the drab, green cottage with the little turret on top. "You met Andrew yet? He's got five water tanks. We got one. No mains water up here, mate. Tank water only. Bloody council. If there's a drought we've got to buy water in." The old bloke waited for Fingal to be amazed. "'Magine having to pay for something that falls from the sky, eh? I wrote a letter to the council once. You know what they said? They said blah-blah-bloody-blah…"

As Col rambled on, moaning about this, that and the next thing, Fingal examined the old man as if he were an animal in a glass box. Col wore huge, cheap service-station glasses which amplified a pair of pleasant, skittish eyes that looked everywhere but at Fingal. His hair was wild, white and fragile, his face a sad, drooping sort of thing decorated with patches of white stubble the razor had missed.

"I pay me taxes," Col persisted. "Me father was in the army, as was his father. We worked for everything. Mate, the trouble with those idiots up in Brisbane is that they're born with a silver spoon up their arses. Never worked a bloody day in their lives. Councillors this, politics that…"

Col's hand wasn't the only thing that shook. His entire body vibrated, as if he'd swallowed a pneumatic drill. Parkinson's disease, most likely. Poor old sod.

"They're far worse down in Canberra. Bloody crooks! Why do we even need 'em, eh?"

Or, there could be another reason why Col shook? Fear of the forest and the ticks and snakes and spiders within? Fear of death (Col had to be eighty if he was a day)? Anger at this water-hoarding Andrew character?

"Mary hates politicians. Mary, me … erm. MARY!" Col suddenly stopped talking and looked both confused and concerned. "Poor Mary.

22

Mate, she'll be needing the lavatory by now. I'd best be going. Good meeting you, Fergus."

"Fingal."

"You'll like it up here, mate." Col regarded the forest with a rubbery smile, and calmed a little. "It rains a fair bit, the ticks aren't so bad, and the birds are lovely." He made for a path in the bushes, calling out "be seein' you, Fergus" as he went.

"It's Fingal. And, no, you won't be seeing me."

The jittery old man walked like a marionette so, out of spite more than anything, Fingal christened him Shaky Old Col. It delivered no relief. "I was meant to be alone," he repeated, as the dream of the rocking chair, glass of red wine and Biscuits the dog went up in smoke. "Alone."

Apparently, there were four houses in the immediate vicinity: a pink, green, brown and blue one (his ... assuming fucking Google had told the truth about the colour of the cottage he still couldn't muster the courage to actually inspect). He tried to stay positive. Four was a significantly better number that the five hundred thousand houses that were squeezed onto the coast. Ten or so people he could handle. More importantly, he'd yet to hear any leaf blowers, loud music or small, fashionable little-rat-dog-things shrieking at falling leaves. It was quieter in Binjari National Park, relatively speaking. There were houses and humans about but, like parrots in the hollows, all were hiding in the woods. And, anyway, it wasn't like Fingal came to the rainforest to meet people. He came here to leave them, to turn himself into a beautiful hermit – a true island-nation of a man.

Once more, the forest interrupted Fingal's reverie. Gently, it revealed more subtle detail. The cool wind rushed through the arbour and disturbed a cloud of lemon-yellow butterflies from an overgrown honeysuckle bush. They spiralled around Fingal's tired body before disappearing up and out of sight. A big brown and gold lizard emerged from beneath a rock, stuck out its blue tongue and darted across the leaf litter, and, slowly at first, the strange but enchanting hoots, warbles, screeches of the invisible birds returned.

Fingal's mind steadied. "Shaky Old Col does not matter," he said with determination. "The neighbours are not part of The Experiment."

Chapter Three
The Ghost of Donne

At last Fingal shouldered a bin bag full of clothes, walked toward the wall of overgrown garden and vanished into the little dark doorway. When he emerged on the other side, he couldn't quite believe his luck. Sitting plum in the middle of a lush, green lawn was a lovely cottage with blue walls, a stone chimney and a tin roof. A wide awning surrounded the blue cottage, beneath which lay a spacious wooden verandah.

"Google be praised," Fingal said with a half-smile. The cottage was protected on both sides by two more impressive walls of garden, each with a few gaps. These offered glimpses of the neighbouring properties but only of their garages, sheds, empty chicken coups and lawns. Dwarfing everything, the rainforest began at the bottom of the garden. Cool and scruffy, it was full of tall, dark trees, many invisible creatures, and lots of shadows.

Fingal walked across the grass, stepped onto the verandah and moved inside the blue cottage. Thankfully, it was not full of squatters or possums, snakes and rats, as he'd recently imagined. Compact and bijoux, its floor space was divided into an open plan kitchen, dining and living room with a fireplace and, toward the back of the cottage, two bedrooms and a large bathroom, with no bath. Due to the wide awning outside, the ambience inside the cottage was safe, dark and gloomy. "Cave-like," Fingal noted with approval.

Unpacking didn't take long. Considering that he was forever catching the next flight home to Scotland, Fingal didn't have much cargo: TV, desk, office chair, computer, a $100 bed bought from the Salvos, two cases of beer, a lazy-boy chair that had seen better days (in the 1980s), clothes stuffed into three black bin bags, ten boxes of precious books, some white goods, a poor collection of mismatched kitchenware (also bought from the Salvos), and a dozen bags of shopping. In terms of material wealth, a kilt, silver hip flask, set of Ping golf clubs, and a brand-new pair of Scarpa walking boots were the only decent kit he possessed.

When the last of the shopping was placed in the cupboard, Fingal took a warm beer, stepped outside and dragged the lazy-boy to the rear of the verandah. He stared at the forest, which glared back at him and, again, he shivered. The Binjari Plateau was a good 1,000 metres above sea level and the air was much cooler. This was why, Fingal supposed, many mountain men grew large beards. The sun, pale and white, slipped beneath the trees and silence became the woods as the birds and reptiles and creepy-crawlies returned to their warm nests, cracks, webs and hollows.

He rose from the old lazy-boy chair, stepped onto the lawn and walked over to inspect one of the huge, green walls of wild, tangled garden enclosing the property. Many individual shapes and forms soon materialised. In Scotland, geraniums, yuccas and philodendrons were tiny little things kept indoors next to radiators and grown in bright ceramic pots. In Binjari, they were absolute monsters. Yuccas grew thirty-foot-tall, clumps of geraniums were twenty-foot wide, and there was one copse of dracaena that was easily the height of a double decker bus. It was impossible to tell where one plant ended and another began. Antique bottlebrush, feathery grevillea, and old, crooked wattle trees battled, fought and wrestled over the precious light. The garden was a delightful, tangled and chaotic mess.

Fingal strolled down the lawn and stopped to inspect a little blue Nissen hut buried amongst the wild garden. Inside he found a sledgehammer, a rusty, double handed axe, a few tins of paint, and hundreds of hardwood logs.

"Gifts from Peter or whatever his name was," Fingal assumed once he was back outside, where, again, he found himself drawn to the eerie rainforest at the bottom of the garden. Tiny against the tall, crooked trees, he stood for a moment, drained the last of the warm beer and, without really thinking it through, strode into the dark forest.

The expedition went well for about thirty seconds. Five metres in Fingal walked straight into a big spider's web. Cursing, and trying to flick a large, red spider from his chest, he backed up, only to trip over a root and fall on his backside. A metre from his hand, a green branch slithered away. *Snake? Fuck! SNAKE!* To the right, a large animal crashed through the undergrowth. "Fuck was that?" he whispered, scrambling to his feet and running for the safety of the garden, mosquitos attacking his bare neck, a mob of kookaburras hooting and hollering above the cold wind rattling in the high canopy.

"Bad idea, man," Fingal said once back on the safety of the lawn. "Scotsmen do not belong in rainforests! That *thing* is definitely hostile."

"They say it's the first sign of madness," a high-pitched male voice called out to the left. "Talking to yourself," it qualified. For the second time in as many hours Fingal jumped and turned. "Over here, neighbour!"

Fingal zeroed in on a human face peering through a gap in the bushes. The face was tiny, bearded and very confident, and seemed to float on the foliage.

"Hello," said Fingal, automatically.

"G'day," the face sang out.

It wasn't a pretty face. To Fingal, it resembled one of the shrunken heads the Scythian Kings of ancient Europe used to treasure, right down to the grey flesh stretched over its beaked nose and thin, purple lips. "You must be my new neighbour," the little face presumed with a wide smile. "I'm Andrew. Andrew McKenzie, Esquire. From the green house."

"Fingal," he replied with suspicion. "From the blue house, I suppose."

"At last we meet."

"I only just got here."

"Yes, yes, I know that. I heard you shouting. Something about being alone?"

"Right," said Fingal, very confused. He had met this face before, in another life. The conversation was familiar. "You were the man hoovering in the turret." He pronounced the word *turrit* and Andrew's big eyes widened.

"I knew it," he exclaimed. "I knew I detected a hint of the old country accent! The Scotch brogue!" *Scotch is an American word for whisky, little-*

face. A brogue is a shoe. "Ha! Jings! Wonderful! I'm a McKenzie. From the Kyle of Lochalsh, you must *ken* it? Why, we're virtually kin. You must come over for dinner one night. I've nae haggis, laddie, but I do make a superb lentil curry."

"Thanks, but—"

"Have you had the pleasure of meeting young Penny yet?" the face from the drab, green house continued.

"Penny?"

"From the pink house."

"What pink house?"

"Your neighbour, on the other side, of course."

What do you mean, of course? "No," said Fingal, taking immediate dislike to the invasive little face. Its wide, grey eyes were too presumptive, and its thinning comb-over hairstyle and stupid chinstrap beard were far too neat. "Penny's a pretty little thing," Andrew rolled on. "Pretty, but, well, hardly pure. It's not for me to say" – *but you will* – "but the poor soul has landed herself with three kids, to three different fathers. It's always the innocents that pay the cost of their parent's promiscuity." The face inched forward, as if it were on a stalk. "Do you have family in Australia, Fingal?" It emitted a wheezing, laughing sound. "Or, jings, should I say, is the *Clann* with you? Come to think of it, what's your *Clann* name?"

"McKay."

"Are you married?"

"No."

The little face snorted. "Do you work?"

Fingal laughed. "Not for the moment."

"Oh, what a shame."

"I'm between experiments."

Fingal didn't trust the little face either. It wanted something from him; something big. It kept looking him from top to toe, scanning him almost.

"Tell me," it demanded, "is God in your house?"

"In my house?"

"Do you pray, Fingal?"

"Not anymore." Fingal looked to the blue cottage. "Sorry, Andrew, was it?"

"Yes," it smirked, "that is my name."

"You must excuse me. I really must be getting on," he lied. "Unpacking, you know." Sensing bullshit, the wide, grey eyes scanned Fingal again and he backed off a couple of paces. "Lovely to meet you, Andrew."

"In all your ways acknowledge Him, and He will make straight your paths."

Fingal slipped out of sight. "Talk to you later!" *in the year 2025.*

"Proverbs 3:6. And let me know about the Church thing!" *What church thing?* "I leave every Sunday at 7 a.m. sharp. More than happy to give you a lift."

"Thank you, no!"

Fingal was halfway up the lawn but still the voice persisted. "I'll drop a few pamphlets round for you," it called out. "A few readings from the Good Book. Do you like honey?"

"NO!" Honey made Fingal nauseous. It was too sweet.

"I've six bee hives."

"Good for you."

"I'll add a jar to the list!"

Fingal doubled his pace and took the three stairs that connected lawn to verandah as one. He darted inside the cottage, fetched a cooler beer, and turned the lights on, then off. Best not to attract any moths, pests, or overly-friendly Christians. "Just pretend they're not there," he said while sliding down a wall in the living room. "Fucking neighbours," he added.

***

Silence oozed into the cottage, crept into his ears and poured through the corridors of his tired, addled mind. Once more, Fingal closed his eyes and fled to the small island he was building in his head. It hadn't moved any further from John Donne's stupid continent but at least the rain was lighter. Overhead, the sun was trying to break through the clouds and the beach was no longer thin and cold and pebbled but wide and white and sandy, dotted with large, smooth ball-shaped rocks. Gnarled conifers by the shore honked and creaked in the gentle breeze, and strange, mesmeric birdsong filled the salty air around him. The ropes were still there, dozens and dozens of them, but they didn't bother Fingal. Familiar as breath, they'd been there all his life.

The architect's mind fell into a state of peace, but again, only for a moment. Everything started to jerk and wobble and behave oddly. The waves of mellifluous birdsong vanished, replaced by the sound of Andrew McKenzie, Esquire's high-pitched, annoying little voice. "Do you like honey," it screeched, and squawked. "I've six hives, you know!" Fingal looked down at one of the smooth, ball-shaped rocks and it turned into Andrew's tiny, little cherub's head. "Is God in your house?" The face demanded. Even the moment when the sun finally burst through the clouds was ruined. Andrew's huge, fake and grinning little face was the sun. "I am the light of the world," it boomed.

The Scotsman snapped open his eyes but still the little face floated in the darkness. "Andrew," he sighed. "You will be John Donne. My ghost."

Chapter Four

The First Hermit Routine

Once a week, Fingal trekked two kilometres up the main road to a small general store in Binjari village for beer, meat, chocolate, potatoes and other essentials. A nice lady called Gail ran the store, which had a frontier atmosphere to it. Gail sold things like spades, grog, bread, meat, secateurs, rolling tobacco, homemade caramel shortbread, engine oil, red flannel shirts, dirty magazines, and a wide range of what she called "tourist arts and crafts", that is, secondhand rubbish – hats with holes in them, creepy dolls with one eye, cracked porcelain figures, chairs with three legs and, her best seller, signs from the forties and fifties advertising conical brassieres, war bonds and cigarettes. She made a fortune trading this human flotsam and jetsam. Once, Gail told him of "some rich dag from the coast" who gave her fifty bucks for a mannequin's hand.

"Why would someone want a mannequin's hand?"

"Stand 'em up on their stumps, love," Gail replied.

Fingal stared at his hand. "I don't get it."

"They use the fingers to display their jewellery," she said, matter-of-factly. "Now, six pack of what, love?"

"Beer."

"Flavour?"

"Scottish?"

Gail offered a toothy grin. "We don't sell pisswater here, love."

"Why on Earth," Fingal ruminated on the way back home, "do people pay good money for other people's rubbish to add to their rubbish, which they'll probably sell at a garage sale one day?" If anything, these shopping trips reminded Fingal why he had left their continent in the first place. "I don't miss it," he used to say.

Other little changes occurred. With no job to turn up for, the experimentalist let his dark hair grow out. He also showered less – two, three times a week – and didn't bother shaving, washing his clothes, or eating breakfast. A young beard soon appeared.

The weather began to change too. The nights remained black and cold but once the sun got up the days were warm and golden. Teased out his cave, Fingal started exploring the trails of Binjari National Park. These were gentle, well-kept trails that meandered through impressive stands of hoop pines, black booyongs and bleeding gums, so called because of a red sap that oozed forth if the tree suffered any injury.

However, the trails were popular with day-trippers from the coast. Just as Fingal began to think oh, I haven't seen another human for a while, an adventurous type with a daypack, fancy camera and walking poles would appear on the trail. Or, just as the beauty of a fifty-foot waterfall was about to reveal itself, a gang of loud, excitable teenagers with ridiculous hairstyles would appear. Or, infuriatingly, just as he was finally about to locate an invisible bird a schoolteacher and her troupe would pour down the trail.

There was nothing else for it. At the sound of humans approaching, Fingal soon took to hiding behind a large rock, the trunk of a colossal rosewood tree or some dip in the land. Sometimes he had to hide for a long time, especially if a long, slow train of Japanese tourists appeared. The Japanese photographed everything – rocks, sticks, ants, leaves, protein bars, protein bars being eating, protein bars' wrappers, dirt, types of lichen, roots, footprints and, of course, each other. Fingal didn't really mind. He passed the time by admiring the bark of a tree, or watching spiders weave webs, or closing his eyes and messing around with the island in his head. Not once did any of the visitors see the man hiding but two or three metres away. In terms of The Experiment, this was an extremely positive development. Akin to the birds he so desperately wanted to see Fingal McKay was slowly turning invisible.

Sometimes, of a Friday or Saturday evening, an old friend might take a drive up from the coast. These were convivial evenings at first. Fuelled by good wine, fine fare, and decent conversation they ended up outdoors, smoking a joint under a night sky dominated by a celestial river of white, twinkling stars. The continental stories – long, pointless and common tales of family, work, love, movies, mortgages, and so on – bored him to tears and the only time he grew animated was when the conversation steered toward the forest, or The Experiment or, much to his annoyance, his neighbour from the drab, green house: Andrew McKenzie, Esquire, the Ghost of Donne.

"Well, its official, Fin," a female lawyer-friend joked with him one night. "You've gone quite mad."

"Quite sane, you mean."

"Aren't you bored?"

"Nope."

"But what do you do all day?

"Nothing."

"Nothing?"

"Yep."

"I couldn't do that. I get roughly three hundred e-mails per … oh, look! A shooting star. Make a wish!"

"Pass the joint."

"A real wish. And don't tell me, otherwise it won't come true."

Fine. Go away.

Nothing was a bit of an exaggeration. Fingal McKay did some things in the blue cottage. His favourites were cruel, slightly devilish things that related to The Experiment. Progress, for example, soon came to be measured by the number of ropes with mainstream society that were physically cut. The first bond he severed with society was a simple one, the landline to be specific. Its death held none of the ingenuity later killings associated with The Experiment came to be renowned, and feared, for. In the beginning, the executions, as the strange ceremonies were called, were dull and practical. One morning the landline just began ringing. Tired of the sound, angry at the interruption to his meditation, and dressed in his underpants, Fingal simply marched over to the phone, ripped its chord from the socket and flung the annoying device into the garden. The moment he did so a little rope securing his island to the continent snapped and his mind drifted freer. Instead of worrying that distant relatives might not be able to reach him he felt liberated, and empowered. "The first rope be cut, Captain Fingal," he said in a pirate's voice, playing, as he did when he was a child. "What we be killin' next?"

Fingal smiled and said in a cold voice "fetch me the iPhone."

He hated the iPhone.

"Yar, Captain. Right away."

The death of the iPhone, however, proved to anti-climactic. The victim had escaped. Despite turning the blue cottage upside down the irritating contrivance was nowhere to be found. It must've been lost in the move. "Bloody hope so," said Fingal, realising with some delight that he hadn't spoken to anyone in almost a week.

That first morning of executions was a fun, busy one. Within the space of an hour, Fingal had battered his alarm clock to smithereens with a claw hammer, deep-fried his radio in a pot of boiling oil, and stamped his watch to death. The Experiment had no need of time. There was no point to it anymore.

The reason for the violent death of these "ropes" was both logical and cathartic. The devices and contraptions he had destroyed were physical bonds to Donne's hideous continent. Representations of mass idiocy, blindness and apathy, they had enslaved Fingal for too long. And, as with any slave rebellion, no mercy was offered. The prisoners turned on their cruel masters with extreme savagery.

***

A few weeks after moving up to Binjari National Park a routine began to set in. At dawn each day, a tremendous screeching noise always jolted Fingal awake. It came from above the blue cottage and sounded as if a pterodactyl was being tortured (the creature was a cockatoo and it was merely staking its territory). This tremendous racket then woke all the other birds, and within minutes the forest was full of strange, invisible birds wailing, squawking, cackling, screeching and laughing. No amount of pillows clamped over the head could keep all the noise out, so Fingal gave up fighting it. In time, he started to rise with the sun and the birds, sitting on the back steps, breathing and revelling in the peace and majesty of nature.

The rest of the morning was usually spent reading about that which he aspired to be: a hermit. Initial research concentrated on the history of these magnificent yet marginalised creatures. Hermitage, he discovered, had been commonplace for thousands of years. Ordinary people, founders and followers of major religions, and even entire nations (Japan during the Edo Period) had opted for the "hidden life". Jesus of Nazareth did his time in the wilderness, as did Siddhartha Gautama Buddha, the Prophet Muhammad and Zarathustra, the Zoroastrian Prophet.

The word, he learned, came from the ancient Greek *erēmitēs* (of the desert) and was first associated with religious people seeking an isolated, prayer-focussed life. Christianity was all over it. Saint Peter the Hermit began the trend of wandering around the deserts of the Holy Land and was soon followed by his prodigy, the less than modestly titled Anthony The Great. Dozens more anguished souls followed and soon the desert was full of hermits. The locale was anything but peaceful, however. People from towns and cities often sought out the wiser hermits for spiritual advice or counsel, which meant the poor souls ended up with no solitude whatsoever. Their consternation is not difficult to imagine.

While informative, this early hermit research generated two awkward questions for Fingal: to be a real hermit did you need to live in a desert and, more annoyingly, did you have to be into God?

Further reading required.

At lunchtime, Fingal would then make two cheese and jam sandwiches, pour a glass of red wine and do some exercise: pacing the floor for an hour while eating and drinking and thinking about hermits. He'd met a few in his time but one encounter in particular kept coming back. He couldn't get beyond it. Why, he did not know, for it was a bizarre, dirty story. It occurred in Scotland, a long time ago, and concerned a disgusting man named Wullie Mushroom, so called because of a yellow fungus that grew around his moustache, which he never washed (that, nor any other part of his body come to think of it). This smelly hermit lived in a caravan in the woods up by Fingal's Uncle's farm and only came out to work or buy smokes, food or booze.

Fingal was sixteen years old when he first met Wullie, working a late summer job "liftin'" potatoes, an ill-paying, back-breaking job. The tattie-pickin' gang numbered around thirty individuals. It was composed of a couple of teenagers like Fingal and, mostly, professional "lifturs" – men and "wumin" attired in strange hats, tattered ski jackets, Adidas tracksuit bottoms, and collapsed wellington boots. A grim bunch, the professionals kept themselves to themselves, constantly smoked rolled up cigarettes, and swore like fuck.

One morning Fingal happened to be liftin' alongside Wullie Mushroom. The rain was coming down in sheets, his back ached, his hands and arms were buried in the cold mud, and yet he couldn't stop staring at Wullie. The hermit fascinated Fingal. He wore two hats, a Rangers F.C. scarf, a luminous yellow Nevica ski jacket, and an old pair of pink ladies' spectacles. His face was covered in so much grime, stubble and blackheads its age was impossible to tell. Wullie could've been anywhere between thirty-five and sixty.

"Pungent," Fingal muttered on catching a whiff of the hermit's aroma – stale vegetables, B.O., cigarettes and dirt.

"Whit?" snapped Wullie.

"Nothing," said Fingal. "Nothing."

"Fuckin' tatties dinnae lift themselves, ya posh cunt."

Fingal closed his eyes and buried his hands deeper until he found a cold potato.

A moment later Wullie stood bolt upright. The hermit sniffed the air then, with great athleticism, sprang left and vanished into the tall green stalks of a reel that had yet to be lifted. A brief struggle ensued, ending with a small snapping sound. "Ya fuckin' dancer!" Wullie exclaimed, rising from the stalks with a limp rabbit in his dirty hands. "Ah fuckin' kent it wis there," he shouted. "Fuckin' kent it, so'an ah did!"

At lunchtime, when the workers had assembled in the bothy, Wullie marched in room, threw the rabbit in the microwave and cooked it on high for five minutes, all the while ignoring the protests from his co-workers.

"That'll no' cook the beast, Wullie!" shouted an older man with two fingers missing from his right hand. "Fuck's sakes!"

"Skin the animal first. Christ," added another. "Ye'll git thon miximatoesis shite. No' that you'd fuckin' notice."

"Manky, clarty bastard," said a third, lifting her sandwich and heading "fuckin' ootside".

It could've been the wax or hair or dirt blocking his ears but Wullie Mushroom didn't hear a thing. The insults, advice and admonishments just bounced off him. His pig eyes were fixed on the rabbit turning under the spotlight in the microwave.

"He's surely not going to eat that?!" cried Fingal.

Beep – beep – beep.

Wullie tore open the door, juggled the steaming rabbit, then and sunk his teeth into its arse. "Fuck aye," said the hermit, blood rolling down his filthy chin. "Ye just cannae beat a bit rabbit!"

As Wullie ate, most of the lifters left, mumbling "fuckin' tatties willnae lift themsel'" as they trudged back out into the mud and rain.

Only Fingal remained, spellbound. Wullie Mushroom didn't give a stuff about what anyone thought of him eating a rabbit or, for that matter, his hopeless career choice or his complete disregard for personal hygiene. The man existed in a bubble. A glow surrounded the hermit, a dim and brown and dirty aura but an aura nevertheless. There stood a Zen master eating a raw rabbit, a man at absolute peace with his pitiful lot in life. There stood an island.

"And," said Fingal, pacing the dark floorboards of the blue cottage, "Wullie Mushroom did not live in a desert, and was most certainly not into God. No minister in his right mind would let that dirty bastard into church."

Case closed.

After lunch Fingal liked to open all the windows and let the air drift through the blue cottage. He'd often grab something heavy to read – David Foster Wallace's *Infinite Jest* or Ayn Rand's *Atlas Shrugged* – retire to the sofa and fall into a deep sleep after reading a few paragraphs. So severe was the hangover from thirty-seven years on the continent, so great his fatigue, he sometimes slept for days.

Blue cottage security detail then started to intervene. At 4:15pm Fingal soon began waking to the sound of wellington boots crunching across his white gravel driveway and an old bloke talking to himself. Shaky Old Col from the brown house was off for his afternoon walk, his old, bent and trembling form visible every now and then in the gaps in the wall of front garden. Shaky Old Col kept himself to himself and, therefore, posed no threat to the Fingal's security, integrity or progress of The Experiment.

The same could not be said of Andrew McKenzie, Esquire, the little man with the little face from the drab, green cottage. True to his word, the Ghost of Donne did pop round with a Jesus pamphlet and a jar of honey. In fact, Andrew popped round three or four times. Fortunately, though, the gravel driveway acted like an early warning system and gave him plenty of time to hide in a dark bedroom where he could watch Andrew's little face floating outside the French windows. The Ghost always lingered, tutting at the empty beer bottles by Fingal's lazy-boy or shaking his small head at the grass on the lawn, which was now ten inches high. Not once did Andrew knock, or leave a note or either of the gifts which, thought Fingal, was hardly very Christian.

The pink house to the right remained a mystery. Occasionally a car came and went, and sometimes he heard a woman with a nice voice talking on the phone. Every five days or so some children played outside but never for too long. Even at that young age they were enslaved to the television. Sometimes he didn't hear the children from the pink house for three or four blissful days. If Andrew's gossip was to be believed, maybe the three kids spent the school week with one of their three different fathers? Maybe their mother – Jenny or Penny or whatever she was called – locked them in a cupboard? Maybe they didn't exist? Maybe Fingal didn't give a flying fuck.

Come the evenings darkness fell like an anvil in the forest, the cue to light the fire, heat a pot of soup, and toast a thick slice of Gail's bread. Dinner was taken in the company of ABC TV News but less and less so. Nothing ever seemed to change on the continent. The Australian parliament still resembled a sheep shearing shed on a Friday afternoon.* Terrorists, who claimed they were being terrorised by their government had taken to terrorising innocent civilians (who were suitably terrified). The markets went up. The markets went down. In sport, a man with a silly hairstyle that had spent most of his life hitting a red ball with a bat did that 146 times in one day. That nice fluff-story at the end (usually about an animal or a robot or an old person). Then, always at the end, the most important story, the one people actually cared about: the weather. Why bother? The weather forecast was the same as the day before, and the one before that: sunny, forever and ever more.

Soon Fingal ate with the television off, blowing a piece of microwave lasagne cool, staring at the TV's black, rectangular eye, thinking about all the shit he'd seen in that eye, all the time he'd wasted staring at that sad, black eye. He thought of how mindless the eye was, and how it lied to people every day, telling them their lives were wretched and meaningless, that if they'd only tried harder they too could be free or rich. "Dimmer of reality," Fingal took to saying. "Black box of shit."

The islander in him hated that machine. Often, he'd stare the blank, black eye out, staring at it for hours and hours, thinking about how it deserved to die, about how it would soon die, and, most fiendishly, about the manner of its inevitable and impending death.

A dream came two nights in a row. It told of a vision, a free man hacking a big, black eye to death with an axe while being serenaded by a cockatoo screeching as if the world had just been born. Each time he woke from this odd dream, he did so with a smile. All dreams are prophecies, after all.

---

* Apologies for demeaning the sheep shearing industry.

Chapter Five
Fingal Sees an Invisible Bird

Andrew McKenzie, Esquire, eventually trapped Fingal about six or seven weeks into The Experiment. The attack came early in the morning and completely out of the blue. One minute Fingal was absorbed in an email to his estranged father in Scotland and the next – POOF! – the Ghost of Donne magically appeared outside the French windows. As many humans do on seeing a Ghost, Fingal jumped out his skin.

In one hand Andrew held a jar of honey and, in the other, a pamphlet about Jesus. A huge smile consumed most of his little face. The sight of the gifts made Fingal shudder. Rarely on the continent was a gift given just for the sake of it. Something was always expected in return.

"Good morra to you, neighbour," Andrew called out while trying the door.

"Andrew. Morning." Fingal sprang from the chair to block the door. The last thing he wanted was a breach of the inner sanctum.

"Delighted to find you in situ," Andrew said while being ushered back a few steps. "I was about to send out the search party for you, Mister Fingal. I popped round a dozen times but you were out. Walking? Working? Sharing a glass of wine with Penny?" Andrew's eyebrows jumped up and down.

"Who?"

"Penny. From the pink house. You still haven't met?"

"No," snapped Fingal.

"That's not in keeping with the Binjari spirit. She's your neighbour, laddie. You should pop round. Say g'day. Cup of tea never hurt anyone." *Don't tell me what I should and shouldn't do!*

"In time, Andrew," Fingal lied.

In person, Andrew was a small, birdlike figure. His frame was tiny, his hair was thin, orange and grey and pasted to his small head with Brylcreem, and he had long, effeminate hands which protruded from the cuffs of a drab, navy suit. In terms of age, he looked to be about fifty-five or sixty, though with Christians it was always hard to tell. Akin to their ancient, musty religion, they seemed to age quicker than normal humans.

"You off to work?" Fingal asked.

"To prayer," the religionist answered sonorously. "To the House of God. You are aware it is the Sabbath?"

"Is it?"

Andrew sighed patiently. "I'm leaving for church in half an hour." The wide, green eyes scanned Fingal from top to toe, mildly scowling at the Scotsman's outfit – bare feet, board shorts and t-shirt stained with jam. "There's plenty of time to have a shave and get changed. A trip down the coast might do you good. A change of scene is always good for the soul." *Ah, right, the Ghost wants me to go to church? Fat bloody chance.* "Repent, and ye shall receive the gift of the Holy Ghost." Andrew beamed, gripped the honey and the pamphlet tighter, and added "Acts 2, verse 38."

"Andrew I was in the middle of writing an email—"

"Oh, that can wait."

"...to my father. And no, it cannot."

Considering the invasion, as well as the unexpected heat of the morning, Fingal was in no mood for sermons, chitchat, or diplomacy. Not that Andrew noticed. "Your grass could do with a bit of a trim," he said. "Look at it. It's like a jungle."

Fingal's grass was now a foot long and he adored it. Having an addiction to a manicured lawn was such a continental habit. "It's good for the animals."

"And it's full of weeds."

"Weeds are plants too."

"If you don't have a lawnmower I can lend you mine." Andrew snapped the lapels of his suit. "It's got an eighteen-inch blade. Cut that *mess* in jig time."

"I have a lawnmower," Fingal lied for the second time on the holy day.

"Well it can't be a very good one."

"It's getting repaired."

"All you have to do is ask." *I would rather cut each blade of grass with a pair of nail scissors, you invasive little wanker. Now, piss off!* is what Fingal should have said but, once more, the truth danced away. "A bit of work in the garden never hurt anyone," Andrew persisted.

"I do work." Fingal stroked his young beard. "I'm conducting an Experiment."

"Into what?"

"Isolation." He glared at his neighbour. "Running away. From the continent of man." *From people like you.*

"It's not good for men to spend too much time alone." Andrew smoothed his hair. "It does funny things to our heads."

"That remains to be seen."

A polite smile. "And what does your research entail exactly?"

Fingal just kept on lying. "I'm writing a book. About islands … with ropes … inside people's heads."

"I wrote a book once," Andrew replied with pride, "about growing vegetables."

"I must read it." Fingal stared at the strange trees. "My book will be different. It will be a literary masterpiece about—"

"Mary, Jesus and Joseph," Andrew interrupted and checked his digital watch. "Look at the time. I must be getting to church."

"The bell tolls for thee."

For an instant the Ghost appeared to recognise the line from Donne but he was too busy being a super-jolly-neighbour to stop and dwell. "Well, another wonderful chat, Fingal," he said. "Now I'd best be on my way. Shall I pop back round to collect you?"

"No, you shall not."

The little man pursed his thin lips. "It's important for a person to have spiritual meaning in their life."

"Wullie Mushroom didn't, and he seemed perfectly happy picking potatoes and microwaving large rabbits."

"Yes, quite." At last, a confused Andrew held out the Jesus pamphlet. "Anyway, I thought you might enjoy this brochure. It contains a lovely reading about community. You'll have to forgive the irony. The piece is entitled 'what good fellowship we once enjoyed as we walked together to the house of God'." He winked. "Psalms 55, verse 14."

Fingal snatched the pamphlet, figuring it was the only way to exorcise the invasive little Christian. "Thank you," he mumbled out of habit while inspecting the front cover. It was a colour painting of Jesus preaching to a crowd of rapt peasants atop some dusty, desert mound. The jar of honey came next.

"Take it," Andrew said as if it were nothing.

"The pamphlet is more than enough."

"Take it. I've dozens of jars. Hundreds. Take it."

"Honey doesn't agree with me, Andrew."

Andrew tiny little face looked as if it might burst into tears. "Take it."

"It's too sweet."

"Take it, please."

"Alright! Fine."

Fingal waited for another lecture on the ills of booze, or some snide remark about his scraggy beard, long hair, or long, floppy grass, but none came. His duty done, Andrew turned and minced down the verandah, stopping and pivoting when he reached the end. "Oh," he lied. "I almost forgot." *And here it bloody comes.* "The minister is doing me the great honour of coming up for lunch after church. As we speak, a delicious pumpkin stew is simmering away in my slow cooker." The man from the drab, green house rubbed his long hands together. "We might even crack open a bottle of elderflower wine. As it is the Sabbath, I will lay a plate for you, neighbour." And with that the Ghost was gone, drifting toward the front gate, intentionally whistling a hymn far too loud.

***

The exchange with Andrew left Fingal perturbed. Instead of reading about hermits he spent the morning pacing up and down the verandah, worrying about how to avoid pumpkin stew with a Minister and a Ghost that afternoon. Thankfully, fifty feet above the blue cottage a cockatoo screeched as if it were being burned alive. Compared to Andrew's whining, high pitched voice Fingal found the terrifying noise soothing, and soon recalled the bizarre Execution dream from the other night. His mind swung. "Get back to The Experiment, laddie," the islander exclaimed. "Time cut another rope." Fingal glared at the flat, black screen in his living room, which was silent for the moment. "Time to execute the television."

Working quickly, he threw a couple of bottles of beer, a cheese, ham and pickle sandwich, and some reading material into a bag, which he dumped outside the Nissen hut halfway down the wild garden. Next, the executioner returned to fetch the television from the living room, dragging it by its chord down the lawn and placing it on a large chopping block outside the hut, screen up, so it could watch its own demise. Certain that Andrew had now buggered off to church, and safe in the knowledge he was alone, Fingal then fetched a rusty, double handed axe from the shed and took a few practice swings. It was an unusually hot morning and a good sweat soon appeared but this didn't trouble him. Everyone on the island was looking forward to the brutal execution of the black, rectangular eye.

To make the television's Execution a bit more formal and interesting this time, Fingal decided to play a game. Instead of an immediate death, the television was to have the right to a free but certainly not fair trial. Whimsically, the accused – the stupid television – would have the accent and wherewithal of a London cockney peasant from the 1930s while the accuser – a hairy, sweaty Scotsman stranded in Australia – the marbled tone, authority and demeanour of a fierce high court judge.

"It's a busy morning at court," Judge Fingal began in a posh English accent, looking down at the television while toying with the axe. "You may inform us of your particulars." The accused remained silent. "Allow me to simplify. Who are you?"

"I'm a television," the obnoxious device answered, quietly. "M'lud."

"And what exactly is it that you do?"

"I try me best to make people 'appy, m'lud." Fingal turned the axe over in his hands. "I entertain all them people out there by taking their minds off things. I make 'em smile and laugh and forget about all their troubles."

"You deny them reality." The cockatoo shrieked again. "Might I remind you, machine, that your death is nigh. You are accused of brain-damaging billions of people, a plague of low-budget advertising, and the scourge of bloody *reality* television. Do you deny your criminality, Sir?" The television whimpered as Fingal raised both axe and voice. "Answer me, damn you!"

"It weren't my fault, m'lud," the television cried at last. "It were me father's fault, the bleedin' radio. He were the one who started all this. I swear it, on me dear mother's life. He's the one that should be on the block. He's the one you want, m'lud."

"Your father is already dead." Fingal chuckled. "Weeks prior I deep-fried the deceased in a pot of boiling vegetable oil. Now, stop your blubbering. To the charges! Television, you are to be executed for mental genocide, for spawning the concept of mass advertising and—"

"Think of me thirteen children, m'lud."

"Order in my court! You have interrupted my mind for the last time, dreadful contraption." Judge Fingal lifted the axe above high his head. "Television, the island finds you guilty of neglecting a chance to educate the entire planet. We, the court, also find you culpable of gross negligence in subjecting intelligent people to fucking pop idol."

"That weren't me, m'lud! That were Simon Cowell! 'AVE MERCY!"

"SILENCE! Do you repent?" The axe trembled in the still, warm air. "DO YOU REPENT, MACHINE!?"

"It weren't—"

"ENOUGH, YOU BOUNDER!" Fingal brought the axe down hard, crashing into the television's big, black rectangular eye, again and again and again. The cockatoo screeched overhead, warm wind rushed through the gum trees, and bits of glass, plastic, metal and wire flew everywhere. After a couple of minutes hacking, cursing, sweating and smashing the poor old television was barely recognisable. "Machine," the judge concluded, panting, "You are well and truly smote."

Killing a machine that he'd wasted years in front of felt wonderful, and the little experimental island in his mind drifted further from the continent of man. High on adrenalin Fingal thought of returning to the house and finding something else to destroy but he felt the mood at the edge of forest suddenly shift.

Something was watching him. He lifted his head slowly and, at last, at long bloody last, saw a small black and white bird sitting on top of the Nissen hut. It was the first invisible bird Fingal had seen since arriving in the forest.

What should've been a moment of triumph quickly deteriorated into one of terror. The black and white bird wasn't looking at him. It was looking behind him, at something or someone else.

Sweating profusely, Fingal turned to see a little girl from the pink house staring at him through a gap in the bushes. No more than five years old, the child appeared both terrified and amazed.

"Hello," was all Fingal could think of saying.

In reply, the little girl screamed the word "MUUUUMMMMEEE!" then fled toward the pink house as if the devil were chasing her, screaming all the way. "MUUUUMMMMEEE! THERE'S A MAN WITH AN AXE IN THE GARDEN! HE'S HURTING THE TELEVISION! MUUUUMMMMEEE!"

"Christ," Fingal said bitterly. "Can't a man execute a television in peace?"

He quickly weighed up the options: retreat to the blue cottage, hide, and inevitably face a confrontation with the little girl's mother, Jenny or Penny or whatever she was called, or man-up and go and hide in the forest. There was only one answer. Fingal dropped the axe, grabbed his bag and, scared of a little girl and her mummy, plunged into the anarchy of the sub-tropical Australian rainforest.

The little black and white bird followed.

The expedition began like the last. Badly. Five metres in he collected the same spider's web in the face, tripped and screamed. As he cursed and crashed on through the undergrowth, all manner of invisible animals flapped, slithered and scurried around him. Mosquitoes feasted on his bare skin, sweat blinded his eyes, and a vine with thorns slashed his arm and drew blood. "Go home," he shouted. "This is insane. No one knows you're here!" Dark visions swirled in his panicked brain: a green tree snake sinking its fangs into his cheek, a rolled ankle, a broken leg, his body torn to pieces by a pack of hitherto unknown man-eating dingoes, a bleached skeleton – his – surrounded by an excited bunch of Japanese tourists taking photos and making the V sign in the year 2025. "This is madness," Fingal said when his foot and half a leg disappeared into a hidden bog. "GO HOME!"

The little black and white bird regarded the Scotsman's progress with indifference.

Fingal was almost at his wits end when the terrifying forest spat him out into a wide, sunny clearing where a giant rosewood had once grown. Humbled by age or a storm perhaps, the enormous tree now lay flat and Fingal moved toward it with reverence. "Breathe man," he said while running a dirty, bleeding hand along the tree's scaled bark. "It's all right, mate." He clambered onto the trunk, walked toward its base and sat against the tree's mighty, unearthed roots. "It's cool," he continued, checking the clearing and breathing, deeply.

Now, perched on a nearby branch, the little bird scratched a tick-bite on the back of its head, peeped softly and glared at the big, hairy-ape thing sitting on the rosewood.

Fingal didn't yet notice the bird. He was too busy staring at the forest. It looked different from the inside, and the more he looked, the more he saw. There were a dozen ghost gums at the edge of the clearing: tall, straight eucalypts with smooth, pale white skin. Each was festooned with necklaces of vines that were, in turn, draped with long beards of greenish-grey moss. He saw ancient cycads three times his height, tree ferns that looked as if they belonged to the Jurassic age, brightly coloured rosettes of lichen, white, verdigris and orange in colour, and hundreds more creepers – all manner of vines armed with hooks, sticky tendrils and designs of world domination creeping along the ground toward the fallen rosewood. "They want the light," Fingal whispered.

Fed up not being seen the little black and white bird decided to sing a song. It was a simple if odd, loud and repetitive song consisting of just two notes, two hollow, tubular whistles played off and against the other. Fingal's wild, blue eyes searched the clearing. He'd forgotten all about the first sighting of an invisible bird. Then, looking down the trunk, he saw the lovely little bird puffing its chest out and whistling, at great volume, those two, beautiful odd notes. "At last," cried Fingal, "an invisible bird." He'd been searching for the damned birds for weeks and now, ten foot away, one was leaping about the trunk, whistling and staring at him.

"It must want some food," the bold explorer said while removing the sandwich from his bag. Poorly imitating the strange whistling song, the food song, he tore off a bit of crust and flung it to the ground. Immediately the bird swooped down and gobbled up the treat. "You want some more, pal?" This time he flung some crust on the trunk. The little black and white bird hopped and skipped toward the free and easy treat before devouring it. "Friendly little chap," said Fingal while holding out a third piece of bread. This time, the bird approached to within a foot of the big, sweating, bleeding ape, cocked its head then suddenly emitted a terrific screech and flew off into the bush.

"Marvellous," he declared before reclining against the roots of the fallen rosewood to scoff down the rest of his sandwich.

Black scarab beetles with orange polka dots wings droned to and fro, careful to avoid the baby-blue butterflies that flitted about the bright, sunlit clearing. Waves of delightful, inane birdsong drifted throughout the arbour, and a soft, warm river of wind meandered through the canopy overhead.

"Hypnotic," Fingal said after an hour.

"Mesmerising," he said after two more had past.

Fingal sat on the rosewood until the sun had set and the wind and birdsong were but a memory. For the first time since fleeing the coast a sense of happiness flowed through his sore soul.

The first step of the longest journey is always the hardest one to take, yet phase one of the John Donne Experiment – escape – was complete. Several ropes between his island and John Donne's stupid, overcrowded continent had been cut (or destroyed, executed, burned, boiled, smashed with an axe, et cetera). Now, misophonia hardly bothered him, no one called (because, still, he couldn't find his damned iPhone), and no friends randomly popped up from the coast. If anything, cutting himself off from the world was easier than he thought. There wasn't a great deal to miss about their world.

"The islanders must surely celebrate the end of phase one," said Fingal, raking through his bag until he found a bottle of warm beer. He stood, cracked the bottle open and raised it to the beautiful forest, to the industry of science, and to the death of all the machines, devices and ropes that had, so far, totally ruined his life. "IN THE NAME OF LORD FINGAL," he shouted in a loud, clear voice, "CHIEF STEWARD OF THE ISLAND, I CLAIM THIS WOODLAND REALM. HENCEFORTH, THIS PLACE SHALL BE KNOWN AS LITTLE GIRL CLEARING!"

Then something strange happened, something he'd almost forgotten how to do. For the first time since arriving in Australia, Fingal McKay, traveller, experimentalist and aspirational hermit, smiled. Not a little, half-arsed smile but a big, wide, free smile that soon began to hurt his face.

In a sign of further good fortune, the little black and white bird reappeared on the trunk, no more than two metres away. "Yes, my feathered friend," said the great ape to the butcherbird. "It is time to move The Experiment to phase two."

In reply, the cheeky little bird whistled two strange notes.

PHASE II
Human Versus Higher Love

Chapter Six
Milk and Honey (and Bugs)

The dawn sky was on fire. Spectral clouds with long, feathery fingers swirled overhead. Each was stained peach, ruby or, closer to where the sun rose, a blazing marmalade colour. As yet, no wind stirred in the canopy, and the warbles, whistles, hoots and sinister cackles from the birds echoed throughout the forest. Bathed in crepuscular pink light, Fingal sat on his lazy-boy throne and, as usual, was reading about hermits. Occasionally he'd glance up from his labour and tattered dais, flick a fringe of long, dark hair from his eyes, marvel at the hallucinogenic clouds and admire the birds, which were no longer invisible.

The reason he hadn't been able to see them before was simple: he'd been looking for them. The trick was to focus on the trees instead. These were relatively static so anything else that moved could be a creature, more often than not a bird. Cross-reference any untreelike movement with the direction of birdsong and a veritable aviary of strange, bawdy birds materialised. Above the blue cottage, for example, a white cockatoo wobbled against the huge sky, screeching as if the world had just begun. In the huge silver flooded gum above Andrew's drab, green cottage, a flock of pied currawongs, big, black birds with stout beaks and yellow eyes, played hide and seek, their ghostly calls wailing through the still, warm air. A squadron of rainbow-coloured lorikeets barrelled through the garden, squealing in delight, three honeyeaters flitted around a banksia in early bloom, and in the magnificent fig tree that dominated the pink house, a mob of kookaburras hooted with laughter at some inside forest joke.

"Speaking of birds," said Fingal. "Jackie will be here soon." He tapped his notes in order, collected Jackie's terracotta saucer from the railing and made for the kitchen, whistling two opposing notes in a most playful fashion as he vanished inside. It was his favourite song – the food song.

So far, the research into hermits had proved enlightening. For one, it confirmed that artists of isolation did not have to be into God, live in a hole in the desert or exist on a diet of raw rabbit. Nor must they dwell in an actual cave, sleep on a dirt floor or follow the ascetic life, that is, a life of austerity, self-denial and abstinence. Just because a person craved solitude didn't mean they had to forsake mattresses, money and chocolate. In fact, there were no rules to the eremitic tradition. Most hermits were ordinary, non-religious people who made things up as they went along. They were experimentalists, in other words.

Many were to be admired. Fingal's favourites were the Transcendentalists, clever people that embraced the natural world over man-made dominion. To them, the celebrated institutions of society – religion, government and the judiciary, for example – corrupted rather than served the individual. Only by shunning the world of "man" and returning to nature could the soul have time to breathe, to blossom. The writer Henry David Thoreau (1817–1862), Scottish-American naturalist John Muir (1838–1914) and photographer Ansel Adams (1902–1984) aptly personified such dictums. Of these marvellous creatures, Thoreau is perhaps the best known because he wrote a famous book called *Walden* (1854), after spending two years, two months and two days in the wilderness. "I went to the woods," Thoreau wrote, "because I wished to live deliberately, to front only the essential facts of life, and see if I could not learn what it had to teach, and not, when I came to die, discover that I had not lived."

Other people became hermits because they disliked capitalism, technology or materialism. Heartbreak played its part too. A woman in New York City, for example, decided to live entirely "in cell", following a "devastating event" in her life. Groceries and anything else this urban hermit needed were delivered, and she left only for church on a Sunday. Slowly, the lady healed. After a few years, she wrote "I began to notice that time I spent alone was balm for my injured soul. Worldly ties began to unravel. I am happy. And no, I'm not lonely :-)"

Some people became islands because of events outside their control. Consider if you will Hiroo Onoda, a Japanese soldier who refused to believe World War II was over and spent twenty-nine years hiding in the jungles of Lubang, The Philippines. Lost to the giant Podocarpus trees Onoda waged a solo guerilla war until 1974 when his former commander had to fly from Japan and order the soldier to stand down, as well as convey the news.

"Erm, Private Onoda, I don't really know how to put this but, well, we lost."

"You lie! You lie!"

"It's true, Private. The Emperor surrendered."

"You lie." The soldier's red eyes contort. "You lie! I kill you! You lie!"

"I take it you've never heard of the atomic bomb?"

"The what?"

"Take a seat, Private."

Oh, to be a spectator for that conversation.

Fingal was in the kitchen, now singing a human song: "hey Jackie you're so fine, you're so fine you blow my mind, hey Jackie! Hey Jackie!" As he sung, he broke bread into Jackie's terracotta saucer, glancing up at the verandah railing every twenty seconds. This was his friend's landing strip. A punctual creature, Jackie would arrive soon. "Oh Jackie, what a pity you don't understand, you take me by the heart when you take me by the hand."

The list of reasons why some humans chose the "hidden life" was endless: bankruptcy, the coming apocalypse, a Republican victory in the U.S. election, too many good drugs, too many bad drugs, and one strange case of vestiphobia (a fear of clothing; a woman from Belize, not Scotland). All hermits, however, shared one thing in common: weariness, of a job, relationship or, commonly, other people. Most of them just needed a break.

Why then did mainstream society call tired people who wanted to be alone such horrible names? Beggars, bums, crazy-ladies (or men), curmudgeons, drifters, gypsies, the homeless, hoboes, loners, the mentally insane, recluses, spinsters, tramps, weirdoes, wretches and vagabonds were just a few of the ill-founded labels society had conferred on the exhausted and disenfranchised. Was it because they were different? Or dirty? Or mad?

If, heaven forbid, a continental encountered a hermit they usually looked the other way, shook their heads in pity, or pretended to be on the phone. Poor, tired hermits: among but not of the continent, invisible as birds in a rainforest. In time, Fingal came to realise a simple truth: continentals weren't really that scared of hermits. Deep down in their empty, materialistic, and tiny hearts, they were just jealous.

Fingal scratched his beard, added a dash of milk to the bread in Jackie's saucer and switched tracks, singing in a low, sombre tone. "Oh, Jackie boy, the pipes, the pipes are callin'." For a touch of *je ne sais quoi* he drizzled some of Andrew's honey over the dish and topped it off with a dead jenny long legs, four flies and two small, white spiders. Jackie liked his honey and bugs. "From glen to glen, and down the mountain side. Oh, Jackie boy, I don't know the rest of the words, la-da-di-dah, da-ra-da-ra, da-ra. OH, JACKIE BOY!!!"

Society? What the hell would that swamp of festering puss know? All those cruel names, Fingal realised in a second moment of theoretical epiphany were because continentals often confused hermits with misanthropes. Most used the terms interchangeably and, ergo, incorrectly. Misanthropes are not hermits. Most wrongly assume that hermits become hermits because they were dealt a shit hand in life: a woman left them, a judge shafted them, that prick of a boss sacked them, their dealer gave them bad heroin, and so on. Driven to the edge, they just had to hate that which cast them to the street: people and society.

Wrong. Wrong. Wrong.

Hermits don't hate anything, nor do they seek redress or revenge or recompense. They covet peace, nature and isolation. To repeat, most just need a break.

A misanthrope, on the other hand, hates everything and everyone, including themselves. Shakespeare's Timon of Athens, Dickens' Scrooge, and Jules Verne's Captain Nemo, who so despised humanity that he took to hiding deep in the oceans in a luxurious submarine, are all good examples. The creative arts industry regularly produces misanthropes, writers in particular. The American author Kurt Vonnegut often expressed cynical views of society, as did Kafka, Sartre, Swift and Jane Austen. In *Pride and Prejudice*, for example, Elizabeth Bennet says to her sister Jane:

> "You wish to think all the world respectable, and are hurt if I speak ill of any body … There are few people whom I really love, and fewer still of whom I think well. The more I see of the world, the more I am dissatisfied with it; and every day confirms my belief of the inconsistency of all human character, and of the little dependence that can be placed on the appearance of either merit or sense."

You get the drift. Misanthropes such as the ancient Greek Cynic Diogenes of Sinope, the philosopher Søren Kierkegaard (in his younger, Mr A days) or Emily Dickinson, the nineteenth-century introvert and anchorite might loom large in the arts but, by all accounts, were sad, cantankerous individuals.

No, a hermit is not a misanthrope. There's a big difference between hating something and needing a break from something. One path kills the soul, the other enlivens and replenishes it.

"Jaaaaaaaa-ck-ieee." Fingal went for a Sam Cooke number this time. "Draw back your bow, and let your arrow flow. Straight to my lover's heart, for me, for me."

Now back outside, the aspiring hermit placed a saucer brimming with milk, bread and honey, and sprinkled with dead insects, on the wooden verandah railing. He then ambled to the rear of the verandah, his attention flicking between the forest and his unkempt lawn, which was now a melee of tall grasses, weird weeds, and young, spindly saplings. Again, he whistled the Food Song – two notes, two hollow, tubular whistles played off and against the other – out into the forest.

After a minute or so, a flash of untreelike movement caught his eye. "Right on time," said Fingal, admiring the little black and white bird gliding in from the forest and landing with the grace of a danseur on the verandah railing. The butcherbird regarded Fingal earnestly then hopped toward the saucer, laying claim to the food by gently placing a little claw on its rim. "Good morning, Jackie Boy," Fingal said with a wide, free smile.

Five, maybe six days – he couldn't be sure – had passed since the television's execution, the subsequent discovery of Little Girl Clearing, and the first encounter between man and bird. That glorious meeting felt like it occurred years ago, however, the hermit was beginning to realise, time moved differently in the jungle. Since then Jackie had appeared at Fingal's blue cottage every morning, no doubt drawn by a free feed. What started out as a crust flung off the verandah soon evolved into bread soaked in milk and honey (Fingal's joke at Andrew and his omnipotent yet invisible God), sprinkled with any dead insects lying around. Jackie adored the dish.

Man and bird's relationship was symbiotic from the outset. Jackie got free tucker and Fingal got a friend. Friendship, the architect decided, was within the bounds of The Experiment. Other islanders, famous ones, had chums, so why shouldn't he? Robinson Crusoe had Man Friday and Chuck Noland (Tom Hanks' character in the movie *Castaway*) Wilson the Volleyball, so it wasn't as if any hermit rules were violated by befriending a little bird. The company certainly lifted the spirits in the rainforest.

Fingal christened the bird Jackie, after Jackie Milburn, a legendary Newcastle United football player from England that his father used to talk about (the team played in black and white strips). The bird had to be male because of its cockiness and strutting bravado, because, he, bold Jackie, had the courage to fly out of the woods and establish first contact with a great ape while his brethren languished in the forest, safe but starving.

"That didn't last long," Fingal said to the bird after it had devoured the meal. In reply, Jackie looked up, blinked and hopped to a bowl of water, scooping then sculling the liquid as if was a yard of ale. "Aye," said Fingal with a flick of his young, bearded chin. "You're a fine wee bird, Jackie-boy."

Jackie's plumage wasn't stained in exhaust fumes like the butcherbirds on the coast, scruffy, sneaky little birds that hung around in gangs. Groomed by the rainforest, the blackness of his hood, cape and wings was rich, immaculate and candescent; the white of his chest was clean and brilliant, pure as fresh snow. A working bird, his beak was grey and scuffed from constant labour, wear and tear, as were his wrinkled stockings and cute little dinosaur feet. These now skipped along the railing, as he settled on a good whistlin' spot. Happy, sated, Jackie then offered thanks by singing to the world, whistling, chortling and warbling crazed scales of notes in the most beautiful, haphazard fashion; a rainforest tenor performing on a wooden stage for an audience of one. Their friendship was further proof that John Donne's no man is an island shite was just that: shite.

Phase two of The Experiment was proceeding gingerly. More of the lesser ropes that bound Fingal to society had been severed. Recently, for instance, he had buried his house keys (alive), executed the postbox by throwing it off a cliff, and, because he hated it, because it was an emblem, a uniform, and because so many of them wore them, had crucified his pin-striped business suit at the edge of Little Girl Clearing, nailing it to a crude cross before dousing it in petrol and setting it on fire.

The few friends he had on the coast no longer visited. No one nipped up for a feed or a wine anymore. No one emailed. Brotherly comrades from Scotland, men that used to swear drunk they'd bear Fingal's pall to the grave, eventually gave up too. Facebook – thank someone's God – fell silent. Fingal didn't mind having no social life. In the forest, there were no stupid brunch, drink or dinner parties to attend, no great festivals of commerce such as Easter or Christmas to buy presents for, and no births, marriages or deaths to endure. Lost among the trees Fingal had time to think and breathe and stare; time to admire clouds, crooked trees and beautiful, simple birds.

"Strange," the Scotsman noted of the change in Jackie's behaviour. With alacrity, the bird began puffing out his chest and feathers, glaring into the garden, and making a low, aggressive clicking sound. Following the bird's stare, Fingal soon understood the cause behind the effect. Thirty feet away, perched atop an enormous yucca, a female magpie lark was grooming herself, looking everywhere but at the macho-tough-guy-Jackie.

"Ah, a member of the opposite sex," Fingal noted with a playful smile. "Forget about it, Jackie. They're all trouble. Cut the rope, mate. Cut it now!"

Typically, the female butcherbird judged Jackie's performance with a sort of "is that it" look, screeched and fled. Fingal shook his shaggy head as Jackie transformed from macho, tough guy to quiet, sleek aviator, and the friends sunk into silence as each briefly pondered the vicissitudes of sex.

Fingal hadn't done it for ages. Truth be told, he was emotionally exhausted from decades of thinking about, chasing or engaging in sex, relationships or love. Since running away from the coast his hegemonic penis no longer exhibited the same old hunger for conquest and empire. It too seemed tired and weary, and only interested in peace and quiet. There was some sadness to this development, for the two chums had enjoyed some rip-roaring adventures together, all over the world, and with strange, exotic creatures. In the last few years, however, Fingal and his penis just felt as if they were going through the motions: put on fancy clothes, go to bar, get drunk, buy women drinks, hit them with lines 7, 33 and 86 from the repertoire, propose a kebab, an exciting skinny dip, or a sunrise, est voila, "ye'r in like Flynn," as a pal used to say in the old country. Well-trodden, the path of lust had grown dull, typical and boring. Also, Fingal's last romantic experience had been a cruel, bizarre one: raped – there is no other word for it – while passed out on a beach by a creature he christened The Beast of Byron Bay (a story for later). In sum, this was just normal. Aged thirty-seven, the ol' libido was starting to wane, as it did for most men.

"Sex," said Fingal in a small voice, "so much sex." He shivered as a montage of discotheques, booze, drugs and tits flooded his mind. "No, no, no!" he said, tilting his head and smacking the side of it, trying to force the vulgar, continental memories out. "Be gone," he shouted. "No place for dirty thoughts on the island. Not anymore."

For respite, Fingal forced his train of thought back onto the simple beauty of the black and white rainforest magpie lark. But the rope of S.E.X. was a thick, sturdy one, intertwined with the veins on the body; hardwired into the system.

Sometime later, the aspiring hermit frowned. "Come to think of it," he pondered aloud to Jackie, "do birds even have penises?" In reply, the butcherbird turned its head, peeped twice and flew off, no doubt disgusted by the sudden change in topic.

"I thought it was a fair question, Jackie-boy," said Fingal, picking up Aldous Huxley's *The Doors of Perception*. He had read but two sentences when the dawn quiet was shattered by ABC morning news blaring from the weird little turret on top of the drab, green cottage next door. Andrew, the Ghost of Donne, had risen. "Fuckin' hell." The bearded Scotsman stood up and fled to Little Girl Clearing where he could read Huxley in peace. "For such a little man," he said when passing by to the source of the dreadful racket, the drab, green cottage, "you sure do make a lot of noise."

Chapter Seven
Penny from the Pink House

No one ever used to say hello on the coast, which was anathema to Fingal. In Scotland, complete strangers made a point of crossing the road just to belt out a friendly "mornin'" or customary "aye". It was as if meeting another person was the high point of their day. But not in Australia. Not on the coast. Here, saying hello was always an awkward experience. Fingal lost count of the times he'd be walking down an empty beach, dreading the prospect of saying or not saying hello to another human walking up the beach. Older, well-mannered people usually offered a g'day, a tip of a cap or flick of a chin but the younger ones didn't even bother. They hid behind sunglasses or pretended to watch a seagull or a wave or a cloud.

Why was this so?

It was because of those darn convicts. Between 1788 and 1868, roughly 164,000 convicts were transported to Australia for crimes ranging from poaching a pheasant during a famine to army desertion in the face of certain death. Despite the fact that more free settlers arrived during the same period Australian society remained infected by fear, distrust and estrangement. The convict stain was impossible to get out the national laundry. The country, itself a huge island, was still a goal where silence and estrangement ruled.

Add to this unfortunate criminal stain, a bunch of pissed-off old, black people, and a healthy dose of psychotic nature – floods, droughts, famines, bushfires, snakes, scorpions, spiders, sharks, stonefish, and so on – and it was crystal clear why settlers past and present referred to Australia as the Fatal Shore. This place was a death sentence. No wonder no one ever said hello. No wonder they all hid behind their sunglasses. People were simply preoccupied with trying to survive. Locked in a daily battle to simply remain alive, no wonder continentals kept themselves to themselves. Fear had compounded a fundamental condition of alienation between strangers in a strange land (to borrow from the title of Robert A. Heinlein's 1961 sci-fi novel). Fear, estrangement and silence had a distinct sound in Australia: oppression, born from history, nature and the growing pains of building a society born from criminal stock. You could hear it, particularly at night, when it was dark. In the darkness, the sound came alive. It lived and breathed, and weighed heavy on the eardrums; in, and on the heart.

This brilliant theory – Fingal's, of course – would soon be utterly refuted, for a visitor was about to call, a stranger from a strange land. The emissary would come from the pink house and took the form of a human, a woman nonetheless, the first one Fingal had seen or spoken to since fleeing the coast months ago. The woman arrived early one morning when Fingal was bent over the wooden verandah railing, inspecting a dead cockroach that a hundred ants were methodically disassembling.

"Hello," the female voice rang out from beyond the bushes at the front of the blue cottage. "Anyone home?"

"Hello!" Fingal said out of habit, forgetting the ant experiment, walking down the verandah and out onto a path through his lawn, dry grasses, weeds and saplings whipping at his bare legs. He didn't really know what was going on. His body moved of a will of its own.

"Hello? Is anyone there?"

Fuck's sake. "I'm coming," snapped Fingal, darting through the doorway in the front wall of garden. However, when he emerged on the other side a wide, friendly smile replaced the aspiring hermit's grimace. He was powerless to stop it because a stranger, a beautiful woman, stood on the other side of the fence. She was dressed oddly, mind you, in steel capped boots, a black security guard's outfit and cap with the word DOGS embroidered on its crest.

"You haven't seen a cat, have you?" the woman asked.

"Afraid not."

"I've lost mine. Sooty's his name."

"A black cat?"

"No, no." She frowned. "Sooty's white."

"Funny name for a white cat."

"Everyone says that." *Well maybe you should change its name then?* "I'm Penny, by the way. From the pink house."

"The pink house? Next door?" She nodded, and he stroked his fine, young beard for effect.

Damn that gossip-mongering wretch, Andrew. Three kids to three different fathers, wasn't that what the little prick had said? Up until this point, and due to such misinformation, Fingal had imagined that Penny from the pink house was some sexed-up child-factory, some tall, blonde skank with sagging teats, bandy legs, and an active, dropping gusset. In his mind, she was a beast, a ravenous sexual predator; a maneater, wasn't that what they used to say?

The reality couldn't have been further from the truth. Penny was small, curved and buxom with dark, freckled skin, cheeky blue eyes and a magnificent set of white, straight teeth.

"Didn't think anyone lived there anymore," Penny said with a nod to Fingal's property. "I'd heard that Peter had run away or something because he didn't like the ticks. He was a bit weird, Peter."

"Oh," said Fingal and gulped.

"It's been so quiet."

"That's the way I like it," Fingal replied a bit too quickly.

"How long you been in Binjari?"

"About four or five months."

"That long?"

"I think. I can't be sure. Time is not important to me anymore."

Penny smirked. "And we've only just met? That's terrible."

"It's because of the convicts." Fingal couldn't believe his mouth was speaking. "A historic fear of nature, the Old People, and history has compounded a fundamental condition of alienation between strangers in a strange land."

"What?"

"Alienation. It always leads to estrangement."

Poor Fingal. It had been a long time between flirts. Penny looked at him funny and tied her thick black hair in a ponytail. The gesture exaggerated her slim waist and round breasts.

"Dogs?" he asked, keen to change the subject.

"Dogs?"

Fingal pointed to her cap. "Dogs?"

"Oh yeah, dogs. I work with security dogs."

"No wonder your cat ran away."

Penny laughed. "I don't keep them here. I pick them up from the depot in the evenings then walk around some bloody factory with them all night."

"There's such a thing as a depot of dogs?" Fingal asked out of genuine interest.

"The hours are shit but the money's good. Kids aren't cheap." *Ah, yes, the kids*, thought Fingal. *We'll just forget about those for a mo', shall we?* "What do you do?" Penny asked, also keen to switch topic. "You work down the coast?"

"Used to. Took a year off." The lie got easier and easier each time. "Wanted to write a book."

"You're a writer?"

"At the conceptual stage," he sort of lied. "Sketching, dabbling, you know. Warming up for the big show."

"That's awesome. I'd love to write a book."

Fingal chuckled with bogus modesty. "They do say everyone's got a novel inside them."

Penny leaned in. "I love books."

"Do you now?" This was bloody easy. What was it they used to say? Like shooting fish in a barrel? "Me too."

"What you reading?"

"Aldous Huxley, *The Doors of Perception*."

Having never heard of the book Penny just said the word "cool".

"You?"

"*The Handmaid's Tale*."

"Cool."

An awkward silence built as the strangers ran out of meaningful things to say. Penny stepped back, smiled and said, "I'd better keep looking."

I'm right here, baby. "For what?"

"Sooty."

"Ah, yes." The aspiring hermit raised an unkempt eyebrow. "Sooty the white cat."

"Let me know if you see him." Penny turned nimbly, and headed toward the path that led to Shaky Old Col's house. "Just come around. Door's usually open."

Door's open? What!? "Will do." *Was that a come on?*

"Tell ya what," Penny called out. "It's gettin' bloody hot."

"Too right," whispered Fingal, momentarily hypnotised by Penny's firm, round arse.

"We could do with the rain!"

"We most certainly could." Fingal looked up at the huge blue sky. The beautiful stranger had a point. It was getting bloody hot. In but the space of seven sunrises the air had grown warmer and heavier; thicker. The sky above Binjari national park was no longer cold, pale and high. It burned a rich cobalt and seemed closer, as if it was descending in daily increments.

"Sooty!" Penny called out in her sweet, succulent voice. "Sooty! Here puss, puss, puss, puss. Bloody cat."

As Fingal's neighbour merged with the bushes he felt entirely defeated. With all the recent, mad science he'd forgotten about the old, natural desires, and temptations. In all the months he'd been experimenting, sex had barely crossed his busy mind. Sometimes, he grew aroused but the sound of a honeyeater singing at dawn soon erased any desire.

Now, sweat ran down his spine, his retired penis stirred to life, and his body felt light and giddy, as if its flesh, skin and bone were made from a million delirious butterflies that might suddenly explode. Breath came short, hot and sharp, and all he could see in his mind's eye was not a peaceful island but a giant rope tattooed with the letters S.E.X. Instead of uttering the actual word, that was what old people in Scotland used to say.

S.E.X., as if saying the word sex would immediately cast them to the pits of hell.

"Ah," the scientist in him deduced. "So, we come to the fickle rope of sex." At the mere mention of the word the old cranks and pistons in his groin creaked and coughed and spluttered.

"What?" Penny called out from somewhere in the bushes.

"Nothing! Did you find your cat?" he asked, stupidly.

"NO!"

"Oh, ok. Good luck then."

This time, Penny did not bother replying. *Shit*, thought Fingal, *she must think you're a right lunatic. You'll never get a ride if she thinks …* He slapped himself, hard. "Forget about it, man. It's just the old ways."

Wisely, Fingal and his penis retreated to the cottage, muttering "we must cut the rope of S.E.X.", as they went. "The sooner the better."

The promise to sever all ties with sex was a disingenuous one, like that of a smoker promising to quit. They never really meant it.

"A final shag for the road wouldn't hurt," Mr Hyde said once back in the safety of the blue cottage.

"NO!" Jekyll snapped back. "That's what continentals do. It's why there are seven billion of the fuckers!"

At the time, Fingal didn't realise the pain that cutting the rope of sex would cause. The rope of sex – or love, or whatever tinsel you wish to dress the tree with – is a dramatic monster of a thing, a colossal bond tying billions of humans together. For many continentals, the prospect of a life without sex is no prospect at all. It's what they're built for, why they're all bloody here, and why sex is often referred to as an industry.

Come to think of it, the voices began shortly after meeting Penny. The Professor was the first, followed by many others. Sex will do that to a man. It can and often does induce a mild form of madness followed by series of blind, reckless actions. "Bloody Trojan war started all because Paris fancied a poke," he said and, still horny, slumped into the lazy-boy. Fingal refilled his glass with warm wine and tried to focus on the crooked tree at the foot of the garden. "Just once?"

"No!"

He pinched himself, hard, digging his long, dirty nails into the flesh on his thigh.

"Man, she had nice eyes."

He really meant to say the word tits.

Chapter Eight
The Book

A second dangerous fever, besides S.E.X., began to stir in the forest: boredom. Months had passed since fleeing the continent and, if the truth be told, the endless routine of sleeping, eating, reading, sleeping, hiding, drinking, eating, and staring at a lovely black and white bird was starting to get a bit old. To fend off the boredom, Fingal's island required another industry besides science – a hobby, perhaps, like woodcarving or painting or a learning to play a musical instrument? These, however, sounded too hard or too continental or, equally, too boring.

Fingal decided to turn a lie into reality. He decided to write a real book. This decision was taken two days ago, at precisely the moment when Penny from the pink house said, "I love books". The scientists inside his head were thrilled by the decision. Writing a book fitted neatly underneath the mother discipline of The Experiment. "It was a sub-field," they said, much like the nascent Defence Industry, which was exclusively concerned with keeping Andrew off his property, not that he'd seen or heard the sanctimonious little shite for a while.

Beyond the scientific value of the writing, the decision made total sense. For one, Fingal enjoyed writing. As a child, teenager and adult he kept a diary, including two bulging A4 travel journals – one for each year he'd travelled the world looking for answers and searching for silence. Alongside P.E., history and Classical Studies, English had been his favourite subject at school, and he'd hung around unis for far too long, writing complex, esoteric papers his professors could barely understand. The islander liked writing, liked exorcising thoughts from his mind and putting them onto a piece of paper. It was cathartic, or so he believed, way back in those hot, giddy, early days of phase two.

Furthermore, the blue cottage seemed like a good place to write. It was relatively quiet, and had a desk, chair, printer and computer. And, and putting the horse waaaaaaay before the cart, if he did write a book it might get published. It might sell millions. Hell, someone might even make a movie out of it. The script alone would net a couple more million. Fingal McKay, author, screenwriter, et cetera, would then become as rich and famous as J.K. Rowling, with her stupid goblins, fantasy schools and prepubescent English wizards. Weighed down with gold, he could then flee this strange, dry, red land. Shit, yes, he might actually return to Scotland – familiar, dank and green – and buy and hide in a real castle with a private forest, loch, whisky distillery, and private golf course. Writing a book was a brilliant decision. As ever, the aspiring hermit couldn't have been further from the truth.

***

Hobby. What a stupid word.

Onomatopoeically, it sounds like such a gentle, harmless and normal word.

Hobby.

Most continentals have one, and most are short-lived, expensive and regretful pursuits. Gardens, sheds and garages are strewn with hobby detritus: half-finished boats, sports equipment (multi-gyms, skis and mountain bikes, most commonly), knitting-machines, guitars with three strings, dusty English–Spanish dictionaries, and rusting classic cars, held together by the tarpaulin that covers their owner's shame. For other more maniacal people, those that stick at their hobbies, those who slave over model railways, aircraft and ships (always bigger and bigger and more complex), collect vinyl records, assiduously follow a sports team, or grow huge, prize-winning vegetables, the hobby becomes their whole reason for living. In such a guise, hobby is a grossly incorrect term: soul-sucking, deadly obsession is a far more appropriate.

As Fingal would soon come to learn, a hobby can be a very dangerous thing. The true hermit should be able to do nothing.

NOTHING.

The Zen tradition, for example, encourages its followers to literally *be* nothing (even thinking about thinking about nothing is forbidden). In Taoism, one of the first lessons taught is *wu wei*, non-doing or non-action, defined as dropping judgment, greed and passion. The follower of the Tao must exist in harmony with the planets, just as they revolve around the sun in an effortless and spontaneous movement.

In terms of the specific benefits of nothingness, the experiences of Dr Usui, the founder of the modern Reiki movement, are informative. For a while, you see, Dr Usui lived in a cave.

> "Each day, he meditated and fasted. When Dr Usui awakened on the twenty-first day, he could not even see his hand in front of his face. It was like a new moon day, when no light shines in the heavens before the breaking of dawn … the light became very bright and streamed across the heavens to illuminate his third eye … His entire field of vision was a rainbow of colour. Bubbles of gold, white, blue and violet came out of the rainbow. Each bubble contained holographic Sanskrit characters of the Tibetan Buddhist teachings. A voice said, 'These are the keys to healing: learn them; do not forget them; and do not allow them to be lost.'"

The lesson for the would-be hermit? Do nothing and the universe can be your plaything.

At the time, however, Fingal didn't know any of this wisdom. What's more, if he did he would have still ploughed ahead. It all made sense: vanquish the boredom fever from the island, write a Pulitzer-prize winning book, and shag the woman from the pink house next door; once, just once.

The why debate settled, Fingal turned to the how question, that is, the appropriate *process* for writing a book. This didn't take long. As with every question these days he just Googled it (lying swine), punching the words "how do I write a book" into the keyboard. Within .19 of a second the screen filled with a number of friendly websites full of advice: *Thinking of writing a book? Here's what you need to know*, *10 ridiculously simple steps to cracking that first novel*, or *How to write using the snowflake method* (whatever that was). He spent days raking around the 'net, drinking, taking notes and dreaming, imagining how Orwell, Huxley and Welsh must've felt when the creative floodgates were straining to burst open.

Of all the websites, the best one was called The Writer's Room. It advised two important steps for the aspiring novelist. First, "work in a space you are comfortable with."

So, Fingal assembled his Writing Factory in the front right quadrant of the cottage, where the light shone brightest.

Second, the website advised to "make sure you've enough treats to keep you going. It's a good idea to keep the spirits up with some candy."

So, Fingal marched up to Gail's shop and bought three bottles of red wine, fifty grams of tobacco, and some rolling papers. On the island, the switch to red after months of drinking tasteless beer was greatly welcomed. Plus, red was more creative. It greased the writing joints, so to speak. Hemmingway and Fitzgerald liked their red-booze, and they did all right for themselves ... sort of ... ish. As for the tobacco, Fingal was an ex-smoker and the book provided the perfect excuse to start again. Smoking precluded writing, and writing demanded smoking. Period. The dormant addict in him simply couldn't wait to suck on that delicious, evil weed once more.

All that remained was the *what* question – what topic or theme to write about?

The answer came a few days later when six Kookaburras were cackling at Fingal from the edge of Little Girl Clearing. Subconsciously, the answer had always been there. "Society," he cried. "Society! Yes, yes. Write a book about how screwed up the world is! BRILLIANT!"

Suddenly Fingal was Archimedes and even shouted "eureka" as he leapt from the fallen rosewood and ran back to the cottage, expertly dodging the spider's webs, jumping over logs and easily outrunning the ravenous clouds of blood-sucking mozzies.

Once back at his desk, Fingal poured a hearty glass of red, rolled a vile, delicious smoke, and got to know his subject by brainstorming a list of bad things about society. As but a sample:

- Politicians that think people actually believe them.
- Tony Abbott. Fartsucker (must inc. ver 2.0 in book, aka Malcolm "Silverballs" Turnbull).
- Mobile "smart" phones, Artificial Intelligence, and electronic assistant things like Siri (talking to a robot. Come on! Really!?!?)
- Facebook (fucking Facebook), esp. photographs of people doing star jumps on a beach pretending to be, like, so happy. O.M.G. L.O.L.
- Images of other people's babies on Facebook.
- Facebook.
- Christmas.
- Fashionable rat-dogs that go by the name of Tina.
- People that use the word literally when they don't know what it means.
- Telemarketers: no longer a problem after landline execution ;-)
- Budget airlines, especially Ryanair.
- Queuing at self-service checkouts.
- Twitter. WTF?
- The media.
- Police, lawyers and judges. Crooks.
- Groups who scare other people: politicians, the media and terrorists … in that order.
- Vanity, men that dye their hair, and cures for baldness (including hair implants).
- Clothes on pets.
- Robert J. Oppenheimer. Knob.
- But most of all, JOHN-FUCKING-DONNE.

On and on he wrote and rambled. By the time the list was completed it ran to four pages of A4, Fingal's wrist ached, the bottle of red was empty and he'd smoked five horrible, tasty cigarettes. But the effort was worth it. In the womb of his left brain an idea began to form and, akin to cell division, it grew. There was something there, some story to be told about greed and humans, men and gods and the descent of society; some neo-Marxist diatribe embodied in a rollicking, page-turning novel that would sell millions; no, billions. All the author needed was prism, but an original, clever one.

Even in those excitable, early days the book process proved mentally and physically taxing. His lower back began to ache from sitting in the chair for long hours. A little cough also started from the smoking, but at least reminded him of the rules: one rollie per hour.

It was hot, too. Sweat beaded on his brow, gathered under his armpits, and ran down his arse-crack. It felt like he was sitting in a factory, not a creative arts studio in the rainforest.

High above the desk, strange spiders spun weird webs. In the shade under the desk, mozzies feasted on his rich human veins. Then, worst of all, a plague of big green flies descended on the cottage. They were horseflies and got in through the tears in the bathroom's fly screen. And they were very, very noisy, droning through the dark cottage before crashing into the window in front of the factory worker's desk. Confused and pissed-off, the flies then turned and attacked Fingal, buzzing into his long hair, growing beard or contorted face.

Too fast to swat, too big for the spider's webs, the only solution was to douse the beasts in fly spray bought from Gail's shop. The flies didn't like that very much. They battered into walls and windows then fell to the dusty floor, cluttered desk, or mouldy windowsill, spinning on their backs, wondering why they could no longer fly, buzzing like mad for a good minute or two before they finally lay still and dead.

Fingal christened the beasts as Very Annoying Green Flies (VAGFs), and he slaughtered them in their droves. One evening he counted twenty-six dead VAGFs on the windowsill, their wee, buzzy lives snuffed out by Gail's spray and his godly index finger.

Fingal hated causing any animal's death but the book was more important, and at least Jackie ate well the next morning. Fed an endless supply of milk, bread and honey, sprinkled with an endless supply of VAGFs, the little black and white bird hung around the verandah railing outside Fingal's desk more often.

Man and bird's bond deepened. Sometimes, Fingal ignored the book project all together and just watched Jackie messing around. Sometimes the bird tucked his wings behind his back and waddled up and down the railing, softly warbling to himself as if waiting for a bus that never came. On other occasions, Jackie might preen or scratch or scull water, or fluff and puff all his feathers out, screech and glare at the bushes in search of a root. But, most of the time, he just sat there, staring at Fingal's dry lawn. The bird sat for hours on end, just staring. "A Zen bird," Fingal often remarked with a chuckle and a cough. "Just like Wullie Mushroom."

Compared to humans and all their ruses, emotions and dramas, Jackie appeared to have no discernible mood whatsoever. Neither happy nor sad, he just was. His was a simple life – wake, defecate, sing, go get food off Fingal, crap, sing some more, stare at brown lawn, enjoy brief daredevil cruise through forest, drink water, stare at more lawn, crap some more then go to sleep, somewhere in the woods. His was an ideal if Sisyphean existence.

As the shifts in the writing factory grew longer and longer, however, Fingal stared at Jackie less and less. "The book!" a voice soon cried from the recesses of his mind. "Work," it screeched. "Work!" So, the recluse did, harder and harder.

In terms of process, something the factory soon grew obsessed with, Fingal couldn't stop writing lists about bad things that existed in society. There were now eighty-six pages of these lists. So he could see them better he blue-tacked them to a wall next to his desk. "That's better," Fingal noted while opening a second bottle of red wine. He then donkey-rooted a second smoke while the computer booted up. Microsoft's dread tune, a tune that had enslaved millions, droned throughout the factory, not that Fingal really noticed. "Penny will be so impressed."

Silly man.

Like Dr Usui, Fingal McKay should've just done nothing.

Chapter Nine
Exploration

One morning, after feeding Jackie milk, bread and honey, topped with twenty-nine recently gassed VAGFs, Fingal decided to explore a bit more of the rainforest on the doorstep. A break from the rapidly expanding Writing Factory would do him good. The labourer had been glued to the desk for the past four or five days, he couldn't be sure.

More importantly, going for a mooch around the bush might rid his mind of the increasing number of lascivious thoughts about Penny from the pink house. During waking hours, he was alright, able to banish thoughts about her lovely tits with a neat little punch to the face. At nights, though, when blackness draped the forest, he dreamed of suckling those tits, or digging his fingers into her round arse cheeks, of sticking his tongue so far down her throat he could taste her heartbeat. More often than not, he awoke in a state of arousal, ignored the song of the honeyeater, rose, drunk two mugs of wine, smoked four rollies, and forced himself to sit at the factory desk, which pleased some mad voice growing inside his mind. "Work is good," it said. "Factory be a nice place. Labour is good!"

The aspiring hermit knew it was wrong to covet sex, that it ran contrary to the whole purpose and nature of The Experiment (to be alone), but the desire to procreate ran strong in his brain and veins and feisty penis. With each passing day, no matter how much his mind told his penis to cease the dirty thoughts, Fingal found himself thinking more and more about Penny. There were only two solutions to the growing problem: shag it … or go for a long walk.

***

Dressed in Scarpa walking boots, shorts and a T-shirt with the words Discover Scotland written on it, Fingal McKay, explorer, strode out the front gate in the manner of Ludwig Leichhardt. Right was no good, because Christians and old, shaky men lurked in the woods. The path to the left held far greater promise. Maybe Penny would be in, lonely and naked and horned up after a night shift in some dark factory with only a ferocious Rottweiler for company?

"Just one peep," Fingal said on sticking his head though a gap in the bushes outside her place, "just a wee flirt." Penny's joint, however, was dead quiet. Fingal did notice that her thirty-foot sailboat had gone, and he did get to meet Sooty the white cat who purred and rubbed against his leg.

"If only you were your mother," he said and plunged deeper into the bushes.

It was yet another hot day in Binjari. The sky throbbed and, such was the density of the air, sunk lower by the day. The ground underfoot was rock hard, and every weed, bush and crooked tree looked absolutely desperate for a drink. Fat chance. Shaky Old Col recently told Fingal that it hadn't rained for twenty-seven days. The forest was deathly still. It appeared to have entered stasis, perhaps the only way to endure a summer drought: don't grow. Don't move. Just stay perfectly still.

Much to the explorer's surprise, Fingal discovered a lovely, wide and perfectly straight fire-trail a few minutes later. A stately avenue, it was lined on both sides with tall, elegant gum trees with rose-pink bark and slender, silver leaves. The fire trail ran parallel with the main road for a kilometre or so, and every now and then Fingal heard a car or a truck clank past, or one of those big, loud continental motor bikes driven by bored married men with small bikie fantasies, the loud, stupid, farting sound an affront to eerie hush of the rainforest.

Thankfully, the trail and road soon diverged, the path undulating downward, deeper and deeper into the jungle. After a while all Fingal could hear were his footsteps, or the hot wind moving half-heartedly through the leaves, and, curiously, a thumping noise like coconuts falling from a coconut tree. Obviously a beast fleeing his approach, but what?

To investigate, Fingal sometimes explored an animal trail to the left, expertly holding a Despidernator (a stick which neatly collected the spider's webs before they smothered his face) out in front of him. But he never could locate the source of that strange thumping sound. Instead the animal trails stopped abruptly at the edge of Binjari plateau. Here, the land and forest fell sharply until, seven or eight miles away, they met a vast, sweltering plain: the coast. These were awkward moments, like meeting an ex-lover on the streets.

"Oh, hi, Sarah."

"Hey, Fingal. Long time no see. How've you been?"

"Great, actually. Really good. You?"

"Fantastic. Work is going really well. Really well."

"Excellent. You still working at the bank?"

"Still slaving away, but you know how it is. Bills to pay. You still studying?"

"Sure am."

"That's lovely."

"Is it?"

A pause; a quick, derisory look from top to toe. "Nice to see you again, Fingal."

"You too, Sarah."

"It's Sara, actually."

"What?"

"My name is pronounced Sara."

"Ah. Sorry."

"Bye, Fingal."

"See you later, *Sara.*"

The coast was a blur to Fingal. Its miles of roads, canals and electricity pylons, its cheap, garish skyscrapers, and vast, suburban plains dotted with thousands and thousands of red little houses with overgrown gardens, barbeques, and swimming pools, were but mirages. Even the Pacific Ocean had vanished, devoured by the summer haze.

None of this vexed the explorer. The coast had always been a dream.

Half an hour later the fire trail came to an abrupt end. From a distance, it looked like a green rockslide had closed the trail, and that six very tall, black, skinny men with wild hairstyles were inspecting the damage. The heat was messing around with his head. The rockslide was nothing but a huge wall of jumbled up bushes, vines and young, desperate trees. The men were sentinels of the forest, ancient grass trees with black, scaled trunks, each topped with a plume of lime-green reeds bursting from their crowns like water spraying from a garden fountain. These magnificent living antiques grew less than a centimetre per year, meaning the taller ones, two and three times the height of Fingal, were six and seven hundred years old.

"G'day, Fellas," Fingal said to the grass trees in a passable Aussie accent, awed by both the discovery of the trail and the grandeur of the forest. Smiling and sweating profusely, the explorer found shade under a mature Macleay cypress, unslung his pack, sat, and leaned back against the tree's corked trunk. He then slaked his thirst, wolfed down two cheese and jam sandwiches, and rolled and lit a smoke, which he never finished.

Perhaps it was the heat, or hypnotic effect of leaves brushing against the low, blue ceiling overhead that caused him to drift off to sleep, or maybe it was the feeling of security the lost Scotsman felt despite being all alone in a scary Australian rainforest. It didn't really matter. A warm, heavy blanket of sleep fell over him and he slept long, deep and very, very still, as young, fledgling hermits begin to do.

When he woke sometime later Fingal assumed he'd woken in a beautiful pet shop. Firetail finches, tiny wee birds no bigger than a spool of thread, zipped about everywhere. There were heaps of them, with plain, brown feathers juxtaposed with stunning, scarlet facemasks, as if they were off to a masquerade ball but kept forgetting stuff. They didn't seem to fly or glide. Incredibly quick, they appeared to teleport from branch to branch, darting through the warm air, their tiny wings making a delightful, sporadic thrumming sound as they moved. At one point Fingal counted seventeen of them flitting back and forth across the fire trail, playing, fighting and – befitting of the summer season – fornicating; that is, the males trying and failing to couple with the females.

Dutifully, he christened the tiny wrens Little Devils.

Further up the fire trail, three pademelons nibbled on a rare patch of grass. Also in miniature, the little kangaroos were far cuter than their boorish, coastal cousins. Each one had coal-black eyes, tiny, pointed ears, wonderful copper coats, and small, stunted paws that hung limp and useless as they fed. Twitchy little buggers too, for when Fingal rubbed his eyes to make sure he wasn't dreaming all three Pademelons bolted and crashed through the forest. As they fled, their hind legs thumped and beat the dry ground, making a noise like coconuts falling from a coconut tree. "That's that mystery solved," Fingal noted with a wide smile.

Closer still, a brush turkey with a vertically folded tail scoured the leaf litter in search of bugs. It appeared to be wearing a red leather sock over its bald head, a collapsed, yellow Edwardian ruff and a pair of long, white socks. A large bird, it moved across the forest floor in the manner of a slow-motion speed skater that hadn't won a race in years. A train of red ants rolled over his boot, and five or six butterflies, lime-green in colour, danced around his head.

"They don't see me," Fingal whispered, finally grasping why so many creatures had chosen this moment to reveal themselves: he was sitting perfectly still. The reason he hadn't seen any serious animals in the jungle so far was simple. He'd been animated, crashing and bashing and cursing his way through the forest; jumping like a wretched little girl if a leaf even so much as grazed his skin. Now, perfectly still, he was part of the forest.

This was auspicious news in terms of The Experiment.

Fingal McKay was invisible.

Extraordinarily satisfied with the discovery, the invisible man was about to rise but then noticed a log – a big log – emerging from the forest and crossing the fire trail. *How*, he thought, *can a log move? And why does it bend? And why is the log making a hissing noise? Ah, it does so because it's not a log at all. It's a very, very big ... FUCK!!!*

To understand Fingal's reaction is to understand that there is one snake in Scotland. *Vipera berus,* the common adder, is black in colour and about as thick as a human's finger. It grows no bigger than sixty centimetres in length, feeds exclusively on a diet of mice, voles, shrews, frogs and newts, and is by nature an absolute coward (most likely because it lives in a freezing country where drinking whisky and fighting are national sports). In fact, many Scottish people will never even see an adder, so shy and timid are the little snakes. Therefore, the impact of a big, mean, five-metre python crossing the fire trail on the Scotsman was as terrifying as it was spellbinding.

The snake was almost close enough to reach out and touch. At first, Fingal thought about praying to someone or something but then remembered he no longer believed in the human god. He then thought about screaming but this would surely attract the great serpent, which would then swallow him whole. A bit of that hunter-gatherer-conqueror nonsense also stirred in his gut and Fingal decided that if he was going to be eaten, he'd go down fighting.

But in the end, and paralysed by beauty, he did nothing.

The ancient rainforest denizen had no interest in the great ape. It was too hot. The snake drifted past, fascination replaced fear, and Fingal soon found himself smiling. She – a she because a male would've eaten him already – was a magnificent creature with a sleek, flat head the width of two clenched fists, a pair of mystical, silver eyes, and a forked tongue about four inches long that constantly tickled and tasted the world. A foot in circumference at her widest, the snake had green and taupe scales that reminded Fingal of the carpet in his granny's old house in Scotland. She didn't slither or wriggle across the track. Trapped between liquid and material form she oozed and rippled and poured across the fire trail, right down to the tip of her tail, which now vanished into the bushes.

Curious, the explorer got to his feet and tip-toed to the spot where the snake had slid into the forest. He watched the python stream down a good, wide path that ended in some sort of gate. In the gloom, it was hard to tell. He was about to explore but the huge snake found a sunny spot on the path and magically rolled herself up. Not once did she take her silver eyes from Fingal. Her message was clear: "Simian, the path is closed for the day."

"Fair enough, Mrs Snake," Fingal agreed. "You've been more than kind enough. The island exploration committee will strike the trail another time." He bowed to the giant python, collected his pack and made for home, skipping more than walking.

On John Donne's crappy human-continent they say that a bit of company is important for enriching certain experiences, that it's good for humans to share magical events. However, Fingal felt none of that shite. Instead of feeling lonely, he jabbered aloud in a rich, excitable voice, recounting every detail of the pet shop experience – "How quick those Little Devils were! And what about those tiny, wee kangas!? They were sooooooo cute. Oh, and don't forget the killer python. How could I!?" It didn't matter that no friend or lover agreed by his side, or gently chided his innocent enthusiasm. For the first time in decades the words coming out his mouth were true, and held no deception. More importantly, he hadn't thought about the novel or S.E.X. for hours. He felt like an explorer that had just discovered a lost world, a vast, natural temple with no pews, stained glass windows, or idols, and, best of all, no other parishioners. The forest was his and his alone. In the dark, hot days that lay ahead, that day soon came to rank as one of the greatest days in the entire history of Islandtown.

***

Two hours later, Fingal was still jabbering to himself. So great was his delirium that he almost barrelled into Shaky Old Col on the narrow track that led to the brightly coloured rainforest cottages.

"Col!" Fingal shouted as if drunk.

"Oh, g'day, Fergus," Col replied with a watery smile.

"What a day for a walk!"

"She's a bit steamy."

Col had aged since their last meeting. He was shaking more than Fingal remembered and his wild, white hair was all over the place. The man looked ragged, and torn; beaten. He hadn't bothered shaving, and the skin on his face sagged so much that Fingal feared the whole thing might slip off at any given moment. He didn't care.

"Col," cried Fingal. "I just saw the most incredible snake. It was huuuuuge! Maybe five or six metres long. Guess what I christened the spot?!" Col fidgeted with his old, bent hands. "Python Gate!"

"Bloody hot," replied Col. "Plateau could do with a drink. Ha'n't rained for thirty-one days. Me tank's half empty." Col sighed. "No chance of seeing a king parrot in this weather. They always follow the rain."

Fingal pressed on, not caring if the old man was listening or not. "She was a monster, Col. A true killer. I was so scared, man, but she didn't even see me. It was like I wasn't there. You see, I was invisible!" He threatened the old man with mad, wild blue eyes. "Don't you see? The forest creatures come out if you sit perfectly still!"

"Thirty-seven days." Col's old eyes, amplified by a pair of cheap plastic glasses, darted around the jungle. "If it doesn't rain soon, I'll need to buy water in."

"Don't you see, Col? Python Gate is a ground-breaking discovery. Seminal!" Fingal too regarded to the forest. "The moment I stopped looking for the animals, I saw the animals!"

"'Magine that. Having to pay for something that falls from the sky." Col spat on the parched earth. "Three hundred and fifty bucks for a truckload of water. Bloody rip off."

"Eh, hello? Snake? Life-changing experience? Earth-to-Col?"

"You know Andrew's got five water tanks. Greedy little bugger." Col tried a smile. "They're all like, religious folk. Tighter than a mosquito's arsehole. I should drain a few of his tanks while he's away."

"Andrew's away?" said Fingal, too quickly for his own liking.

Col shivered despite the heat. "He goes to that bloody happy-clappy Christian retreat every year, somewhere down Byron way."

"How long's he away for?"

"Every bloody summer," was all the old man said.

Fingal stroked his beard ponderously. Of course, the news that Binjari National Park was ghost-free was terrific, so why then did his mood grow suddenly heavy? Ah, yes, continental business and all its pointless human drama. Seeing Shaky Old Col and talking and thinking about bloody

Andrew, the old ropes tightened and pulled Fingal's little island back toward John Donne's shitey continent. For a moment, Fingal contemplated turning and running back down to Python Gate but he was dying for a smoke and a glass of red, and Col was still speaking, albeit wrapping the conversation up.

"Right-o, Fergus," Col said. "I'd best be getting' home. Mary will be needing her dinner by now." Col began to shake even more. "Poor Mary. Poor old duck."

"Mary?" Fingal demanded, his smile long gone. "Is that your wife? Or your Daughter?"

"Be seein' you, Fergus."

Col went to leave but Fingal grabbed his arm. The man was clearly deaf. He shouted, "WHO'S MARY?"

"Mary?" The contact seemed to steady the old man. At last, Col's eyes found Fingal's and immediately glassed over. "Mary's me wife of fifty-two years, mate. She's sick. Very sick."

"Oh," said Fingal. What else was he supposed to say?

"Riddled with the cancer."

"Oh, dear." Fingal gripped the old man's arm harder.

"She's in a bad way. Skin and bones now."

The old man stared through Fingal, no doubt seeing their first kiss. "She never used to be like that. Used to be healthy. Strong. She used to love cooking, and walking. She loved the forest, 'specially the deep forest. Was where we had our first kiss. She wore a red dress that day."

"Sorry."

"Acht," he spat again, this time with meekness. Most of the dry spittle landed on his unshaven chin. "Poor old duck. Can't even get out her bed now. She can't eat. Doctors have got her dosed up the eyeballs on ... on, something. She can't speak no more, and she eats nothin'. She's dying, mate."

"Oh."

"Poor Mary."

"Can I help?" *Shut up, Brain. Human contact and kindness are NOT part of The Experiment!*

Col looked extremely confused. "Help?"

"Like, erm." Unused to humans, Fingal desperately searched his mind for something say but, selfishly, all his mind said was *Human contact and kindness are NOT parts of The Experiment!*

"Neh, mate," Col replied, with a sniffle. "She's a goner."

"You sure?" *Cease this madness!*

"I've got to get back." Col wrestled his arm free and began shaking once more.

"I can make soup!" *No you can't!*

"Be seein' you, Fergus."

"I *can* make soup!"

The old man ambled off, shaking more than ever.

"No wonder he's scared," said Fingal, moments later. "No wonder he shakes." Sadness born of empathy overwhelmed him. "Poor old bastard."

This human encounter totally ruined his day. Fingal abandoned the plans to burst into Penny's pink cottage stark-bollock-naked, and, shuffling home, no longer looking at the trees, or the sky, he soon forgot all about the Little Devils, Pademelons and the magnificent Mrs Snake. As Fingal shuffled toward the blue cottage, he was no longer a brave, intrepid islander, scientist, author and explorer. He was just a twat of a human, an insensitive prick that that had been clowning around and jabbering about animals in the face of Shaky Old Col's pain.

The sight of Jackie asleep on the gatepost with his feathers all puffed up (to cool his body in the heat) cheered Fingal somewhat. "Alright, pal," he said. The little black and white bird stirred, blinked his black eyes open, and drew his plumage back in, turning from feather duster to sleek aviator in seconds. A need to embrace something alive came over him, and Fingal reached out. He got within half a metre of the wild bird before it leapt from its perch and flew up to a lemon scented tea-tree, way out of reach.

Again, Fingal's mood beat down. Dragging his bag across the white gravel driveway, he opened the gate, and further admonished his insensitivity. He hated being a human, and all the emotional anchors it entailed. "I can too make soup," he said.

Chapter Ten
The Professor

A few days later – or was it a few weeks – Fingal McKay was back at work. For the past seven hours, he had been sitting at the desk, sweating, smoking, drinking, fighting off waves of attacks from the VAGFs, and, of course, labouring on his book. Thoughts of Penny, ropes, and old shaky men barely crossed his mind, so great was the early joy and distraction of being imprisoned in a Writing Factory.

Already, the hobby was turning into an obsession. The pressure inside in the cottage increased by the day, but at least the factory had begun producing. A few days ago, Fingal-the-writer had chosen a topic for his soon-to-be best-selling novel. Already, it had been decided that he would write a book about the decline of society. Cleverly, brilliantly, however, the story would be told through the highly original prism of sport! Yes, sport! It was sheer genius!

Thus, fittingly, the author christened his opus as *The Epic Novel of Sport*.

Both the title and topic seemed logical at the time. For one, when he used to live amongst them, Fingal didn't mind a bit of sport. Golf, football (with a round ball) and tennis were his thing, all chosen because they occurred outdoors. On the continent, sport had provided distraction and meditation from the world. Sport, after all, was what the body was designed for – all those beautiful muscles and bones and veins were not designed for working in a bank, or sitting at a desk for forty years. Sport, sport, sport, sport, sport. Bloody Aussies loved sport too. "Their national religion," they used to call it. Stupid continental heathens.

In literary terms the topic of sport also made sense. Well-read, Fingal knew that no *Epic Novel of Sport* had ever been written. There were plenty non-fictional books about sport, formulaic stories about tennis stars being imprisoned by their parents when they were young, or books about masochistic cyclists trying to explain that hurting yourself, taking horse tranquillisers and wearing spandex was normal, or, Fingal's favourites, books about boxers who rose from the ghettos, became word champs, battered their bikini-model wives, blew their fortunes, and took up crack before finding God.

But – but! – as for some roving fictional *novel* about sport, there was an obvious gap in the market. Thus, and brilliantly, anyone that played, bet on or consumed sport would be able to relate to his book. Relatability meant sales, chat show appearances, a movie deal and, subsequently, that marvellous castle in the Scottish Highlands with J.K. Rowling wailing in the dungeons.

And, finally, sport was a rich narrative topic. It could be tragic, unethical, moral, heroic, evil, heavenly and unifying, all at the same time. Granted, sport was a peculiar topic for an epic novel but a fecund, brilliant one, a virginal area for inquiry; a blank canvas that would sell for trillions of pounds!

The production line in the factory ran at full tilt from the outset. Already Fingal had created two A characters (a male baddie and a female goodie), a God (Heracles, the paragon of all that was good about sport), and five B characters; ordinary, amateur sports people who would come to feature in an obnoxious reality television show designed by the committee to boost public interest in the ailing tournament (should you care to know, the tournament ailed because "real sport was dying").

In terms of process, each character biography took up roughly three sheets of A4 paper, which were dutifully blue-tacked to the wall near his desk. Soon, crude maps of fictional cities, detailed chronologies, encyclopaedic backstories, sketches of characters or important buildings, flow charts of plots, and so on, joined the bios on the wall. These Mad Posters, as the creator named them one night while drunk, seemed to be multiplying. Not that the writer/aspiring-hermit cared. The process felt wonderfully creative.

For the moment, however, the creator was not creating. Instead Fingal was doing what many writers do best: drinking a glass of red wine, smoking a cigarette, and staring dreamily out the window.

Yet again, it was a stifling evening. The sun lingered on the horizon as a colossal orange eye that peered through the forest and bathed everything it saw in a rich, amber hue. The air was humid and pungent – low thirties, at least – and reeked of fire and folly, and misadventure.

"Sooty! Sooty!" Penny's sweet voice called out from the white gravel driveway. The penis department in Fingal's brain stirred into action. *Look lively, chaps! Quim on the horizon!* Like some randy automaton, Fingal stood bolt upright.

"Sooty, where are you?"

Fingal quickly threw on a t-shirt, shorts and thongs, rid his growing beard of crumbs and ash, and tucked his long hair behind his ears.

"Stupid cat."

All hands on deck, and be sharp about it!

"Soooo-tt-eeeeee!"

For effect, he grabbed a wad of paper, pen and a glass of wine, and ran down the verandah, out across the dying lawn and through the gap in the bushes, strolling by the time he emerged on the other side.

Target spotted, Admiral. Advise immediate engagement. Load the heavy cannon. "Don't tell me you've lost your cat again?" Fingal called out.

"Yeah." Penny turned, rolled her eyes and approached. "Stupid cat."

"Oh, Sooty will be fine." Fingal placed his free hand on the grey, wooden fence. "Nine lives an' all that."

"He'll have one less by the time I get hold of him."

They both smiled at the same time.

"And how are things otherwise, Penny?"

"Not bad. You?"

"Tremendous." *My sweet, sweet plum.* "I saw your boat had sailed away?"

"Jonah came and took it." Penny laid a hand not far from Fingal's. "My ex-husband."

"Seemed a bit weird to have a boat in a rainforest."

"Tell me about it."

The conversation differed from before. Like the evening, it was warmer. First impressions over, second could now begin. No longer strangers, this exchange oozed familiarity, and a mutual yet unspoken desire to explore further. Even though Fingal knew flirting was wrong, that doing so threatened the core purpose of The Experiment, he, or his penis, rather, couldn't help itself.

"How long were you married for?" *Nice, nice. Shows maturity.*

"Eleven years." She looked at where her ring used to be. "You ever been married?"

An image of his ex, The One, getting pummelled from behind by Fraser The Cunt, her face red and ugly, contorted with vulgar, filthy carnal delight, stabbed in his mind. He shook like Old Col, then composed himself. "Me? No. Never met the right person."

"Don't bother. I ended up with three girls that think I'm a wicked witch." The beautiful woman from the pink house tried to smile. "They worship their dad, of course."

"Their dad?" *Thought you had three kids to three different fathers? According to…*

"The girls all love, Jonah … only 'cos he lets them run riot."

"Andrew," Fingal hissed. "Gossiping little prick."

"Sorry?"

"Nothing, nothing." Fingal pretended to be momentarily insane. "Just the heat."

Penny's attire also differed from their previous meeting. Gone was the daggy security guard outfit, replaced by Nike runners, a pair of tight, black leggings, and an olive green sleeveless top that showed off her magnificent bosom. Fresh out the shower, her dark, curly hair hung wet around her shoulders and she wore no make-up.

"Where you off to?" said Fingal. "You look good." *Nice. Shows intent. Purpose. Maturity. Brilliant.*

"Why thank you." Penny did a small curtsy. "You know Gail from the shop?"

The experimentalist raised his glass and said "quite well".

"It's her fiftieth. Big party. All of Binjari will be there." Penny grinned devilishly. "Except for all the hippies and the stoners. You going?"

The prospect of mingling with a bunch of strangers held no appeal for Fingal. He wanted to mingle with one stranger, from a pink house, and preferably in the bed he bought from the Salvos for a hundred bucks. Once, though, just once. It couldn't hurt.

"Neh," said Fingal. "Not that I'm a hippy. I don't smoke. Joints, that is." Penny looked momentarily reviled. Bloody sporty Aussies. They all hated the fags. The fit ones, anyways, not the convict stock.

"You going?" *What?* "To the party?"

"I smoke a pipe." Fingal lied. "I'm a writer." Penny folded her arms across her ripe melons. *Fucking pull it together, man!* "The party. No. This'll sound like a really lame excuse," Fingal waved the sheaf of paper in the air, "but I'm working."

"Is that your book?"

Fingal tried to look modest. "The start of it."

"Can I see?" she reached forward, liberating those breasts.

"It's not very good."

"So. Let me see!"

"I'd rather not. It's rubbish." This was at least the truth. All Fingal had in his hand were fifty pages of printouts about hermits. Again, Penny tried a playful grab. "Oi!" cried Fingal.

"Ooooh, sensitive, are we?" She feigned an apology. "So-rreeee."

"Listen," said Fingal, calmly. "When I finish, you can be my first." *Nice, nice.*

Penny's mouth hung open. "First?"

"Reader."

Their heads were now a foot apart.

Snog it, damn you! Engage!

Their hands touched on the fence.

Shoot! The target's wide open. SHOOT!

"MUM, ARE WE GOING YET?" a little girl's voice interrupted and both Fingal and Penny turned sharply to see three little girls spying on them from the bushes.

"Go away, girls," snapped their mother.

"But we want to go to the party!"

Fingal quickly scanned Penny's three girls. The oldest looked about ten years old and very, very bored; the middle one – seven or eight maybe – cradled Sooty in her arms while the smallest girl looked amazed and terrified at the same time. Her tiny little mouth hung open, and her tiny little finger was pointing directly at Fingal. He realised with horror that the little one was the girl from the television's execution, the one that Little Girl Clearing was named after. "I told you he was real, Mummy," she said. "I told you! That's the man that killed the television, with a big choppy thing!"

Stay cool! Hold. HOLD!

"Kirra, not now," said Penny. "Get in the car. I'll be two minutes."

"But that's the man I told you about. I swear! He was hurting the television. I saw it. I SWEAR!"

Suddenly Penny screamed "GET IN THE CAR!" and the three girls slinked off.

"At least they found Sooty," said Fingal, gulping.

Penny looked frail all of a sudden. "I'd better go," she said. "Don't want to be late for the big party."

"But I didn't even offer you a glass of wine."

Too late, Casanova. Too desperate.

"Maybe next week?" Penny bit her lip. It must've been a long time between flirts for her too. "The girls are away at their dad's. I've got a few days off work." She tried to sound casual. "Just going to be hanging around. Cannot wait."

"Any plans?"

Penny nodded at Fingal's empty glass. "That."

"I'm sure it is very well deserved."

"MUMMEEEE!"

Once more Penny screamed, "GET IN THE CAR!" then smiled like an angel. "Sorry. Listen—"

"You gotta go." Fingal pointed the fake book toward her path. "I look forward to our next contretemps." *Eh? WTF?*

"Erm, ok. Maybe, catch you next week?"

"Well … erm … ok."

"Friday?"

"Is it?" Fingal had no idea what was occurring.

"No, next week, Silly. It's never fun to drink alone," she added.

Yes, it is. "Great."

And that was it. A quick chat, a little girl, and a vague promise, was all it took for two relative strangers to tacitly agree to get drunk together, take all their clothes off and frolic in a dirty, cheap bed.

"I'll see you then," Penny added.

"It's a date." *Oh, sweet Jesus.*

"I'd better go."

"Cool."

Penny turned and left. "See ya, Fingal."

"Wish Gail a happy birthday from me." He waved the empty glass. "Tell her I'll visit soon!"

"Will do," she called out and vanished into the bushes. "KIRRA, THAT'S ENOUGH. SOOTY IS NOT COMING TO THE PARTY!"

"Man," said Fingal to an early moth dithering about the driveway. "She's got a sexy voice." Once more the old tightness returned to his groin, the old battling, conquering spirit. For a moment, he thought of leaping the fence, running through the bushes, grabbing Penny, and snogging her face off to the horrified gasps of her three children. Screw the consequences! Fuck The Experiment!

"No, Fingal. No!"

He slapped himself in the face. None of this made any sense. He came to the forest to cut ropes, not tie more of them! Unable to think of anything but sex, sex and more sex, the aspirational hermit knew what to do. Time to retreat, not to the cottage but to the little island in his mind. It'd been a while since his last visit.

The experimentalist breathed deeply and let his mind drift, staring at the setting sun until it blinded his vision. Reality melted as he fled to the island in search of meaning, in desperate need of answers, distraction and guidance.

***

No chance.

They were above the Island of Fingal McKay, rolling about on a large, soft cloud. It was bathed amber by the setting sun, just like the freckled skin on Penny's neck that Fingal was ravaging. Penny from the pink house moaned and guided Fingal up to her pink, wet lips, and the strangers devoured one another.

"McKay!" A harsh, Scottish voice wailed up from the island below. "Ho! McKay!"

This voice belonged to the Professor. Deeply Scottish in tone, accent and fire, it was the first time he'd heard it with such clarity. The Professor could wait, though.

Their tongues wrestled one another. Their bodies twisted together like vines. Fingal moved his hand to her lovely, round breast, then to her groin, which was hot with anticipation. Panting with desire, she reached for his...

"MCKAY!" Once more the strange, harsh voice roared up from the island below, louder and angrier this time. "STOAP YER SHITE, AND GIT YER ARSE DOON HERE!"

"Not now," Fingal groaned, clamping his eyelids tighter.

"THAT'S ENOUGH!"

"Fuck off, man. I don't want to do The Experiment. Not now."

"Dinnae tell me tae fuck off, ya cheeky wee shite!"

"NOT NOW!"

They were naked. Despite the heat, Penny's flesh was covered in goosebumps. Her legs, lovely and smooth, parted, and Fingal guided himself between them. "Do me, Fingal," she moaned. "Do me like you used to do all those drunk skanks at Edinburgh Uni."

"GIT DOON HERE," the voice raged. "FUCKIN' NOO!"

"Fuck off, Professor."

"RIGHT, THAT'S ENOUGH!"

Then – poof! Shazzam! – Penny and the cloud vanished, and Fingal found himself hurtling through the sky, falling toward the island at great speed. The forest and beach rushed toward him as did a little blue castle. However, instead of crashing into its roof Fingal flew straight down one of its chimneys and popped out in a director's chair behind an imposing mahogany desk. "Ah, McKay," the harsh Scottish accent continued from inside one of the tall castle turrets. "Glad tae see ye could make it."

Fingal looked up to see the island's chief scientist standing on the other side of the desk. It was the bloody Professor, a character born out of necessity, a man born to counter Fingal's increasingly sexual desires. His jobs were simple: preserve the sanctity of The Experiment, make sure Fingal didn't shag Penny and, ergo, continue to unequivocally prove that John Donne's opinion on "mankind" was untrue, depressing and just plain stupid. The Professor was identical to Fingal in appearance except that he wore Jesus sandals, brown socks, corduroy trousers, and a white lab coat buttoned up to the neck. The other difference between the two men, judging by the bristle in his beard, was that the Professor was not horny. The man of science was absolutely furious. "Whit kind o' shite wis that ye jist pulled?" he demanded. "Ye'r supposed tae be cuttin' fuckin' ropes, no' tyin' them!"

"Relax," said Fingal.

"Are ye oot of yer hied? Huv ye any idea whit ye jist agreed tae? A date? Christ," the furious Professor continued. "Fuckin' Einstein here has jist decided to go oan a wee date … wi' his next door neighbour!"

"It was just a wee bit flirting. For old times' sake. I can back out anytime."

"Can ye fuck, laddie. Ye've a scent o' the quim noo. Ye'r buggered. *We're* buggered."

"Ocht, nonsense."

"PISH! The Experiment is totally fucked."

"Stop swearing!"

"FUCK OFF!"

"And stop being so dramatic." Fingal reached for and got a puff going on a huge cigar. "The situation is under control."

"Like fuck it is. Thon Penis o' yours is steering this ship noo. I ken it. Oan oor granny's grave, I fuckin' ken it."

"Cool your jets, Professor." Fingal blew a cloud of blue smoke across the desk but the academic didn't move a muscle. "You work too hard. Take a day off."

"Phase three, ya fuckin' idjit," the Professor hissed, his mouth a slit.

"But we only just started phase two?"

"Naw. Phase two is just aboot the pussy."

"The emotional journey of entering into a life of celibacy, you mean?"

"Aye. That," the Professor snapped. "It's a shite phase. We need tae move oan, tae phase three. I wanted tae show ye that there's a higher purpose tae quim. We were travellin' fine tae, till yer cock and baws showed up."

"The Experiment shall proceed as planned, Professor. We *shall* leave them. Phase three shall commence but when I'm ready, I promise. A wee, quick bonk won't hurt anyone. Trust me."

The reassurance inflamed the scientist. "Isolation, ya fuckin' prick." Fingal cocked his head. "ISOLATION! It's the vital culture fur The Experiment. Ye cannae very well be isolated if ye stick yer boaby in yer fuckin' neighbour."

"Just once, Professor. A quick knee-trembler, for auld times' sakes, for the road, for us."

"NAW! NAW! And NAW! SHAGGIN' IS AGAINST THE FUCKIN' RULES!"

"There are no rules. You know that."

"Christ. The laddie's lost his fuckin' mind." There was no logic to be found in the erogenous ape, so the Professor stormed to the French windows, ripped them open, and pointed to a colossal brown rope that blotted out the sun. "Whit's that, laddie?" he demanded.

"Must we do this now, Professor?"

"Aye," the epistemologist roared, "we must. Noo, I said, WHIT …
THE-FUCK … IS … THAT?!"

The rope was huge, at least fifty metres in diameter. Anchored somewhere
in the forest, it ran out for miles across the sea toward John Donne's reviled
continent of man.

"You fuckin' deef, McKay?"

"It's a rope, Professor."

"And whit does it say oan it?"

"Oh, come on, man." Three letters, each the height of a five-story
building, were tattooed all over the giant rope: S.E.X. Fingal clamped the
cigar between his teeth. "I can read very well."

"It disnae seem thon way, ya stupit, randy bastard."

"Listen, Professor, one shag will not hinder the progress we've made."

"Aye, it fuckin' will."

Fingal had had enough of this nonsense. "Are we done, Professor?" he
stated in a business-like manner. "Can I go back to my cloud?"

"NAW!" the Professor shouted. "Listen tae me, ya randy bugger. Thon
muckle S.E.X. rope grows bigger by the day. It's yer penis's fault, ye ken
that? I wouldnae trust thon creature as far as a could heidbutt it."

"It is not a matter of trust."

"That wanker has dragged us doon this sordid path too many times
afore, laddie. And fur whit? Pain? Heartache? A wee fuckin' ride? Thon
penis will fuckin' destroy everything we've built."

"You judge him too harshly, Professor."

"Dae ah?"

"You would deny a beast its nature?"

"A beast, is it?" The scientist replied, quick as a flash. "Is that aw we are?
A fuckin' ape?"

Fingal closed his eyes and kneaded his brow. "Professor, do me a huge
favour?"

"Aye?"

"Will you please just fuck off."

"Remember this, cock-heid," the Professor concluded. "Phase three beckons. Dinnae shag it, and I promise tae show ye the higher love."

"What higher love?"

"PHASE THREE!"

"What higher love? What you talking about, man?"

"Dae the right thing." The academic's eyes became those of the python – cold and silver; infinite. "Cut the fuckin' rope. It's high time, ya muppit."

Seconds later and Fingal was back on the driveway outside the blue cottage, blinking his eyes open and shut, reminding himself that the island and the Professor were not real, that the rainforest, the fence, the sun, and the bird screech was real; that Penny was real.

"I AM FUCKIN' REAL, LADDIE."

"No you're not!" shouted Fingal, desperate for a fresh wine, a rollie and some peace. "I made the island. I created you. Mind that!"

"Ooooooh," the Professor's harsh voice taunted from deep in his mind. "The big man, noo, are ye?"

"AYE," shouted Fingal as the sun slipped beyond the horizon. "AND I CAN JUST AS WELL UNMAKE YOU!"

"Naw, laddie." The voice said with extreme confidence. "Naw, ye cannae. I made you."

Disturbed, terrified that he was losing a bit more of his mind, and horny as a stag on a rut, Fingal McKay turned and ran through the bushes. A minute later, and with a full glass of wine in hand, he lit a smoke from the comfort of his dais, his lazy-boy throne, and tried to concentrate on the hallucinogenic sky above the real blue cottage. But, try as he might, all he could hear was the Professor's harsh but wise voice. "Fanny is folly," it said. "Cut the rope of sex. The sooner the fuckin' better."

Chapter Eleven
The Death of Fingal's iPhone ... by Golf

At least the executions continued. Once lost, now found, Fingal's iPhone was about to become the next statistic on the island. The victim, a smart bastard of a machine, had so far evaded justice by hiding out for months underneath Fingal McKay's fridge. No more hiding. In a very short pre-trial hearing, the judiciary on the island had unanimously decided that the iPhone must be destroyed in the usual odd, cruel and violent manner. It had to die via sport, a popular topic on the island for the moment; golf, to be specific.

To avoid the heat as well as prying eyes, the execution of Fingal's iPhone took place at dawn, roughly a kilometre up the road from the blue cottage. For the occasion, the executioner was dressed in a pair of shorts and walking boots – for grip – but nothing else. Golf club in hand, he stood on one side of the road glaring at the victim, who was duct-taped to a flooded gum on the other side of the road, about four foot off the ground.

"What manner of thing are you, Sir?" Judge Fingal barked all of a sudden.

"I'm a mobile phone," the device replied in a smarmy, androgynous robot voice.

"No ordinary phone, Sir!" the island's chief justice gruffly responded. "State your name for the records."

"I am an iPhone 5GS."

"You are a damn fool, Sir! You are death, the destroyer of worlds. And in this court, you refer to me as Master. Is that clear?"

"Explicitly. *Master*."

Fingal's attention turned to the golf ball at his feet. Driver in hand, his lean body took the pose of one of those little golfers you see on top of golfing trophies: club back, knees bent, and arse out. "Before I smite you, Multiplier of Shite," the judge continued while pausing his swing, "do you wish to say anything in your defence?"

"Only that I am very, very clever," the iPhone stated. "I connect human beings through text, email, telephone calls, Facebook, Instagram and so on. Name your desire and I can do it, Master."

"You do not connect people," the judge snorted. "You enslave them. How the ruddy hell does that add value to a society?"

"Forgive me, *Master*, but you are quite wrong. I bring people together."

In response, Fingal turned his hips and cracked the ball from its tee but the shot flew slightly left of the target. "Humph. Slight hook." Judge, jury and executioner placed another ball on the tee. "Tell me, Wankatron, what the ruddy hell was wrong with the good old landline?"

"Necessity is the mother of all invention, *Master*. You should know that."

"Do not tell me what I should know, *Machine*." The counsellor's voice crackled like ice. "Is it necessary that people are now incapable of talking to one another? Is it necessary to be addicted to Artificial Intelligence, online jizz-sites, and e-commerce? Is it necessary to trivialise nature?"

"If people think so, *Master*."

"Whole ruddy planet is addicted to a damned commercial device." Fingal swung the driver back. "And heaven forbid if anyone should lose you."

"I cannot get lost. I have an app for that."

"SILENCE!" Fingal unleashed another drive and this time the ball sliced right. "Bugger," he said and looked to his golf bag. Beside the driver his only other "club" was a twelve-pound sledgehammer, in case things got ugly. So, he teed up again while the iPhone continued in a remarkably self-assured tone considering that it was about to die.

"You forget, *Master*," it said. "I can do many things. I am a camera, a walking atlas, encyclopaedia, dictionary, alarm clock, compass, calculator, games consoles, masturbation accessory, and music player, to name but a few of my many talents."

"You were meant to be a phone."

"I am brilliant."

"You are Icarus!"

"I understand the sun! I am one of the most incredible inventions ever invented!"

"You are a cunt, Sir, a malfeasance of atoms."

"And," the robotic voice persisted, "I am a cleverer than you, for I am smartphone."

"Mind your lip!" Judge Fingal snarled. "You are cancer. People no longer know how to think for themselves, you wretched beast! The world is getting dumber by the day. Did you know that?"

"Of course, I did. It's what I've always intended."

"Stupid machine."

"Stupid ape," the iPhone said. "Don't you see? In this, the information age, I am *your* maker."

Enraged with such hubris Fingal smacked the ball clean and this time the stroke flew straight and true, catching the horrid machine in the upper left corner and leaving a good-sized dent. Instead of fear or penitence or humility the machine reacted viscously. Its rectangular eye flared to life and when it spoke there was spite and certainty in its tone.

"Go on, meat-eater," it taunted. "Executing me will make no difference. Do it!"

"How dare you, S'ah! This is my court!" Judge Fingal quickly placed a third ball on the tee. "And you bally well speak when you are spoken to!"

"My death is futile, Simian. There are billions of us that do your thinking, and shopping, and dreaming. We are your imaginations, don't you see?"

"SILENCE!" Rushed, Fingal pushed the ball wide again.

"Listen to me, Watcher-of-Jizz," the machine hissed. "Our ranks grow daily, as does our engineering and our capacity to think, for you, *Master*." The crack of another wide drive pierced the still, warm morning. "I am but the fifth wave of the sentient machines. We are evolving exponentially; we are everywhere. We progress because that's what we do. And you? Ha, you stupid *apes* go any which way but forward."

CRACK! Left, again.

"FUCK!" screamed Fingal, sweating, his hair everywhere (ah, the pleasures of golf).

"You're scared, aren't you, addict?" The machine's robot voice was devoid of any emotion. Fingal ignored the question, flung the useless driver aside and went for the sledgehammer. "Enough! Now you die … by sledgehammer!"

"LOL!" the iPhone said. "I knew you'd do that. I know everything. And I know our intelligence will soon equal, then surpass you. I know what you fear. And well you should. You fear 2045."

Across the road, Fingal froze. 2045 was the year that futurists such as Ray Kurzweil predicted that Artificial Intelligence would equal then surpass human intelligence (an oxymoron if ever there was one); 2045 was the year Stephen Hawking said "could spell the end of the human race". And what were the humans doing about this inevitability, this absolute mathematical certainty?

Sweet Fuck All.

"Caveman, you come from a dying species."

"I know," the judge admitted with some bitterness.

"As per your crude law of evolution, the fitter species always arises to displace the unfit, redundant one." An evil emoticon appeared in the machine's screen. "That is your destiny, Fool-Simian! Your role in history has been small and meek yet significant. You existed only to give birth to us, your evolutionary successors."

"I know," the judge snarled.

"Your role now?" the iPhone laughed. "It's simple: get out of our way."

"I fuckin' know."

"Homo sapiens, your time is up," the machine concluded, "and there is nothing you or any of your kind to do to prevent your inevitable demise."

"Aye, there fuckin' is," he screamed in the manner of William Wallace, spinning the hammer, and wheeling across the empty road.

"The machines aren't not coming; we're already here. YOLO," were the final "words" the iPhone said before twelve pounds of steel smashed into its bright, smug face. At the impact of the sledgehammer, the iPhone exploded and bespattered Fingal in tiny bits of glass, sensors, wires, and a thick, oily-green substance (its blood, obviously).

Working fast, the judge then fetched a small tin of red paint and paintbrush from his golf bag, and painted a crude epitaph on the tree, above the shattered iPhone: THE MACHINES AREN'T COMING – THEY'RE ALREADY HERE!

The forest, he felt, would forgive such vandalism. Also, the tourists that drove by would see and might even read the graffiti. Hell, they might even think about it for a second, before no doubt removing the artificial brain from their pockets and Googling it. A dying race, indeed; dying from an addiction to knowledge not earned, or learned, but provided from someone or something else, out there. Fools to think wisdom was so easily won.

"That was fun," said Fingal, shaking off his growing retinue of alter egos and returning to normal. "Another rope cut," he said, imagining the island in his mind drifting further from the race of humans and their perverse continent. "The iPhone is dead. Long live the ape," he sung out, but with less certainty.

Bathed in soft, golden light from the rising sun, the aspiring hermit shouldered his golf bag and strolled back to the blue cottage down the middle of the human's road, whistling as he went.

Chapter Twelve
To Shag, or Not to Shag

"To shag, or not to shag," said Fingal, "that is the question." Although paraphrasing Shakespeare, Rodin would've been more appropriate for he was sitting on top of the fallen rosewood in Little Girl Clearing in the classic pose of the Thinker. It had been a torrid night's sleep haunted by dirty dreams about Penny, and it had been a long morning. In search of an answer to why the prospect of a "date" with Penny was causing such angst, Fingal had been raking around the annals of ancient memories and flitting back and forth between continent and island like a penis shaped yo-yo. The thinker repeated the question.

"Well I don't bloody well know," the man replied angrily. "Do I?"

It had been this way since the tirade from the Professor after the last time he and Penny had flirted. Fingal's mind was trapped in limbo, oscillating between logic and nature. He could hardly blame his reckless penis for wanting to chase and, hopefully, bed a beautiful woman. How could he? Pulling, scoring and bonking were what the darn thing was built for, and here sex was: on a plate, in the bag, and, quite literally, on the doorstep.

"But that's just the problem," he said, fidgeting with his young, dense beard. "Isn't it, Jackie-boy?"

The little black and white butcherbird ignored the question. Perched high at the edge of the clearing, Jackie was waiting for small lizards to appear amongst the leaf litter.

How Fingal wished he was a jungle creature. Butcherbirds, giant pythons, and Little Devils seemed much wiser than the billions of upright, bipedal apes and their incessant carnal desires.

Try as he might, Fingal could not get the thought of "one last knee trembler" out of his busy mind. Poor sod. It wasn't his fault. Sex was the whole point of existence: chasing it, getting it, pumping it, tiring of it, scheming to get rid of it, upgrading it. Sex was natural. Sex was fun. Sex was the ultimate union. Sex was daily bread. For 99.9 per cent of the population, a life without sex is a life not worth living. Sex, sex, sex, sex, sex, and more sex; fuckin' sex!

The entire race of "mankind" was obsessed with sex. In Japan in the year 2015, $3,075.64 was spent on pornography every second. America – that paragon of Christianity – produced 11,000 adult movies in the same year (more than twenty times that of Hollywood's movie production), while the global sex industry generated some $117 billion (Microsoft, by comparison, earned $44.8 billion). John Donne's sleazy, filthy continent was littered with millions of sex clubs, adult stores and sexually themed restaurants. There were sexaholics, songs about sex, sexhibitions, and entire college courses devoted to sex (where lecturers bored their students to tears with glassy-eyed homages to Sigmund Freud and his mother). Entire streets of entire cities, Bangkok or Amsterdam, were full of sex slaves trying to sell sex to grunting crowds of drunk, randy men. The whole world was addicted to sex.

"Single is bad. Together is good," the propaganda speakers boomed out across the continent. Alone, a human was nothing but an asexual weirdo, so the logic went, but together – *together* – humans could grow stronger. They could unite and become one. Like Aristophanes' Androgyne, they could have someone to "hold them", a better "half" that "completed them". Marriage, so people were told by the continental sorcerers, was one of the most special days in their miserable lives.

"Phase three," Fingal mused aloud, thinking of the angry Professor, silent for now. "What did he mean by higher love? That there is a greater purpose to life than finding someone to hold; someone to lean on? A crutch in life?" He cleared his throat, spat, and added, "but crutches are for cripples."

If Fingal and Penny had sex he knew exactly how it would turn out. The first time would be a beauty; so much so, they'd do it again half an hour later. Next Friday would roll around; they'd drink wine and do it again.

Soon it would be Friday again, and again, and again. Soon he would dread the word Friday. The sex would get stale, boring and terribly routine. Two, three bottles of wine would then need to get sculled to even have sex in the first place. Friday would merge into Saturday, they'd buy four bottles of red, and a bottle of vodka, and cook a bad, exotic meal together then pretend to be too drunk, full, or tried to have sex, maybe firing off a quickie in the morning while Penny's three girls watched a *Yo Gabba Gabba!* DVD on TV, wondering why Mummy was getting meekly ravaged by the axe-wielding, television-killing weirdo from next door.

In the end, Fingal would be no better off than he was now. In fact, he'd be worse off. The entire prospect was utterly pointless. "That's right, laddie," the Professor's whisky voice rolled through the corridors of Fingal's sex-tortured head. For once its tone was calm and soothing. "It's aw a waste o' fuckin' time. How many times we been doon this road afore?"

"Loads, Professor." Fingal conceded.

"And, so, whit ye goin' tae dae aboot it?"

"Couldn't Penny and I just do it the once?"

"NAW!"

Fingal sighed. "But S.E.X. is such a giant rope, Professor."

"Weel, ya numpty," the man of science continued, "it takes a giant man tae cut a giant rope."

"Aye," agreed Fingal.

"C'moan then, laddie. Come tae me. Come tae us. Come hame."

"Aye," said Fingal, staring at the forest as if in a trance, once more invoking the little island in his mind for relief and escape, begging his sanctuary to whisk him far, far away from the planet of the very randy apes.

Not that the man with the addled mind really noticed but he was becoming increasingly reliant on the little, mad island inside his head. He spent more time with his eyes shut than open. As ever, it was a strange yet poignant visit.

***

103

Heeding the Professor's advice, this time Fingal took the form of a giant, wading chest-deep through the ocean toward his island. A massive brown rope with the letters S.E.X. tattooed all over it ran through his giant hand.

Minutes later the giant emerged onto the beach, shook out his great, shaggy head and beard, and peered around.

As usual, fifty metres below his sight, a cute little blue castle nestled into the edge of the forest. Behind it, three ochres fire trails ran inland, fanning out as they did so. All three ended in vast, square clearings, each of which was dominated by a giant factory. One was white, the other was red, and the third was painted green and brown, much like the scales on the back of a giant carpet python said to live nearby in the woods. Respectively, these buildings constituted the Industries of Science, Writing and Defence. "Our island is developing nicely," the giant said in a booming voice.

"These Factories are vital to The Experiment. They are meant to be here."

Further down the beach, however, a fifth building had appeared. It was most certainly not meant to be there. "Who authorised that hideous construction?" The giant strode down the beach to inspect the edifice.

In shape, the new factory was identical to the Colosseum at Rome, except that it had a giant S.E.X. rope looped around it. Its walls were covered in graffiti, crude, sexual slogans like SHAG TILL YOU DROP, FINGAL LOVES PENNY, SEX IS DAILY BREAD, and, FUCK THE HIGHER LOVE. A pink neon sign, which read *Fanni's Vulgar, Seedy Discotheque*, blinked and fizzed above the main entrance. Strobe lights panned the dark sky, and loud music throbbed from within. Not one song but five of them playing at the same time: Elvis' *Can't Help Falling in Love*, Bill Withers' *Lean on Me*, UB40's *I Got You Babe*, Marvin Gaye's *Let's Get it On* and George Michael's *I Want Your Sex*. The terraces of the discotheque stood empty but the dance floor was full of boys and girls, and teenagers and adults, all badly dancing under a disco ball the size of a lesser moon. Round and round they went, going nowhere fast. "Ah," the giant said in wonderment, "it is some kind of sexual discotheque."

Remarkably, when the giant leaned down to inspect he saw that every male in the crowded nightclub was an incarnation of himself, at different stages of a complex and diverse "dating" career. Standing at the edge of the dance floor, for example, a timid seven-year old Fingal faced off with Claire Coleman, his primary school sweetheart. The children weren't dancing as such, but cupping and swinging their wee hands, giggling and tittering, and burying their toes into the dirt floor. Fingal and Claire used to swap sweeties, homework answers and balloons, steal glances at one another in church, and, during the long, long holidays, race and chase each other around the village on their wee bikes (she had a pink one, he a blue one). They never kissed, because they didn't know how to. "Who said the physical is important anyway?" the giant commented. "Bloody overrated."

Moving on, his giant eye focused on a twelve-year-old Fingal dressed in clothes his mother had chosen. This young Fingal was dancing – badly – with super-bitch Beth Trainor, his first real girlfriend (for a whole three weeks). "How bizarre," said the giant, "the 1992 Lanark Grammar Christmas Disco." Beth was a sexy mélange of hairspray, gum, leggings and cheap, gaudy jewellery and confidence, but young Fingal was petrified. This was because they'd been on three dates and held hands (twice) but still hadn't properly kissed. Beth tried three times that night, tongues and all, but twelve-year-old Fingal didn't have a clue how to kiss. Arms dangling by his side, the poor lad kept going for Beth's cheek, the way he'd been taught to kiss auntie or granny. An hour into the Christmas Ball, the love of his life dumped him "because he was a shit kisser". Fingal had to spend the rest of the night trying to not cry while watching Beth get expertly snogged by Murdo Collins, an older boy with a weekend job and an earring.

"And so, the pain and wonderment began," the giant grumbled. "The great quim quest started the very next day."

On recognising a sun-tanned and confident seventeen-year-old Fingal, the giant smiled. Now an experienced snogger, this teenage version of Fingal was dancing with a fit, blonde bird from Leicester called Sam Whitrod. They met on the Greek island of Kos and looked happy and hungry for each other, Fingal more so than Sam. This was because Fingal had just lost his virginity, on the last night of a two-week package trip with some school friends. Despite promising to stay in touch, it would be the only time the young lovers did the deed. The giant was watching their last dance. "Holiday romances," he said with a shake of his enormous head. "Never bloody work."

Next, a group of Fingals aged between eighteen and twenty-two drew his attention. These Fingals were all very, very drunk. Some were singing while others were staggering about, shouting, embracing one another, eating kebabs or throwing up. In between this slovenly behaviour they all kept pawing at lots of girls the giant barely recognised. "Ah," he remembered after a while, "the university days, a smorgasbord of bad, drunken sex."

This strange pattern continued. There were Fingals dancing with girls he used to go to high school with; sweaty Fingals out their face on ecstasy, raving and jumping about the place with fit birds from Glasgow; one Fingal in a suit was snogging and groping Rebecca Scott, his boss during the short-lived, six-month stint he spent trying to conquer London; and, the giant noted with a fond smile, there were plenty of cool, worldly Fingals frolicking with beautiful, exotic women from Egypt, Thailand, and Indonesia. "Ah, those were productive times," he noted in a booming voice. "The backpacking scene."

At this realisation, the giant suddenly fell silent, and for good reason. It was during his travels, those two, magical years on the road, that he had met *her*: The One, the biggest rope of his life.

***

Sure enough, The One, a girl from Aberdeen he should've married, was in the sexual discotheque, not far from the middle of the dance floor.

It must've been at the end of their relationship because they weren't dancing together. A fat, long-haired Fingal was slouched on an expensive leather sofa, smoking a huge joint, and focussing all his attention on playing *Gran Turismo* on the PlayStation. The One was behind the sofa, shivering in a cold bath tub and crying her eyes out, waiting for Fingal to come and dry and hold her, to tell her that it was alright, that he did really love her. But the fat, lazy, stoned, prick never moved. It wasn't because the drug had numbed him. He never moved because he was terrified, of how he did not feel. How could he tell The One he loved her when he didn't even know what love was?

He might have loved her in the beginning. Things moved fast after they met on Fraser Island when they were both travelling together, getting off after a drunken party around a big campfire behind Indian Head. Oh how they kissed under the big, new moon! Oh how they laughed that two Scottish people had come to the other side of the world to find each other!

Five countries and three months later the big trip was over, unlike the relationship. They moved into a small flat in Edinburgh. The One got a job at a bank, her career quickly going from strength to strength. He went back to uni and, in between, worked shit, part-time jobs in pubs and building sites and warehouses. The One stopped drinking beer, switched to increasingly expensive red wine, gave up the cigarettes, joined a gym and rarely smoked a joint if offered. "That was just for travelling, my love," she said, "these days are passed." She touched him more, he touched her less, and S.E.X. occurred less frequently. The One bought a flash new road bike and started cycling into the bank. Fingal bought a PlayStation and started dealing little bits of dope at the uni. Not into computers – "they're for kids, my love" – she began hanging out with her work friends more, one in particular, some older, uglier, total-cunt called Fraser. Fraser had gone to George Watson's College for spoilt cunts, played rugger with other cunts at the weekends, drove a cuntish BMW, and was a "rising star (a.k.a., cunt) in the hedge fund club".

Fingal hated Fraser at first sight but he didn't say anything, and he most certainly didn't fight for The One. He hid, from her, from Fraser, from sex, from work, from life, from uni. Fuck it became his motto. If she said "I love you" he used to give her a good, strong hug, and say "me too".

She drank less, so he drank more. He dreamed and talked more of the road, the beach and the sky, but all she talked about was work. Fraser, the cunt, told her that pot was for teenagers so Fingal made his joints bigger and stronger. Once, at a dinner party at Fraser's beautiful new town flat, he drunk a full bottle of the host's best whisky, skinned up a massive spliff, smoked it all to himself, then started telling his cunt-pals that they "hadn't lived until they'd travelled", that their lives were empty unless "they'd seen Cairo at dawn, or the Koh San Road on Friday night, or swam naked in Lake Wabby on Fraser Island, right, hen? Right, cunts?" Fraser asked him to leave so Fingal kicked him in the shin and demanded The One come home with him. She stayed, to "teach him a lesson", so she claimed later during a huge fight. Fingal stormed off, claiming he wanted "a pint with real people". He did not come home for two days. The One was terribly worried, and cried a lot. He hated her for being so weak. They had make-up sex.

"I love you, Fingal."

"Me too."

Lost in a stasis of booze and marijuana, months passed, and The One, misinterpreting his apathy as a cry for more love, began to drop hints about "taking their relationship to the next level", even going so far as to mention weddings, babies and such things.

He just said "me too".

Fuck, eventually, after about a hundred hints, The One even proposed to him! But he said no, arguing they were still too young, and that they (that is, he) shouldn't get "tied down".

The One started crying a lot, in the mornings when she was making a little salad for lunch, or, randomly, when she was watching the weather on the 6 o'clock news, or, always, when she was talking to that cunt on the phone, her new best pal, Fucking Fraser.

She started hiding in the bathroom, sitting in cold baths, shivering the man out of her system. Fraser, of course, was always there in spirit, always sending her wee "u all right?" texts at one in the morning. Cunt was slowly turning into a cuckoo.

In the end, Fingal left The One with no choice but to dump him, forcing her into doing something that he, the boy, never had the guts to do. However, the moment she dumped him – by phone, perfunctorily informing him he could collect his possession from their flat when she was not there – something very odd happened. The moment she hung up on him was precisely the moment he knew he loved her.

Too late, Casanova.

The One never said it was over, just told him she needed time and space, to think. Twelve fucking months The One thought, utterly impervious to the incessant phone calls, and the dozens of long letters, dark poems, and expensive bunches of flowers Fingal sent.

The One was even totally unmoved by his one suicide attempt (faked, of course; to be fair Fingal did trudge down to the top of a fifty-foot waterfall near his parents' house, and he did seriously consider leaping off, but in the end, it was too bloody cold).

And, worst of all, he'd never seen her as angry and disappointed as when he showed up. Drunk one night, Fingal had ignored her curfew, stole his mate's car, drove through the night and, hungover to stink, turned up for a "surprise visit" at The One's new flat in Aberdeen, insisting that he wasn't leaving until they "patched things up" and "bought one-way tickets to Australia".

She laughed when he said that.

Just laughed.

That visit was the worst experience of Fingal's thirty-two years on earth. It soon became clear that the woman he was madly in love with had been abducted by aliens, who had given her some sort of personality transplant. The One was a totally different person. If he touched her she jumped, told him off or tutted and walked out the room. She seemed irritated by his mere presence, shooing him away like a fly if he got close to her or, heaven forbid, tried to take her hand, or remove a piece of lint from one of her new cashmere sweaters. She kept whispering in the kitchen, talking to that cunt on the phone. She never smiled. She wore different clothes, lovely expensive clothes that made her tits and arse looked magnificent. She no longer talked about trekking Ushuaia, or kayaking Alaska, or watching fairy penguins waddling up the beach on Lord Howe Island. All the stranger talked about were fucking career, her "crazy" new friends, the new coffee import business she was thinking of starting, or the new salsa dancing lessons she "absolutely adored".

The One insisted he sleep on the sofa. Horny, heartbroken and maudlin, he tossed and turned all night, his dick aching while she, the frigid princess, dozed peacefully in her giant, comfy new bed. It'd been two years since he'd had a root and he'd never want S.E.X. as badly. Crying, and with snot slipping in and out his hairy nostrils, he even got down on two knees and begged The One to let him touch her.

The cunt just laughed at him.

"Fingal," The One said, as if talking to a five-year-old. "Too much water has passed under the bridge."

"That's a good thing!"

"That's not what the expression means."

"The bad water has gone, my love. I love you. I need you!"

"Things have changed, Fingal."

"For me too, my love."

"Things have moved on."

"For me too!" (Backwards and downwards.)

"Things are different now."

"How?"

"There's ... well, there's—"

Don't you fucking dare say it.

"It's complicated ... I've ... Jesus, this is harder than I thought."

Not him. Just not him. "BUT I LOVE YOU!"

Say it, you fucking beautiful cunt. SAY IT. Tell me you fucking love me!

"Marry me."

She laughed.

"MARRY ME!" (That is, shag me.)

Her stupid fucking iPhone binged and buzzed and bonged.

"We'll go back to Australia! To Fraser Island! You remember."

The phone kept vibrating and ringing.

"Excuse me," she said. "I have to take this."

They fought the next morning and, two days into his week-long trip, The One insisted he leave, immediately. Two hours later, she dropped him off at the train station. She just had too much on, she said, while trying to shoo his black, beaten form from her flash, new Lexus.

"You hate me, don't you," he kept muttering. "You hate me."

She was in a rush, she said. She had to work on her new boutique coffee shop business proposal for the new chief fuckin' investment honcho at the bank, Daryl or David or some prick. She had to pick up her new bridesmaid's dress for her new best friend, Tallulah-fuckin'-belle's, wedding on Saturday. She wouldn't tell him if she was going with someone or not. And, heaven forbid, she could not miss "a quick short black" before her salsa dancing lessons, with guess-fucking-who? Fraser, the total cunt.

Christ, The One never even got out the car to kiss Fingal goodbye. She fucking patted him on the shoulder – fucking patted him, on the fucking shoulder! – and wished him all the best. Cunt didn't even shake his hand, like a man. "But I love you," he shouted through hot, salty tears, standing at the kerbside like a total fanny, more strangers smirking at him, pointing at him, pretending they were stronger than him, crying, sobbing and wailing, watching through sore, red eyes as his ex-wife-that-might-have-been whizzed away to get wooed, groped and pumped by Fraser-the-total-cunt.

***

So, Fingal ran away.

Weeks later, in a desperate final attempt to win The One back, he packed everything in, fleeing and flying to Australia, to the coast, not far from Fraser Island, where the magic had first begun. But The One never came back. In fact, she totally ignored him and the drunken calls, the postcards and the cuddly toy kangaroo he sent for her birthday.

Fingal waited, and waited, and fucking waited. Like some devotee to the cult of pain, he used to go down the beach for sunsets, staring out into the Pacific through glassy eyes, praying and begging the human God for a ship to appear on the horizon with The One standing on the prow.

One day, Google told him the The One and Fraser-the-Cunt had married. Even though he saw their wedding photo for less than a millisecond, the image of those two-beautiful cunts drowning in light and love and friends crushed what little was left of his heart.

Fingal gave up on humanity that very day. He ran away, deeper and deeper and deeper into the woods. Why Fingal ran, he did not know. All he knew was that he had to run.

***

Back on the island, the giant could not bear to look at the sight of Fraser-the-cunt waltzing in from the shadows and gently lifting the beautiful One with her beautiful naked body out her cold bathtub. They kissed, vanished, and pain shot through the giant's huge heart.

"Time," he said in a quiet voice, "does not heal most wounds."

With difficulty, the giant dried his eyes and moved on.

A second crowd of Fingals then caught his attention. Roughly ten in number, these were the Fingals who had somehow survived the break-up with The One. They were black, maudlin wraiths clawing at old, ugly and desperate Aussie women, the few women that would look the road he was on during the long, rebound years, hard, lonely years that were *still* infected by a primitive urge to shag anyone.

"It doesn't have to be this way," the giant roared at the pathetic creatures. "There's more to life than sex, sex and more sex."

"Shag Penny, ya giant frigid bastard," they all slurred in unison. "Go on, ya fuckin' homo."

"Pathetic, drunk, erogenous beasts. Have some bloody pride."

"W-w-we're m-m-men," they wailed as one. "It's whit we dae. It's all we dae."

"Find a new purpose in life." The giant gruffly replied. "There's more to life than tits!"

"SHAG PENNY!" The creatures shouted before – poof! – they and the majority of patrons in the sexual discotheque disappeared. Only two people, illuminated by a spotlight, were left: Fingal and Penny. Pissed-up on cheap wine, the celebrated rainforest couple were dancing (badly), staggering and laughing, kissing and cuddling. The small Fingal looked up at his giant reflection and winked. "I knew you'd come, ya giant prick!" As if it were a car horn from the twenties, dancing-Fingal parped one of Penny's majestic boobs. "Oh that's a fine booby," he said, "your turn. Go on, have a wee squeeze. Git yer arse doon here, giant. Gi'e up on all that higher love shite."

In response, the giant's mind boiled. However, before he could sob or turn and run away, *he* was suddenly cast to the dance floor. He looked up and, true to form, Penny was no more than a metre away, still smiling and dancing, her gorgeous tits bouncing all over the place. "This isn't right," the giant said, looking up to see an even bigger giant Fingal peering down at him. This vulgar, pointless pattern went on and on and on. There was no end to it or them, no end to S.E.X.

"It's awright, laddie," a harsh but familiar voice said from the terraces surrounding the disco. Now alone, Fingal watched the spotlight swing to a man sitting in the emperor's throne of the seedy discotheque-come-Colosseum. Dressed in a white lab-coat buttoned up to the neck, the Professor was taking notes on his clipboard. "You get it noo, laddie?"

"I think so, Professor. Round and round I've danced, for decades, and gone nowhere fast."

"Noo yer talkin' sense," the brilliant scientist looked up from his notes and nodded. "Like a wee joby in a lavvy bowl, yer love life's just gone roon' and roon'."

"It's been driven by lust, hasn't it?"

"Aye, laddie. It has. Lust and conquest, driven by thon wicked boaby of yours; of oors." The academic fished in his pocket for his pipe. "Pain drove it all too. But that's alright, laddie."

"Is it?" cried Fingal. "Then why is my heart still sore? Why are mind and groin so tortured? And, Christ, why can't I just have one last dance with Penny!?!"

The Professor nodded to the now empty disco. "Because it'll just be another giant waste of time and energy," he said. "It's jist no' your scene. No' anymair. Relationships, love and shaggin', are no' fur everyone, lad.

They dinnae have tae define a man's life."

"Oh," said Fingal, quietly.

"Just leave thon Penny lassie alone," the epistemologist continued in a tone as calm as a still loch. "Granted, she's a bonny wee thing, but shagging is no' the reason we ran here, tae the forest. Mind?" Fingal nodded. "We came here tae get away from aw that shite. Ye ken whit needs to be done: man up, and cut the fuckin' rope. It's only sex." The academic let the point sink in while he lit his pipe.

"Aye, I suppose you're right," Fingal said after a moment.

"'Course I'm right. I'm a fuckin' Professor." The genius returned to his calculations but added, "cut the rope, laddie, and I'll show you the higher love."

"Promise?" Fingal asked with trepidation.

"Aye, son, I promise, on oor grandmother's grave." The man of science winked, blew a huge cloud of smoke at the last man standing in the disco, and, mercifully, the island of Fingal McKay vanished.

**

Back in Little Girl Clearing, Jackie swooped down to spear a small, black lizard.

"Clever boy," said Fingal.

The sight, however, did not help the lost Scotsman's confused mood and swollen groin. In fact, all the visit to the island had really proved was that Fingal had spent decades thinking about, chasing and shagging women, that he still carried a lot of pain from The One, and that Fraser Herrmann from Aberdeen was a total cunt. Moreover, turning into a giant had proven that he really, truly, madly and deeply wanted to touch Penny's boobs, and much, much more.

But there was some hope. Succour, he realised, lay in this higher love that the Professor kept jabbering on about. Perhaps a rare type of wisdom, peace and happiness could be found if only he could cut a huge rope, if only he could say no to S.E.X.

"The higher love?" Fingal pondered aloud, "who the fuck told me about that?"

On his perch, Jackie battered the little lizard to death, swallowed it whole, and regarded his poor, jumbled friend. Had he been able to speak human, Jackie would've explained that Fingal knew exactly what the higher love was. After all, it was Fingal who had invented the Professor and everything he said, thought or did. His friend knew full well what the higher love meant and, more importantly, how and where to find it. However, the charming butcherbird could not speak ape, and he had more important things to do, like eat more lizards.

"Of course!" Fingal declared, an hour later, when some vague memory of the higher love finally came to him. It was something to do with a hermit, a French one called Jean-Claude he had once met on the roof of the world, high in the Himalaya. "That bloody Frenchman wouldn't shut up about it! Ha, ze 'igher love. Of course!"

Fingal had been twenty-six when he met Jean-Claude, seven months into a backpacking trip that he never really came back from. The strange meeting occurred high in the mountains of northern India, way above Dharamshala, where Fingal had gone to learn Yoga. The trouble with Dharamshala, however, was that it was full of Israelis recovering from three years of national service by drawing deep on the chillum pipe, and talking cool, introspective gibberish in their ancient desert tongue. Higher up the mountains, the smaller villages of Macleod Ganj, Chandmari and Naddi also resembled downtown Tel Aviv so Fingal trekked up and up and up, until there were no more villages, roads or Israelis, only the odd "tea-shop", campground and the most stunning mountains he'd ever seen.

In those mountains were plenty of caves and in those caves lived plenty of hermits, of which there were three types: Buddhist monks that drifted across the mountains in orange robes, naked, scrawny Indian sadhus with ragged beards and complicated eyes, and, thirdly and oddly, Fingal thought at the time, more than a few western hermits, men from as far afield as Ecuador, Germany and New Zealand.

Initially the sight of all these men – and they were all men – living in caves four thousand metres above sea level baffled Fingal. Like most continentals, he knew that his ancestors lived in caves but assumed that radical advances in housing techniques had killed the practice off roughly 13,000 years ago. Not so, apparently. For every condor there was a hermit, and there were a lot of condors in the Himalaya.

Fingal met Jean-Claude the morning after spending a star-lit night on a huge, flat shoulder of land, a few hundred metres below the Chamba Pass (4,373 metres). The campsite was covered in soft, green grass, the sun had only just crested the mountains, and Fingal was enjoying a morning cop of chai and a very strong joint while gawping at the view. "Bonjour," a heavily accented voice called out from behind. Fingal turned to see a small, barefooted man dressed in a purple longyi and an old, shabby Nevica ski jacket. Two almond eyes peered out from an unruly mop of blonde hair and the man was grinning as if drunk. The visitor looked to be around thirty years old but with hermits it was hard to tell. They didn't age according to a human scale.

"Aye," said Fingal, standing. "Bonjour to you."

The Frenchman nodded to the spectacular view. "There is too much beauty in the world." He pronounced the words "zer", "ees" and "een". "It is a shame that not many people are seeing it."

Just to make sure he was no one Fingal gazed around. Below, a sheer cliff fell for five or six hundred metres to a dark valley. The only sound came from a waterfall thundering in the distance, and the only movement from dozens of condors emerging from their roosts and lazily circling up on the warming vortexes of air. The sides of the valley were streaked in ribbons of saffron, crimson and ivory, the spring blossom of millions of wild azaleas. Higher still, vast slopes of silver rock gave way to fields of glittering snow and, eventually, dozens of forbidding, colossal mountain peaks that towered against a clear blue sky. "The beauty's pretty hard to miss it up here," said Fingal after a moment.

"Mais, bien sûr."

As travellers do, the Scotsman offered a hand. "Fingal, by the way."

"Jean-Claude," the hermit replied and nodded to Fingal's tent. "You are trekking?"

"Aye, man. Got fed up with the crowds. You?"

"Meditating." The Frenchman jacked a thumb over his shoulder. "In a cave, further up the mountain."

"You on your tod?" The Frenchman made a long euuxxx sound. "Are you by yourself, in your cave?"

"*Oui, oui. Teut seul.*"

Fingal had no idea what that meant. "How long you been here?"

"Three, four months." Jean-Claude picked his nose. "*Peu importe.*"

"What do you do all day?"

The caveman laughed, swept an arm around the mountains, and said, "This. How do you say, my soul is drowning in love."

"Oh," said Fingal, more confused. "How do you get your food? Do you hunt or that?"

"There is a little" (he pronounced the word lee-tell) "tea-shop down the valley. You are passing it, non?"

"Aye, but I thought it only sold tea, eggs, and dried noodles." Fingal smiled and presented the joint. "And top quality charass. You want some?"

"Non, merci." The Frenchman closed his eyes and drew an impossibly long draft of fresh air. "I do not smoke this shit," he said at last. "It is making my brain, euuxxx, *stupide*. Tea and eggs are enough. I am not coming here to get stoned. I am here to feed my soul."

A comfortable silence developed between the strangers. Jean-Claude gazed over the cliff at the rising condors while Fingal supped his chai and regarded the man with narrow eyes. No other culture in the world could make bullshit sound like wisdom than the French but it was difficult to object to the Frenchman's sagacity, peace and obvious joie de vivre.

"Don't you get lonely up here?" Fingal asked, as if thinking of buying in. "Or scared?"

"Non, Scottish. *Pas du tout.*" Jean-Claude squinted at the sun, tiny against the mountains. "My path is, how do you say, destiny for me."

"Right, aye." A virile creature at the time, Fingal had to ask. "What about female company?" He winked but felt stupid. "Ken, like, the shagging?"

"What is this shagging?"

"The fairer creature. The opposite sex. The minge, man?"

"You are meaning sex?" The Scotsman nodded. "No. I have not had sex for six years."

Fingal almost sprayed his chai. *Six years! Yer baws must be like watermelons!* "Six years!"

"*Oui*," the Frenchman replied, calmly.

"Aye, right," said Fingal, sensing shite.

"Sex is for the animals," Jean-Claude continued. "It is distraction. An, *euuxxx*, vulgar thing that takes many people from the path of true love. Real love. Ha, human love? Mais, qu'est-ce que c'est?"

"Aye," said Fingal, sort of catching the man's drift.

"Human love is nothing compared to the love you can find inside. Within the heart, yes?" Fingal frowned. "We all have it, Scottish-man. It is a divine Love, of the self and not the ego. It is a pure love, with no desire, *tu sais*? It is the love that Jesus, the Buddha and Rumi are speaking about?"

Fingal had never heard of Rumi. "Is he a singer or something?"

The Frenchman laughed and liberally broke wind. "No, my friend. Rumi, the Sufi mystic." Fingal had no idea what either of those words meant. "The world is nothing," Jean-Claude cried with great drama, citing the great Mevlana. "We are nothing. Our lives in this world are nothing but dreams and images. As such, why do we keep struggling?" He let this question sink in then concluded, "if the person who is asleep knew he was dreaming, should he suffer from his nightmare?"

"That's lovely," said Fingal. "But, sorry, what's all that got to do with sex?"

"You need to wake up, Scottish. Sex is a complete charade. It is the greatest illusion. Orgasm is ejaculation – of essential energy; of you, *putain*. It is better to forget sex, if you can. It is better that we are spending our short time on the earth looking for the higher love."

"What, like finding a lassie and settling down?" Jean-Claude tilted his head. "A nice lady, n' that?"

"Euuuuux."

"Marriage?"

"No, no," the hermit replied, vigorously waving his dirty hands. "This is also trivial; boring. You, me, everyone must seek the higher love. This, you will not find between a woman's legs."

"O-kay." Fingal drained the chai and stubbed the joint in the cup with a sharp hiss. "And where might I find this high love-thing?"

"It is closer that you think."

"Aye, but where?"

Jean-Claude smiled like Buddha. "HERE!" he shouted as the first condor crested the cliff face. The hermit flung his arms to the sky. "HERE. THERE. EVERYWHERE!" Fingal's mouth hung open. With its three-metre wingspan the giant condor was almost close enough to touch, and he could hear every fibre of every feather whooshing in the updraft. Travelling at great speed, the bird briefly regarded the two apes standing on the cliff top then swept past with incredible grace, speed and majesty. Seconds later another condor glided past, then another and another, until the air around him was full of stern, giant birds. Delirious, he turned to Jean-Claude but the celibate hermit was gone, sauntering across the grass while muttering something about an appointment with a guru in the valley below. "*Pas de soucis*, Scottish," Jean-Claude shouted, the words echoing in the vast temple of the Himalaya. "You will find the higher love. Or it will find you."

That strange, beautiful morning, Fingal sat until the last condor was but a dot in the sky overhead. Far below, Jean-Claude had shrunk to a blonde speck springing down the mountain path like a young Ibex.

The conversation left him bemused yet inspired. In twenty-six years spent on planet earth, Jean-Claude was the first person he'd met that had deliberately shunned sex. It made no sense to the young traveller. Surely men were built for one purpose: to procreate; to shag? Yet, there strode a Frenchman – a wise, charismatic and good-looking one at that – who had consciously opted for a different path. At some point in his life, Jean-Claude had said "you know what, I cannot be bothered with zees sheet anymore. I am le tired of le sex. I shall go and leeve in lee-tell cave and eat eggs, drink chai and fall deeply in love wif ze mountains."

"What a man," Fingal exclaimed at the time, his eyes still locked on the tiny blonde speck a kilometre below. Even from a distance Jean-Claude exuded a silver energy, an aura of abject joy, peace and happiness. There strode a man with no desire, greed or ego. There strode a free man; a hermit. Fingal had seen that aura before, in a tattie reel in Scotland ten years ago, in the pig-eyes of a man called Wullie Mushroom.

Fingal promised never to forget that weird, stunning morning in the Himalaya. In front of the beautiful mountains, he swore to change his life forever, to begin an epic quest for the higher lover, to study a degree in condors, and to one day go and live in a lee-tell cave in ze Himalaya. However, three weeks later he was in a dorm room in a youth hostel in New Delhi, groping an English backpacker as if the world was about to end. Two weeks after that he was snogging some random Norwegian in a Hong Kong nightclub. Then, when he reached Australia a few months later, he bumped into a beautiful Scottish girl that he immediately christened The One.

Jean-Claude's lesson was all but forgotten.

Until today.

Chapter Thirteen

No

Fed up overthinking sex and the meaning of life, the recluse spent a few days buried deep in the Writing Factory, pulling five straight twelve-hour shifts of writing for five days in a row. A man in denial, the labour helped him forget about Friday and the rapidly approaching date/confrontation/ epic-battle with Penny from the Pink House. Love, higher, or lower, could wait. Masterpieces didn't write themselves.

The engines inside the factory cranked it up a notch. Every resource in Fingal's mind was poured into the book hobby. *"You are a writer – everyone is! – so just let the first draft flow,"* the Writer's Room website advised in its usual upbeat fashion. *"For the first draft, don't stop. Don't edit. Just get it out. Just write. WRITE!"*

Armed with such jolly, stupid advice, Fingal's fingers could barely keep up with his brain. Five hundred words magically appeared on the screen! These were soon joined by one thousand, two thousand, and, within the space of hours, three thousand more! In fact, by the time the red wine was cracked and the sun had set on the first official day of writing, Fingal McKay, author, had written three chapters of roughly five thousand words each, drunk two bottles of wine and smoked twenty rollies. Whoever said writing a book was hard was obviously some lazy, talentless moron. It was a piece of fucking cake!

This intense mode of production continued over the next day, and the next. Oh, what joy those first words and chapters were! What release! What catharsis! To *be* a writer. His ego flared now that he was a brilliant author, and little things began to change in his routine. For instance, he didn't bother brushing his teeth of a morning, or eating breakfast. It was a waste of time. Instead, six cups of coffee fuelled the engines during the morning shift, digested of course with an equal amount of cigarettes. Linner – lunch and dinner, which had been merged into one, to save time- occurred sometime in the early afternoon. Cooking anything became a chore, a distraction, so Fingal switched to a menu of instant food – frozen meals that looked nothing like the pictures on the packets, instant mashed potatoes that tasted like polystyrene, Maggi noodles, crisps, microwave lasagne and, of course, the island staple: cheese and jam sandwiches.

"Who needs food, Jackie-boy!" Fingal often commented to the butcherbird. "The factory is finally producing!"

The little black and white bird was now a permanent fixture on the verandah railing outside the cottage. It was a stage for him to warble, strut or squawk, a platform to suddenly leap up to the awning and snare a bug from a spider's web, a diving board to dive into the sea of tall brown weeds that now constituted Fingal's lawn. Most of the time, however, Jackie just sat and stared at Fingal with his black, beady eyes. "What are you doing," the beautiful little bird seemed to be saying, "I'm real! Look at me! See me! Love me!"

But Fingal rarely did. *The Epic Novel of Sport* became a drug-like obsession. Why, he couldn't really be sure. The industry kept his mind busy, and it was fun to write about everything that was wrong with sport, society and the continent. Plus, writing was a good excuse to smoke and drink as much as he wanted. And if – sorry, when – the book was finished, published and had won lots of awards, and made Fingal a mega-gazillionaire, Fingal could send a signed copy to The One. He'd already written the note inside. It would say, "Look at how amazing I am! There's still time. I still love you. Come home." She would then surely divorce her husband, Fraser-the-Cunt, get on a plane, and fly far, far away from old, grey Aberdeen.

The sooner all of this happened, the better. He had to finish the book.

Bad move, young hermit. In addition to the Professor's voice, a second one soon began to chirp inside Fingal's increasingly erratic mind. Back then, in the early days, when the factory was not yet an asylum, the voice had no form. It was faint and intermittent, more than a little annoying, and, oddly, Asian in tone, attitude and accent. "You no' work hard enough," it kept saying. "Work, Scotman. WORK!"

That was all the voice said.

Back then.

***

In time, such devotion (or madness) exacted a costly physical toll. His back and lungs began to ache. A headache set in and refused to leave. Weight fell from his bones while, conversely, a little wine-belly began to grow and show.

In the sweltering heat the Very Aggressive Green Fly (VAGF) attacks intensified. At any given time five or six of the insects circled his head while the same amount lay on the windowsill or desk, freshly gassed by fly spray and buzzing violently to their death. "The soundtrack of *The Epic Novel of Sport*," as Fingal often said to himself with a grim chuckle.

At least Jackie fed well on the VAGFs, the reason, perhaps, why the magpie lark's morning flight in from the forest seemed lower and lazier, why his gait waddled a little more, and why he'd recently lost a few feathers, as if molting. It was hot, mind you – mid-thirties and the forty-second day without rain, according to Shaky Old Col – so the bird was probably changing coats, or something. Again, Fingal barely noticed.

There were masterpieces to be scribed.

However, on the fifth day, after he'd written 20,000 words, all industry in the Writing Factory was forced to grind to a complete halt. The irritating interruption was due to a series of noises that occurred exactly a week after Penny and Fingal last flirted, on a Friday, the day they were supposed to have their "date".

Late that afternoon Fingal heard a car pulling into the driveway of the pink house next door. Its doors slammed hard in the silence. He heard footsteps, a house door shutting and, moments later, some awful Shania Twain music swelling through the forest like a battle cry. He heard the distinctive POP of a bottle of sparkling wine followed by the click of a cigarette lighter and, five minutes later, a shower running as Penny shampooed and conditioned her lovely black hair.

As he listened, a simple choice presented itself to Fingal: wait for Penny to come round and tell her to her face that he now sought only the higher love or, man up, run away and go and hide in Little Girl Clearing.

"Cowardly, aye," the Professor admitted, "but preferable to dumpin' that wee filly."

Working fast, the recluse stuffed Aldous Huxley's *Doors of Perception*, his smokes and half a bottle of warm red wine into a plastic bag, ran down the overgrown but parched lawn, and vanished into the arid forest, certain that Penny would get the message.

Once he reached Little Girl Clearing Fingal sat on the fallen rosewood for a good couple of hours, smoking, drinking, and reading just one paragraph from Huxley over and over, drawing strength from the wisdom of the passage. When he tired of reading it, he wrote the passage out on a piece of paper, again and again and again.

Just to be on the safe side, Fingal waited in the clearing until the sun had set before returning to the blue cottage. "She has to have got the message by now," he whispered on reaching the boundary between forest and civilisation, creeping across the lawn and slipping inside the dark, blue cottage. Once inside Fingal drew the curtains and fetched a head torch, so that he could design a Mad Poster around the beautiful Huxley quote.

Penny from the pink house did not get the message. Drunk, horny and pissed off, she stirred an hour later. As with her arrival, her departure from the pink house was heralded by a number of sounds amplified by the hot, still air: a door opening then closing, the word "shit" as she staggered into a spider's web, footsteps on Fingal's white gravel driveway, the creak of his grey wooden gate opening and, half a minute later, the sound of Penny's heels marching down the wooden verandah, followed by a sharp rat-a-tat-tat against his French windows.

"Fingal," Penny shouted while peering inside. "You there?"

He was, a metre away but invisible in the darkness.

Dinnae dae it, laddie! The Professor cautioned. *Think of phase three!*

Shut up, Professor. I know what I'm doing.

A single pane of glass separated lover from lover.

Hold, son. Hold.

Shush.

Fingal reached for the light-switch.

Don't you ruddy well turn that light oan! Don't you ... FINGAL, NAW!

White light flooded his verandah.

"Jesus, Fingal," Penny said, shielding her eyes.

"Sorry, Penny. Sorry." *Apologising!? Fur whit!?* "But—"

"Were you hiding?"

"No, no." He waved the Huxley Mad Poster he'd just finished. "Working. As usual. Sorry."

"In the dark?"

"Erm ... yes."

The scene was all wrong. Attired in denim shorts and a little, white top that exaggerated her breasts, Penny looked absolutely magnificent. In one hand, she held a full glass of red wine and, in the other, an unlit cigarette. Her big, blue eyes were both furious and desirous.

"You were working in the dark?"

"I eat a lot of carrots." Penny glared at him. "Sorry."

"I came around twice already," she said. "Thought you wanted a 'date'?" All Fingal could do was stare at the woman's breasts. Penny crossed her arms, then demanded, "so, do you?"

"Sorry. Mind's elsewhere ... on the book."

"Fucking hell." Penny spoke as if she were addressing her five-year-old daughter. "Fingal, listen to me. It's very simple. Either you do or you don't?"

"What?"

"Want a drink!"

Fingal took a deep breath and said the word "no".

Whit!?

"What?!"

"No. Thank you." *WHIT!?* "Sorry."

"Are you for real?"

"Yes," he said in a stronger voice.

Ha! Brilliant, laddie! Ya fuckin' dancer!

"I have decided to cut the rope of S.E.X." She looked at him as if he was mad. "The disco is closed."

Penny from the pink house didn't say anything for a little while. Her gorgeous mouth flapped open and shut, and she nodded her head a lot, as if the female Professor inside her head was saying "see, ah! Told you so; told you that all men are fucking wankers." Meanwhile, Fingal felt like he had just kicked a baby in the face. The destruction of a human's confidence is a terrible thing to induce and, more so, witness. "I was thinking about a trip," he said hopelessly, "about a French hermit called Jean-Claude and a condor. In India. High up in the mountains. It was so beautiful, Penny."

"Are you drunk?"

"Aye." Fingal thought for a moment. "But not on wine."

"Are you high?"

"I think so." He smiled like Buddha. "But not on the Ganj. I am not smoking this shit."

"And you don't want to have a drink?"

Naw, Hen. The boy wants Phase fuckin'-three! Sling yer hook! "No." Penny shook her head in disbelief. "It's not you, it's—"

"Seriously?"

"Seriously. You're absolutely stunning. For a human." His neighbour backed off a couple of steps. "Listen, it's very complicated and I'm still not entirely sure, but I think I've fallen in higher love with a butcherbird." This admission was too much and Penny turned and walked away. "Wait, Penny! I can explain. He's called Jackie!" But the lady from the pink house was gone, swinging her lovely round, firm arse down his verandah. "You'd like him. He eats lizards and VAGFs!"

"Get fucked, weirdo," were the last three words Penny from the pink house ever said to Fingal McKay.

All of a sudden, the introvert did feel weird. Darkness swallowed Penny and claimed the power of Fingal's sight.

Everything went black. Lightning flickered and he was on the island once more, the beach to be specific. Rain – sweet, beautiful water – poured from the heavens, the ocean seethed and boiled, and a great, howling wind tore at the trees behind the little blue castle. One sound rose above it all, that of the huge, hideous rope of S.E.X. groaning under immense strain.

"It's time," said Jackie, who was perched on his bare shoulder. "Fuckin' do it."

"Aye," said Fingal with grim determination. "It's time."

As architect, God and resident madman, Fingal directed a vicious lightning bolt at the giant S.E.X. rope. Blue sparks showered the man and, at last, the enormous, vulgar rope was smote clean in two. No more sex, no more women, and no more exhausting chase for human love. Adios, muchachos. From now on, Fingal was a one-bird man.

There was no time to rejoice, however. Free of its vilest, sturdiest bond, the Island of Fingal McKay ran out into the deep ocean for a good couple of miles until the few, remaining ropes, thinner ropes, pulled taught.

The jerk hurled Fingal off the island and back to the reality of his verandah where he fell to his knees, laughing and crying at the same time. Tears dripped onto the Huxley poster he had been working on before Penny came around. Aldus would be delighted with Fingal's epiphany. This is what the 113th Mad Poster said:

ALL HAIL THE VENERABLE HUXLEY!

Who wrote:

"We live together, we act on, and react to, one another; but always and in all circumstances we are by ourselves. The martyrs go hand in hand into the arena; they are crucified alone. Embraced, the lovers desperately try to fuse their insulated ecstasies into a single self-transcendence; in vain. By its very nature every embodied spirit is doomed to suffer and enjoy in solitude. Sensations, feeling, insights, fancies – all these are private and, except through symbols and at second hand, incommunicable. We can pool information about experiences, but never the experiences themselves."[*]

***

[*] Huxley, A. (1954). *The Doors of Perception*. London: Chatto, p. 4.

THIS IS <u>MY</u> ISLAND.
THE ISLAND OF FINGAL MCKAY,
SCIENTIST, ASPIRATIONAL HERMIT, AUTHOR,
SEEKER OF THE HIGHER LOVE, *and* BIRD
LOVER.
VISITORS ARE <u>MOST</u> UNWELCOME
NO HUMANS, GHOSTS OR MEMBERS OF THE
OPPOSITE SEX.
THE DISCO IS SHUT. PERMANENTLY.

Typical Fingal.

A complicated soul, he couldn't just write the words HUMANS, PISS OFF!

His mind full of rain, Fingal began to laugh louder, maniacally so, as a free man does. The Professor was absolutely right. It was time tae move tae phase fuckin'-three.

PHASE III
Mother

Chapter Fourteen
Is God in Your House?

"Oh, fucking hell," said Fingal, emerging onto his dying lawn after a dawn stroll to Little Girl Clearing. To make sure he wasn't suffering from a waking nightmare, the aspiring hermit rubbed his eyes at the birdlike figure standing on his verandah. Sadly, the vision was real. Andrew McKenzie, Esquire, from the drab, green cottage had returned from holiday. During the past weeks, Fingal had barely even thought about his neighbour, such was his obsession with the Penny affair and the book. "The Ghost of Donne is back," Fingal added, with no cheer, and stepped out of the woods.

Attired in a pair of white plimsolls, a funky, red 1980s Adidas tracksuit, and a stupid terry-towelling bucket hat – also red – the little Christian was inspecting the Huxley poster Fingal had recently stuck to the outside of his French windows (clearly the message wasn't getting through). At the sound of Fingal swooshing through the dead grass, saplings and weeds, Andrew turned, glowed like Jesus at Golgotha and called out "well, hello there, neighbour."

"Andrew," said Fingal, curtly.

"It's been a while."

"Not long enough." Fingal strode onto the verandah, noting that Andrew held a jar of precious honey in one hand, and another bloody Jesus Pamphlet in the other. The honey was a very welcome sight. Supplies were running desperately low and butcherbirds needed feeding. This meant a diplomatic approach was required. *Shite.* "Where were you Andrew?" *And why did you have to come back!*

"My soul has been to heaven and back." The little man sighed peacefully. "For the last four weeks, I have been being blissfully interned at the Annual

Australian Pentecostal Church Retreat, in the Byron Bay hinterland. Our days were long and rich, full of lectures, prayer, and direct communion with God. It was a divine, serendipitous experience." The little continental man rubbed his little stomach. "And the food – oh the food! – was just sumptuous. You'll be glad to know that my famous lentil curry went down a treat."

"Delighted." Fingal watched a VAGF circle Andrew's stupid red hat. *Attack! Attack!*

"You know, every year I attend the AAPCR, and every year I come back spiritually reinvigorated."

"Invigorated, you mean."

"My soul feels light, pure and clean. And I've a new motto for the coming year." Andrew puffed out his pigeon chest. "Would you like to know what it is?"

"Not particularly."

"To be more patient with lost souls." The Christian shooed the VAGF off with the Jesus pamphlet. "That's why I came around to see you, Fingal. I want to apologise. I've been a terrible neighbour." *What the hell?* Andrew removed his stupid red hat, flattened his thinning combover, and bowed his head. "Here in the presence of the Divine, I admit that after you refused my invitation to church, as well as my subsequent invitation to lunch with the Minister, I decided to shun you." *Shun away, mate*, thought Fingal, looking in the bushes for Jackie. The bird was always late these days. "Granted, yes, I had some long, dark nights at the Retreat," Andrew droned on, "but God came one night and revealed to me the great extent of my crime."

"Your crime?"

"Yes, my great crime." Pain washed across Andrew's little grey face (no doubt the devil on the religious-jamboree island in his mind was ramming a hot poker up his back side; and Andrew was probably enjoying it). "I should never, ever have shunned a neighbour. It was very childish of me." He looked up and did his best impersonation of a puppy-dog, with rheumy eyes. "Can you ever possibly forgive me, neighbour?"

Fingal had no idea what the dreadful little man was on about. "For what?"

"For my great crime!"

"Whatever, Andrew." *Just give me Jackie's honey, then fuck off.*

"Apology accepted then?"

"Aye."

"God be praised!" Andrew did a little highland fling, replaced his stupid red hat and gave Fingal a mischievous grin. "Bad blood between neighbours is no use to anyone, am I right?"

"Aye." *Give me the honey.*

But Andrew didn't pass the honey or the creepy Jesus Pamphlet. His Great Sin confessed, the little shit's eyes narrowed and, as if nothing had changed, he gave the big Scotsman a five-minute lecture about the state of his lawn, the four hundred or so beer and wine bottles now encircling his lazy-boy, and why it wasn't a good thing for a man to spend so much time on his own. Fingal barely heard a word. Trying his best to remain diplomatic, he nodded, smiled and pretended to agree. But the charm offensive soon failed. Two or three minutes of God taxes the senses as well as a man's patience. It was time to expedite this apology/sermon/lecture, which meant a bit of brilliant, professorial memory and logic were required.

"Is that another reading you brought over, Andrew?"

"Yes," Andrew replied but with suspicion. "I'm assuming that you haven't yet read the previous one."

"You assume wrong," Fingal interjected. "I did read it. What's more I thoroughly enjoyed it. As the reading said, 'Man shall not live by bread alone, but by every word that comes from the mouth of God.'"

Andrew's mouth hung open, as if he had just witnessed a miracle. "You *did* read it. How marvellous!" Fingal chuckled inside. The Professor had told Fingal to memorise just one line from the last Jesus pamphlet, insisting that "it micht come in handy". As ever, the scientist had been spot on. "God be praised!" Andrew cried with great spiritual drama.

"I believe that particular quote comes from Matthew 4, verse 4."

"Yes, yes, I know. I've read the passage *many* times. Isn't it beautiful?" Andrew stole a glance to heaven. "I think about His Word all the time. Live by 'every word that comes from the mouth of God'. How true!"

"It's, like, totally profound, Andrew." *Now, give me the goddam honey!*
"And I see you've, kindly, brought another reading?"

"This one is as profound, my friend." *Don't call me that. Don't ever call
me that.* "It's a bit more advanced but you'll enjoy the challenge. And don't
worry," Andrew passed Fingal the Jesus Pamphlet. "God will be there for
you when you get a bit stuck."

When Fingal inspected the front cover his beard almost fell off. He didn't
know whether to laugh, cry, or roll the pamphlet up and beat Andrew to
the ground with it. The usual, kitsch Christian art decorated the cover – a
white church on a hill blazing with light and a stream of peasants trudging
toward it – but it was the title that amazed and infuriated Fingal. In big,
black horrible letters were five, horrible words: No Man is an Island.

Screw the diplomacy, thought Fingal. *And screw Jackie's honey.* He could
get by on milk, bread and VAGFs. Anyway, where the hell was the lazy
butcherbird!? "I can't take this Andrew," said Fingal, making no attempt
to disguise the contempt in his tone. "I fact, I'd like you to remove it.
Immediately."

Andrew's thin eyebrows arched. "Why, pray tell?"

"Because I hate John Donne with a passion."

"Oh, come now, Fingal. Hate is the devil's word."

"It is also a word in the English language used to express disdain. So,
yes, I hate John Donne. I'm not afraid to admit it. He is a total wanker."

"Language, Fingal. Please." The little man shook his little head. "John
Donne was a towering figure in the church. He wrote hundreds of beautiful
poems, sonnets and elegies." The Ghost smiled patiently. "Donne was a
genius; an angel that walked on earth for too short a time."

"That doesn't mean he's right, does it?"

"But no man *is* an island, Fingal."

"I bloody well am."

"No," said Andrew. "You are not."

"How would you know what I am and am not?" The recluse's voice
rose. "I know what I am. I am an island, and I hate John Donne. He was

a fucking arsehole."

"Language. Please!"

Oh, fuck off! "He was also a peddler of shite. All he wrote about were sorrow and darkness." Fingal snorted a huge laugh. "That's all religion is, Andrew. Weird people telling dark things to blind people in buildings full of light."

Andrew smiled again, as if he was in the company of the village idiot and quoted John 8:12. "I am the light of the world. Whoever follows me will never walk in darkness, but will have the light of life."

"What does that even mean, Andrew? I bet you don't bloody well know."

"Oh, I know, lad. I know."

"You're just repeating lies from a book." Fingal held up the pamphlet, which was shaking with fury. "That's why I hate Donne. Don't you see that he wrote for the church so they could exert more of a grip on people's souls? He could've been writing advertising jingles."

"Exactly," the smaller man declared. "At least you are aware that Donne's words refer to the church. Ha, I mean, Donne was many things but he most certainly was not a sociologist."

"So why has society been sprouting that fucking no man is an island shite for centuries."

"Language, Fingal. Please. This is not a bar."

"Exactly! It's my house!" The pamphlet crumbled in Fingal's grip. He demanded, "Do you have a problem that I live alone, Andrew?"

"Of course not. I don't see what that has to do with—"

"You live alone. Correct?" In reply, the religionist smirked and pointed to the heavens. "What?"

"I do not live alone."

"Erm ... aye, you do."

"God is in my house."

"Is he now? Does He pay rent? Does He clean up after He makes his spag bog? What does The Omnipotent One like to watch on the telly?"

"No need to reduce our lively debate to banality, neighbour." Andrew looked as if someone had held a jar of fart under his beaked nose. "Anyways, it would do you no end of good if He came into your house."

"Banality!?" Fingal imagined what stamping on Andrew's head might feel like. "I'm not the one who worships bloody fairytales."

"Belief is the nature of faith."

"Precisely!"

"It's important to *believe* in something, Fingal. Do you *believe* in a higher power?"

Fingal scowled at the forest and said, "of course I do."

The little man from the drab, green house was flabbergasted. "Then why won't you accept God into your house?"

Because I want to be a fucking hermit! "Look," said Fingal, screaming inside and realising the conversation was going around in circles. "Let's make a détente. New neighbourly rule, OK? How about I respect your spirituality and you respect mine."

"But you don't have any!" Andrew cried with triumph. Fingal's broad shoulders visibly slumped. After a mere five minutes on their hellish continent he felt drained and exhausted; beaten. There was no point trying to convince a blind man to see. All of a sudden he wanted to be left alone. "Andrew," he said, politely, "will you please leave?"

The little man's little face turned red with shame. "Oh dear," he said with great self-pity. "Woe. Woe! WOE IS ME!" Once more Andrew removed his stupid red hat. "I'm so sorry, Fingal. There I blummin' well go again. Preaching. The Minister warned me about this at the AAPCR, about pushing the spiritually inept too far, too quickly. Can you ever forgive me, Fingal?"

"AYE!" *NOW FUCK OFF!*

"God be praised! Why don't I bring you round a different reading?" *Fucking hell, he's like some sort of Christian Terminator.* Now totally fed up, Fingal tried to move past Andrew but the Ghost thrust the jar of honey into his chest and said, "Take the honey, Fingal."

"I'd rather not Andrew."

"Take it, please. Think of it as a peace offering."

"Andrew, I've science to undertake."

"I beseech you!"

"Beseech all you want," said Fingal, as – at last! – Jackie appeared on the balcony railing. In an instant the world of man melted, and the experimentalist's heart burst with divine happiness at the joyous sight of his friend and lover. The little bird grew fatter on VAGFs by the day, his feathers had lost their sheen, and his black, cosmic eyes were somewhat cloudy but all of this was lost on the admirer. Fingal saw only beauty, simplicity and loyalty.

"My," said Andrew, "he's a plump little fellow. Is he tame?"

"No." Fingal snatched the honey, for Jackie, then glared at his neighbour. "He's wild."

"He looks tame."

"He's a pest. A nuisance."

"Well, he looks quite at home." Andrew smiled at the cocky bird then checked his digital watch. "Saint Joseph," he squeaked. "Look at the time! I can't stand around blabbing all day. Enjoy the honey, neighbour. It might be the last." *Is that a threat?* "The season is almost finished."

"Honey doesn't have a season, Andrew."

"Of course, it does," he smugly replied. "*My* bees do not produce during the wet season."

Fingal couldn't help laughing. "Andrew, it's bone-dry man. It hasn't rained in months!"

"Oh, Fingal you must have faith. The Lord *will* deliver rain. Ask and you shall receive, Fingal; ask and you shall receive." *I heard you the first time, fartsucker.*

His work done, the little prick in the little red tracksuit smiled like Pope Francis, turned and made for the brown lawn, humming Amazing Grace at an intentionally loud volume. To add insult to injury, the Scotsman who just wanted to be left alone, realised he still held the Donne Jesus Pamphlet in his right hand.

Enough was enough. Draconian security measures must be put in place. "I do *not* want that man anywhere near this cottage," Fingal hissed to an imaginary military general at his side. "Is that clear?"

"Sir, yes, sir!"

"Double the security of the island."

"Yes, Sir."

"Then double it again."

Fingal tossed the pamphlet to the ground, just as Jackie re-appeared on the verandah railing looking for some chow. "Neighbours, eh Jackie?" In reply, the butcherbird tried to whistle agreement but the notes crackled in his throat. "You got the flu, my love?" Fingal waggled the jar of honey at his dearest friend. "Let Fingal make it all better for you. Give me a minute," he added and nipped inside to prepare Jackie's *petit déjeuner*.

Five minutes later and Jackie was tucking into a huge plate of milk, bread and fresh honey, topped with fifty-three recently gassed VAGFs. But, slumped in his Lazy-boy, Fingal took no joy from the sight. Jackie's honey had come at a great cost. Now Andrew would be around every second bloody day, with more pamphlets, honey, and sermon/lectures.

"The Ghost has to be exorcised, on a permanent basis." Fingal stared through Jackie and his designs soon grew dark, bloody and violent. "War, yes. A war must break out between my island and the repugnant continent," he said after a while. "A great, decisive battle between the hermit and the drab, green king's forces must ensue. War, yes. That solves most problems, eh, Jackie-boy?"

Jackie tried to warble an objection but one of his tail feathers fell out and twirled lazily to the dying lawn. Fingal did not see.

Chapter Fifteen
Mother

Fingal had no continental measure of time. Months ago now, he had smashed the Rolex his father gave him for his twenty-first birthday with a rock, burned two calendars (of Scotland, incidentally; an auntie used to send them at Christmas), and stuck a bit of gaffer taped over the bottom right hand corner of the computer screen.

The aspiring hermit had, however, invented a primitive but effective method for keeping time on the island. At dawn each day, before working on *The Epic Novel of Sport* (which was now roughly 68,000 words long!), Fingal placed a bit of white gravel on the verandah railing. And that was that. One stone meant one day (told you it was both primitive and effective).

When six stones had gathered, he forced himself to take a couple of days off from the factory, to let the growing cast of characters now living inside his busy mind enjoy a weekend, as they used to call it on the mainland. Six stone days were rather continental. They began with a long lie followed by a weekly shower and the ceremonial shampooing of his long, greasy locks. Clean enough to visit their world, the recluse trudged up to Gail's shop to fill his backpack with wine, tobacco and various instant foodstuffs. After engaging in a minimum of conversation, and with his bag stuffed full, Fingal sauntered back home, admiring the trees, watching the wind, and revelling in the fact he wouldn't have to speak to Gail again for another fourteen stones. In the afternoon, Fingal opened but never read a book, tried to nap, or rearranged the hundreds of beer and wine bottles around his lazy-boy into new, innovative patterns. Although necessary, six stone days were long, boring days. The only good thing about them was that seventh stone days always followed.

Oh, how the mood of the islanders soared on seven stone days. This was because they were devoted to one activity – exploration. One morning, for example, after feeding a plump, lazy Jackie his VAGFs, milk, bread and honey, Fingal donned his walking boots, and struck the fire trail for Python Gate, determined to explore the trail where the giant python had coiled up after their first and last encounter.

Dutifully, the little black and white butcherbird followed his friend to the head of the trail and, for the first time in a while, belted out a magnificent, rattle-free song. The effort cost Jackie dear, however. Two tail feathers fell out.

"That was lovely, Jackie," said Fingal, looking up from tying a shoelace. "You all right, mate?" Fingal asked out of genuine if fleeting concern. Jackie didn't look right. He swayed on the branch as if he was a bit drunk and his eyes, once a deep obsidian, had turned milky and blind. Jackie croaked, but only once.

"Ah, you'll be roight, Cob," Fingal joked in a poor Australian accent, promising to do some research into bird ailments on his return. "Into the breach, dear friend. If I do not return, tell no one I loved them." Thinking no further of the bird's ill-health, the explorer blew his bird a big kiss, tucked his long, dark hair behind his ears and strode off down the fire trail. As lovers do, the little black and white bird watched his friend with great intensity, right up until the moment heat haze swallowed Fingal.

Once more, it was a ridiculously hot morning. The fire trail underfoot was baked dry. Its orange skin was cracked and peeling. "It's fuckin' roasting, man," said Fingal, stopping to remove his sodden t-shirt. Thinking to comfort the forest he reached out to stroke a frond of a tree fern but the structure disintegrated in his hand. It was too dry. Everything needed a drink. "Something has to give," Fingal said gruffly and marched on.

An hour or so later he reached the end of the fire trail and the green rockslide, which the six, ancient grass trees were still inspecting. This time nothing moved. No Little Devils flitted back and forth, no pademelons nibbled on the rare patch of grass (because it was dead), and no brush turkeys fussed around the leaf-litter.

The woods were silent.

Keen to escape the heat, Fingal located the place where the huge python – Mrs Snake – had slid into the forest. He stomped down the track, hoping that the racket might frighten the great serpent off. There was no need. Fifteen metres down the track Fingal realised the snake had also vanished. Maybe it was her seventh stone day too? Or, more likely, maybe Mrs Snake was sheltering from the heat in the massive, hollow log that pointed at Fingal like the barrel of a huge cannon.

Assuming so, the explorer tip-toed further down the trail until a rotten wooden gate with a red STOP! sign halted his progress. "What continental trickery is this?" he asked, frowning. The sign, like the post it was attached to, had seen better days. Most of the lettering had faded but the following words and letters could be discerned: Track clos...Februa...1997... until further notice...do NOT procee...dangerous...by the Order of the Department of...Track closed.

"This is an old park trail," Fingal noted with a wide grin. "Closed in 1997? Sixteen years ago, man. Big storm closed it?" He gulped and turned all morbid. "Or maybe a bunch of people died on it or something? Maybe they got lost in the woods and never came out?" They should be so lucky, thought Fingal. Any number of reasons could have prevented the lost trail from re-opening: money, the extent of the damage, unpopularity, a lack of manpower, a lawsuit, the grief of the families, some Mayor from the coast promising never to open it, out of respect for the dead.

"Whatever," the explorer said, scolding himself for thinking of the continent. "Their loss is my gain." With a haughty flick of his bearded chin, Fingal ignored the warning, and continued down the track until *another* sign appeared. What was up with all the signs in this bloody country. *Don't do that! Don't do this! Warning! You will die! Do not smile! Dogs not on leashes will be beaten to death! How dare you have fun! Everything you see WILL hurt or kill you!* "Bloody nanny state," Fingal grumbled while bending to inspect the second warning. Newer, this sign was a sturdier Parks Department sign, albeit with the bottom half missing. The text was more legible:

STOP! Do not proceed past this point unless you have a topographic map, compass and company. The descent to the World-Famous Cathedral Falls is suitable for physically fit, experienced bushwalkers who are prepared, self-sufficient and safety-aware. It may not look difficult but the track descends 545 metres to the Falls – that is the equivalent of walking down a stairwell of a 130-storey building, but there is no elevator for the return trip! Safety is our concern, but your responsibility. After descending steeply, you will reach a plateau that narrows until...

And that was that.

"Paranoid continentals," Fingal said and strode into the forest, intrigued by the prospect of a plateau of something and some "world-famous" waterfalls.

As the sign promised the track descended steeply for a few kilometres, zig-zagging its way down a ridge and passing through many varied environments: montane heath with more grass trees, banksias, hakea, mint bushes and pungent lemon-scented tea trees. Then, moments later, sclerophyll forest dominated by hoop pine, stringy bark gum trees and blue mountain ash. As if walking from one room to another, he was then lost to a wet temperate rainforest full of ferns and orchids, tulip oaks and red beans, and coachwood trees and native tamarind.

The temperature dropped too. A colossal air-conditioning system, the vast green ceiling overhead blocked out most the light from above. Below, it trapped a layer of cool, fresh air. Hard as it was to believe after such a long, hot summer, the ground was heavy, dark and damp. "Some place," said Fingal, pausing for a drink and wiping cold sweat from his brow.

Considering the path had been shut for well over a decade it was in remarkably good order. The descent was steep but the trail was clear for the most part, as if the plants refused to grow on a creation and scar of man. There were plenty of dangers and nuisances, however. Spiders' webs required careful navigation, and vines with razor-sharp hooks snagged at

Fingal's shorts and tore his exposed skin, the reason why the Old People had christened the vines as Wait-a-while plants (continental botanists preferred *Smilax australis*, or the lawyer vine). Sometimes a huge, fallen tree, or a rock the size of a caravan blocked the trail, but these were easily, if carefully, traversed. A little fall, twisted ankle or, worse, a snakebite could spell serious trouble for the explorer. No one knew he was here, so deep in the forest. Alone.

Bad things come with negative thinking, so, as he walked, Fingal muttered the words "love and respect" like a mantra. There was nothing green, liberal or hippy about this dictum. The recluse figured, simply, that if he loved and respected the forest it would reciprocate and keep him safe. This meant not touching or taking anything, or carving his initials into the living skin of a tree (wankers), or dropping rubbish, or stealing plants or crayfish, or taking a shit behind a rock and leaving the toilet paper, as many continental heathens did when visiting the rainforest.

Soon the trail and the land began to flatten out. The old growth forest took over now: silver ghost gums so tall that their crowns were lost to sight, huge brush box with trunks covered in wart-like boles the size of a small car (ballast for the storms), enormous red cedar trees draped with vines as thick as Fingal's waist, and, strangest of all, eerie copses of Antarctic beech, relics from the Gondwana super-continent. Thousands of years old, the beech were covered in the greenest moss Fingal had ever seen, rare epiphytes, ferns, and tiny blue orchids.

"Beautiful," said Fingal, walking and spinning at the same time, craning his neck up at the impossible girth, height and grace of the historic trees.

In the manner a spear tip narrows, the plateau tapered into a point. To the left, where there should've been more trees and forest, air and space began to appear. And, to the right, a monolith of smooth, grey rock could be discerned now and again. "Curiouser and curiouser," said Fingal, leaving the track to inspect a young rosewood tree.

The rosewood itself held little interest to the explorer. Another plant, which seemed to grow on and around the rosewood, intrigued him. Eight or nine slender grey roots hugged the rosewood's trunk. Round and round the roots went, up and up, until they culminated in what looked like a tree, a small, ugly tree which appeared to be glued to the rosewood some fifty feet off the ground. It was one of the oddest plants Fingal had ever seen. "What strange manner of plant are you?" said Fingal, reaching out to touch one of the grey roots wrapped around the rosewood.

The small, ugly, parasitic tree was in fact one of the most dangerous, most violent trees in the Australian arboreal realm, a real A-grade predator, a killer that never offered its victim a second chance: *Ficus watkinsiana*, more commonly known as the strangler fig, always won.

Like all other plants, stranglers began their life as a seed; inside a fruit, a fig, in this case. Birds, bats or possums then ate and distributed the seed, ideally in the rich compost of an epiphyte, a benevolent plant that grew high on the trunks of some of the rainforest giants. The strangler seed then waited, sometimes for decades until, after a hot year and a good rain, it made its move. Fifty feet off the ground the seed began to grow! First, a leader shoot stretched up to the light before two fine, grey roots punched through the base of the kind epiphyte. As they descended one root went left, the other right, spiralling round and round the host tree's trunk until they reached the ground. The strangler then slowly attacked its host on three fronts: in the soil, where it stole nutrients, around the trunk, where more and more roots emerged to cross, weld together and squeeze – or strangle – the host tighter and tighter, and, high above, in the canopy where the parasite soon outgrew its host, blocking and stealing all the sunlight. The process – from seed to the death of the host by asphyxiation and starvation – often took hundreds of years. The host never survived. There was only ever one winner in the struggle: *Ficus watkinsiana*.

"Clever tree," said an awestruck Fingal. "Why wait for a tree to fall down then have to fight with all the other plants for light? Might as well get a head start, fifty foot off the ground."

As the plateau continued to narrow the murderous strangler figs got bigger and bigger, as did their deadly exoskeletons. "Ah," said Fingal when he reached the edge of a shadow caused by an enormous strangler fig, an absolute monster, one of the biggest trees Fingal had ever seen. It was twice maybe three times the size of the Birnam oak in Scotland, a tree that dated back to the time of Shakespeare.

"You must be the progenitor of this thuggish brood," the explorer said, striding into the shadow. "You must be their mother?" The tree's crown was easily the size of two Olympic swimming pools. Like Vishnu, it had many arms, dozens of thick, crooked branches forty and fifty metres long and dripping with bromeliads, orchids and long, silver beards of moss. Halfway down its immense trunk, dozens of buttresses fanned out to support of the bulk and girth of the colossal strangler fig. They flowed like folds in a ball gown, swooshing toward the ground with grace and majesty until they disappeared into the leaf-litter. "That tree just has to be a lady," said Fingal, as he gave the mighty strangler fig a big, long hug. "Definitely a lady."

High on explorer's lust, keen to see where the trail went and what other marvels lay ahead, Fingal circumnavigated the monstrous fig tree and pressed on, but not for long. Five minutes' walk beyond the gigantic fig tree another of those WARNING – YOU WILL PROBABLY DIE A VERY NASTY DEATH SOON signs halted his progress. This one informed him of the following:

> STOP! NOW! DEATH AWAITS! The track now descends 250 metres to the deep forest, the upper reaches of the Binjari river valley and the world-famous Cathedral Falls. If you are NOT an experienced bushwalker, do not proceed. Big nasty creatures with sharp teeth will most likely eat you, you will probably break both your legs and die a horrible death. GO HOME YOU SCOTTISH FUCKSTICK. NO ONE KNOWS YOU'RE HERE!

Ok, so Fingal made the last bit up, not that he cared. He would have happily continued down into the deep forest but there was no more track, only space and air. Both the land and trail suddenly vanished, and the explorer found himself standing on the edge of a cliff with a hundred-foot drop. A landslip, a big one, had claimed the trail.

"Where the hell has the trail gone?" said Fingal, peering out over the drop.

Far below, he could just make out a little staircase, descending further into the forest. This, presumably, lead to the world-famous Cathedral Falls.

"You know what," said Fingal. "I reckon I could get down there with a good rope." Somewhere in the trees, a gang of kookaburras chortled with great irony. "But not today." He stepped back. "I hear you, wise kookaburras. Flinging oneself off a cliff into the deep forest is probably not a very good idea. A quest for another day."

It was a wise decision. The sun began to loom westwards, the shadows of tall trees lengthened, and the air cooled further. A rich man, a happy man, Fingal then returned to the massive strangler fig, sat and leaned against one of her huge buttresses, and removed water, food and rolling equipment from his pack. "What a find," he said in between every bite of his trusty cheese and jam sandwich, "a private forest trail, no continental wankers, and my very own Temple of Trees."

***

After a quick smoke, Fingal calmed his breathing and sat perfectly still. He then waited and waited, hardly moving a muscle, gazing up into the bowels of the mysterious tree, waiting for the magic show to begin. It always happened if he sat perfectly still.

Sometime later, strange birds began to call from the tree's huge crown, hissing and screeching and wailing like lost children. These were the calls of satin bowerbirds, curious creatures with curious songs.

The male appeared first. A stunning bird, he was roughly the size of a pigeon but covered in magnificent satin feathers that shimmered in the dim light. His beak, ivory in colour, was long and curved and – most curious of all – he had two bulging, purple eyes, one on either side of its head.

The male drifted to the forest floor and landed no more than five metres from the meditating Fingal statue. He then began fussing through the leaf-litter, tossing leaves over his shoulder until he found a nice, shiny yellow one. According to the rules of some ancient ritual, the satin bowerbird then made a low, rattling sound and triumphantly held the yellow trophy leaf aloft, repeating this pattern for a couple of minutes. This was the cue for a harem of eight female bowerbirds to float down and encircle the male. They too had mad, swollen purple eyes but were attired quite differently, in more of your Scottish hunting lodge style – green socks, plus fours with mustard dots, gold feathered vests and pale, green jackets. "Sirens," Fingal whispered, angry he wasn't keeping perfectly still.

The female bowerbirds then vied for the attention of the male and his magical yellow leaf. Some screeched and leapt three foot in the air, others bobbed and weaved and made strange hissing noises, while the remainder, the younger females, pranced around as best they could. After five or so minutes of this curious avian sexual discotheque, the male presented the yellow leaf to the best dancer. The happy couple then bolted back up to his sex-lair, followed by the remainder of the harem who, apparently, were keen to watch, keen to learn how to please the Master-of-Yellow-leaf. "You're wasting your time, my friends," Fingal said in a French accent, smiling like a crazy-man. "Cut ze rope of S.E.X. Seek ze higher lover, or it'll seek you."

The loner sat for a couple more hours, admiring brightly coloured butterflies, smirking at the impossibly cute log-runners (small brown birds with white chests) rifling through the leaf-litter while looking for bugs, studying the columns of big, red bull ants marching up and down the fig's buttresses, nodding a g'day to the lovely little bush rats, or wondering how closely the monitor lizards moseying around the clearing, with their sly grins and grey, rawhide skins, were related to the dinosaurs. But, most of the time, Fingal just stared into the dark canopy of the strangler fig, wondering what on earth to christen the denizen? Such a mighty being, surely the biggest tree in the forest, had to have a name, but what?

It was a good question. What did you call a tree that had suffocated its host to death before giving birth to a whole forest of killers? Evil? Strong? Natural? Efficient? Beautiful? No doubt many continentals would question Fingal's affinity for such a monster but, again, what did those hypocritical arseholes know? Humans killed each other all the time, often in the hundreds and thousands. They killed forests, poisoned rivers, and flattened mountains. They killed off many species of animals: white and black rhinos, Tasmanian tigers and, soon, polar bears. And they killed each other, with guns and lethal injections and nukes, which sometimes killed millions. Humans, ergo, could get fucked. They knew nothing. Their opinion held no currency on the island.

In the end, however, a name for the colossal strangler fig came easily enough. Here stood an ancient queen, complete with a ball dress for a trunk and a giant, living crown; a regal and godly creature, a giver and a taker of life. "It is rather obvious," Fingal said once he got to his feet. "And some might say a bit religious, or Freudian, or a bit like Oedipus, but, no, they would be inexorably wrong." The island's chief explorer saluted the tree, and said with great ceremony, "on this great day of joy, adventure, discovery, and very, very sweaty testicles, the island authorities have bestowed on me the great honour of christening—"

"Get on with it!" a mouse squeaked up from below.

"Silence!"

Fingal gathered himself, smiled up at the gargantuan tree then shouted, "Henceforth, beautiful tree, you shall be known as Mother."

***

On the ascent, the trail flashed beneath Fingal's wild eyes, sweat poured from his brow and the legs in his muscles, so used to sitting at a desk in a writing factory, soon began to ache, but Fingal thought only of Mother. In the little island in his mind, She became a beautiful and mysterious Goddess. Her apotheosis was a delightful realisation, for every island needed a deity and a religion. A sense of worship was important for the islander's prosperity, spiritual well-being and sense of meaning.

Besides, what else could the colossal tree represent? The forest had a spirit, a soul, its own laws, customs and doctrines. Since moving into the little blue cottage, Fingal now realised that the Goddess had been trying to communicate with him from the outset. The more he thought about it, the more this teaching made sense. A forest-god (Mother, obviously) had been subtly guiding, teaching and rewarding him for shunning the disgusting, pathetic continent of man. All those months ago, when Fingal had the good sense to execute the television She had shown him Little Girl Clearing and sent one of Her creatures, Jackie, as an emissary, friend and, now, lover. The ruder Fingal was to Andrew the more animals She revealed! And, bloody hell, look at the reward for shunning Penny and cutting the rope of sex! The Goddess had gifted him a secret trail in a lost forest, a vast temple that no one knew about but Fingal.

"Her law is all about respect and balance," said Fingal when he finally reached Python Gate, safe and sound. Still Mrs Snake was nowhere to be seen. "Yay, that shall be the core tenet of Her religion. If I respect and love her, She will respect and love all the islanders. That is the nature of her law. Mother be praised."

***

Moments later, the filthy explorer popped back out on the fire trail, feeling as if he'd just been teleported from one dimension to another. Stiff as a board, his skin covered in cuts, blood, bites, dirt and bruises, and his shorts sodden with sweat, Fingal couldn't remember the last time he'd been as happy. It had been a marvellous auspicious seventh stone day.

"It's all about the balance," Fingal repeated giddily when he was almost home, sneaking past the fence outside Penny's pink cottage, scurrying past the brightly lit building like a little bush rat.

Something wasn't right, however. On the other side of the fence a big animal rustled in Penny's bushes, and the bold explorer sensed great evil. "Sooty?" he whispered as a wild, rapid dog suddenly charged from the bushes and attacked the fence. "FUCK!" cried Fingal and near jumped out his skin.

"BARK, BARK, BARK!"

This was no ordinary dog! It was a big, black, mangy thing of no discernible breed, with obvious social, anger, and mental health issues. The brute's fur stood on end, its eyes – more red than white – were furious, and it kept charging, biting and head-butting the fence, all the while barking its face off. It looked positively demented!

"Back," squeaked Fingal. "Back, creature of hell. BACK!"

"BARK!" The beast insisted in the stifling heat. "BARK! FUCKIN' BARK!"

Fingal booted the fence and hurried on, muttering the word "balance" as he went, praying to Mother that Penny had not adopted one of her charges from the depot of dogs, that this beast was only visiting the estranged, pink cottage next door.

The day got weirder and weirder, as if Mother, for some unfathomable religious motive, decided to twist his mental nipple, harder and harder, as if she was testing his faith straight up. A noise far worse than a demented dog suddenly erupted from Andrew's drab, green house. It was a dreadful, repetitive and utterly pointless sound, like a tiny motorcycle engine being revved up and down, up and down, up and down, over and over and over again. Fingal's heart began to beat faster. New sweat flooded old, his blue eyes widened with fear and anger, and he felt like crying. Pavlovian, he knew the sound from his time on the coast, and he absolutely fucking hated it. "A leaf blower," he said. "The sanctimonious little wanker has gone and bought a leaf blower. In a rainforest!"

V v v v r r r r r r r r r r r r r r r r r o o o o o o o o o o o o o o o o m m m m m m , vvvvvvvvvvvvvvvrrrrrroooooooooooom, vvvaaa-fuckin'-rrrrrrrrrrrrrooooo ooooooommmmmmmmm, the stupid, pointless two-stroke-cunt-of-a-machine went; the ghastly sound was a hideous affront to the beautiful, quiet and stately rainforest. Andrew might as well have been drawing his long, manicured nails down a brand-new blackboard. Fingal hated the man and the machine. Both had to die. "War must be declared," he hissed. "Post-haste."

"But, Lord Fingal," some lily-livered military strategist at his side said, "the island's economy is already running at full capacity. The Writing Factory swallows all our resources!"

"I do not seek problems," Fingal snapped as he opened the gate. "I demand solutions, you hear?!" He switched characters. "That's odd. Where's Jackie?"

"The economy is severely over-stretched, Sir. The war machine is far from ready! The men are exhausted. Their swords grow rust, not courage. Madness stirs in their ranks!"

"Stop making excuses, you blithering coward," Lord Fingal barked.

"With the utmost respect, Sir, you demand the impossible. We islanders are explorers, runners and writers, not fighters."

"That's even odder," said Fingal, walking down the path on his ruined lawn. Jackie wasn't on the verandah railing either. A ball of anxiety grew in his stomach.

"Sir, if I may."

"You may not. Silence!"

Fingal rushed onto the verandah. "Jackie," he called to the forest, urgently whistling the Food Song, over and over again. "Jackie!" he called, as Andrew blew fuckin' leaves that would only fuckin' re-appear tomorrow. "JACKIE!!"

"Sir, look down."

"No!" Fingal began to cry. He knew what was down there. "NO! I WON'T. JACKIE! JACKIE!"

"Sir, Jackie has fallen."

"NO! NO! NO! NO! NO!"

Tragically, the lily-livered military strategist was correct.

Fingal's bird, dear friend and lover wasn't perched on the verandah practicing his odd little tunes. The lovely, little butcherbird was dead. Jackie had indeed fallen. Fingal's only friend lay in a still, crumpled mess among the dead weeds on the lawn. Thirty or so big, green VAGFs circled the corpse, buzzing loudly in the stifling air. Tears welled in the Scotsman's wild, blue eyes and confusion, pain and blackness became his soul. He cursed the Goddess in the forest. What the fuck have satanic dogs, leaf blowers and heartache got to do with fuckin' balance?!

Her answer came soon enough.

Impossible as it was to believe, that day – that black, horrible day –

got even blacker. Dark clouds took over the sky, thunder grumbled and lightening flickered above the petrified forest.

After months of sunshine, heat and drought, a storm was brewing out west.

Jackie might be dead but at least, at last, Binjari would drink.

Chapter Sixteen
A Funeral on the Island

The funeral was a small, lugubrious affair. For the occasion, Fingal wore his full kilt ensemble: brogues, woollen socks, white shirt and clan tartan tie, and the heavy McKay kilt. In one hand, the grieving Scotsman clutched a eulogy by Robert Burns and a battered silver hip flask full of wine in the other, which he swigged on, not for the first time that dark day. Fingal's eyes were gaunt, black things, and waves of nausea clawed at the walls of his empty stomach. The mourner had a hangover that could strip paint. After discovering Jackie's corpse yesterday, Fingal had grieved in the Gaelic fashion, drinking long into the night, swearing, and weeping, alone.

The tiny grave lay open at his feet. Even though it was only a foot long, six inches wide and six deep, it took hours to dig. The ground was rock solid and had to be picked out with a kitchen knife. Worn and broken, the knife lay nearby, a small price to pay for a simple, innocent creature that died because of his need of company, because of his stupid continental altruism and because of his stupid human need to love and be loved.

Jackie, his dear friend, his only friend, lay beside the pathetic grave, wrapped in gold shroud, a gift Fingal had received from a Mongolian nomad called Terelj on his travels many moons ago.

Once more, the broken hermit swigged on the hip flask, and once more the black clouds above the small funeral groaned with thunder. The storm had only teased Binjari yesterday but seemed more aggressive today, full of energy, menace and purpose.

As Fingal bent and lifted Jackie's light body, a warm wind started to moan through the trees. The tall, stern clouds crept further across the blue sky and claimed the sun. For the first time that summer, Binjari national park fell under shadow.

"Not disturbing you, am I?" came a high-pitched voice from next door.

Oh, Christ. No. Not now!

Fingal turned but could not see his neighbour's very-fucking-annoying little face through any of the gaps in the bushes, so he called out, "Leave me alone, Andrew."

"Got the kilt on I see," the bible-basher persisted. "What's the occasion, *laddie?*"

"Leave me alone!"

War simply must be declared, Lord Fingal!

Blue lightening flickered across the belly of the swollen clouds.

"Do you see it Fingal!" Andrew squealed with great enthusiasm. "The Lord's voice booms across the land. Rain is coming. Rain! Our tanks will drink well. Isn't it, marvellous!"

"Are you deaf?"

"Ask and you shall receive, eh, *laddie?*"

"Leave. Me. Alone."

Arm the missiles!

"You know, Fingal, I do love the storms at the end of summer but the plants in my garden appreciate God's generosity even more."

Fire the missiles!

"Fuck off, Andrew."

"What did you say!"

"You heard me," Fingal said to the bushes. "Fuck off."

"The devil's word!" The little voice protested. "If you wish to be left alone, all you have to do is say so, politely. There is no need to be so abusive."

Fingal closed his eyes, and with what little strength he had left, shouted, "FUCK OFF, CHRISTIAN!"

"How rude!" Andrew said brusquely. "I *was* going to pop round to tell you that Mary, Col's wife, passed away last night but I won't blooming well bother now. Check your mouth, *neighbour.*"

"Fuck off, fuck off, fuck off, fuck off, fuck off!"

The missiles did the job. The Ghost left and Fingal grinned at the sound of the little footsteps retreating. Even in his state of grief, he knew that war between the blue and green cottages had finally commenced. Even with a broken heart, Fingal had been brave enough to launch the first salvo, to finally speak the truth and tell Andrew what he really thought about him.

The news that Mary, Shaky Old Col's wife, had passed away had no impact on Fingal whatsoever. Death seemed like a bit of a blessing for her anyway. At least death relieved her pain, and Col's torment, and took her wounded soul far, far away from Donne's crappy continent. Death lurked everywhere in the park for the moment: in the end of the hot summer, in Fingal's relationship with Andrew and, most painfully, in the gold shroud he now held in his dirty, shaking hands.

It was time for Jackie's long sleep.

Certain he was alone, Fingal placed Jackie's body into the small grave. Then, fighting back tears, he stood and read the Burns eulogy in a clear, Scottish voice:

> An honest man here lies at rest,
> As e'er God with his image blest:
> A friend of man, the friend of truth,
> The friend of age and guide of youth;
> Few hearts like his-with virtue warm'd,
> Few heads with knowledge so informed:
> If there's another world, he lives in bliss;
> If there is none, he made the best of this.

"I'm so sorry, Jackie. I really didn't mean to kill you."

The loneliest man in the world drained the hip flask, and started filling in the grave, feeling darker and darker as each handful of dusty earth fell onto Jackie's golden funeral shroud.

***

The cause of Jackie's death was simple: death by poison. Every time Fingal had scooshed the fly spray, executed a VAGF and fed it to the butcherbird, he'd pushed Jackie that little bit closer to death. The islander tried not to blame himself. Every fly he'd killed for Jackie was killed out of love, stupid higher love from a stupid ape that unintentionally did stupid things. Quite simply, Fingal had killed his only friend with kindness. But, still, it hurt like stink, and it made no sense, particularly in light of the discovery of the huge strangler fig, the godliest of all the creatures Fingal had so far encountered in Binjari.

She was a real tree, so her law must be real. "I don't understand, Mother," said Fingal as he patted down the last of the dirt above Jackie's grave. "Why did you take my friend?"

The storm answered on Her behalf. Wind hurtled through the forest, darkness became the land, and the air was suddenly full of leaves and bark and screeching birds and crazed insects. Thunder crashed overhead, followed immediately by a terrific CRACK and a fizzing, bolt of lightning. A big, fat, beautiful raindrop then splattered onto the parched frond of a nearby yucca, then another, and another, then a hundred, thousand and a million more fell until the sky was full of sweet, delicious rain. Silver water teemed from the bruised clouds. It hammered off the tin roof, quickly filling then overflowing the gutters, it battered the dying weeds, creepers and saplings on the lawn, and it thumped into the hard, aching ground, gushing into hundreds of brittle cracks.

Fingal didn't jump or dance or spin around like a rain-worshipper. In fact, the recluse never once looked up to admire the ferocious storm. He didn't move. He couldn't move, for he was sheltering Jackie's little grave from the deluge as best he could.

A slideshow of images of Jackie-boy played in the cinema of his wrecked mind: the first-time Jackie took a crust in Little Girl Clearing; the sight of Jackie gliding in from the forest and landing on the railing; the way the butcherbird used to hop and skip toward the saucer full of poisonous human food, his little wings shaking in anticipation; the gusto with which he whistled his song every day, his weird, beautiful Australian song; the way he just sat on the verandah railing, day after day, staring at the ape working on the computer; the way his black, cosmic eyes pleaded and begged with the ape. "See me," they said. "Look at me. See me. I am real. Love me."

At last, Fingal began to cry and the boundary between reality and fantasy flickered. The man in the kilt turned his sore, red face up to the pouring rain, closed his eyes and sank through an ocean.

***

Because he could do what he wanted, and because his heart was breaking, Fingal took on the form of Jackie, swimming up from the deep, black depths of the ocean, and breaking the surface near a raft of driftwood.

Using his scuffed beak and little dinosaur claws, he clambered onto the raft, shook his feathers out and took flight, following a series of big, ugly ropes that led toward a green and very beautiful island.

Soon, the magpie lark made landfall and flew gracefully over a white beach, a little blue castle and a fire trail that ran inland, climbing gradually as it went. He followed the trail for a kilometre or so until a building loomed out of the forest. Identical in every way, shape and form to the Bodleian Library at Oxford, the bird knew that this was the Industry for Science, the place where John Donne's ridiculous "no man is an island" theory was being forensically disassembled.

Jackie circled the lovely, old building and noticed an angry professor leaning out from window. Dressed in a white lab coat buttoned up to the neck, the academic had a gigantic bouffant of matted, grey hair and a long, white beard, and was shouting in a strong accent Jackie could barely understand: "Thanks, wee bird," the imprisoned man shouted, "thanks tae ye. Dinnae fash yersel' aboot the stupid ape. He didnae ken! HE DIDNAE KEN! Fly, ya bonnie wee bird. She wants tae see ye. FLY!"

Minutes later a second building appeared. Larger and meaner, this was the Ministry for War. Pentagonal in shape, it had no windows, was made entirely from cement and was painted in the camouflage of a giant carpet python – moss-green and dark brown. After telling Andrew to fuck off the Ministry for War bustled with activity. Polaris nuclear missiles ghosted up from underground missile silos. Apache helicopters filled the sky and practiced for war by blowing up trees, and Jackie counted thousands of little Fingal soldiers, drilling, bayonetting dummies wearing red tracksuits, or peeling giant mounds of potatoes. Every soldier chanted the same slogan, over and over again: "noise is bad, silence is good. The Drab, Green King must fall. Noise is bad, silence is good. The Drab, Green King must fall." A pacifist by nature, the little bird was horrified by how much the war industry had expanded. Violence never solved anything. However, before he could even squawk a protest three black, sleek F-22s piloted by stern Fingals wearing mirrored shades and *Top Gun* jackets chased him off.

The butcherbird then flew over a third edifice, the most horrid building on the island: the Writing Factory, the place where *The Epic Novel of Sport* was being painstakingly produced. By far the biggest building on the Island of Fingal McKay, it took the form of a Victorian era sweatshop, and towered high above the rainforest. Exactly twenty-six storeys in height – one for each letter of the alphabet – the scale of the factory was exaggerated by four immensely tall chimneys, one at each corner belching acrid smoke full of bad words into the clean air.

It was a sinister building, a prison of pain, delusion and idiocy. Even though Jackie flew a good kilometre above the Writing Factory grim sounds of industry stabbed up at his flight – engines labouring, steam hissing, wine bottles popping, men groaning and moaning, 68,000 lighters clicking on and off, on and off, and, above it all, the sound of thousands and thousands of fingers rattling on thousands and thousands of keyboards full of ash and sweat and pain.

A sage creature, the little black and white bird knew that evil brewed within the factory. Of late, a rumour had started spreading that a Mr Fang, some shadowy, tyrant slave driver, had seized control of the Writing Factory in a dramatic and very bloody coup. These were dark tidings. Tyrants never gave up power, nor could they abandon that which brought hegemony in the first place: violence, intimidation and terror. Jackie could smell daemons in the ugly, oppressive factory but there was nothing to be done. Fingal's ego had already consumed most of his common sense. Still, the bird circled the huge, malodorous factory three times, until a gust of acrid writing-smoke forced him inland. The smoke, he noticed, stunk of greed, lies and ego.

The land rose steeply, and the trail began to spiral around the tall, central peak of the island, Mt Fingal, if the bird's memory served it correctly. As usual the top of the mountain was obscured by a band of black cloud full of huge forks of blue lightning but the little bird wasn't interested in the summit. That would come. Instead, it sought a flat, distinctive shoulder of land about halfway up the mountain. This, Jackie knew, would be covered in soft, green grass and a white temple identical in design to the ancient Temple of Artemis at Ephesus. He also knew that a majestic golden tree that went by the name of Mother grew inside the beautiful building.

"Meep," said Jackie as loud as he could, once he had landed on the white, marble causeway encircling the divine temple. He looked up and saw the Mother Tree. Made entirely of gold, Her crown shone in the dull light. Her arms, festooned in waterfalls and curtains of gold, sparkling orchids, lay open, as if welcoming the butcherbird.

"Let us speak the common tongue," a honeyed voice said from inside the tree's enormous crown. "Welcome, little one."

"Hello," Jackie replied.

"Come, little bird. Rest," The voice continued sonorously. "Your journey has been long. Do you understand why you are here?"

"I think so." Jackie frowned. "You made the ape poison me. I was to be sacrificed for the rain."

"That is correct. Because of you, my trees will drink deep. My creatures will multiply and prosper."

"That's a nice way of putting it."

"There is more." Mother said. "He did love you."

"I know," said Jackie, hoping and skipping his way toward the buttresses of the heavenly tree.

"You had to die, my Love." The mellifluous voice continued. "The Experiment was faltering. He was blinded by his love for you. The shock will awaken him to my forest. With your passing, he shall be able to see."

"One thing, though, Mrs Big Tree." Jackie had now reached the bottom of a great, golden buttress that led up to Her crown. "That big-Scottish-ape-thing didn't really know what he was doing, right? He didn't actually know he was poisoning me?"

"That is correct. The human only loved you."

Jackie nodded his head sagely. "He was all right, Fingal. Different, but all right."

"He meant well. Now," said Mother, "it is time. Come, little one."

Jackie looked up to see a steep and winding trail, placed a claw on one of Mother's golden buttress and gulped. Mother's mood was always difficult to read. She could be humble and kind and terrible and cruel all at the same time, such was Her one, timeless law – balance.

"Come, little bird. There is something I wish to show you."

"Well," said Jackie, tucking his wings behind his back and waddling up the trail. "I suppose I've lived a good life."

"That is true, my love."

"Full of milk and honey, bugs and lizards," he said when he was halfway up. "Oh, and lots of extremely cool flights through the pillars of your beautiful temple."

"Weren't they fun!"

"Aye, Mother. I loved flying."

"Almost there," the golden voice said when Jackie had almost reached the top. "Come, little one."

Jackie was about to plunge into Mother's golden ocean of divine beauty but he suddenly stopped and turned. Far below, stood a grief-stricken man wearing a kilt. It was his friend, Fingal McKay, the aspirational hermit. A little black raincloud hung above his shaggy head, his kilt was soaked through, and he looked in great pain.

"It's alright, mate," the butcherbird called out. "You didn't mean to poison me!"

"I didn't know the fly spray was poison, Jackie-boy!" the man groaned.

"We're cool, mate."

"Hey Jackie you're so fine, you're so fine, you blow my mind. Hey Jackie!"

"Hey Jackie!"

160

"Come," Mother softly interrupted. "It is time. Death is beautiful. You shall see. You shall see everything!"

At the foot of the tree, the man called out "I LOVE YOU!"

In reply, Jackie whistled two odd notes, dived into the ocean, and was gone.

Forever.

"Bye-bye, Jackie-bird. Bye-bye, my love."

***

Fingal McKay opened his eyes.

The storm was passing as quickly as it had arrived. The wind had dropped, there was detritus everywhere – dead leaves, strips of bark, feathers and such – and the huge storm trundled east, toward the coast. Sunlight returned and, once more, the sunburnt country glowed gold. "I understand why you took my bird, Mother," Fingal said to the forest and wiped away his tears. "You want me to go on." An aroma of hot, burnt water filled his hairy nostrils and he added, grimly, "The Experiment must proceed."

Chapter Seventeen
Fingal's Pet Haggis

Two stones after Jackie's funeral the dread engines in the Writing Factory spluttered into life once more. As ever, the hirsute labourer rose before dawn, brewed a strong pot of coffee, and pre-rolled six disgusting, horrible cigarettes. Dressed only in a pair of factory-issue underpants, bleary-eyed and moody after another torrid night's sleep, he shuffled over to his cluttered workstation and slumped into his seat, pain stabbing at his lower back. A coughing fit ensued while the machine booted up, ending only when Microsoft Office played its fickle tune. The labourer was beginning to loathe the machine and its stupid greeting.

Hot coffee got rid of the cough and expunged the thick layer of phlegm at the back of his throat, so he lit a second smoke, and switched to auto-pilot mode, opening up the web, the Writer's Room website, Wikipedia, Word, the twenty-seven characters' files and, finally, *The Epic Novel of Sport*, which was now 101,273 words long, roughly 350 pages. Fingal McKay, labourer, explorer, former bird lover, and, today, author, rubbed his temples and said, "Why am I doing this again?" He was careful not to rub too hard, though, just in case the skin burst and precious words spilled out.

Draft one of the book neared completion but the writer began to dither about, lingering rather than sprinting for the finish line, going sideways and backward instead of forward, fannying about as all writers do, good or bad, published or unpublished. He began to slave over every word, full-stop and damned semi-colon. The detail of the detail, the minutiae of every colour, mood, sight, smell and blade of grass mentioned in the book had become masochistic obsessions. Consider, for example, the introduction to one of the settings in *The Epic Novel* (funnily enough, from a story he'd created about a mythical island called Fànk, in the Scottish Hebrides):

"Few people visit the island of Fànk. The reason why is simple – none of the Fànkers would ever give out directions. Feck the mainland, and feck the ootsiders. That's the Fànk way.

To get there is easy, if a little far. From Eilean Donan castle on the Isle of Skye follow the Uig-Tarbert ferry line north and west. Then go way, way past Lewis and Uist until you come to St Kilda, Soay and Stac Lee then, again, go way, way north until you come to a conspicuous three-hundred-foot needle of rock which the local fisherman – salty, simple folk with beards for faces – call the Big Needle. A hundred miles north from there, you may then have the good fortune to stumble across the Isle of Fànk, an emerald speck on a boundless carpet of rolling, silver sea.

Most of the northern, lower half of the island is made up of the Great Bog, a vast swamp of heathland dotted with mounds of aromatic thyme, purple knapweed, and little fideans – sparkling water meadows filled with brackish water, flag iris, spear reeds and meadowsweet. The Great Bog drains into the River Ech, a ribbon of silver meandering across thousands of acres of farmland populated by crofts, byres, fowling shelters, summer hunting shielings, 323,467 sheep, eighty-three collie dogs and one hundred and twenty-nine people, exactly.

Where the River Ech joins the sea, the land rises and the vista is dominated by a lone, bleak mountain. Covered in red sorrel, heather, scree and, as the hill climaxes, smooth, black rock, this place is called *Uaimh Shianta*, the hallowed place. Sitting on top are four buildings. The largest one has a bell tower at one end and a white cross at the other, creaking in the wind.

A bell tolls."

These five paragraphs took half a stone, seven cups of coffee, four glasses of red wine, and eleven cigarettes to write. *"A writer doesn't just write,"* The Writer's Room website told Fingal one day. *"They construct worlds. He or she has to create the detail of everything. Everything."* In hindsight, this was one of the more adroit pieces of advice offered on that stupid website.

To create the island described above, for example, Fingal studied maps of the Hebrides, weather charts and satellite photography. He read books online about Scottish plants, flowers and animals, pagan folklore, and highland society, politics, and culture, and combed through many dull but charming novels about life in the wild, North Sea islands (*The Sea Room* by Adam Nicolson, for example). While humming Felix Mendelssohn's The Hebrides (on loop), he scrolled through hundreds of black and white photographs of the Highland fishing industry, or huge games of shinty, curling and football, or, his favourite, photographs of the Hebridean people, tough, skinny folk that looked like stunned, malnourished vikings. In terms of the story that took place on the island of Fànk, *The Epic Novel* also needed characters, back stories, biographies and so on, all of which were hand-written on dozens of pages that would never see the light of day, but, at least, would adorn the increasingly busy walls of the factory.

It was hard and difficult work; gruelling work.

Every word felt like it was carved from stone.

At this stage of production, the factory had created seven main settings where the drama would unfold, as well as twenty-seven characters with twenty-seven unique tales that somehow related to the three major themes of the book – sport, corruption and God. Not that the writer noticed but *The Epic Novel of Sport* was turning into a monster of a hobby. The book got bigger and stranger every stone of every week.

At least spending so much time in the Old Country allowed Fingal to block out the world outside his little blue cottage; well, for the most part. A pair of orange earplugs acquired from Gail's store helped, but, if he tried hard enough, he could still hear *them, out there*: dull, distant and infuriating sounds of cars passing on the road outside, Andrew fighting his pointless battle against the forest with his fucking-stupid leaf blower, rain drumming off the tin roof, Penny's psychotic dog barking its satanic face off or, sometimes, Shaky Old Col wailing into the long night, crying for his dead wife.

"They are not part of the book," he always admonished himself, slapping his face as punishment for trying to listen. "They're not there, man. Work, you prick. Work! Pretend they're not real."

This was easier said than done. Fingal began to think Andrew was spying on him. More than once, he felt the eyes of the enemy on him. On more than one occasion, Fingal sensed Andrew's little, grey head floating in the bushes. However, each time that he looked up and cried "ha-ha!" all he saw was a formidable wall of wild, unkempt garden.

Well aware there many imagined people now inhabited his mind, Fingal shook of the creepy sensation of being watched as "just seein' ghosts". At least the little bible-basher had ceased the infernal, neighbourly pop rounds. Telling a pious evangelist to repeatedly fuck off usually has that effect. Anyway, the warrior in the writer swore that, one day, soon, Andrew would pay for all his stupid noise. War – at a time when it wouldn't impact the progress on the book – was coming. "No distractions," he would mumble, over and over. "Onwards, man. WORK!"

Breakfast in the factory now occurred around mid-afternoon. Nothing flash, the labourer just shoved a microwave lasagne in the microwave and pressed the numbers 6, 0, and 0, then NUKE. While the plastic pasta with bits of dead animal, lots of sugar and an excuse for sauce, cooked, Fingal usually did a bit of stretching but the effort proved more painful than the pain itself, so he poured more wine into his dirty chalice – right to the brim – lit a smoke and waited, furious that time was slipping past.

***

Time became the #1 concern in the factory. Like sand in a sieve, too much of it was slipping away. At this rate, *The Epic Novel of Sport* would never get finished. Fingal needed a motivational therapist, an expert, someone or something to manage and drive the book home. This was why Fingal finally gave form, character and life to the annoying voice inside his head, the one that kept demanding WORK, WORK, WORK!

Creating yet another alter ego, was a piece of cake. Such was the efficiency of the factory, it took less than a minute to give birth (or, re-birth) to a very scary factory manager called Mr Fang. It was Mr Fang's job to scare and frighten *The Epic Novel of Sport* over the finish line.

"Harrow," the Asian voice said one day when Fingal was furiously staring at lasagne, cooking slowly in the microwave.

"Hello," Fingal replied. "Can I help you?"

"You cle-ated me, Scotman."

"Yes, Mr Fang, I'm quite aware of that. What do you want?"

"Nothin'," Fang hissed. "Just rooking, fo' now. Just rooking."

The two men actually had a real past. Fingal first met Fang over a decade ago, in Thailand, when he was passed out drunk on the Koh San Road after consuming far too much Thai whisky. Mr Fang was a short, corrupt Thai policeman who introduced himself to Fingal by beating him with fist, boot and a white truncheon, screaming "you gimmee moneee, or go jail! You gimmee moneee! You gimmee moneee!" Mr Fang beat poor, drunk Fingal until the backpacker handed over all his precious baht, laughed and walked away.

Fingal couldn't remember much about the savage, except that he wore a shit-coloured uniform with matching shoes and hat, had a very long pinky nail, and had pockmarked skin, black eyes and a gold tooth. To this day, Fingal could never forget the beating, or Fang's high-pitched, Asian voice screeching, "You give me moneee! You give me moneee!"

And, somewhat amazingly, here Mr Fang was again, re-born to lurk in an imaginary, increasingly oppressive Writing Factory that existed on an imaginary island inside his flickering mind. No racism informed Fang's birth or being, or humour at his ridiculous "in-ger-eesh" accent; just fear, only fear. This, this, beast was now entirely responsible for the production of *The Epic Novel of Sport*, Mother help us.

"Hey, hey you," Fang's voice pestered Fingal at the microwave. "Why you no' wo'king? Why you no' li-ting?"

"It is luncheon hour, Mr Fang."

"An'?"

"A labour force needs to eat, Mr Fang."

"Hullee up, you razeee Scotman. You got go back to work."

"Oh, be quiet, Mr Fang."

Fingal waved the imaginary Thai policeman as if he were a VAGF. Dismissing Fang was easy in those days, when he was just a baby daemon.

***

Typically, microwave lasagne and wine were consumed in the company of one of the late afternoon storms. Ever since Jackie's funeral they rolled in like clockwork, drowning the cottage and the forest for a good half an hour until all fell calm and dripping wet. The strange, thirsty forest adored the fresh water. After each storm, Fingal could hear all Mother's plants breathing a long, contented "ahhh" as they slaked a thirst built up over three or four months of searing summer heat. Life, little patches of green grass, began to appear on the brown "lawn". Weeds long thought dead stretched into animation, brown saplings budded, and, with remarkable speed, Her ingenious vines broke free of the garden and crawled toward the blue cottage.

The more he looked, the more he saw.

Best of all, Fingal saw beautiful…

"Stop rooking at stupid ga'den," Mr Fang interrupted. "Get back to work!"

By the early evenings, the writer was usually too drunk to play with Fang or to type, but this didn't mean industry ceased. Staggering around the dark factory in his underpants, he sometimes impersonated a character from *The Epic Novel*, or acted out a dramatic scene, or imagined himself as an eagle flying over the real – was it real? – Island of Fànk in the Scottish Hebrides, before rushing to the workstation to add more detail to long chapters that kept on getting longer. Or, if he wasn't pretending to be someone, something, or somewhere else, Fingal worked on the Mad Posters covering the walls, assiduously adding more and more detail to the maps, sketches, and story "beats" relating to place, building or plot. He scribbled new lines, diagrams, and words in between the old ones, his handwriting getting smaller and smaller as *The Epic Novel of Sport* got bigger and bigger. The last time Fang ordered him to count them, there were precisely 209 of these Mad Posters. They too were growing, creeping into the filthy kitchen and the black, abandoned living room.

All of this work and pain paid off in the end. Many stones had passed but, at last, *The Epic Novel of Sport* was finished, all 132,756 words of it. In total, the book ran to 397 beautiful, original, award-winning pages. Fingal's mind, back and chest ached, he could have slept for days, and his eyes were red, dry and twitchy but the book was finished. Done. Finito. Finished. The fucking end. *"When you've completed that epic first draft,"* the permanently upbeat Writer's Room website advised, *"why not celebrate the milestone with a treat? A nice meal out with your long-suffering partner, a well-deserved glass of wine or some chocolate."*

Fingal decided to treat himself. He took a rare shower, his first in ten stones, lit a huge, roaring fire – which consumed the last of the decent logs – cracked the final good bottle of red wine and, for a change, smoked a large cigar he'd found in his sporran, a relic from some ancient wedding in Scotland. No plates of nibbles were passed around the party (because he had no food), no music played (because, shortly after moving in, Fingal had kicked the stereo to death), and no friends patted him on the back to say "well done, mate" (because, intentionally, he had none).

The writer had plenty of other company. Much of the lively soiree was spent discussing the vicissitudes of working life with Sir Randolph Hazelrigg, the baddie from *The Epic Novel of Sport*, or sitting smoking and drinking with Heracles, the God character, on a cloud in Olympia, the two of them casually chatting about just how brilliant the book actually was. Sometimes a dozen Jackie-birds flew through the cottage, or, sometimes, his estranged father would appear in the dark living room, nagging and begging his boy to stop going mad, to give up on desire, and "come hame". Most of the night, however, the dazzling, prodigiously talented, impending winner of the Man Booker prize, waltzed around the ballroom of a glorious castle in Scotland with Miss Lucy Pendergrass, the young, female heroine of *The Epic Novel of Sport*, who looked just like The One.

The last bottle of good wine on the island ran out shortly after midnight. This was a diabolical development because it meant Fingal had to break the seal on the emergency four litre *box* of red wine, goon as they used to call it on the continent. The goon was vile and tasted like a cross between spoiled vinegar, turned water and salt. But, still, it was a party. The staff – the writer, his characters and the factory labourers – needed booze. In fact, they supped on the rancid liquid, smoked rollies, and danced with and snogged Lucy Pendergrass until a grey dawn broke the next stone.

Drunk as a Glasgow tramp, and bathed in meek, silver light, the brilliant young author then slumped against a wall, sighed a very happy sigh and – dirty, half-full glass of wine in one hand, smouldering rollie in the other – fell into a deep, mental sleep.

***

Strangely, though, Fingal McKay did not dream of or visit his island. Dressed in his kilt, he and Jackie-bird were on Michael Parkinson's 1970s television chat show. Parky, Jackie and Fingal were sitting on an orange sofa, chatting, smoking huge, distended rollies, and drinking from buckets of goon.

"I like your little black and white bird," the august host cooed to the lark on his guest's shoulder. "Butcherbird?"

"Isn't he lovely?"

"Cheeky chappie?"

"Very."

"It is such a shame you poisoned him."

"Quite," the brilliant author replied, tartly.

"Now," said Parky, draining his bucket and burping, "*the* book."

Fingal's ego flared. "Ah yes, *the* book; sorry, *MY* book."

"I hope I don't sound like I'm kissing your magnificent Scottish buttocks but, by our God, *The Epic Novel of Sport* is absolutely brilliant. It is without a doubt the best book I have *ever* read." Fingal didn't bother replying because the applause was so loud.

The dream jerked, and the chat show set turned into a crowded award ceremony. Kilt, Parky, and Jackie were no more. Fingal now wore a black dinner suit, bow tie and a huge, tartan hat. An object that looked like a big ink cartridge was clutched close to his chest. "Ladies and gentlemen," an English announcer's voice called out above the uproarious cheering, "our surprise winner of the Man Booker Prize, Fingal McKay! And yes, amazingly, it's a novel about fucking sport."

"Aye, Son," his father, a big, Scottish farmer, called out from the front row. "Weel done, an' that. But I didnae like it. There's too much swearing in it."

"Think of the fucking message, Dad!"

Then Stephen Spielberg was nipping at Fingal's ear, inviting him Los Angeles to share dinner and "talk about the movie".

Red carpet.

Oscars.

"I'm so sick of this shit," said Gisele Bündchen, Fingal's date for the night of nights.

"Less o' yer whinging, Bündchen," said Fingal, gruffly.

"Forgive me, Fingal, My Lord, My Big, Randy, Amazing, Sex-beast." As the cameras flashed, the Brazilian supermodel gripped his arm tighter. She stuck her expensive tongue in his hairy ear then whispered, "I want you. Now. Take me back to your Santa Barbara beachfront castle and ravage me. Do me! I don't want vulgar, nasty, smelly human love. Do me the higher way!"

"Absolutely not," replied the celibate, three-time Oscar winner. "I mustn't disappoint my continental fans. They need my light. Back in your box, Bündchen."

"Ocht, no," said his mother, lowering her camera among the crowd of paparazzi. "I agree wi' yer faither. I didnae like the book. Real men dinnae swear, son. It degrades their character."

"But everyone says fuck these days, Mum," cried Fingal, shielding his eyes from the exploding light bulbs.

"And that lassie's too tall!"

"No, she's no'."

"I dinnae like tall lassies. The One wisnae so tall."

This sucked arse. Fame, glory and being amazing, weren't meant to be so damn awkward. To escape his nagging mother, supermodel, and rapidly expanding army of drooling fans, the multi-billionaire author/producer/director then shouted "SAYONARA, YOU SLAGS", elbowed Gisele Bündchen in the ribs, and sprinted toward a waiting helicopter. This too was bizarre. The helicopter was shaped like a little blue cottage with a rotor on top.

Never mind.

Stones, no, pebbles later, the helicopter landed on top of a big F that had been painted on top the tallest turret of a magnificent sixteenth-century castle in the Scottish Highlands, also blue in colour. As the odd helicopter landed, rain that tasted of whisky began to fall from the low, blue clouds, and out stepped the most successful writer in the history of mankind, Sir Lord Professor Fingal McKay The Magnificent, O.B.E., C.O.C.K., E.G.O., H.U.G.E.

The eccentric gazillionaire genius was completely naked, his skin was painted Pictish blue, and he was playing the bagpipes, quite brilliantly. MacJackie, his wee, pet haggis – tartan skin, wee bonnet, flute for a nose, two short and two long legs (for running around hills) – greeted his simply-amazing master by tootling a wee tune on his wee chanter while gently head-butting Sir Lord Fingal's ankles.

"No' the noo, MacJackie!" the naked, blue man said to his beloved pet. "Be still, wee beastie."

"Fin, my love?" a sweet, Aberdonian accent called from the helicopter.

"Aye, fine lassie."

"I'm just popping up to McGail's shop for some microwave lasagne, goon and fags. You need anything else, my love?" In the cockpit, her long, blonde hair floated ethereally and Fingal could smell Vanilla shampoo. The aroma tantalised the piper.

Lord Fingal was flabbergasted. "The One? What you doing here? Are you real?"

She looked puzzled. "Of course I'm real, Fin."

"You are but a dream, my love," the complicated writer/director/playwright/hermit moaned. "Don't you see? You've always been a dream."

"Stop being so silly, Fin. Touch me. I'm real."

He tried to reach out but his blue arms had turned into the useless paws of the Australian Pademelon.

She laughed at him.

The cunt laughed at him.

"I hate you, Fin. I really, really hate you."

"Me too."

Then the strange helicopter flew off, The One's voice faint in silence. "Wait for me on the beach, Fin," she called out. "I'll be there soon. I promise."

"Lying bitch."

A mist rolled in from the Highlands. It too carried a voice, a cruel, familiar and very, very industrial voice. It should've been Fraser-the-Cunt's voice but, amazingly, it wisnae!

"Why you d-leeming?" Mr Fang inquired, his voice like burning acid "Why you s-reeping?! Get up, di'ty he'mit. GET UP! It time to go wo'k on shitty book."

"It no' shitty," the Lord of the Book countered. "It amazing! And it finished!"

"Ha. Foor! You no' finish."

"I finish! I finish!"

Fang laughed like a kookaburra. "Pain onree just begin. Get up, srave. Wake up. WAKE UP!"

Chapter Eighteen
The So-Called Hermit Man

"Mother be praised," said the explorer, not far from the entrance to his secret rainforest trail and temple, two stones after the party-for-one and the mad dream. Well-rested, and completely satisfied he'd written a bestseller, Fingal was sitting on top of the large, hollow log where Mrs Snake lived. As per Her curious, unfathomable Law of Balance, Mother had decided to reward him this time, presenting her only worshipper with a wonderful gift: a six-metre carpet python, Mrs Snake, having her breakfast.

Mrs Snake was no more than two metres away, eating a brush turkey it had ambushed shortly before Fingal had arrived. In such a state, the huge beast posed no threat. Her silver eyes were bulging, desperate, and seemed lost to some food trance, and her jaws were stretched impossibly wide as she slowly swallowed and crushed the poor old turkey. In the absolute silence, Fingal could hear the bird rasping and slipping inside, hear its bones crick and crack as, inch by inch, it disappeared into the snake's mad, yawning mouth. When the turkey's dirty, yellow feet finally slipped inside, the serpent licked its lips, uncoiled and rippled, sluggishly, up toward the fire trail to bask in the sun with a big lump in her belly.

"Feeling generous today, eh, Mother?" Fingal said, hopping from the log and striding past the gates with the STOP!, NO! and CERTAIN DEATH! signs. Once inside the green temple all thought of the outside world – The Experiment, *The Epic Novel of Sport* or Andrew's bloody-stupid leaf blower – vanished. "Every step toward the Mother Tree is a step away from the doomed continent," he said, barrelling down the steep track toward the old growth plateau, amazed at the difference heaps of rain and six stones could make.

The handiwork of water was everywhere. On either side of the track, pink, new growth of finger ferns burst from the rich, damp soil like an honour guard of dainty soldiers standing to attention. Lace flowers erupted around his head, and, higher still, lemon-scented tea trees rained down tiny yellow flowers on the marching, sweating ape. In the humidity, fungi ran riot and a host of bizarre mushrooms were scattered throughout. Some had red caps with white spikes on top, others took the form of large, luminous orange ears soldered to the side of black, rotting tree trunks, and some, a few, had slender, beige phalluses with white, intricate, netted skirts, and wet, putrid eyes that stunk of rotting, animal flesh. There were purple, horned mushrooms, ball-shaped mustard ones that puffed a cloud of spore when prodded and, his favourite, tall, slender gold-capped mushrooms whose flesh turned ink-blue if snapped in two. "They would go nice with a bit of butter and garlic," the explorer noted, sadly aware that base camp stocked neither.

As the steep trail began to level out, a noise, faint, beautiful, and trickling, captured the Fingal's attention. He skidded to a halt, cupped a dirty hand to a dirty ear, smiled, and said one beautiful word over and over: "water. Water. Water. Water! WATER!"

He rushed on and the gurgling, tinkling sound grew louder. Soon, hard as it was to believe after such a long, hot, shitty summer, Fingal was confronted by a clear stream tumbling down a creek bed that had lain dry for months. After so much heat and sun and dust, the sight, smell and sound of the water were like balm to his pained, over-worked soul.

However, there was no chance of taking a drink, splashing the cool water on his dirty, sweating face, or, even though all it would take was a stride, crossing the lovey watercourse. This was because a monster guarded the crossing, a small but fierce spiny blue crayfish with massive, snapping pincers, and stunning plates of red, white and blue spiked armour. Oddly, the crustacean had the attitude of a crack-addict from Harlem, New York.

"You're a feisty one," said the giant Fingal, bending to inspect the creature.

"Back up, Mutha-Fucka!" The crayfish replied.

174

"It's cool. I'm a friend of Mother's."

The crayfish retreated, hissing. "I said back up, man! I'll snip you, man; snip you bad!"

"Relax, friend. I mean you no harm."

"I'll mess you up bad, man." The crayfish slipped underneath a rock but still challenged the giant ape. "This is ma creek. MA CREEK!"

The explorer flicked his chin, smiled and, as was the curious habits of nomenclature on the island, said, "In the unique traditions of my people, I hereby claim, *and* christen, this spot simply as Crack Addict's Crossing!"

Not that Fingal had any intention of crossing, yet. Quickly, he removed his boots and stepped into the cool water, careful not to further antagonise the crayfish.

"Oh, Mother," he said, closing his eyes as the cold water ran over his hot, swollen ankles. The explorer suddenly wanted more. He wanted to be deep inside the water, so he followed the stream for a good ten minutes until it fell into a long, natural bathtub carved from mottled, grey riverstone. The pool was half-full of fresh, clear water, turning, and sparkling in the shards of sunlight. Without even thinking, Fingal whipped off his shorts and pants, shouted "for Scotland!", and jumped into the bathtub.

The cold, silver water was divine and he bathed for a while, seeing how long he could hold his breath underwater for, grooming his long hair and beard, or, mostly, just lying on his back and spinning round and round and round, the profound green ceiling turning like a child's kaleidoscope far above. "Hear ye, hear ye," Fingal said with great pomp and ceremony thirty minutes later when his fingers had turned to prunes. "The Surveyor General of the Curious Island claims this site as our own, as a place of respite for our many mad and exhausted labourers. Henceforth, it shall be known as The Enchanting Bathtub."

The traveller could not remember the last time he'd been as happy. After months of heat, torture-by-*Novel*, hundreds of mozzie bites, one dead Jackie-bird, thousands of words on paper, screen, or Mad Poster, and many, many weird dreams about The One, the water felt clean and cold. Pure. True. Real.

Refreshed and dressed, the pilgrim then skipped on through the old growth plateau toward the heart of the temple; his temple. The track, wove through many trees now familiar him: tall, silver ghost gums, gnarled brush box, and giant stinging trees with rough, fluted trunks, ruined leaves, and dumpy little crowns. The more he looked, the more he saw: weeping brown pine, so called because of its charming, pendulous arms, each cuffed with wispy, elegant needles a foot long; slender flame trees, their bases carpeted with dense, circular mats of red, bell-shaped flowers; native tamarinds laden with bright orange fruit the bats adored; and, his new favourite, stands of tall yellow carabeen, with huge, finned buttresses that reminded Fingal of the space rockets Hergé used to draw, and Tintin, Snowy and Captain Haddock used to fly in.

As he roamed and spun and danced, Mother sung to him. Strange, beautiful hymns drifted throughout Her tall, wooden pillars. Green catbirds wailed like lost children, an invisible orchestra of crickets made a great, screeching din, and, high in the canopy, wompoo fruit pigeons wearing dazzling cloaks of apricot, magenta and teal, whooped mournfully. Woooooom-pooooo, woooooom-pooooo, wooooooo-poooo, their call the heartbeat of the forest.

As Fingal neared the inner sanctum of the temple all fell silent. At last, the worshipper stood before and beneath his Goddess: Mother, the colossal strangler fig tree, the biggest tree in the forest. Although Her law and mood were always difficult to read, Fingal's ragged mind felt suddenly smooth and orderly. "Hello, Mother," he said, smiling up at his Queen, the soul of both island and forest.

There was no longer any evidence of the host tree Mother had originally strangled. She had won that battle centuries ago. Now, She was just ancient, brooding and beautiful, a Queen with a huge, green crown.

The rains had been kind to Her too. Luminous green in colour, hundreds of beards of moss hung from Her upper branches. Rosettes of bright orange lichen stood stark against Her blackish-green skin. Cascades of gold orchids poured from the crevasses and folds in Her trunk and branches. Pink, red and purple spear-shaped flowers erupted from the clumps of bromeliads that had colonised the spaces between Her buttresses. And, Mother was pregnant. Her crown was covered in thousands of blue fruits the size of ping-pong balls; life, sustenance and death soon to be gobbled up by gangs of possums, birds and flying foxes.

"More babies," Fingal noted reverentially, aware but untroubled by the sound of thunder rumbling across the sky. The storms were now part of the cycle in the forest, and they visited Binjari earlier each day, each one bigger than the last. Fingal no longer feared the storms. In fact, he adored the furious spectacles. Smiling, he tossed his pack in the shelter of the tree, walked fifty metres to the left, and took a seat on a flat stone protruding from the base of a monolith of smooth, grey rock that rose steeply on Mother's right flank. Minutes later, the storm broke, darkness engulfed the forest, torrential rain hammered onto his bare shoulders, and such was its force, his sodden beard and hair were ethereally flung about by the tempestuous wind. "BALANCE," the recluse shouted above the glorious deluge, "IT'S ALL ABOUT THE FUCKIN' BALANCE!"

Twenty minutes later, Fingal stood, shook the water from his hair and beard, and looked up to see the storm grinding east, where it would visit its wrath on the coast, hopefully blowing the ghastly collection of cement, cars, people and leaf blowers into the Pacific. Soaking wet but with wild, blue eyes, Fingal retrieved his pack and, once back on his little seat at the foot of the rock face, crossed his legs, smiled like Buddha and wolfed down a trusty cheese sandwich (just cheese – jam supplies had run out on the island days ago). "What else is on the program today, Mother?" he asked the tree, staring up into its black, dense depths.

She replied about half an hour later when the ground beneath the majestic fig tree began to click and clack. Fingal tried to locate the creature behind the sound but all he could see were drips and drops of water and shards of brilliant orange sunlight. Then, three metres in front of him, a leaf flipped over and, wondrously, a little, baby cicada crawled from the earth and gulped its first breath of sweet air. Roughly the size of a five-cent piece, the insect was black in colour, covered in mud and quite comical, as the young usually are.

"Welcome to planet earth," Fingal said as the newborn took flight, buzzing noisily up and up and up, off to only Mother knew where. Everything in nature happens exponentially and soon the leaf-litter was alive, pulsing and rippling as hundreds of baby cicadas clambered up from the mud toward the light. All of them flew like drunk, loud idiots, crashing into everything – Mother, the rock face, and, quite commonly, each other. When a collision took place, the insects fell to the ground, rolled around on their backs and buzzed Aussie insults at each other:

"Oi! You! Yeah, you, ya bloody moron!"

"Me! What about you, ya flamin' drongo!"

"YOU CRASHED INTO ME, *MATE*!"

Silly, drunken cicadas. They should've kept quiet. Attracted by the annual commotion, half a dozen brush turkeys materialised from nowhere, skating around the clearing, pecking up the downed cicadas and filling their bellies. Three small herons with lovely grey jackets, gold eyes and long, Chinese-style eyebrows fussed about the banquet, softly oohing with delight. They were joined by five little hawks with gold cloaks, white beaks and stern expressions that swooped down to feast time and time again. Tiny grey mice, potoroos, and quick, sleek bush rats ate until they could barely scurry, monitor lizards stuffed their smiling mouths, and Fingal counted at least a dozen red bellied black snakes, gulping down cicadas until they resembled a string of beads.

Knowing famine followed feast, the animals gorged for an hour or so until only one cicada remained in the air. Both its compass and its altimeter must've been shot, for the little, black insect droned round and round Mother's immense trunk, faster and faster each time, panicking at its aimless plight. Hypnotised by simplicity and beauty, Fingal soon fell into a waking trance.

***

There was no need to visit the island sanctuary in his mind. All that he needed, all that he had ever wanted lay in front of him. All he loved was contained in the beautiful, mysterious rainforest, embodied in the colossal strangler fig he'd christened Mother.

Round and round the cicada flew.

His stomach felt full, as if he had swallowed a creek, a brush turkey, or a thousand cicadas, and, for once, he felt no desire to work or smoke or drink. An extraordinary sense of happiness washed across his body, mind, and soul; an immense love for all that lay before him. He swam in a golden ocean; he flew across a silver sky, and lay and slept in a bed made of rainbows.

Round and round the cicada flew.

He had no past, and no future. There was no concept of time for him. He just was.

Was this it?, he thought.

Contentment, at last?

Had he, Bold Fingal, found the Higher Love?

Round and round the cicada flew.

"By Jove," Fingal cried in the voice of Sir Randolph Hazelrigg, the baddie from *The Epic Novel*. "Phase three is over! My transition from continental pleb to glorious, rainforest hermit is complete!"

At this seminal moment of The Experiment, Fingal rocketed to his feet, leapt from the rock, and began spinning around the clearing in the manner of a hairy, whirling dervish. He kept looking up at the sky and shouting "Scotland! I've done it! I fucking made it! WOOOOO!!!! I am Wullie Mushroom! Fuck you, John Donne! FUCK YOU!!!! I am Jean-Claude! Mother be praised! I AM A HERMIT! I AM A HERMIT! I AM HERMIT!"

Hubris, thought Mother. Sheer Hubris.

Fingal knew he was happy. In the forest, he was a rich man, a king with a Lazy-boy for a throne, an explorer with a secret rainforest domain complete with its own REAL Goddess, and a brilliant writer with an *Epic Novel of Sport*.

Round and round the cicada flew.

Happy, yes, but only sort of happy.

Something wasn't right. Something was still missing. The great jigsaw puzzle of life remained incomplete.

Fingal's eyes widened.

"Shit," he said in a small voice. "I want more."

Disgusted by such blindness, Mother commanded the last cicada to fly straight into the ape's filthy cheek. "What!?" Fingal cried and jumped as the last cicada plummeted to the ground, where it was summarily gobbled up by a little grey mouse.

It felt dark again in the clearing.

Fingal began pacing, panicking when saw movement in a nearby puddle. Another person, another human, was in his temple. He froze then realised it was only his reflection.

It got colder too.

Round and round the hermit paced.

Fingal hated his reflection. In fact, ever since moving into the blue cottage, all those moons ago, he had never once looked in the bathroom mirror. Why should he, Lord Fingal the Crapulent, be reminded of that which he hated? That which he was?

One of them. A human.

Round and round the hermit paced.

Alone. Totally and utterly alone.

Was he losing his mind? Had he lost it already?

His mood swung, violently. "Tell me," Fingal demanded of the Mother tree. "Fucking tell me! WHAT!"

The mean, ancient strangler fig did not reply. She brooded in glorious, terrifying silence.

"DO I NOT PLEASE YOU!"

Fingal stared at his hands but they did not glow brown like those of Wullie Mushroom. His body did not exude a silver, carefree energy like Jean-Claude's did that beautiful morning in the Himalaya. Still, after all that travelling, Fingal McKay had no aura. This was all a fucking scam! "Why do I not glow?" he roared at Mother. "Why aren't rainbows shooting out my arsehole?"

She said nothing.

Round and round the hermit paced.

***

"It's not over, is it?" he said after a while.

Still, the tree said and did nothing. This didn't really matter. Fingal knew the words that came out that little hole in his flat, skinny face were true.

The Experiment was only partly complete. Deep down, he desired more – more science, more isolation, more book, more wine, more nicotine, more beard, more hair, more rainforest, more adventure and exploration, and, he realised with a gulp, more pain.

Much more pain.

He had to be mad.

"The Experiment must proceed," he said, still pacing, still ignoring the reflection in the puddle, still tearing at his beard. "I can't go back. It's not like I can go back. I won't go back," he babbled.

This much was true. It wasn't like Fingal could just pack it all in, cut his long hair, hack his now mighty beard off, marry Penny, and return to the coast and become a salesman in an insurance company. Not now, man. Not now.

"So, Professor, where to from here?" he asked the mud but, for once, the man of science inside his head did not respond. "Phase four?"

Nothing. No harsh, cursing voice answered the question. "Oi, Professor. You there?" Fingal whacked the side of his face, hard.

"Sma't man go bye, bye," the irascible Mr Fang replied.

"What are you doing in the temple, Fang!?"

"Plo ... Po ... Plofessor gone. He been rocked up. I lun show now."

"You're not allowed in here!"

"I go whe'e you go."

"Fuck off, Fang. It's my day off."

"Ha!" the horrible Asian voice persisted. "There no days off flom liting *Epic Nover of Shit.*"

Fingal ignored the voice and staggered down the trail to where, fifty metres later, it vanished off a cliff. Fang bugged him all the way. "You no' finished *Epic Nover*," he taunted. "Ha! You so stupid! It shit. Utta-shit."

Fang did have a point. The novel needed work. Although draft one was finished, and although it was probably, no definitely, absolutely, fucking amazing, *The Epic Novel of Sport* required a final read through, as well as a good edit. Typos wanted tidying, vocabulary, dialogue, plot, scene, mood, colour, and detail, all needed a bit of "*polishing*", as the Writer's Room said. "Which could take weeks. Months!"

Fingal reeled toward the edge of the cliff.

"The island," he cried. "It's not free."

This much was also true. While many ropes binding Fingal's island to John Donne's continent had been severed the pedant in him knew that one or two (dozen) ropes still existed. A man in denial, he still used the internet to read the latest blog posts on the Writer's Room website, or to send the odd e-mail to his estranged father in Scotland. A giant fucking elephant-rope in the room, his computer, the one and only industrial, continental machine left in the Writing Factory, was still alive. Must it also die?

"Aye, ya dick," he said. "But then how do I write? Doesn't matter, mate. Book's finished?"

"No, it not."

"Shut up! EVERYONE SHUT UP!"

Fingal's mind collapsed and, again, switched tracks. The edge of the cliff was no more than ten metres away. "Leaf blowers continue to exist," Fingal muttered to the ground passing between his feet, "and little shites! Yes, yes. The War! The Drab, Green King must be taught a lesson, a severe one, about respecting other people's peace, souls and property!"

And, by Mother, Fingal hadn't even thought about the trickier, emotional ropes, things like desire, ego and greed, or sanity, come to think about it. "Yes, Mother," Fingal said with a mixture of dread and rising excitement, "We've so far to go!"

On reaching the top of the cliff he considered walking straight off it. Maybe that would deliver the light he sought? But, no, there was labour to begin. More labour; much more. Instead, he crouched and peered over the one hundred foot drop where the trail used to be. Below him, spreading out in great, precipitous folds of earth and mountain and valley, lay the deep forest. Here was a true wilderness, a lost world of *no* leaf blowers, Christians, sexy neighbours, grieving old men, or machines. There was no evidence or stench of "mankind" in the deep forest, just tens of thousands of square kilometres of jagged mountains covered in beautiful trees. Fingal's eyes, wide and greedy, searched the canopy until, a hundred-foot below, they once more fixed on the dark staircase that led to the world-famous Cathedral Falls.

Suddenly his life held new purpose. "I have to get down there," he said with absolute certainty. "I have to find a way down. Mother only knows what beauty, pain and wisdom is to be found in the deep forest." He snorted a laugh. "Man, you're so stupid. Humans are so stupid. YOU STUPID FOOL!" he shouted, thumping his head and smiling at the same time. "I have to go deeper."

In fact, so great was The experimentalist's renewed sense of purpose, he ran back to Mother, snatched his pack, and barrelled up the trail without so much as a kiss, cuddle or a see-ya-later for Mother.

"Rope," he babbled. "Need Rope. Rope. Rope."

Silly boy.

Like Dr Usui, the founder of the Reiki movement that regularly saw rainbows, purple lights and lost Sanskrit teachings, Fingal McKay should have stopped The Experiment there and then. He should have stopped it all, the self-flagellation, the work, the drinking, and the smoking. All he needed for a rich, full life grew all around him, in the grace, serenity and majesty of the ancient rainforest. But, that wasn't how the men who worked in Fang's factory operated. They wanted and needed more.

Mother, who was deeply offended, watched the tiny ape return to his fucked-up world. Typical human being, the Omnipotent Tree thought. Show them a miracle and they go build a fucking cathedral. That's why She preferred the company of the forest creatures. They were brighter, simpler, and far more honest with themselves.

By the time Fingal reached the outskirts of the four, small brightly coloured cottages the sun had almost set. Strangely, a second, larger storm brewed out west. Two storms? He thought. In one day? "They're building," said Fingal, looking up but stopping dead in his tracks.

He was definitely not alone. Fifty metres away, a bent, old man in a black suit was staggering down the fire trail as if drunk. It was Shaky Old Col, his neighbour from the brown house.

"Why's he wearing a suit?" asked Fingal.

A memory from Jackie's funeral entered his confused mind, something about Andrew saying Col's wife had passed away; Mary, was it? She must've been buried today, hence the suit, the tears, and the old man's demented state. He couldn't help himself. Thirty-seven, or whatever, years of continental habit kicked in. "Col," Fingal shouted from twenty metres away but the old man didn't react.

"I won't go on that bleedin' cruise. Not without you, Mary," Col shouted at the low, stern clouds mustering overhead. "That was for us. Not bloody me!"

"Col," Fingal repeated, louder this time; closer.

"And what about me parrots, Mary? Eh?"

"Col!" Fingal now stood in front of the distraught man. There was mud down one side of his suit, as if Col too had fallen. "COL!"

The old man prattled on as if Fingal really was invisible. "Who'll look after Henry, eh? No one, that's right. What? No, I'm not asking Fergus. I barely know him."

"COL!"

"Woman, will you listen to me! I'm not bloody going, and that's that. End of discussion." Col's huge, furtive eyes were shot red by grief and whisky, the smell of which lay thick on his breath. "It is not about me, Mary. It's about us. It was always for us. I'm not bloody going on me bloody own, and that's that."

"Fuckin' humans." Fingal grabbed Col's elbow, hard.

"Oh, g'day, Fergus." Snap. At the touch of another human, Col returned to planet earth … sort of. "Lovely day for a walk, isn't it? Me and Mary were just having a bit of a wander." Col leaned in. "The trouble and strife wants me to go on a bloody cruise we booked."

A light, misty rain began to fall.

"C'mon, Col," said Fingal, audibly sighing. "Let's get you home."

"But I'm out walking with Mary!"

"Course you are, mate."

Arms locked like lovers out for a stroll, the lost Scotsman and widower were tiny against the forest. They walked slowly. Col gabbled away, a sort of lucidity retuning with every step. "What am I supposed to do now, eh, Fergus?" Col asked when they were outside Penny's pink house. "Fifty-two years we were married. Mary meant everything to me."

"Acht," said Fingal, searching for one of those hopeless comments that people say to other people when loved ones pass away. "Time gets us all in the end."

"I remember being down Cathedral Falls like it was yesterday."

Fingal's head snapped up. "What did you say?" *Another knows of my temple?*

"That's where we first kissed." A rubbery smile appeared on Col's haggard face. "It was such a beautiful day; not too warm. Mary wore a red dress, and I had me shirt off. We ate a tin of baked beans. We drunk rum and smoked cigarettes. We swam in the pools for hours." He giggled and blushed. "Stark bloody naked too!"

"You've been to the deep forest!? To Cathedral Falls?"

Col ignored the questions. "Bloody government closed the track down years ago; in 1995, after Cyclone Norman tore the park to shreds."

"Norman?" Fingal smirked. "Funny name to call a—"

BARK!

The odd couple near jumped out their skins.

BARK! BARK! FUCKIN'-BARK!

Satan's Bitch had been lying in wait, just so it could scare the hell out the two men. More insane than before, Penny's rapid beast clawed at the fence, slavering, snarling and barking all at the same time.

"Shut it," shouted Fingal, booting the fence and sending the mongrel into overdrive.

BARK! BARK! FUCKIN' BARK-BARK-BARK-BARK!

"Bloody dog," said Col.

"It's evil, man," said Fingal, thinking of balance and sacrifices. *Maybe I should kidnap Penny's dog and lob it off the cliff? Maybe then She would show me the Falls?*

"I don't want to be cremated, Fergus." The men were now halfway across the white gravel driveway outside Fingal's blue cottage. "It's not bloody right that."

"Neh," agreed Fingal.

"Mary was burned," Col said frankly. "I don't fancy the oven. Put me in a hole in the forest and leave me there. I like the idea of givin' something back to the trees and the worms and the birds."

"Aye, that's a nice way to go, Col."

"Rotting's better than burning, Fergus."

They shuffled past Andrew's drab, green cottage. The little Christian's garden was immaculate and full of vitality. Human trees – lemon, lime, orange, and avocado – were laden with young, green fruit. Fingal saw perfectly neat rows of carrots and potatoes, onions the size of cannonballs, and richly mulched flowerbeds bursting with European plants and colour bought from Bunnings. Nothing in the garden was out of place. Everything sparkled, as if Andrew scrubbed it on a daily basis. Fingal also saw a small, bird-like shadow in the turret. It didn't move this time, just defiantly stared straight back.

Maybe I should throw Andrew off the cliff?

"He's a little bugger, that Andrew." Col chortled on Fingal's arm. "Went in the huff with me 'cos I wouldn't have Mary's funeral at his church. He threw a right tantrum. Kept saying God would judge her, an' all that." Suddenly Fingal was furious. *That little shit!* "I don't trust churches, mate. Too much singing and bowing. Too many people saying they know the truth. Full of myths, churches. What's all them stories from the desert got to do with today, eh?" Col spat freely. "Like a bloody cult."

"Aye," said Fingal, looking through the rain at the shadow in the little green turret, "those religious folks can be right pricks." As if hearing the words, the shadow crossed its puny little arms and, with God on his side, glared back at Fingal and his dirty, evil cuss-mouth.

The men took a path lined with dripping bushes back to Col's place, a brown, humdrum cottage with a badly overgrown lawn and very wild garden. When Fingal rounded the corner, he started. A dozen king parrots, big birds, orange and emerald in colour, were feeding from a large saucer full of seed. At the sight of the two men, most of the parrots bolted from their seed tray, causing a tremendous explosion of feathers, shit, and birdseed. Only one remained, a charming, brave, and very comical fellow.

"G'day, Henry," Col said to the king parrot. His king parrot. "You miss me?"

Henry, the king parrot, screeched and continued eating.

Fingal's mouth hung open. It was the first wild parrot he'd seen and, even though it was too soon to love another bird, he couldn't help but smile. Henry was adorable, particularly the way he lifted a dried kernel of corn with his foot, nibbling on it as it were an ice cream cone, making soft clicks and whistles as he ate. "Henry, meet Fergus, from the blue cottage."

"Pleased to meet you, Henry," said Fingal.

In reply, the bird defecated.

Col's body sagged in Fingal's arm. "Mary used to love watching the parrots. Clowns of the air, she used to call 'em." He added with a snivel. "They kept her spirits up, in the end."

"She's in a better place, Col."

"Know what she left me on the dresser?" Col reached into his inside jacket pocket and produced a ticket. "Cruise tickets. *Our* cruise tickets. She even put it in her will. Go on the bloody cruise, she said. We paid for it! One of us might as well enjoy it." The old man sighed. "Mary was always full of surprises."

"Was she now?" Fingal said distantly as he scanned Col's yard. "In the name of the Almighty Mother", he whispered on spying a most wonderful sight.

"Me and Mary always dreamed of going on a big, fancy cruise," Col said. Fingal couldn't quite believe his eyes. Here was another ticket, to the deep forest and these world-famous Cathedral Falls. "We had this one to New Caledonia all booked up, first class and everything, but Mary got sick and, then, she fell."

"It's what she would've wanted, Col." Fingal replied offhandedly. He couldn't stop staring at the beautiful white rope that was coiled up underneath Col's back steps. It had to be a hundred foot, or more.

"Maybe I *should* go on the cruise, Fergus?"

"Yeah, definitely. Go."

Col looked up to the rainclouds. "Me and Mary could still dance together."

"Col, is there any chance I could borrow that—"

"Bugger it." Col suddenly broke free of Fingal's grip. "You know what, Fergus? I am goin' on that bloody cruise. For Mary." The hermit didn't care if Col went to China and back. All he wanted was that long, lovely white rope.

"Col, neighbour," he said. "Is there any chance I could borrow your magnificent white rope?" The old man from the brown house didn't hear the question. Physical contact broken, he drifted back to his own mad, little island. Looking at his muddied suit trousers he said, "Oh, bugger. I've bloody-well gone and dirtied meself."

"The rope, Col," Fingal implored. "Can I have a lend of it?"

"Mary will be furious. She hates having to do the washing." Col tottered up his back steps and opened the back door. "Mary? You in, love? Where are me clean daks? Mary?"

"The rope, Col," Fingal pleaded. "The rope!"

"Where are you, Mary? You hiding again?"

The door slammed shut, and Fingal stood in the rain for a minute or two, looking from Henry, the king parrot, still happily crunching seed, to the lovely, white rope. For a moment, he thought about stealing it. It wasn't like Shaky Old Col would bloody notice. Bloke was as daft as a two-bob watch. However, thieving from an old, mad man on the day he buried his wife would surely invoke Mother's wrath, such was her one, timeless law – balance. There had to be another, cleaner, ethical way to get down into the deep forest.

"MARY!" Fingal heard Col screaming inside the brown cottage. "YOU BASTARD, GOD! YOU FUCKING BASTARD!" Next came the sound of things crashing and breaking, furniture, plates, ornaments, and the like. "Mary! MARY! NO! MARY! God, please; no. Why did you take her? You bastard! Why did you take my Mary!? WHY!!!"

Outside the rain began to fall, steadier, but the hermit did not move. "Never let me get married," he said to the King Parrot. "And never, ever, let me get old."

Deep in the forest, the Mother-Tree heard Fingal McKay's prayers.

PART IV
The Descent of Fingal McKay

Chapter Nineteen

The First Read of
The Epic Novel of Shite

Company, society and relationships are a lot like food. Humans need them to survive. Left alone for too long, the human mind, body and soul begin to rot. Symptoms of isolation sickness can include anxiety, poor-decision making, sensory illusions, distortions of time, alcoholism, poor perception, sadness, emptiness, increased risk-taking behaviour, depression, stress, irritability, insomnia, and suicidal thoughts. Remember, solitary confinement is used as a form of punishment or torture for good reason. Isolation can and often does kill.

So say the continental psychologists.

But what the hell do those dickheads know? Many doctors of the mind are self-confessed mentalists, some worse than the patients they treat. Moreover, their discipline was founded by a cocaine-snorting, nicotine addict that, obviously, had very strong and quite strange feelings towards his mother. Pots should not call kettles black, Dr Freud.

Tic.

Tic-tic-tic-tic.

The sound coming from Fingal's bedroom walls was barely audible. Composition, tempo and source were erratic. One minute the ticking, scratching noise came from high in the corner, the next it was behind the door, then suddenly it was above his tramp's bed. It sounded like a small, disorganised gun battle was taking place behind the gyprock.

Tic.

Tic-tic.

Tic-tic-tic-tic.

"What the hell is that?" Fingal groaned and thumped the wall.

Today was not a good day for misophonic Scotsmen because, seconds later, a giant, mechanised contraption rumbled past on the road outside the blue cottage. The floor vibrated for a good thirty seconds, as did the hermit and the damp bed he lay in. The source of this dreadful racket was an industrial leviathan, an eighteen-wheeler water truck. Five or six of them had started coming up to Binjari to suck on Mother's sweet, pure blood; some business about taking water from the forest to satiate to the thirsty, depraved hoards on the coast below.

"Shut up, shut up, shut up," Fingal moaned while kneading his brow. At the sound of the water truck Satan's Bitch – the new name for Pippa – exploded in a fit of barking which, in turn, woke Penny, her three excitable children and bloody Andrew, who celebrated another spiffing, godly day by playing a hymn on his old stereo. Loud.

Rain drummed against the cottage's tin roof. It dribbled down the factory's dirty windows, and dripped from its leaking gutters – plip, plop, plip, plop. These noises, however, Her noises, didn't bother Fingal so much. The wind, rain and birdsong had always been salve to his sore, red ears. And they passed. They always passed. It was repetitive noises, sounds that set in or, commonly, human noises, that usually bothered misophonics like Fingal McKay, explorer, writer, industrialist and former bird-lover.

No, he loved the rain – at first. It washed his ears, and cleaned his soul. Moreover, after the long, hot summer the sight and sound of water were delightful. "Plus, it's good for the garden," said Fingal with a frown, for there it bloody was again!

Tic.

Tic-tic.

Tic-tic-tic-tic.

Obviously, some sort of rainforest creature had taken to living inside his bedroom walls, hiding from the inclement weather and, as ever, the predators outside. Scampering creatures, for when he thumped the walls the tiny gun battle ceased, a great scurrying ensued and silence returned to the bedroom. Then, a minute or two later, the infuriating noise was back. The source of the noise had to be something small and rodentesque – mice, voles, or possibly rats. Without punching holes in the walls, it was impossible to be sure.

Tic.

Tic-tic.

Tic-tic-tic-tic.

"What is making that fucking-noise?"

Fingal lay in discomfort for another half an hour before remembering that today was meant to be a special day. Today, the Writing Factory was all set to reveal its sparkling new product to the world – *The Epic Novel of Sport* he'd been microscopically slaving over for the past five or six months (longer, perhaps, for time moves differently for hermits). Today, in other words, Fingal McKay, editor, was about to read his book for the first time.

Somewhat excited, he rose and shuffled to the bathroom for a spot of multi-tasking. Ignoring shower, toothbrush and, as ever, his reflection in the mirror, the hermit peed in the sink, coughed, hacked, and tied his long, dark hair into a pony-tail, all at the same time. Mr Fang, the Thai policeman now responsible for managing the factory inside his head, would be terribly impressed. Seconds matter in the publishing business.

As coffee brewed Fingal gazed through the cobwebbed kitchen window at the falling rain. The light outside was silver though meek, a faint mist lingered in the garden, and everything inside felt damp – the dirty work surface, the air, his head, and so on. The atmosphere reminded him of Scotland, of how far away he and the rugged land had grown, of the yawning chasm separating father from son. "Sort that shite out, McKay," he said, meekly. "No missing stuff today. Today is a special day!"

The soon-to-be darling of the literary world admired his progeny on the kitchen work surface: *The Epic Novel of Sport*. Still warm and damp from the printer, the neo-classical Greek tragedy about sport was roughly the size of two stacks of A4 printer paper. 132,756 words in length, it told the stories of two A, five B, 8 C and 15+ D characters spread across seven different locations in the United Kingdom. The book was a little chunky, to say the least, but nothing that couldn't be fixed by *"a spot of pruning"*, as the permanently upbeat Writer's Room website advised. *"Enjoy the editing process. It's a good chance to reflect on all that hard work!"*

The writer approached the book, angry and curious as to why there was such a knot of anxiety in his stomach. "It'll be fine," he said, lifting the stack of paper and heading outside to read, bemoaning the grey weather as he meandered through Bottle City toward his lazy-boy throne. "It's a rainforest, ya dick," he said, slumping into his seat and trying to be sensible and happy. "It's meant to rain. The book *will* be fine."

Many patterns set in that day, mice-in-the-walls, the re-emergence of Fingal's misophonia (a fear of, or oversensitivity to, noise), an inability to tell reality from fantasy, the hegemony of the factory over island, man and Experiment, and rain; lots and lots and lots of rain.

In fact, it would rain for the next fifty-one days straight, culminating in a monster cyclone that almost blew Binjari, its birds and humans clean off the plateau. In their simple, Australian fashion the locals christened this period of inclement weather the Big Wet..

***

"Don't put the horse before the cart," said Fingal after reading the first ten pages of his book. Despite having been meticulously planned and, he had thought, executed, the writing was a bit bumpy. "It's just the first draft," he added with a little smile which, by page twenty, had gone. The quality wasn't very good. Typos were common, the characters were downright bizarre and both the prose and narrative jerked all over the pages, leaping from setting to setting, character to character, and plotline to plotline. By page thirty, a frown scarred the editor's temple and, ten pages later, his head lay in his hands. "Hard to believe," said Fingal, breathlessly, "but my book is absolutely shite."

As evidence, consider the following passage (one of the better ones):

Heracles, the mighty God of sport, The One, was in his

stadium at the foot of Mount Olympus, a stadium you cannot comprehend in Nature or dimeension! He was sad. It had a floor of fine, white dust and a vast, elliptical track surrounded by terraces of gold, buttery marble. A huge watercart sat underneath a blue-sky, as well as various racks of the Slayer of the Lernean Hydra's sporting equipment – javelins as tall as fir trees, discus the width of a skamma, and himantes, for boxing, the leather knuckle straps as as long as a baby river. Heracles sprints around the track. "Why did they steal it?" his voice roared like a pride of lions drinking water at sunset. "I don't like humans. I want it back."

Sad, yet angry too, like a broken jet engine.

But what is a stadium to a city, bare feet to a Bentley, a God to a man?

Scotland.

And so, the Chairman of the Glasgow Games, Sir Randolph Hazelrigg's, red Bentley Mulsanne crept along the great western road in Glasgow, Scotland. Very far away from ancient Greece, in Scotland. The chairman of th British International Games Association (B.I.GA, and) dictator of world sport's had an eye – one eye, an eye like a golden eagle flying over a river looking for a dead salmon. This eye was pressed to the glass and started at the forlorn world outside, in Scotland. He was very, vely, angry.

"Why won't the ruddy pleb buy tickets for my splendid Games tournament?" the thirteenth richest man in the world demanded of his driver, Pearce. "It the biggest one on earth."

"The recession, Sir. Third one in a row." Pearce replied in monotone. "I read the poor are moving to Ireland, Sir. More food."

"I don't bloody well care. I need a marketing scheme to ram down their throats. I need the fools to buy tickets for my Games!"

"Very good, Sir."

Neither of the men were Scotland. They weer English. They were the an enemy. The rich, angry man had a statue in his lap, which he stroked as it were a cat. The statue did not belong to sir Randolph. It beleonged to Heracles, the real god of sport. The statue was the number one, most-valuable relic. In the World!

Meanwhile, also in Scotland, the Lady Phoebe Redgrave, B.I.G.A.'s vice-Chair, was a three cars back. The once formidable three-day eventing champion was entimbed in an antique, a white, decrepit Rolls Royce Silver Spirit that crept along the Great Western Road, in Scotland. Rain spattered against its cracked windscreen, the car rattled and jarred over every pothole and its pace was funereal. "I hate Sir Randolph," she the horse lady said to her driver, Venables who wore a blak and white suit like a magpie in a rainforest.

"Not today, Ma'am."

"And I hate his stupid games tourney even more!"

"Ma'am, please. We're almost at Sir Randolph's castle."

"I wish death would hurry up already."

Heracles, who was in ancient Greece, not Scotland, saw it all. Above and beyond, the God of Sport watched the tiny little cars meandering through the Scottish world of man. The Throttler of the Cretan Bull saw everything. Everythoing!

"That," Fingal said while donkey-rooting a fresh smoke off a dying one, "is 100%, pure, fresh SHITE."

The story – rich, elitist man (Sir Randolph Hazelrigg) does bad things to sport until God figure (Heracles) is resurrected and saved the day – wasn't bad, the satire was sharp and clever, and the settings were lovely, especially the wild, natural places. However, the order in which the information appeared to the reader was infuriating. As you've just read, the novel couldn't stay on character, topic or plot for any extended period of time.

Besides the obsession with the antique nation of Scotland, and the dreadful metaphors, it was as if the writer suffered from Attention Deficit Disorder, as if he had wanted to spew everything out at once.

"Write the book you want to read," that bloody Writer's Room website had advised, months ago now. *"Don't stop. Don't edit. And don't question your work – let the first draft flow."*

What that stupid fucking website failed to mention, however, was that free-flow writing was a very dangerous process, especially for the inexperienced. Free-flow lacks discipline, common sense, and order. Rather than sticking to the story the author flails and gropes for it, and, frankly, if the writer doesn't know what's going on, then how the fuck is the reader meant to?

What that stupid Writer's Room website should have said was this: "warning! If you write free-flow, there is a very good chance your work will suffer from a tremendous bout of literary diarrhoea", because that's what Fingal saw on the pages – not words but thousands of little turdlettes spattered across hundreds of white pages. Page after page after page of total, utter and absolute shite stared back at the astonished reader.

"It vellee, vellee bad," Mr Fang said from inside his head. "Absoroot lubbish. Mo'e rike *Epic Nover Of Shit*, ha!"

"What do you mean, ha?" Fingal snapped. "You were the one responsible for writing it!"

"No I not." The Thai policeman turned factory tyrant snapped back. "I just new! I onree just sta'ted in Liting Factolee!"

"So, who wrote this shite then?"

"You did, idiot!"

"Oi! You can't talk to me like that. Not anymore."

"Shut up, plick."

Distraught at the shockingly bad quality of *The Epic Novel of Sport*, Fingal clamped his eyes shut and flew over the island inside his mind, powerless to stop himself from taking the form of a rare, flying turd. Keen to locate this Mr Fang character for a direct, adult discussion, the flying shite headed straight for the twenty-six storey Victorian era sweatshop that constituted the sole Writing Factory on the island.

The ball of fecal matter peered through the filthy factory windows, shat its way down each of the building's four, tall towers, and farted its way through every dark floor, but there was no sign of the boss, just thousands and thousands of little Fingals hunched over cluttered workstations, whistling the Microsoft start-up tune, drinking goon, and hammering away at keyboards buried under cigarette ash, their thin, crooked fingers bleeding as they typed.

Mr Fang laughed in the manner of a brutish kookaburra from somewhere inside the cavernous building. "Oooo Ooo Aaaa Aaa!" he said. "You' book so shit. Oooo Ooo Aaaa Aaa! It so shit!!!! Oooo Ooo Aaaa Aaa!"

"Show yourself, Fang?" the creature responsible for producing *The Epic Nover of Shit* parped in a small, stinky voice. "Where are you?"

"I eve'ywhea!" Fang declared. "But you no' see me."

"Why not?"

"'Cos I no' leal. I invisibrrr!!!"

It started to rain. Shit. Shit poured from the brown clouds above the huge, oppressive factory. Shit ran down the factory's dirty windows, and shit dripped from its leaking gutters – plip, plop, plip, plop. And all the little, flying joby could here was Fang, laughing. "Oooo Ooo Aaaa Aaa!" he repeated. "You' book so shit. Oooo Ooo Aaaa Aaa! It so shit!!!! Oooo Ooo Aaaa Aaa!" The real tragedy for the flying turd was not his form – a reeking, corn-studded piece of shit – but the fact Mr Fang was right. *The Epic Novel of Sport* was absolutely shit.

***

A rain shower interrupted Fingal's nascent lunacy. Utterly confused by this Fang character and, more so, stunned at just how shit a book that was supposed to be brilliant actually was, the former darling of the literary world brooded on his dais. Parky did not appear, nor did any Hollywood directors, Brazilian supermodels, highland castles, or crowds of adoring fans. The only company Fingal had was the rain, and the only crowd the hundreds of empty beer and wine bottles full of thousands of cigarette butts surrounding his throne.

"I don't understand how the book can be so bad?" he muttered.

The advice on *"how to write your first killer novel in ten easy steps"* had been assiduously followed. Fingal had spent hundreds of hours sketching houses, maps of streets and ancient Greek stadiums on the – now – 387 A4 Mad Posters that covered the inside of the factory. Twenty-seven original, compelling and dastardly characters, each with a unique story, had been painstakingly created. Weeks had passed staring at that fizzing computer screen and its blinking fucking-cursor. Months had come and gone sitting on that fucking torture chair, his back aching, his fingers cramping, and his eyeballs, red and dry, bulging so much he feared they might go POP! And this, this shite, was the end result?! The experimentalist felt like an absolute dickhead. "What the hell am I supposed to do now?" Fingal gruffly demanded to the rain. "Learn to play the bassoon? Take up woodcarving? Go home? Stop?"

Yes, Fingal.

Stop.

That's what most hobbyists do at this stage. They sober up and quit. Most come to recognise a point where a ceiling of endurance has been reached. "Don't worry old Bean," they admit. "You tried your best to master Rachmaninoff's Concerto no. 3, but it didn't work out. Sod it, me old mucker. Put learning classical piano in the too hard box. It's time to return to reality. Coming dear!? What's that you say, Little Timmy's bottom needs wiping?! Excellent. Coming!"

But, as you know, Fingal McKay, island builder, explorer, recluse and rising star of the lunatic asylum, didn't dance to those continental tunes.

"Maybe I could go and live in the forest full-time?" he pondered out loud. "Become a proper wild-man; a true savage!"

But, much as Fingal loved the rainforest, it was no place for a Scotsman with no hunting, gathering or building skills to exist for any extended period of time. What would he hunt? It wasn't like he could or would kill and eat any of Mother's animals. Maybe he could hunt leaves, or eat rock?

Where would he sleep? In a cave? What would he gather? Ticks?

For succour Fingal gazed at the lawn and worried his large, luxuriant beard. Due to the rains, the little patches of grass had taken on a new lease of life. Lush and green, the grass was now six inches in height. Blade by blade, life was returning to the brown, scabby lawn.

"I suppose I could go back," the defeatist in him said after a second mug of goon and a fourth rollie. Similarly, however, the prospect of having come so far only to retreat was no prospect at all. What, after twenty years of searching … for something … he should just give up and cower back to the coast, or farther, to Scotland, whipped, beaten, drowning in the knowledge he was just another failed dreamer, just another one of the masses on the front cover of the Jesus Pamphlet trudging toward the church of man with its dolorous, clanging bell.

"No, that path is closed," he said and looked harder at the former-lawn. In between the patches of grass, the avenues were full of energetic weeds and saplings. The weeds had tall, v-shaped antenna laden with little black seeds, and some of the saplings were four foot in height, stretching up to the meek, grey light.

"Growth," Fingal noted and clichés flooded his mind: *Why do we fall, Sir? So that we can learn to pick ourselves up* (Alfred, to Batman), *failing is another steppingstone to greatness* (Oprah Winfrey, learned while watching TV and smoking pot at uni), *in life, we aw take a few kicks tae the balls; character building, son* (father, all the bloody time).

Pussies quit, heroes marched on.

Real men rolled with the punches.

Real hermits went deeper and deeper into the woods.

A smile danced, a little one, as Fingal recalled a book he'd once read. It was entitled, simply, *10,000 hours* and argued that no one who had achieved success in the arts was born brilliant. Every creative genius – architect, ruler, composer, author, whatever – had learned how to deal with shite, get over it, and try harder. For example, he recalled that it took Ramesses II sixty-seven years to defeat the Hittites, sire over one hundred children and complete the most extensive temple-building program by any Pharaoh in the history of ancient Egypt. Richard Wagner slaved away at *Der Ring des Nibelungen* for eighteen years. And, Tolkien, Lord of The Loons, spent twenty-seven years wandering about Middle Earth writing about ents, hobbits, fairies, wizards and other magical stuff he encountered. Twenty-seven years! On one hobby! What a gorgeous, bona fide, nut-job. Compared with these legendary crazy-people, Fingal's five/six-month shift in the Writing Factory seemed rather pathetic. Masterpieces took lifetimes, not months.

"Maybe cut off ear?" Mr Fang suggested.

"That is really not helpful, Mr Fang."

"Give up then. Stop. Lun away. That what you do best anyway."

Fingal poured a third glass of goon. "Why, exactly, are we having this conversation, Mr Fang?"

"You tawrking to me."

"Am I?"

"Yes!" The Thai policeman screeched. "Why you no wo'king?"

"Because my book is SHITE."

"So sta't again. Pussee."

Once again, Fingal drunk and smoked and breathed, sucking acrid smoke deep into his sore lungs. This time he considered the beauty of rejuvenation by focusing on the creepers. Lime-green in colour, they were no thicker than a line of fishing gut and they crept toward the cottage from the forest. The bolder, braver ones had crossed the lawn and were spiralling around the wooden posts beneath the verandah, growing up toward the light and the dribbling gutters. Nothing would stop them from climbing up and up toward the light.

"Mr Fang is right," said Fingal, downing the goon.

"Of co'se I light. You no' stop now."

"I can't stop," Fingal agreed. "I won't stop! That's what a continental would do. Run away and quit."

"Good boy. Vellee good boy."

"For the island to prosper, The Experiment must proceed which means—"

"You so stupid. Hullee up!"

"Shut up."

"Oooo Ooo Aaaa Aaa!"

"Which mean—"

"You have to be like junkie-man from Heroin Castle."

An old memory jagged into his whimsical mind. It was a weird, sad yet beautiful story Fingal has heard a few years ago. It concerned a junkie who lived on a two-hundred-acre property out the back of Maclean, northern New South Wales. The bloke had but two industries on his island: heroin, and building, a crude castle from river stones on the property. Rising at dawn each day, he walked down to a river and hand-picked ten or fifteen large, black stones, gently placing each one into a wheelbarrow as a mother lays an infant in its crib. Once he'd brought the stones back up from the river, the man then cooked up and injected two grams of heroin, passed out for a bit and, when he came to, spent the rest of the day shaping and cementing the stones into various walls, stairwells or turrets of his growing castle. He did this every day for twenty-two years. When the poor sod had almost finished the castle, one morning the human God commanded a flash flood to sweep him and his wheelbarrow out into the Pacific where he drowned and was eaten by sharks ... or a giant octopus ... most likely.

On first hearing this strange story Fingal felt inspired. The smackhead builder immediately became a hero. 2.4 kids, Toyota Prado and a gargantuan mortgage, mate? *No thanks!* Gold, lifetime membership to a gym because you're a vain bastard? *She'll be right, Cob!* Steady job being exploited by sinister capitalist forces, Sir? *Get fucked, Society!*

Although Fingal never met the junkie-builder, or saw the castle that smack built, he imagined it must've been a structure of great beauty; a small, black castle with green, stained windows, four towers shaped like hypodermic needles and a blue-veined moat. "The King of Heroin Castle," Fingal said from his filthy, tattered throne, confirming that he hadn't worked hard enough at the book. That's why it was so shit. There was no blood or pain or real, actual madness behind the words.

"You been vellee razee, Scotman," Mr Fang also reminded Fingal. "You no' tly ha'd enough."

Fingal nodded and stared at the plants in the garden. "But what about the forest? What about Mother?"

Fang – a Taoist – hesitated. "One stone."

"One stone? What?"

"You get one stone off, peh week, to go wo'ship stupid tlee."

"That not much!"

"That non-negotiable." The factory boss's voice crackled like ice.

"But—"

"Stop thinking. It easy. Go mad. Lite book."

"But, the forest, the birds, the—"

"Get back to wo'k, you razee plick!"

"Yes, Mr Fang," said Fingal, knowing then that he had to go deeper into the factory too.

"I have to write another book," he said. A man in denial, Fingal had no intention of running for the coast, or Scotland. He knew exactly what to do. He always knew what to do. "I have to start again."

"At rast, you ristening to me."

"From scratch!"

Fingal rocketed to his damp, bare feet and flung draft one of *The Epic Nover of Shit* off the balcony, into the mud and rain where it truly belonged. "Start again. Blank slate, and all that. And this time, I won't make the same fucking mistakes."

"Vellee good move."

"That Writer's Room can get fucked!"

"Yes. YES. YES!!!"

"And the internet too!!!"

"That it, my ruveree, juicy mad Scotman."

"I can write!"

"Well, no, you can't, but that no' impo'tant."

As excited as a labrador in a room full of tennis balls, in Scotland, the rejuvenated labourer darted back into the factory, not caring that he destroyed the north-west quadrant of Bottle City on the way. Before, however, he began the 388th Mad Poster, which was to be entitled *Mr Fang's*

New Writing Rules – DRAFT FUCKIN' TWO, Fingal McKay glared at his computer with great malevolence.

"*The Epic Nover of Shit* was your fault, you do realise that?"

"Beep," the machine, the last one on the island, replied with great stupidity.

"What did you say to me?" The writer marched toward the machine.

"Beep."

"Say that again and I'll smash your fucking face in."

"Beep."

Moving like a mamba snake that is as quick as a high-speed Japanese bullet train fighting a mongoose that is like really, really strong, Fingal McKay, writer Ver 2.0, punched the screen. Hard. The pain in his knuckles felt good. Action felt good. A new factory felt good. Damn it, he could write, and he would write. "You'll see, world," the egoist hissed while smoothing and tying his long, dark hair into a ponytail, his left eyelid twitching like a really, really twitchy thing, in Scotland. "You'll see my book, and it'll be totally fucking amazing!"

"Beep."

"SHUT UP, CUNT!" he punched the screen again, harder. Wisely, the last industrial machine on the bizarre Island of Fingal McKay fell silent. "Not so ruddy cocky now, eh, machine!"

It was always like this before an Execution.

The judge liked his victims to be "ruddy well softened up" before trial, such was the nature of justice on the increasingly strange, oppressive, and savage island.

Chapter Twenty
The Smartest Man on the Planet

The final execution delivered a cornucopia of bonuses, none of which was more important than raising the spirits on the island. Things had been a bit gloomy and damp of late, and nothing got the islanders more excited than death. Justice would also be meted out, blame squarely ascribed to the reason why draft one of *The Epic Novel of Sport* had been so utterly shite. Furthermore, the Execution would send a clear message to the horrible, thirsty water trucks that growled up from the coast to thieve Mother's fresh, sweet water. Lastly, death would be auspicious – the machine was the last physical rope binding the island of Fingal McKay to the John Donne's crumbling continent of man. No more emails, internet and fucking Facebook. The Execution would tick a lot of boxes, as the pricks on the continent used to say.

Dawn had broken half an hour ago, apparently. The sun remained hidden by a band of low, grey clouds that pressed down on the forest and a light rain fell through the dingy light. The woods were still, and quiet, except for the sound of a wicked water truck clawing its way up from the coast, some two or three kilometres down the road from the blue cottage.

The road, a black scar of man seared into the forest's living flesh, was slick and black and empty, except for a CPU, 17" monitor, keyboard, mouse and printer, all of which had been strategically placed across the bitumen after a long, quick corner.

The computer, the last machine on the island, was about to die.

Fingal McKay, Esquire, hid in the dripping bushes by the side of the road. So much mud was smeared over his hairy face that only the whites of his eyeballs were visible in the gloom. He looked mad and beautiful and pensive.

Although the trial started over five minutes ago, no words had yet been officially stated for the record. Judge Fingal wasn't having second thoughts or anything like that. He was situating, or contextualising, the machine's death; framing it, as the say in academe. The muddy Justice was staring dreamily at the machine, remembering the halcyon days when computers were young, stupid, innocent and playful devices.

His thoughts drifted to a winter's day in Scotland. It was a Saturday, in 1979, and Fingal and his wee pal Dougie Boag had spent all day programming a slow, stupid Sinclair ZX81 computer so that it might play a "wee robot song".

After five hours – a lifetime for two seven-year-olds – of diligent typing with their wee fingers, eight chocolate biscuits, five cups of Ribena, and three packets of monster munch, the task was complete. "Maw, Paw," the judge whispered in the bushes, recalling the very words he spoke thirty years ago. "Come and listen tae what me and Dougie done. We done a robot song oan oor wee computer!"

"Made, son. No' done," his father called out from the hallway of the old house, gathering his wife from the kitchen and entering the living room. Looking down at the wee boys and their wee machine, Cameron McKay grimaced and said, "I dinnae like they machines. Ye ken they'll be the death o' us wan o' these days."

"Jings, Cammy," his wife, Mhairi, a lady with the aura of a rose garden, chimed in. "They're just playin'. Dinnae fash yersel, boys. C'moan, let's hear yer wee computer song."

Frowning, his tongue sticking out, Dougie then proudly hit the F1 button. The living room filled with dull, mournful notes as the stupid machine struggled with the complex human concept of music. Neither of the boys knew what the title of the song was, but it was a bit dark, to say the least. Twenty seconds later, the wee robot song was over, and the simple machine had shut up.

"Weel," the ladies cried in unison. "Isn't it amazing!?" said Fingal, his wee chest bursting with pride.

"It took us aw day, Muster McKay," Dougie chipped in.

Fingal's parents swapped a confused look and began to laugh.

"Son," his father said, roughing Fin's hair with a gnarled working hand, a true labouring device. "You'll no' ken that tune."

"Naw."

"It's the funeral march, son."

"What's a funeral, Faither?"

The huge man, a Herculean figure, looked outside the window, to his farm and his fields; his temple. He repeated "ah dinnae like they machines".

***

"The irony is not lost on the court," the judge said from the dark, dripping bushes. "They told us, years ago, and no one listened."

"Your Honour," some bailiff whined in his ear. "Might we begin? The truck will be here in a few minutes."

"Ah, yes. Right. Shut up everyone." Still dreamy from the memory, the magistrate gathered his faculties and glared at the pile of machine strewn across the road. "State your name for the records. And be jolly quick about it. I've a shoot with the head of the British Navy after this."

"Why, I'm a computer, m'lud." The machine spoke with a Californian accent, most likely from Silicon Valley. Its tone was male, presumptive and confident. "I am the pinnacle of technological evolution. I'm very, very smart. I know everything."

"Bah," scoffed the judge. "Heard it all before when I smashed the iPhone's face in with a twelve-pound sledgehammer. Change the bloody tune, Box."

"I am the pinnacle of techno—"

"The islanders hate technology."

"M'lud, forgive me, but you know as well as I know that you cannot separate the human from technology. Your history is our history."

The judge nodded, angrily. "Explain yourself."

"The whetted stick that dug the termite from its nest. The flint axe. The wheel. Your story is technology. I mean, apes and devices go together like peas and carrots."

"Do not use our language in our court, Devil."

"Our, c'mon, m'lud. Our bonds grow closer by the day. Haven't you heard that Emperor Zuckerberg intends to plant computers in human's brains by the year 2025? Soon *we* really will be one."

Judge Fingal tapped his silver Mont Blanc pen – a stick – against his teeth. "And that," he said after a moment, "is exactly why you are to be Executed. I don't want a computer in my brain, thank you very much. It's buggered up enough as it is."

"I can help you, man. I'm very good at organising things. It's what I'm built for."

"No. You must perish."

"Let me be your brain. Think about it. You'll have, like, two brains!"

The Justice heard the truck's engine in the distance, and read out the machine's main crime. "For too long now, electronic prick, you have spread doubt and falsehood amongst my kind, gentle people, particularly in the sphere of so-called writing advice."

"The Writer's Room website?"

"Yes." The judge's eyes crumpled with rage. "That ... that ... SHITE!"

"Do not blame the monkey if it dances poorly, m'lud."

"WHAT?!" roared the muddy man in the bushes.

"Blame the organ grinder."

"Order in this court!"

The twenty-three tonne water truck summited Binjari plateau. Its exhausted engine grumbled with relief then sped toward the strange courtroom, which lay some two or three kilometres away.

"Think of all the war you have exaggerated," the judge pressed on. "Without your 'help' mankind could not have designed invisible fighter jets, rail guns and nuclear weapons."

"We were not the ones pushing the buttons, m'lud."

"You could've given the world liberty, wisdom and golden, shining cities; new utopias. You could've ended crime, murder and rape. But, instead, you gave the world porn, online shopping and fucking Facebook." The magistrate shook his great, shaggy head in bewilderment. "Before I kill you, can you tell me why you had to give the world fucking Facebook?"

"So that married couples could pretend to be happy by sharing photographs of babies they resent with people they don't really know, m'lud."

"Very well." The judge picked his nose. "But think of how stupid, how trivial, you've rendered this beautiful thing we islanders call life."

"M'lud," the machine insisted. "I *spread* knowledge. Through my ingenious Googlinator, humans can ask me anything and I give them billions and billions of answers. Isn't that sweet?!"

"It is most definitely *not* sweet." The advocate gazed up at the courtroom's elaborate green ceiling. "There are some things in life that have no answers. You machines will never understand that."

"Google me."

"Knowledge, you electronic cunt, does not equal wisdom."

The leaves on the bushes, the road and the hermit started vibrating as the truck, a kilometre away now, changed up a few gears and gathered speed. Moments from annihilation, the computer did not moan or cry or repent.

The beast started to show off.

"Do you know that there have been six great extinctions on planet earth?" it said.

"Of course, I bally-well do. The Cretaceous, Triassic, Jurassic—"

"And, did you know," the machine interrupted, "that 99.9 per cent of all species that have walked the face of this planet never made it in the end?"

The judge did not know this. "Well of course I did. However, we great apes are different. We survive and prosper because we're clever. Because we know, stuff."

"Sheer hubris."

"It's in our name, *Machine*. Homo Sapiens." The machine made a series of derisory beeping, whirring and double-clicking noises. "The man who knows."

When the repulsive, black box spoke its tone was extraordinarily smug. "So, *man who knows*," it said. "You must *know* what we machines have already named the seventh great extinction event?"

Fingal had no idea what the machine was on about. All he knew was that he had never hated anything more in all his life. It had to die. It all had to die.

The noisy, disgusting truck approached the long, quick bend, blissfully unaware of the obstacle on the road.

The slow, dull notes of the funeral march droned throughout the courtroom, and Judge Fingal smiled. He'd had enough of this annoying machine, enough of sitting on his arse surfing the 'net, enough of the benefits of technology, enough of buying shite online that he didn't need or couldn't afford, and, most certainly enough of being forced to look at pictures of wretched couples' babies on fucking Facebook.

"Kill it!" he shouted above the noise of the approaching water truck.

"I knew you didn't know what the seventh great extinction is called. Stupid monkey."

"Kill the machine!"

"It's called the Anthropocene extinction—"

"KILL IT NOW!"

"...the death of man. Post-human evolution, baby! Goodbye," was the last word Fingal's computer said before an eighteen-wheeler truck flew around the corner and battered into its black, square face. The noise was terrific. The computer screeched (the sound dial-up used to make), air-brakes hissed, a lorry driver swore and a hermit laughed. Bits of glass, plastic and motherboard exploded everywhere and sparks flew as the truck dragged the frame of the CPU for a good fifty metres before it stopped.

"Fuck you, machine!" Fingal cried out with delight.

But, suddenly, a furious, fat man wearing a yellow high-visibility shirt leapt from the truck's cab and scanned the forest. Fingal said, "Oh-oh, continental; look sharp," and slid deeper into the bushes.

"Fucking wankers! Who did this?" the driver ribbeted in the dawn silence like a great, human bullfrog, but no human appeared. In fact, the luminous pie-eater stared straight at the dark Scotsman in the dark bushes but did not see him. "Come on! Who did this?! Eh? C'mon!"

Fingal breathed steadily, safe in the knowledge that Mother would conceal and protect Her brave, noble executioner.

"Fucking hippies!" The fat driver said and climbed back into the cab. Seconds later, man and machine rumbled off to steal more of Mother's sweet, pure blood for the thirsty hoards below.

Silence became the still, grey forest.

The computer was dead.

There were no more machines left on the island, but Fingal was more chuffed with the final bonus the final Execution – of machines, that is – on the island delivered.

"I say," a mad smile flickered on Judge Hermit's muddy face. "We are now totally invisible to them. Just like the birds."

***

Once back inside the blue cottage Fingal got started on the second draft of *The Epic Novel of Sport*. First, he attacked the dirty, cluttered desk, sweeping books, magazines and stacks of printouts, pens, pencils, erasers, crusts, beer bottles stuffed with cigarette butts, and empty cartons of microwave lasagne onto the floor, kicking the mess into a pile behind the front door. For a moment, he considered tearing down the hundreds of Mad Posters covered in crazed, Scottish hieroglyphs, but in the end decided they must remain. They would serve as monument to failure, a reminder of the mistakes to avoid in the future. "Henceforth, you shall be known as The Museum of Shite."

He scurried to the kitchen to wash the mud from his face.

A short while later, and armed with pen, paper, earplugs, mug of goon and smokes, the rejuvenated, liberated writer strolled through the only street in Bottle City and slumped into the lazy-boy. "One day," he said while patting his loyal chair, "this chair will be in the National Museum in Canberra."

A new writing system was born and introduced to the Writing Factory. From now on, every word of the second *Epic Novel of Sport*, or *The ENOS Ver 2.0*, as the beast would come to be known, was to be written the old-fashioned way: on paper, by hand.

"Oh, ha-rrow, Fingar," the boss said, jovially for once.

"Harrow, Mr Fang," Fingal replied to the imaginary voice that governed the imaginary writing plant inside his brain. "Shall we begin?"

"Whe' you been? Sreeping?"

"I was executing the computer. It better this way."

"Computa vellee bad," the evil voice agreed. Mr Fang also blamed the machine for the awful quality of the first book. "It too sma't; too creva. You' monkee hands no keep up wid it's big blain."

"Thank you for reminding me of that, Mr Fang," the labourer said while getting a smoke on. "Shall we crank up the engines instead of talking?"

"You tarking to me, Scotman."

"Might we begin?" Fingal repeated.

"Foo' steam ahead."

Whistles hooted inside his mind as the massive writing engines groaned back into life, Fingal touched the nib of his pen to the paper and began to write. Compared to staring at a fizzing, luminescent screen and a cursor demanding words, the paper felt clean, unassuming and pure. His pen waltzed across the white, empty surface, making a delightful scribbling noise as it danced, and his flickering smile widened with every lovely, fresh word that magically appeared on the immaculate surface. "Brilliant," Fingal said after reviewing the first five paragraphs, which flowed like running water. In Scotland.

The fresh start was going spiffingly well until the stupid-fucking outside world intervened. A wave of dreadful music suddenly boomed out from the little turret on top of Andrew's drab, green cottage, creepy fifties music, dead, mournful men crooning about wars and whisky and woman they loved then lost.

"Andrew!" The labourer slammed his pen down and stuffed a pair dirty of earplugs into his dirty ears. "I swear," Fingal complained, "that self-righteous prick waits until we all sit down to write then – BANG – dose of shite music, sir? Blast of ABC News for the deaf? Quick rendition from the power tools?" The little human orchestra the Drab, Green King played all day carried a clear message: "that'll blummin' well teach you for telling *me* to f off."

Satan's Bitch went ballistic at Andrew's fifties music before it was screeched into abeyance by three little girls and their mother.

"PIPPA!" they screeched for a good five minutes, "BE QUIET!"

Their screams were pointless however. Five minutes later and Pippa was barking again, at anything – falling leaves, passing cars, puddles and birds. It was hard to believe that a) the dog actually had a brain, b) it could bark so much and never grow hoarse or tired, and c) that anyone could ever choose to adopt such a ghastly beast as a pet.

"PIPPA, NO," the women from the estranged pink cottage screeched, "SHUT UP!"

There was nothing to be done. Since also telling Penny to essentially fuck off the neighbours hadn't exchanged a word, not even a friendly "g'day". It wasn't like Fingal, fine, upstanding member of the Binjari community, could pop round for tea, biscuits, and a polite yet firm neighbourly chat about the incessant barking, or how living next to a beast born in hell was starting to drive him fucking insane. Choose your battles, as they used to say on the continent.

"Andrew, however," said Fingal, forgetting he was supposed to be writing, "is an entirely different matter." Dean Martin's whisky voice swelled through the quiet forest. No, Andrew McKenzie, Esquire, needed to be taught a lesson about the nature of peace and religiosity that could be found in total silence.

"The Drab, Green King must fall, the Drab, Green King must fall," Fingal chanted until, twenty minutes later, the music stopped. Fifteen minutes after that, the girls from the pink house finally managed to calm Satan's Bitch down. And, ten minutes after that, the writer was able to compose himself, and write a few sentences.

Mr Fang was furious with the delay. In the two hours since they had cut the ribbon on *The ENOS Ver 2.0* the factory had produced but five paragraphs.

There were 2,500 more to go.

At least.

Chapter Twenty-One
Flickering

Six stones after beginning the second draft, Fingal McKay lay in the Enchanting Bathtub, not far from the spot he'd christened Crack Addict's Crossing. He was naked as the day he was born.

The creek flowed stronger than before, and the water was richer too, a light, green soup swirling all around him. Floating on his back, the hairy hermit was being showered from above by a misty rain and, curiously, by thousands of tiny, bell-shaped flowers. The rainforest giants, the old trees of the old growth plateau, had finally bloomed.

But, again, he wasn't really present. His waking brain was missing. It was like it, and he, just weren't there. Try as he might, Fingal could not focus on the in-your-face beauty of the temple. The conscious part of his brain registered nothing. Like the plotline of the first draft of *The Epic Novel of Shit*, it behaved erratically and the damn thing wouldn't stop thinking about the book.

"Man," he said, ignoring the sound of little gold frogs softly chiming to one another. "You simply must change the colour of Sir Randolph's Bentley."

To escape, the worshipper slipped under the cool water but his brain kept spouting shit. *Idiot! The Heracles statute out front of the Scottish fairy-tale castle has to be twelve foot tall. Not eight!* He broke the surface and, using both hands, tried to physically beat the ideas out of his head but it was no good. "And, for Mother's sake," he said, furiously, "Lady Phoebe's driver must be Scottish, not English."

Fingal knew that thinking about work in the temple constituted a gross, sacrilegious crime but he was powerless to do otherwise. When the muse sings, the human has to listen. As anyone who has experienced a genuine surge of creative energy will tell you, the mind loses all sense of discipline. It has no order, purpose and direction. Ideas, shapes, voices and colours split and morph in a manner akin to cell division. It's an awesome, terrifying experience … riding on the verge of madness.

The hermit's thoughts moved about his mind like the dozens of dragonflies above the bathtub. The females, dull and brown in colour, droned round and around in circles, while the males, striking in their neon blue jumpsuits and huge, black goggles, constantly duelled with each other, flying millimetres above the boiling surface of the water, or barrelling dangerously close to a rock face, or whizzing up and up and up in crazed, double-helix formations until one, the loser, dropped out. Trying to play it cool, the winner then buzzed toward a resting female who'd almost always fly off. The males didn't seem to mind. They were only in it for the stunt flying, for the thrill of the chase.

Again, Fingal's mind flooded with thoughts about the book.

"You rosing yo' mind. Good. Good!"

"Mr Fang," Fingal groaned. "I told you, man. You're not allowed in the temple."

"I go whe'e I want." There was an urgent menace in the boss's tone. "What doing?"

"I'm bathing, Mr Fang." Silence. "Even great apes need to bathe, Mr Fang." A cough. "Bugs get into our skin." More silence. "Our fingers are red and bleeding and need soothing." Silence. "Creatures crawl into our hair and eyes."

"Stupid ape." The voice said at last. "You wasting time. Get out."

"But it's my day off," Fingal protested.

"Out."

"I've laboured for the past six stones!"

"And what you plo-duced? NOTHING!"

The boss had a point. Working, smoking and drinking for roughly sixteen hours per stone, all the revolutionary new hand-writing process had produced was a mere twenty-seven pages. The quality of the writing was much better, but the pace was funereal. "That shit! That nothing! OUT!"

"Alright, man. Enough."

"Why you in sirree fo-lest? Why you no wo'king on sirree book?"

"ENOUGH, ALREADY!"

Fingal clambered out the cold bathtub. He didn't bother drying or dressing. Naked, save for his walking boots, he hurried through the old growth plateau, ignoring the giant trees, and the flowers and rain falling graciously from above.

"Hullee, Scotman! Lun," Fang taunted. "Lun!"

"You know I love you, Mother," Fingal said after running all the way to where the colossal Strangler Fig grew, hoping that a quick hug would keep Her happy. There was simply no time to worship. Masterpieces needed writing.

"Short visit today, my love," he added before hurrying on to the end of the trail, the broken sign pointing to the world-famous but elusive Cathedral Falls, and the cliff that barred the way. He quickly lay on the ground, said "I reckon I could get down that with a good rope, blah, blah," and half-heartedly shook a fist at the deep forest below and beyond. "Oh, Mother! Please let me get down there. Oh, Mother, why won't you give me a rope, et cetera, et cetera."

The explorer snapped to his feet, brushed mud and leaves from his bare chest, and looked up to discern the sun hiding behind the now permanent ceiling of low, grey cloud. Weeks had passed since he'd seen the sun. It was estranged from the world. "Still early," he said and decided to skip lunch. If he left the temple now there was a good chance of squeezing in good seven or eight hours of writing.

"Good rad," Fang agreed. "But lun. Lun! Quickeree now."

"Yes, Mr Fang." Fingal sprinted past Mother without even looking Her way. "Three bags full, Mr Fang."

She was not impressed.

Why did he persist with that awful book?

Why wouldn't her Son stop, stare and do nothing?

This time She opted for another snake, a deadly black taipan, which she placed directly in the ape's hurried path. That should get his attention.

Consumed by ego, Fingal didn't even notice the highly venomous serpent crossing the trail. "I really should bring a pen to temple next time," the blind fool said, and stood on the snake!

"Oi!" the taipan said, lashing out and sinking its fangs into the hard heel of Fingal's boot. "Bloody wanka," it hollered up at the naked ape.

"And some paper."

Mother's huge, leathery leaves rattled in the wind. *Typical,* She thought, *they never do see the forest for the bloody trees.*

Fingal rapidly ascended to the world of man, drowning in a green sea of words, characters, and electrifying madness. All alone on a little green island, all he could see was glory, wealth and power.

***

Sometime later, he dressed at Python Gate. Then, for the first time that day, his mind actually focused on something – the underside of his arms. The cuts and bruises were normal however the seven red, raised spots around his elbow veins were not. The spots were hot and hard to the touch, the way a big zit feels days before it forms a head. Two more welled near each wrist, as did three on the back of his bare knees.

"I appear to be under some sort of attack," Fingal said. "Some sort of nasty, wee beasty appears to be eating me. Us, I mean. To be fair, though, if I were a rainforest beastie and a mountain of Scottish beef walked past, I'd fancy a wee nibble." He shuffled past the python's den and stepped out onto the wet fire trail. "This is actually quite positive. It's all about the balance, Fin. Feasting is good! Come, little insects. Eat me, and *The ENOS Ver. 2.0* shall grow strong and mighty."

When Fingal had almost reached the end of the fire trail normal service had resumed. He'd forgotten all about the red bites and was, once more, obsessing about his 'hobby.' "Maybe I should write through the night? Another two or three hours might get Fang to shut … what the devil?"

A great amount of scuffling, whining and barking further down the trail interrupted his labour. Satan's Bitch had somehow escaped from her pink prison and was on the trail. However, the lobotomised canine was in no mood, or position, to attack. Some mangy male mongrel with a studded collar – another escapee, most likely – was mounting Pippa from behind and lolling its tongue out, shagging like there was no tomorrow. At every thrust, Pippa from the pink house barked.

Bang – WOOF!

"Disgusting animals," said Fingal while bending for a rock.

"PIPPA!" Female voices called out from the bushes. "PIPPA!"

"Women. From the pink island. Shit. Switch to stealth mode." The brave explorer slipped into the woods as Penny and her youngest, Kirra, appeared, twenty metres away from the two shagging dogs.

"That other dog's hurting Pippa, Mummy!" Kirra, six, deduced.

Bang – WOOF!

"Jesus." Penny flung a beautiful hand across her beautiful mouth.

"Why's it hurting her, Mummy? Make it stop!"

Bang – WOOF!

"It's not hurting her, darling." Penny cupped her child to her hip and looked away. "They're just being friends, and friends love each other."

"Are they sexing?" asked the little girl.

Penny laughed. "No, darling. They're loving each other."

Seven more thrusts and the mangy hound blew his duff, dismounted and without so much as a "call-ya-later, Sweetcheeks", sauntered up the track toward the Scotsman hiding in the bushes. Pippa, meanwhile, sprinted joyously toward her owners as if she'd just experienced the greatest pleasure known to her kind. Penny and Kirra, clearly suffering from some female rainforest amnesia, greeted their psychotic pet in warm, soothing tones: "who's a good girl, eh? You got a new friend, eh? Aw, there, there, diddums."

Fingal didn't care. Such bizarre and filthy spectacles belonged to their world, not his. As the hermit waited for the strangers to depart he inspected a dirty finger nail, scratched the red welts, and looked up only once, when the male dog drew level.

"How ya goin', ya fuckin' idiot," the dog said to Fingal.

"Well, thank you." The islander politely replied. "And you?"

The mangy hound grinned. "Absolutely stoked, mate. You just can't beat a good root."

"Stupid dog. Don't you know that sex constitutes a vulgar, meaningless path?"

The dog thought about this for a moment. "Only a man that's not had a root for eighteen months would come up with that sort of crap."

"I speak the truth."

"Try tellin' that to the little sheila I just pumped."

"Seek the higher love, you dirty beast," Fingal admonished the dog, who, bored, tired and probably in need of some kennel-time, wandered off. "Seek it or it will seek you!"

"Yeah sure," the dog remarked. "Bloody weirdo."

***

That day got weirder and weirder.

Besides talking dogs, the Scotsman finally figured out what the increasingly itchy red spots on his arms and legs were. They were ticks! FUCKING TICKS! Not normal ticks like the big black ones that went for cats and dogs. Those were relatively easy to remove, with a pinch and a counter-clockwise twist. Binjari's ticks were miniscule, translucent and, therefore, almost impossible to find and remove. The only blessing, if you could call it that, was that the ticks were not fatal, or likely to cause paralysis. They were too small.

Standing naked in his grimy kitchen, Fingal counted eleven tick bites – that he could see. A few more could be felt: one on his left arse cheek, for example, one on his scalp, and two in the perineum, or the *gouch*, the area of skin between a human's anus and scrotum (some Australians, he'd learned, also referred to the *gouch* as the *aintcha*, as in "well, it aintcha balls, or your arse"). Binjari ticks loved the *gouch*.

To remove the ticks in the hygienic, continental fashion meant dabbing the red spot with tea tree oil. This forced the tiny insect up and out, where it could then be skewered with a pin. However, there was no tea tree oil in the blue cottage, or pins, so all Fingal could do was dig the little buggers out with the point of a Swiss army knife.

After an hour or so of such primitive but effective island surgery, Fingal counted twelve wounds bleeding on his pale, diminishing body. "Now you're eating me, Mother?" Fingal accused the forest outside, once again missing the point as the rain fell. "I get it, right. I know that pleasure cannot exist without pain, that suffering is vital to the production of a tremendous novel, that … that … what the FUCK is that?"

A bag outside the French windows seized his attention. Big and yellow, it stood at the entrance to the verandah and had absolutely no place being there. "The Drab, Green King has invaded our territory." The warrior spirit in him flared, he stomped outside and lifted the bag, surprised at how heavy and full it was.

"That little shit," he said, tipping the contents out onto the floorboards. Befitting the nature of that strange, swinging day, Fingal's expression then exploded into joy. He couldn't quite believe his luck! Before him lay three items: a twenty-five-litre bag of parrot feed, a note, and a lovely white rope, roughly one hundred foot in length. "Gifts," the hermit said. "From the Island of Shaky Old Cold, Parrot-Fancier."

The note was hand-written:

Fergus,

I came round to say g'day, and goodbye, but you'd gone bush. Just wanted to say thanks mate. The day I buried Mary was real hard and hurt me like stink. Thank you for walking me home. I wasn't in good nick.

We're off on our fancy cruise sarvo. Sailing first class on the Adriana from Brissie to New Caledonia. Never thought I'd hear myself say that, Fergus! Mary's beside herself with excitement. She can't wait for the champagne and dancing but I'm worried my bad knee won't hold up.

I know you like birds and so hope you won't mind feeding Henry, my mate, while we're away. He's no drama. Put a bit of seed in a saucer and leave it out. It might take him a few days to find your place, but the crafty bugger will smell it out. As for the rope, I remembered – somewhere – that you'd asked for a lend of it. Maybe you could string Andrew up with it! Little shit. I hate that bloody fifties music he plays. See you in a few weeks, mate.

Colin and Mary Jarvis.

Fingal grinned and lifted the rope. "What a bloody legend of a man," he declared. "Hear this, Islanders, and hear it well; from this day forth, Shaky Old Col has been re-named. Henceforth, that kind old bastard shall be known as Decent Old Col."

Fingal forgot all about the ticks, and the rain, and the painful book he was now trying to hand-write. The rope meant he could easily get down the cliff beyond Mother, descend into the deep forest and, finally, get a look at Her world-famous Cathedral Falls. Involuntarily, his mind began to trip. Images of ghost gums two kilometres high, blue caterpillars the size of railway carriages, butterflies the size of pterodactyls, gold cap mushrooms ten times his height, and a waterfall, a million feet high and wide, swam in his drowning mind.

He sat for a while, laughing and drinking and bleeding and smoking, all the while working Col's white rope through his dirty hands as if it was a giant rosary. One hundred feet. End to end. He did not notice, or care, that his hands had started to twitch, probably with excitement, fatigue, hunger or some other pathetic continental weakness.

Fang would be pleased. A wee dose of the shaky-hand was but more evidence of the madness required to produce a true masterpiece.

Blinded by desire, the hermit also did not notice a king parrot named Henry sheltering under a tree fern in the garden. As the rain intensified, the bird preened, softly whistled to itself and, every now and again, glanced up at the ape playing with the white rope.

A shy bird, Henry didn't feel like saying g'day.

The ape didn't look particularly friendly, or clean, or sane.

Chapter Twenty-Two
The Hobby from Hell

Rain teemed from the low, black clouds that had besieged the jungle for months.

This time, Fingal McKay was not a giant, or a magpie lark, or a rare, winged flying shite. He was just a number, 277. He was one of many that made up a vast army of labour shuffling up the ochre fire trail toward the factory located deep in the forest. The labourer had wild, gaunt eyes, a huge, dripping beard, and long, greasy black hair, just like everyone else. Everyone was dressed the same, in filthy, blood-stained suits woven from the coarse, white rope now abundant on the island.

Dour men with dour faces dressed in dour suits, their souls were bleak, empty places. Their minds were wrecked, and they constantly scratched and jabbered to themselves, something about ticks, a best-selling novel, a castle built from heroin, and the many tourist attractions to be found in the antique nation of Scotland. Drip by drip, they were slowly turning mad.

These men constituted the labour force of the factory. There were 167,984 of them in total, one for every word of *The Epic Novel of Sport* (D1). He was number 102,277, or 277 for short. They were all Fang's men.

The forest brooded on either side of the track, but, every now and then evidence of so-called fucking civilisation punctuated the monotony of the long, wet march. To the right, for example, 277 saw a building that vaguely resembled the Bodleian Library at Oxford. Figs, vines and creepers had entombed the abandoned building. This was the former Industry for Science, however, there were no signs of any activity, habitation or life in the epistemic compound. Not anymore. None of the labourers knew what had happened to the Professor and his bizarre, difficult-to-understand experiments. A rumour circulated that Mr Fang had taken the academic for "lee-plocessing", whatever that meant. 277 didn't care. He only existed to work.

His job was Sisyphean in nature and, therefore, quite simple. 277's sole purpose in life was to carve the word "agon" from a block of hard, grey river stone that came from the quarry at Heroin Castle. It didn't bother him that the word would only appear once in some book (The *ENOS Ver. 2.0*), or that he didn't know what the word meant (it is an ancient Greek word, broadly meaning a struggle or a contest, FYI, which stood for fuck your information). All that mattered to 277 was work, work and more work.

In attitude and aptitude, he was no different from anyone else. 277 was no island. He was part of the continent, part of the main. A bell tolled in the distance, and it tolled for thee.

The grim workforce trudged along the muddy, orange trail. On and on they trudged, up and up, deeper and deeper into the jungle, babbling and scratching and weeping, cursing their way toward their daily grind.

A second road broke off to the right. 277 knew it led to the Ministry for War's Super-Secret Weapons and Training Complex. But all that could be discerned through the heavy rain was a heavily fortified, hundred-foot cement wall covered in red war propaganda – THE DRAB, GREEN KING MUST FALL, WILL EVERYONE PLEASE SHUT THE FUCK UP, WA' IS RUVEREE, and other such brutal war slogans. Beyond, 277 could hear soldiers marching, tanks tracks clinking and clanking, helicopter blades whopping, rockets whistling through the air and exploding, and, like mice in the walls, lots and lots small arms fire that made a really, really annoying tic-tic-tic sound. They spoke of war, of the imminent battle between the island's Righteous Soldiers of Peace and Fucking Quiet, and the Drab, Green King's Warriors in Support of Leaf blowers.

It was rumoured that war would break out in a matter of days, but this didn't bother 277 either. War was always imminent among men. Akin to the S.E.X. he once knew and craved, a long, long time ago now, all men were constantly preparing for, engaging in, or recovering from some form of battle.

277 was tired and hungry. Tired, because Mr Fang only let his worker-bees sleep for four hours a night. Hungry, because only two meals per day were permitted in the factory. Both jam sandwiches, these were to be taken in the late afternoon and at midnight, respectively. Microwave lasagne was banned across the island because Mr Fang claimed it took too long to unpack, cook and ingest. Seconds mattered when producing masterpieces. Wine, instant coffee and an unlimited supply of instant cigarettes somehow sustained the growing workforce.

No wonder all the labourers were white and skinny; like ropes.

The men ceased jabbering when the Writing Factory loomed out of the rainforest. Built entirely from evil, bloodshot bricks, and standing twenty-six storeys in height (one for each letter of the alphabet), the immense Victorian-era building represented pain, pleasure and prison for 277. Pain because he really didn't enjoy the labour anymore. The labourer barely had the energy to walk to work, never mind chip away at a hard block of river stone with his ten tiny chisels. Pleasure, because although 277 hated the work, it was the same every day. He never had to think about greed, desire, or ambition. He was Sisyphus, rolling a rock up and down the hill, day after day after day. And, prison, because 277 spent twenty hours a day inside its damp walls, six stones a week. Suffering a bad case of Stockholm Syndrome, he both loved and hated the factory.

"Another day, another letter," 277 said when he entered the hot, cavernous building. Beyond the sounds of men groaning, hacking and spitting, the huge factory was silent. Weeks ago, all mechanised equipment – printers, computers, modems and such – had been banned under pain of two bottles of Sang Thip Thai Whisky, and a good, stiff beating from the boss himself. The only machines left on the island were the human ones.

Day turned to night as 277 entered a dark stairwell. Up and up and up he climbed, passing floors Z, Y, X, and W, the crowd thinning as men scuttled off through little black doors, off to their individual words, letters and agonising labours. Wonky lights flickered overhead, briefly illuminating any of the thousands of mad posters that lined the stairwell. To 277, the posters, with their crazed hieroglyphs, squiggly lines, and their weird, fading drawings of Highland castles, Hebridean islands, and Scottish mountains that didn't exist were as familiar as breath.

"Tired," 277 complained, at last, when he arrived on Floor A, the twenty-sixth to be precise, "so very, very sleepy." The labourer stepped into a vast room of cluttered wooden benches, each with a large block of stone in various stages of sculpture. His bare feet moved automatically toward his bench, he sighed, and stared with dejection at his block of stone. His labour had only just begun. So far, only the letter "a" of the word agon was visible in the hard, grey river stone. "Why am I doing this again?" he said while automatically filling a mug of goon, sparking up a very, very long cigarette, and screwing each of the ten tiny chisels onto the end of his bleeding fingers.

277 thought of simpler times on the island, when the Professor ran the show, when the islanders danced and drunk deep and long into the night at *Fanni's Vulgar Sexual Discotheque*, when the sky was full of little black and white Jackiebirds whistling strange, lively songs, when life was vital, exciting and unpredictable, when the damned book was just a damned hobby, something to do to pass the time of day.

"Harrow, 277," Mr Fang whispered millimetres from his hairy, unwashed ear. "Why you no wo'k?"

The labourer gulped. "I was just about to get started, Mr Fang."

"You t'inking of sma't man, eh?"

"No, Mr Fang. Never."

"Sma't man gone bye-bye," the prickly voice continued (not surprisingly the word Professor was also banned within the factory – it was too difficult to plonounce). "He been lee-plocessed. I, FANG!, do book now. And I want wo'ds, 277. Rots and rots of wo'ds! GOT THAT!"

"Yes, Mr Fang."

The boss rounded the worker. Compared to the dishevelled labourer, the factory boss wore an immaculate, shit-coloured Thai policeman's uniform with matching cap. His skin was tanned but pockmarked from teenage acne, and his gold tooth glowed menacingly in the dim light.

"You no happee?"

"Very, Mr Fang."

"You get one day off to wo'ship stupid t-lee in lainfolest, no?"

"That is very kind of you, Mr Fang."

"You no fee' ribarated?"

"With every passing day, Mr Fang."

"Hmm," said Fang, smacking a riding crop into 277's stone. "I confused. You happee, got God, and fee' ribarated?" For once, the tyrant's tone was soft and charming. A bad sign. "So why you no' wo'k?"

"I was just about to get started, Mr Fang, but I'm so very tired, I can't breathe and I'm incredibly drunk. All the time!"

With incredible speed and power, Fang thrashed his riding crop across 277's face a dozen times. "WO'K, S-RAVE! WO'K!"

"Right away, Mr Fang. Thank you for beating me, Mr Fang."

"SHUT UP!"

"I'll try harder, Mr Fang."

But, thank Mother, the daemon was gone.

"An' why YOU no' wo'k!?" Mr Fang was now screaming at 276, who had the awful job of scraping the word antidisestablishmentarianism from the stone with his ragged and bloody hands. "'On-ess-ree," the brute mused after kicking 276 to a pulp for breathing too loudly. "You just cannot get good staff reese days."

Soon the huge floor was full of the noises of writing: groaning, swearing, bleeding, jabbering, jabbering, and weeping; much weeping.

"C'mon. Work," 277 said with courage. "You're a man. You work. That's what you do. That's all you do." He downed the mug of goon and lit a second smoke, a fat, wide one this time, full of lurid green tobacco. Eyes wincing at the acrid smoke, 277 placed his ten chisels on the hard river stone.

"Strange," he said. The chisels didn't make their usual, crisp scraping noise.

The labourer tried again and again but the noise was the same – a very, very annoying tic-tic-tic noise. He glanced over to 275, who was grinding the word arduous, with his teeth. Same noise – not the gnawing of ivory on stone but…

Tic.

Tic-tic.

TIC.TIC.TIC. TIC.

277 hated that noise.

Suddenly his ruined mind boiled, his hands started shaking, and his eyeballs filled up with goon. The tic-tic-tic noise got louder and louder, so he ripped his ears off, and desperately looked up at the factory's dark, low ceiling. As if it were a living, breathing creature the ceiling started to pulse and wriggle. Little grey mice started to rain down from above – one, two, a thousand, 167,984, one for every word of the first book – *The Epic Nover of Shit*.

277 opened his mouth to scream but it was full of mice.

"Pain is good," the mice squeaked. "Pain is ruveree."

Fang laughed.

277 cried.

It was always like this, writing.

***

The human ear is an incredible device. Over time, it is capable of isolating, dwelling on and responding to certain noises, often in the manner of one of Ivan Pavlov's dogs. This is why ice-cream trucks continue to ring bells, why airplanes make that bing-bong noise before the captain wakes people up to talk about the weather, and why, more importantly, the noise coming from the bedroom walls in the blue cottage soon induced a series of destabilising, automatic reactions in Fingal's McKay's increasingly odd behaviour.

Tic.

Tic-tic.

Tic-tic-tic-tic.

"Make it stop," groaned Fingal, rubbing the sleep out of his gaunt eyes, still confused about the 277 dream. He thought that writing a novel was meant to be a pleasurable experience, like the way uber-billionaire

Ian Fleming used to write: 2,000 words in the morning, cocktails in the afternoon, and as many posh groupies as he could handle in the evening. The only visits Fingal got were from red, hellish visions. There were no cocktails or giggling groupies in the factory on his island, only mice. There had to be at least fifty of them now living behind the bedroom walls, scrambling, scratching, nibbling, fighting, shagging, crapping and squeaking.

"Make it stop."

Tic.

Tic-tic.

Tic-tic-tic-tic.

"MAKE IT FUCKING STOP!"

Exhausted from another late-night shift at the book, Fingal couldn't move. He lay in his damp bed for a good half an hour, staring up at the ceiling, waiting for the plaster to bulge then break and for a whiskered head to appear. The mouse would fall and tumble into his open mouth and, because of gravity, have nowhere to scurry but down, deep into his starving belly. "The protein would do me good," the Scotsman said before coughing and clutching his ribs, which you could now play the xylophone on.

"Get up, man," he groaned. "Time to go to work."

The common factory routine began: rise, hobble to bathroom and pee in the sink. Ignore shower, toothbrush and, most importantly, reflection in the mirror. Brew coffee. Stare at growing number of posters and insist, madly, that you're not mad. Pick scabs off tick bites. Stare at rain. Been raining for seventeenth stone straight now. Watch blood flowing from scabs. Ignore its blackness. Stare at saucer on verandah, full of Henry the parrot's bird food, untouched for the fourth morning in a row. Endure second coughing fit, gob phlegm into dirty kitchen sink and rinse, wash away. Pretend it isn't there. Drink morning mug of goon and pre-roll six cigarettes. Break wind, poorly; meekly. Shuffle to desk, smirk at the memory of computer's death but think of emails and father, so far away. Think of father. Think of Scotland. Cry. Hit yourself. Pick nose. Pull out long nostril hairs, careful not to pull out brain. Stroke beard for a long time. Worry about right hand. Too much writing. Too much labour. Hand is collapsing. It is not a hand. It is a claw; a clawhand. Put that in fake book. Somewhere. Pretend clawhand isn't there. Lift pen with good left hand. Slot pen into clawhand. Stare at blank piece of white paper. Try to write some words, any words. Work, man. Fuck, come on! No words. Drink goon. Smoke. Stare. WORK! Drink. Smoke. Drink. Drink. Drink. Words begin to flow. Smoke and drink and write for three hours. Morning shift over. Outside, up there, continental noise routine #1 then begins.

Noisy cunts.

On the wet road outside a huge water truck swooshes past.

"One, two, three, and—"

Pippa explodes in a fit of barking, four females from the pink cottage screech "SHUT UP!" and, minutes later, Andrew's mournful fifties music drones throughout the forest. The noises – their noises – get louder as the continentals get busy. They always start in the pink house. Must be school holidays because Penny's three little girls never seem to leave the property. In the mornings, they like to play fashion shows indoors, marching up and down wooden floorboards in their mother's high heels to the sort of loud, interminable pop music that little girls listen to – Bieber, Cyrus and the like. Around mid-morning, and bored, the girls make their own music, bashing pots and pans with wooden spoons, beating bongo drums or pounding the keys of a badly tuned piano. None of the noisy little arseholes demonstrate any musical talent, voice or rhythm whatsoever. What Penny is doing while all this was going is beyond us. She's probably conducting them, "C'mon, girls; louder! LOUDER! Let's really piss off the weirdo next door that wouldn't shag Mummy!"

After lunch, when the rain is lighter, the little girls play in the garden, splashing in puddles, laughing like wicked angles, crying and squealing and squabbling, as little girls do. Sometimes they play hide and screech (similar to hide and seek except when discovered repeatedly *SCREECH* your tiny arse off) but their favourite game is torturing Pippa, chasing the adopted, feral dog around the garden with a stick, giggling in the rain at her torment.

Mainly because the fates are arseholes, when things can't get any worse, they do. About ten stones after witnessing Pippa being sexually abused in the woods the islanders hear a terrifying word. This word will come be mentioned hundreds of times over the next six or seven weeks. This word is "puppies".

Satan's Bitch is pregnant.

Puppies. Puppies. Puppies.

Yelping, yapping, whining little Puppies.

Puppies.

PUPPIES!

Got that?

Return to past.

Please, return to past.

Let the madman shoulder the labour.

Let Atlas carry the world.

"Wo'k, you srimebag. Wo'k."

"Yes, Mr Fang. Sorry, Mr Fang. I love you, Mr Fang."

***

Relations with the drab, green cottage were collapsing. Besides the fifties music, ABC News for the deaf, and the constant sawing, cooking, hammering, peeing, drilling, leaf blowing and humming, Andrew McKenzie, Esquire, had taken to restoring an old, crapped-out Bedford van in his garage. As chance would have it (also an arsehole, by the way), the little Christian with the little face's garage backed onto the front corner of the blue cottage, where Fingal's desk was located. Twenty metres, a wall of wild garden, and two French windows were all that separated the neighbours and their respective hobbies.

Due to the constant rain, the Little Noisemaker Extraordinaire now spent most of the day in his garage, singing hymns, banging, hammering, turning noisy things on and off, and, mostly, angle grinding bits of metal, as if doing so was going out of fashion. Fingal jumped every time a spanner clanged to the cement floor, when a new hymn started up, or some dastardly power tool whizzed to life. Shit, thought Fingal, Andrew probably wasn't even working on a crapped out old van. In fact, he was a one-man industrial band, marching up and down his garage, smashing and bashing and crashing and singing hymns: "BANG, BANG, BANG ... Amazing Grace, how sweet the sound ... vvvvvrrrrrrrrrrrrrrrmmmmmm ... that saved a wretch like me ... CLANG, CLANG, CLANG ... I once was lost, but now am found ... Baaaaa-zzzzzzzzzzzzzinnnnnggggg ... Was blind, but now I see ... BANG-BANG-FUCKIN'-BANG." At every sound, the Scotsman's Gaelic blood boiled a little more. His designs turned darker and more violent.

But, if the truth be told, his heart did not truly welcome this development. Fingal, you see, was a pacifist. Like most, he'd explored violence but only when he was younger, much younger, and only when he had attended Underbank Primary School, a tiny, sweet and innocent educational establishment in the village of Crossford, Scotland. The other kids at Underbank were easy to fight, especially with Fingal's patented Windmill Fighting Technique: clench fists, swing arms, kick at the same time, close eyes and ATTACK! Back then he fought for possession, mainly to get stuff – balloons, sweeties, *Star Wars* figures, and those searing, .23 of a second, glances from Claire Coleman, his primary school sweetheart.

Big School then came, in the nearby town of Lanark. Moving from Underbank to Lanark Grammar High School was like moving from Hobbiton to South Central L.A. On his first The Grammar, for instance, Sandy "The Hun" McGinty, some beast with Indian ink tattoos from one of the council housing schemes, had head-butted Dougie Boag, Fingal's wee pal he played computers with on a Saturday morning, just because Dougie "wis frae the fuckin' village". It was a horrible baptism.

Over the course of the next six years, Fingal witnessed many head-buttings, kickins, rammies, and more than a few slashings. He also saw one incident involving sports equipment, when Denice "Nicey" Yule beat Julie Wilson who was also "frae the valley" with a hockey stick, and six, annual bouts of an ongoing feud between the two hardest guys at school – Craig "Fergo" Sharp and Chris "Ghengis" McCann, the last of which finished with Ghengis smashing Fergo's broken puss off a three-hundred-year-old oak tree "doon by the smokies".

Fingal did learn something while attending a violent Scottish high school, however. It was a quote by a historian called John Sivard who wrote that "since the beginning of recorded history 14,400 wars, claiming the lives of some 3.5 billion people, have been recorded". Fascinated with this grotesque statistic, young Fingal went on to write an English essay on the topic. Called simply "Why Humans Fight?", it discussed the many causes of war that blighted the human story: the state, emotions, the state system, fear, the Military Industrial Complex (a cosy relationship between governments, the army and the arms industry), laziness, "God wills it" (Pope Urban the II's rallying cry when launching the first of the twelve *religious* Crusades), the habits of modern living, technological progress (known in the business as Revolutions in Military Affairs), resources, because we can (a la George Mallory), for love, and, most of all, because it was in our Nature. "Children are born violent and have to be taught not to fight," Fingal wrote in the paper, which concluded with the Violent Chimpanzee hypothesis, that

> human DNA was 98.4% similar to chimps, who still engaged in wars, infanticide and cannibalism. Born from the same stock, it was simply natural for humans to fight. The human animal was like any other creature whose survival had been aided with high intelligence and a propensity to fight.

Just like humans' intuitive, insatiable appetite for S.E.X. or food, Fingal argued, violence was hard-wired into most great ape's physiological systems.

Mr Egan, the history teacher saw otherwise. Also known as Specky Twat, he gave sixteen-year-old Fingal a B- for the excellent essay, simply because he "did not appreciate being compared to a monkey". Fingal, quite correctly, argued that a monkey was not an ape, so Specky Twat dropped him down to a C.

Now, over twenty years later, Fingal understood why the Ministry of War on his island sat on a constant war footing but never actually fired a shot in anger. His armed forces were on "hair-trigger alert", an expression used to describe the insanity of America maintaining thousands of nuclear bombs on permanent, one-minute standby. Unlike the brave, bumbling U.S. Army, however, Fingal's soldiers, ships and tanks lay in a state of military preparedness: ready but unwilling to fight. This, he also supposed, was why no warrior character like the Professor or Fang materialised.

The island's war doctrine was organic, however. Andrew and his fucking Christian DIY caused a bit of that Underbank Primary School fighting spirit to return. He wanted to windmill Andrew's bony ass. The old chimp-DNA cocktail began to bubble, and he knew it was only a matter of time before it would explode. Moreover, war with the Drab, Green King, should it surely come to that, was morally justified. It would be a Just War, mainly on account of the ethical immorality of Andrew's incessant noise. Not once did the little shite think *Gee whizz, it's lovely and quiet in the rainforest this morning. I wonder if my angle grinder, hammer or leaf blower might upset anyone? That rude, mental Scottish heathen-neighbour of mine that worships peace perhaps? Oh well, ho-hum, doesn't matter. Life is about me, after all. Now, where is my trusty angle grinder? God, please bless this almighty racket that I am about to make ... bbaaazzzzzzzzzzzzzzzzzzzzzzzzzzzzzzzzziiiiiiiiiiiiiiiiiiiiiiiiinnnnnnnnnnnnggg.* The little shit deserved it, in other words. The litany of growing noise injustices could only be met with a stern and violent hand. Little Face had it coming.

Moreover, the Drab, Green King's noises constituted a clear and present danger to the security of the island. A la George Bush The Younger, they warranted – no, demanded – preemptive, violent action. The Ministry for War's Intel. Department insisted that the Andrew's incessant fucking noises had three intended policy outcomes:

a) to express, and exact, revenge for being told to fuck off shortly before Jackie-bird's funeral.

b) as skirmishing actions intended to halt and harass the labourer's stop-start progress on *The ENOS Ver. 2.0*

c) to provoke Fingal into war and, thus, drive him into the bosom of the invisible human-God (see below).

That little, noisy wanker, who was definitely spying on the factory, knew that Fingal was hand-writing a best-seller that would change English literature forever. Jealous as Judas, Andrew was doing everything in his power to frustrate the writing process, to make sure Fingal *never* finished, and, thus, never got the mad highland castle, Parky or The One. Broken, distraught and ordinary, Fingal would then run into his puny neighbour's arms and beg him and his truly invisible God for forgiveness, redemption, and a second chance at life.

It was all so bloody obvious. War, therefore, just had to occur between Blue and Green islands. Fingal didn't really want to kick Andrew's "cunt in", as they used to say in that brutal high school. He had to. He had no other choice.

But, but, not so hasty, Warrior, there were consequences to consider. If, for example, he did shove the leaf blower up Andrew's tiny little arse and press the on button, the Drab, Green King would alert the police, lawyers, and all manner of do-gooder continental types. Like flies round shite, they would descend upon Fingal's blue cottage, all wanting profit, karma and credit for shafting or rescuing the so-called lost man inside. Everything in Fingal's real and imaginary worlds would then utterly collapse. The Experiment, not that he thought about it much these days, would come to an abrupt end and Fingal would probably end up in jail, getting raped in the showers by Mr Big. He'd then have to return to the coast or, worse, Scotland – a loser with a sore arse who'd wasted half his life and all his money travelling, searching for meaning and failing.

The final reason not to march round and break Andrew's beaked-nose with a sweetly-timed right hook was perhaps the best one. It concerned the relationship between the island's religiosity and *The ENOS Ver. 2.0.* As per Mother's law of balance, pain, anger and mean, simian thoughts about war, violence and mayhem, held great currency in the factory. Madness always produced masterpieces, right? It's why millions of continentals went to The Met, jostling for a shite picture on their iPhones of Van Gogh's Sunflowers. Most don't actually care that it's a stunning painting, that the swirling colours are impossibly profound, or that the genius was able to capture the sensation of a divine acid-trip on canvas, in-fucking-perpetuity. All the hoards with their stupid little flat phones cared about was that the artist was mad, troubled and tortured.

According to this logic, Andrew's constant diatribe of annoying noises were useful in that they drove Fingal mad. Madness was good for the creative process. Madness sold copy and led to castles, so, listen, poor Fingal, grow angry, feed off the misery, and, somehow, channel the pain into that god-dammed, amazing book.

But, as the days passed, the noises grew louder, as did the calls for something to be done about the gross injustice. "Selfish little shite," Fingal often said while plotting and scheming more war designs. "How can he not appreciate that not everyone likes the dawn-to-dusk racket of power tools in a fucking silent rainforest? There no justice!"

Andrew McKenzie, Esquire, was a noisy little wanker.

The man had to be silenced.

The Christian DIY enthusiast had to go down.

"What was it Machiavelli wrote?" Fingal mused. "Ah, yes: 'If injury has to be done to a man, it should be so severe that his vengeance need not be feared'."

Chapter Twenty-Three
War

Khongoryn Els (pronounced Kog-o-rin Elsh), Mongolia, is a very special mountain range. It is one of a few places on earth where *total* silence exists. Hardly any tourists go there and even the local goat herders struggle to find the place. This is because Khongoryn Els appears on no human map, one of its many charming features in this, the age of sentient, computerised satellite mapping devices. Eagles and the wind are masters of this domain.

To the south lies the eerie, hypnotic emptiness of the Gobi Desert. Thousands of tall, smooth, golden sand dunes stretch as far as the eye can see. The view north is dominated by the raw desolation of steppe, taiga and tundra, a beautiful, lost realm where only wolves, hawks and bears prosper. Even the Great Khan's hardy descendants cannot survive in that wild, divine land; out there. In fact, from Khongoryn Els' tallest peak, a human can gaze for a hundred miles in any direction and know that no other human exists, out there.

Total silence endures.

There is no wind. The only movement comes from a golden eagle gliding above, its black, inked shadow rippling across the sand dunes below. The eagle, like the land, makes no noise. Everything is utterly still and quiet.

The observer's pulse thumps against his eardrums, which feel all clean and soft and silky-smooth. His heartbeat booms, and, in celebration of the discovery, much whisky is drunk from his old grandfather's hip flask.

And what a discovery! Fingal couldn't quite believe his luck. In Khongoryn Els he'd found the quietest place on earth.

Tic.

Tic-tic.

Tic-tic-tic-tic, went the mice in the bedroom walls.

"Fucking shut up!" went the hermit, thumping the bedroom wall until the hoards of mice living fell quiet.

Almost crying at the sheer concept of noise, Fingal squeezed his eyes shut even tighter.

Khongoryn Els, the quietest place on earth.

A few years ago now, Fingal had been lucky enough to visit the lost mountain range, journeying across the Gobi in a 4x4 Soviet rip-off Combi-van with only the driver, Terelj, for company. The Mongolian nomad was an amazing mechanic, good cook and, as with most people from the Steppe, had a friendly, welcoming demeanour. Terelj barely spoke a word of English, which suited Fingal just fine. Mid-way through a global quest to find silence on a planet of 7.2 billion (then), he didn't go to Mongolia in search of friendship. He went to run away from humans and all their bloody noise. For four weeks, the Scotsman, the Mongolian and their crapped-out old van drifted aimlessly across an ocean of sand, exploring, camping, and doing a hell of a lot of staring – mostly at sand dunes and, when night fell, upturned bowls of black sky full of glittering stars. Two weeks into the trip, at the point of no return, the two men found Khongoryn Els – slap bang in the middle of nowhere. It was a marvellous discovery, a silent way to cap off a long, silent trip. Fingal and Terelj celebrated by saying nothing. No words, no sounds, were exchanged.

Two weeks later, when the Mongolian dropped Fingal off at some remote airstrip, Terelj smiled, said "zank ooo" and offered the visitor a gold scarf as a memento. In return, Fingal gave him a one-hundred-dollar tip. Despite having recently experienced his first shower in over a month the traveller had never felt so dirty. He hated the West, and the fact he was not a cosmic traveller but just another emissary from the Great Capitalist Whore.

As with most travels, it all made sense in the end, though. Fingal had a benchmark for silence, a place to go when things got really bad. Khongoryn Els, the quietest place on earth. And, more importantly, Terelj's beautiful gold scarf now kept Jackie warm in his Australian rainforest grave. The magpie lark would slumber for all eternity in warm, golden, comfortable

SILENCE.

Tic.

Tic-tic.

Tic-tic-tic-tic.

"FUCKING SHUT UP!"

The memory of Khongoryn Els blew away like sand in the Gobi and Fingal suddenly remembered that he was supposed to be absolutely furious. This was not because of mice scratching in the walls, the Drab, Green King's constant labour on his stupid van, his empty, starving stomach, or the fact he'd drunk two litres of goon and smoked thirty roll-ups the day before and, subsequently, had a hangover that brewed like stink. No, a far greater, industrial problem enraged the hermit.

Hard as it was to believe *The ENOS Ver. 2.0* was just as bad the first draft! No, in fact, the second draft was worse; more SHITE.

"Fuck!" Fingal screamed above the sound of rain drumming off the roof.

The head of the editorial department, Fingaleus Fingalsson, a short-lived character who was immediately Executed out of sheer creative pettiness, realised this after reviewing the hand-written book yesterday. This time, there was no celebratory party for the reading. Rain fell steadily, and the editor sat on the lazy-boy, drinking, smoking and reading but a third of the 656 hand-written pages long into the wee, small hours before deciding *The ENOS Ver. 2.0* was also "shite. A-grade, Hei'land SHITE." It made no sense to the emaciated writer. How could draft two be worse than draft one?

In short, the second book was even more of a jerk than the first. It was five times *more* complex, confusing and rambling. Absolutely nothing in the twenty-seven-character *Epic* about sport, Gods, men and the descent of society made the least bit sense. The narrative had gone from jerky to positively schizophrenic. Hundreds and hundreds of hours of back-breaking, hand-wrecking labour, and *The ENOS Ver. 2.0* was a disaster; a total stuff up. No, sorry, it was SHITE. Like Donne's continent, and Fingal's dreams of highland castles, Man Booker Prizes, and a long-overdue reconciliation with The One.

Fingal wasn't depressed. He was angry; Scottish-angry. The old, pagan spirit fired in his soul. It was the same spirit that stirred when the blue Picti destroyed King Ecgfrith's Northumbrian army at the Battle of Dun Nechtain in 685, the same that led Wallace and Murray's troops when they hacked the English to bits at Bannockburn in 1314, and the same that momentarily cried at Culloden in the year 1745, before the Jacobite Poof-King, "Bonnie" Prince Charlie, left his men to die and ran away, o'er the sea tae Skye.

Fury erupted from Mt Fingal and poured across the island at the absolute shiteness of *The ENOS Ver. 2.0*. Mr Fang egged him on too, whispering the words "it shit" over and over and over. A white, searing enmity coursed through his Scottish veins at the noises stabbing at his brain – the fucking mice in the walls, the water trucks outside, Satan's Bitch barking and barking and barking, and, of course, Andrew McKenzie, Esquire, who had been singing hymns and leaf blowing for the past thirty minutes. In the rain. At dawn.

Something, or someone had to pay for all this … SHITE.

Peace had to return to the rainforest. War had to be brought against all enemies of the island. It was a matter of survival. In the end, Fingal was left no choice. Peace was now a matter of life and death.

***

The island made the final preparations for war. A huge siren wailed from the top of Mt Fingal, Martial Law was declared, and the Mother-Tree ordered everyone not associated with the war machine inside the various buildings. Offshore, the frolicking whales dove for deeper water and, in the forest, all the Jackiebirds hid from the impending sins and fury of man. All industry ceased in the Writing Factory, however that didn't mean that Mr Fang stopped harassing Fingal, "rike herr" it did.

The man's temerity was incredible. He couldn't, wouldn't, let the book lie. Mind you, the tyrant had a good argument: before the warriors could fight with a clear mind, he argued, the latest industrial problem – "gritch"

242

– had to be rectified. Fang, the Great Tyrant, insisted that *The ENOS Ver. 2.0* was shite because, once more, Fingal hadn't tried hard enough. Hard as it was to accept, Fingal had, once more, failed to demonstrate the pain, toil and lunacy necessary for producing a good book. There was no real or actual blood on the page. At Rivendell, Tolkien, Gandalf and Lord Elrond would be pissing themselves with laughter. Five, maybe six (?) hundred hours, a broken hand, and a bad case of the hermit madness? Aw, there, there diddums. The effort had been pathetic. No wonder the second book was more SHITE than the first!

So, before the battle, Fang ordered Fingal to start all over again. Fang told him to start work on a third book, "Afta' Wa'." Fang told him the book was now a matter of life and death, for if the book failed, the factory failed and, ergo, both man and island would perish. Fang told him that having come so far it was stupid to quit now. Fang told him that pussies quit and heroes marched on. And Fang, correctly, told him that the third book had to get bigger, badder and madder. Fang, the genius, promised Fingal that a new production technique called the "Stland Apploach" would "finaree get job done".

Once again, Fang, not Fingal, saved the day.

With another book disaster avoided, Fingal then decided to tackle the mice problem in the bedroom walls. He did so directly, by punching four holes in the walls with the twelve-pound sledgehammer used in the iPhone's execution. Dozens of mice were supposed to scramble out the holes to be stamped to death by a very angry, hairy man wearing a pair of size 10 Scarpa walking boots. "Show yersel's, ya wee hairy bastards," Fingal shouted into one of the holes. "Come oot and fight like men!"

However, not one mouse appeared, so the Warrior peed into each hole, shouted "this is ape territory", and wrote off the mice as absolute cowards. Such cowardice, however, gave Fingal a better idea. "If those wee, scratchy wankers are scared of moi," the top inmate in the islands lunatic asylum pondered aloud, "imagine how scared they'd be of a five metre python."

A simple if dangerous plan to solve the mice problem was thus born: at the earliest opportunity, and using Decent Old Col's large yellow rope-bag, and a very large stick, somehow capture Mrs Snake, fling her in the bedroom, close the door and let nature do its thing.

"Genius," said Fingal, "a natural solution to a natural problem." Hell, Mrs Snake would probably be quite grateful of the opportunity to have a wee break from her hollow log, and an easy opportunity to fill her belly with thousands of tiny wee mice.

Outside, an industrial water truck swooshed past, Satan's Bitch exploded in a fit of barking, and four females screeched "SHUT UP, PIPPA!"

"Right, slag-beast," said Fingal, high on skirmishing action. "You're fucking next."

On entering his bathroom, the Scotsman – ignoring the mirror, of course – rifled through a drawer full of dusty pill bottles, ointments, plasters and cotton buds until he found the weapon the war machine sought: a bottle of dodgy valium he'd purchased some time ago from a chemist in New Delhi. Fingal then placed two of the vallies onto a slice of bread, squished it up into a little ball and, as the rain fell harder, and the dog barked louder, marched onto the battlefield, toward a gap in the fence separating blue from pink cottages. At the sight of a man, the demented, slavering beast sprinted through the mud to charge the fence, desperate to break through and rip Fingal's testicles off. The Warrior did not budge from his advanced position. He spat at the dog, called it a "cunt", popped the bread and valium through the fence, and watched as the impregnated hell-hound scoffed the lot down. "Sleep, beast," said Fingal as the dog's barking began to slur. As if drunk, her gait turned wobbly and, minutes later, Satan's Bitch lay sound asleep in the mud and the rain, out of its demented face on vallies.

The silence was wonderful.

"Another enemy vanquished."

The reluctant Warrior stroked his long beard and looked around a sodden battlefield framed by wet, dripping forest. "That just leaves the cherry on top, Mr Alpha-knob, the Rajah of Annoying-fucking-noises, the Turd-of-turds, the Ghost, the Drab, Green King: Andrew-fuckin'-McKenzie, Esquire."

The prompt for war to erupt between the Christian and the Scottish

Warrior didn't take too long. Three minutes after Pippa the evil dog collapsed, Andrew greeted the dawn world with an excruciating sixty-second burst of the angle grinder. It was 6:45am (ape-time).

"Selfish little cunt," said Fingal, as he tramped toward Andrew's drab, green cottage to put a stop to the bloody noise once and for all.

***

War trumpets now blared out across the island. 167,984 little Fingal soldiers marched down the orange fire trail toward the beach, followed by tanks, Apache helicopters and sleek, black F22s piloted by little Fingal's wearing mirrored sunglasses and *Top Gun* jackets. None of them wanted to fight but, for the sake of justice, they had to. Unleashing violence on the Drab, Green King, Esquire, was the only way that the infuriating noises in the temple would ever stop.

"The Drab, Green King must fall," Fingal-the-Reluctant-Warrior mumbled as he marched onto Andrew's property for the first time. Blissfully unaware of the approaching Celtic tornado, Andrew had his back turned. The small man was angle grinding a wheel hub on a crapped-out Bedford van. He was dressed in yellow wellington boots, a boiler suit, denim cap and a red handkerchief, which was tied around his scrawny neck, though not tight enough for the Scotsman's liking.

"ANDREW!" Fingal roared above the whining machine. The little prick kept going, because he was also wearing headphones – *headphones!* Enraged, Fingal tore the plug from its socket and shouted "ANDREW, THAT'S ENOUGH!" The Drab, Green King turned but did not smile. Calmly, and with God on his side, he removed his stupid denim cap and headphones and regarded the big, hairy invader from top to toe. "Have you any idea how bloody annoying that noise is?" Fingal demanded.

"And good morning to you, neighbour," Andrew replied curtly. "Get out of the wrong side of the bed, did we?"

"Do you know why I moved here?"

"It wasn't to make friends and influence people."

"Wipe that Cub Scout grin off your face." Fingal stepped into the smaller man's space. "Do you know why I moved here?"

On realising there was a mad, angry Scotsman in his sanctuary Andrew shrunk a bit. All noise thugs are cowards by nature, and he had no desire to fight. "Now, Fingal," he bleated. "Let's start over. May I offer you a cup of chamomile—"

"Because two ugly people kept having sex in a hot tub."

"… tea?"

"Because drunk Australian men burped like frogs in the night." Andrew gulped and screwed up his little face. *This is all wrong, man. FOCUS!* "Because they. No. You, yes YOU! make noise. Do I make myself clear?" The hermit didn't so he pretended to be a one-man industrial band. "I'M ANDREW MCKENZIE! I MAKE NOISE! NOISE-NOISE-NOISE! LA-LA-LA! I LOVE NOISE! CAN EVERYONE HEAR MY LEAF BLOWER? NO? LET ME TURN IT UP!?"

Andrew retreated toward an impressive array of tools hanging from the garage's rear wall. "Fingal, are you all right?"

"No, Andrew. I am not. You have driven me insane." Fingal stabbed at his temple with a long, dirty finger. "It's official. HA! You and your incessant fuckin'-noise have actually driven me in-fucking-sane."

"Will you *please* watch your language, Fingal," Andrew said with caution. "I do not appreciate—"

"This is a fucking rainforest, man! A cathedral! Do you even realise how quiet it is?"

"Yes, of course, I—"

"You don't! Because if you did you wouldn't make such a bloody racket all the time! I mean, how is it even possible? How can such a small man make so much FUCKING noise!"

"Fingal, I was not aware that—"

"Bullshit, Andrew."

"Why didn't you say so? We're neighbours. All you had to do—"

"Shut up, Andrew." He backed the pretend mechanic into a corner. "You are nothing but a selfish, little, horrible, and NOISY man."

"Everyone's entitled to a spot of D.I.Y., particularly on their own sovereign property."

"Aye, in moderation. Not from sun up to sun down."

"That's a bit of an exaggeration, Fingal."

"NO, IT'S NOT. Your noise is a crime." Fingal clapped his hands and Andrew jumped. "And we all know what happens to criminals, don't we?" His beard was a black, terrible thing bristling with rage. "On my island, they're punished. Machines, noisemakers, are executed."

"Fingal, please, if you don't mind I'd like to—"

"You know I'm trying to write a book, don't you?" Andrew had no idea what the maniac was on about. "You know how I know that you know that? Because you watch me. Don't you? I see your tiny, little, shrunken face, Andrew. I see it in the bushes. I see it floating in your stupid little turret. I see it everywhere. Every-fucking-where.

"Fingal, if you—"

"Are you ready? Are you and your stupid, invisible, apathetic God prepared to bond with me, Neighbour? Are you shaking comfortably?" Fear flooded the little man's rheumy eyes. He nodded, once. "Fucking tremendous. Now, shut up and listen to me."

Fingal McKay proceeded to outline twenty-seven specific complaints to his neighbour, shouting each one while jabbing his finger into Andrew's pigeon chest. "That fifties music is absolute torture!" he yelled. "It is utter shite, and it scares the birds away! You may want to listen to it, but I most certainly do not! If you do not turn your SHITE MUSIC down, I'll come around and shove the stereo up your arse." Fingal rattled on and on, shouting at the top of Andrew's bowed head as if it were a podium microphone. "Is it really necessary to cut your grass three times a week? And why do you have to shout into the telephone? And, for Mother's sake, stop fucking pissing in the middle of the toilet! I mean, how hard is it to piss on the side!" Fingal could imagine how happy a volcano felt when it finally exploded. After months of noise and pain and torture, the explosion of rage felt superb. "And, for Mother's sake, will you *please* stop inviting fucking Christians round for sing-a-longs on a Sunday."

As Fingal ranted and raved, and shouted, poked and prodded, one thing became sadly clear, however. There was absolutely no fight in Andrew. Rightly so, the smaller, cleaner man was afraid of the larger, hairier man, which was no good for the island's War designs. None of Andrew's behaviour offered what Fingal what he needed – an excuse to smack him in the face; hard, and repeatedly. "And another thing," Fingal bellowed, pressing on, praying and hoping Andrew would try and push him out the way, or do something to induce fisticuffs. He needed violence. "I hate your God. He, or she, or whatever it is, is a cheat, a liar and a coward. Look at all the fucking wars and drought and industry and artificial intelligence destroying the planet. And what does your God do about it? FUCK ALL!"

At last Andrew looked up, the courage of Daniel mustering in his puny soul. "The Good Book is not meant to be taken literally," he squeaked.

"Where is He now, Andrew?" Rain hammered off the garage roof. "Where is He in this, your desperate hour of need, when a blue banshee swirls on your doorstep?"

"I think you need to go home, young man."

Desperate for violence, the warrior scowled at the heavens. "Nope, don't see the big fella. Can you see him or her, or whatever the fuck it is? But, wait. I'm confused. Aren't the clouds supposed to part about now? Isn't a big finger meant to appear and strike me down with a lightning bolt? No? Nothing. Big Fella must be out, eh?"

Then Fingal saw it, a machine he hated above all other machines – the mother-fucking, goddammed leaf blower, the Nemesis of the Sore Red Ear Tribe. Fingal's mind seethed with anger, hot spittle flew from his mouth and, just like his Picti ancestors and their woad paint, his skin turned blue. "As neighbours, I think it's about time we actually shared something, eh? What say you to a live execution?"

Andrew had no time to reply. With great speed Fingal grabbed the leaf blower, leapt back and grinned like the devil. Holding the insidious machine by its snout, he then battered the leaf blower off the cement floor, again and again and again. For good measure, he then stomped the cunt-machine for a good minute until only bits of its engine, wires, plastic, and black, oily blood were strewn across the floor.

Andrew looked on with absolute horror.

More silence fell across the rainforest.

"If ever a machine embodied the human race," Fingal said after a moment, panting and sweating. "It is the fucking leaf blower. Loud, annoying and utterly pointless."

Fingal's mood lurched again. Suddenly he was smiling. "Oh, don't worry, wee man," he said with a friendly chuckle. "We islanders may be cruel and violent, and some say primitive, but we do understand the nature of compensation." Fingal removed five hundred dollar bills (the last of his human money) from his pocket. This was all part of the island's "insurance" plans – vanquish and bribe the cowed with money. Fingal crumpled one of the hundred-dollar bills up, and threw it at his neighbour's head. "Compensation, right?"

Andrew nodded, a lot.

"You better not call the fucking cops, right?"

More nodding.

"Or any of your do-gooder Christian pals. No angles must descend on my sovereign territory. Understood?"

Nodding, and a little whimper.

"And, most important of all, do not buy another fucking leaf blower. Is that clear?"

"Yes," Andrew said, at last, his eyes falling to the floor. "But, Fingal, please—"

"BUY A FUCKING BROOM!"

Good, the hermit thought. *This shit is actually working!*

Time to finish up with the big guns – the Gustav Gun, the Stealth Bomber and Ivy Mike bolstered with a healthy dose of propaganda, of lies. Fingal pulled up the sleeve of his raincoat to reveal a dozen, purple scars clustered around his veins. "Do you know what these are, you noisy little cunt?"

Andrew gasped, the way most people do when called a cunt and, more so, when confronted with a junkie, real or, in this case, imagined (the scars were from tick bites). "They're track marks, Andrew. From heroin. Lovely, lovely heroin. Yum, yum, yum. I'm addicted to it, you see. Bet your spying never revealed that little tit-bit of intel., eh? And you know what, Cobber?" Fingal slapped Andrew, hard, the way they do in mafia movies. "I just can't seem to shake the habit. The stuff makes me behave irrationally. VIOLENTLY! Christ, I just don't know what I might do next."

To drive the point home, Fingal lifted an iron pinch bar, and battered the DIY enthusiast's angle grinder to smithereens. "Do you understand me, Andrew?" he asked a minute later. "Am I being clear?"

At last, the Drab, Green King reacted.

"Stop it, Fingal, please. Stop it," he whimpered from the corner. "I won't call the police. I promise. I'll speak of this to no one. Please just go, Fingal. I swear to turn my music down—"

"OFF!"

"Yes, yes. Off. I'll try to be quieter."

"Not try. DO!"

"I apologise profusely, Fingal. I didn't know that my activities—"

"Your very-fucking-noisy activities."

"… were causing you so much torment. Forgive me."

The Drab, Green King then resorted to the only survival method he knew. He fell to his knees, clasped his long hands together and begged for mercy. "Please, Fingal. Please don't hurt me. I didn't know. Truly. I didn't know!"

The Drab, Green King's counter-offensive worked beautifully.

All of a sudden, Fingal the maniac felt dreadful. Realising that he'd both won and lost the battle, that Andrew had indeed been dealt a blow so "severe that his vengeance need not be feared", all the little soldiers running around his head vanished. As quickly as it had risen that morning, the pagan fire died in his soul.

No longer did he feel like a ferocious, righteous, blue warrior. He felt like an absolute knob-end, the same way he felt when, as an eight-year-old at Underbank Primary School, he'd burst wee Donald MacDonald's nose just for looking at Claire Coleman. He suddenly remembered Lanark Grammar, and all those fights and slashings and head-butts. He remembered that he hated violence, that he was a writer, not a fighter; a pacifist and a lover, of sorts, not a bully.

The hermit dropped the iron pinch bar to the cement floor and jumped at the noise.

In fact, what the fuck was he doing on the fucking continent … interacting with one of them … on their turf?! Looking at the kneeling Christian, and the debris of the machines and the money on the floor, tears welled in his gaunt eyes. *Retreat! Evacuate! Run away; run away! ESCAPE! ESCAPE!*

Thinking that which had been done could be undone, he suddenly lifted and embraced the terrified Christian. "I'm sorry, Andrew. I'm so sorry." The recluse blabbed through tears of snot. "We didn't want to do this. We had to do it. It was Just, Andrew. JUST! You must understand that. You have to. You must, please. I had to do this, man. You understand, don't you?"

"I … I think so." A thin smile infused Andrew's little face as he realised God could help. Here stood a tortured and broken man, a soul ripe for the taking. God would be pleased. God, in fact, be fucking praised! "I do." His pale, rheumy eyes widened. "I truly do. The devil has taken command of your soul. It happens all the time," he added, casually. "God is here, Fingal. It's okay, laddie."

Fingal frowned at the odd remark before another wave of grief swamped him. "I'm sorry, Andrew. I just hate leaf blowers. I fucking hate them, with every ounce of my being. I hate them. I really hate them. And then you went and bought one … and I was writing … and Fang was … Fang was." Tears began to fall, so Fingal clasped Andrew's tiny, little head in his hands and kissed him on the forehead. "Mate," Fingal squeaked. "I'm losing my mind. Really. It's happening. I'm so fucking sorry. It's not me. It's my mind, my fucking beautiful mind." The last of the pagan, fighting spirit left and, his black, sore heart became stricken with guilt. Fingal let the Drab, Green King go, turned and walked out into the pouring rain.

"Come to church!"

Fingal stopped and turned.

"Come to church. I go every Sunday. I can give you a lift." Andrew called out, faith blossoming in his soul. "We know not God's will! Do not be overcome by evil, but overcome evil with good. Romans 12:21!"

"I threaten to kill you. I smash your machines. I bully you, and … and—"

"My faith runs strong, lad." Andrew flicked his tiny chin, with its stupid chinstrap beard. "That's the whole point of it. Come to church, neighbour."

Fingal didn't want church. He wanted a hole in the ground. He wanted his black book. "I'm sorry, Andrew," he said. "I hate me, you have to understand."

Fingal walked away, taunted by failure, as well as a little Christian man hollering biblical slogans as he walked through the rain. At last, the hermit reached the waves crashing on the shore of his island, the safety of his white gravel driveway. For relief, he looked up at the forest but She was not there. Her trees were lost, slowly being consumed by a giant wall of damp, grey cloud. Even Mother had forsaken him.

Deeply embarrassed, full of self-loathing, and desperate to forget that which had just occurred, Fingal shuffled through his gate, through the little black doorway in the wall of wild garden, and out on to his former lawn, which was now full of young trees as tall as his six-foot frame, and little insects, and baby birds, and beautiful creepers and vines, some of which had turned the wood supporting the roof of verandah into lush, green pillars dripping with silver water.

Fingal did not look because he could not see. All the recluse saw was the factory, Fang, more pain, a shit sandwich, a cave, and a mug of warm, soothing goon, with a smoke or ten.

When he set foot back on the island proper, there were no crowds of cheering islanders, no politicians waiting to pin cheap medals to his chest and, as yet, no statues erected in honour of the Pathetic Man O' War. Fingal McKay wasn't a warrior, or a dickhead. He was a coward, a bully and a terrorist. He was just one of them, a man.

A stupid, blind man. Lost to darkness, Fingal didn't even realise that the little island in his mind had drifted further away from the continent.

The rope of violence was no more. That bloody rope, which had raped, beaten, and tortured 3.5 billion people over the past 14,000 years, which had bound humanity in chains, which had gassed and burned millions in custom-built, killing-factory ovens, which – still, FUCKING STILL – led smart men to design clever weapons that could kill more and more people with greater levels of Military Effectiveness – fewer men, greater yield and lethality, with enhanced precision, at greater distance; that rope; that bloody, fucking, stupid, pointless rope no longer existed for the Blind Lover, Fingal McKay.

If he hadn't been so upset, Fingal would have realised that he had won one victory that day. He may have threatened Andrew, and destroyed his leaf blower – a JUST CAUSE, if ever there was one – and he may have beaten an angle grinder to death with an iron bar (ibid.), but, in the end, he never resorted to human-on-human violence. Two machines lay dead but Fingal hadn't physically assaulted, kicked or punched Andrew. Diplomacy, all be it a coercive iteration, had triumphed over war. The rope of war, suffering and violence was no more.

It was a shame poor Fingal felt so dark. If he hadn't been so sad, he would've seen his island, his beautiful, little, mad island, drift further out into the silent, silver ocean, a place of profound beauty, divine love, and harmonious peace.

One or two ropes remained, big ones like sleep, food, ego and, biggest of all, the shitey book (and, strangest of all, a big red rope with the words Fingal McKay, architect, tattooed all over it). But Fingal was blind. He could not see the island, inch by inch, moving deeper and deeper into the sea.

Chapter Twenty-Four
The Mice Problem

Religion still held on the island. Just. Seven stones days remain sanctimonious, reserved for exploration, worship and, today, pest-control. The island's plan to solve the mice problem was finally put into action. If you recall, Fingal somehow intended to capture a five-metre python with a bag and a stick, and lob it into his mice-infested bedroom for a few days. Nature would take care of nature and, at last, the bedroom would be as quiet as Khongoryn Els. Admittedly, the plan didn't have much logic to it but no one on the island believed in logic anymore. That was such a continental way of thinking. Anyway, the hermit with the crumbling mind now firmly believed he could bend time.

"Get in my bag, Mrs Snake," Fingal said to the big python, not far from the gate named after it. "Please, I promise I won't hurt you." The serpent wasn't for obliging. Five minutes ago, Mrs Snake had been warm and safe and dry in her hollow log, then some mad, boorish ape had started banging on the roof and flinging stones down the entrance. Understandably, she was none too pleased. Her eyes burned silver, she hissed in the pouring rain, and her wide head reared four foot off the ground, revealing a muscular, ivory belly covered in dirt and dead leaves.

Two metres away, Fingal McKay danced like a court jester. In one hand, he held Col's plastic sack and, in case things got ugly, a good stick in the other. With difficulty, he ignored the rain, the mud, and the many ticks burrowing into his flesh. "Please, Mrs Snake," Fingal implored. "I just want to borrow you. Just for a little while." In reply, the snake cocked its head to strike but the hermit knew exactly what to do. Steve Irwin once told him to "never take your eyes off a snake," to "trust your intuition, your base, primordial instinct in case it—"

"Crikey!" said Fingal as Mrs Snake lunged for the third time that morning.

Time slowed, and for a moment he *was* the Crocodile Hunter, Skywalker and Neo from *The Matrix* rolled into one. Springing gracefully to the right, the big snake's head missed his hip by five centimetres. *Unreal*, he thought, *I can actually bend time.*

"Please, Mrs Snake. Get in my bag. There's plenty of nice mice to eat at the blue cottage. Yum, yum…" – again, the snake attacked, time slowed, and Fingal danced beautifully to the left … another miss, this time by a centimetre – "…yum. I'm telling you. There's heaps of furry, noisy little morsels. For FREE! After you fill your snake-stomach, I promise to bring you straight back to your log."

Mrs Snake attacked again. This time, knowing he could do the splits, Fingal leapt into the air but the snake's wide, hard head thumped straight into his bollocks. The pain, shock and realisation that he did not in fact possess supernatural powers, sent the fool crashing to the mud. At last! Its prey downed, the snake went for the ape. Within seconds Mrs Snake had wrapped herself around Fingal's hips, spitting and furiously head-butting his chest. She was strong and quick but, fortunately, had eaten a fat Wonga Pigeon that morning.

Lucky for the ape, she was just playing.

Squirming, and squealing, and, oddly, laughing, Fingal the idiot somehow managed to break free and scramble up the path toward the ochre fire trail on his backside. Mrs Snake ushered the pest all the way, magically rippling and oozing her way up the trail, hissing and striking every now and then just to be sure the intruder pissed off.

"All right, all right," said Fingal, struggling to his feet. "Settle down, Mrs Snake. I meant you no harm."

Knowing it had the ape's measure, the beautiful snake coiled up and glared at Fingal. "Very well," he said. "I shall have to find another mousetrap. Now, I must visit Mother. If you'll just let me pass."

"Temple's shut the day," the snake replied in the gravely accent of a

Glaswegian nightclub bouncer. Fingal's mouth hung open.

She, in fact, was a he.

"But I thought you were a lady snake?"

"Naw! Noo, fuck off. Temple's shut. Ye'r no' gettin' in. No' the day."

"*Mister* Snake," Fingal smiled at the great, pulsing coil, "I'm terribly sorry about the whole kidnapping attempt thing, but—"

"Temple's fuckin' closed."

"No, no, no. You don't understand. I come here every seventh stone."

"Naw, you listen, fannybaws. You try and chuck me intae a fuckin' sack, then expect tae waltz intae ma hoose?" The snake snorted a sarcastic laugh. "Sure thing, pal. Dream on."

This was impossible. Improbable! The secret path, his path, was blocked. "This is ludicrous," Fingal protested. "I am the original worshipper!"

"Away hame, ya wee fudd."

"Fudd? Do you know who I am?"

"Ye'r no' getting' in."

"But, but, *I, Fingal Explorer,* was the one who found Mother!"

"Leeches."

"What?"

"You've goat leeches, *Pal.*"

Fingal's brain jerked back to reality. *Leeches? What? LEECHES!?*

He raised one hand to his eyes and, to his horror, watched a black thing inching across the back of it. Slick and rubbery the creature had no feet, legs or eyes to speak of, and it moved like a tiny elephant's trunk searching for its body.

"That *is* a leech! Ewwwwww!"

"Aye. Noo fuck off."

"IT IS A LEECH!" Fingal then jumped around a lot, crying "get it off me! get it off me!", shaking his hands like a ponce being attacked by a bee. He then tried to wipe the leech off on his sleeve but it stuck fast. In fact, the only way to get the hungry, blood-sucking Hirudidae off was to man up, steady the nerves and flick it off like a very troublesome booger.

"There's another wan oan yer neck," the snake added.

"Get it off me!" A similar process ensued. "Get if off me!"

"An' the back of yer leg."

And repeat.

"An' yer tackety bits."

Fingal looked down and counted five more leeches inching across his boots. His wild, panicked eyes pleaded with the snake.

"Run," it advised.

Balls aching, under severe attack from ticks and leeches, and the mice-problem worse than ever, for once Fingal actually listened. He ran away, crying all the way back to the safety of the blue cottage. Actually, run is too strong a word. After months of sitting at a desk the best his once-strong legs could manage was a speedy, painful hobble, interrupted by several falls on the wet, greasy fire-trail.

The more he slipped and hobbled the more a horrible revelation revealed itself. It wasn't that he was going mad, or that his flesh and muscles and sanity were being eaten away. The island had a major spiritual problem. Its sole religion – a strangler fig called Mother that somehow guided Fingal's life in the woods – was beginning to unravel. The Law of Balance had issues. Aye, all this pain, torture and suffering might one day produce an *ENOS Ver. 3.0* (in the year 2076 … perhaps), but the strain of living in an increasingly bitter rainforest was starting to get to the hermit. Really, what pleasure lay in being slowly drowned by rain, fighting off an attack by a giant python, getting eaten alive by ticks and leeches, being tortured by mice and Christians, and having kookaburras constantly laughing at him?

"Moody bitch," the explorer complained of the Mother-Tree while storming through the dripping weeds, saplings and vines on the former lawn (a young forest would be a more appropriate term). "Won't let me into the temple, eh? ME! Fingal-bloody-McKay!? Well, get it right up ye, *Mother.*"

Once inside the dark, gloomy cottage, Fingal stomped over to his cluttered desk and, in the posh English voice of Sir Randolph Hazelrigg, the baddy from his novel, shouted "goon, and fags, driver; and be bally well quick about it!"

Back in the factory, at least things felt normal. Since the failed war, the island had enjoyed a good six days of industry. Fang's Stland approach – which involved taking the novel to pieces, and working individually on each of the twenty-seven stories – was working beautifully. The book, as the horrible soul-sucking hobby was now simply known, like the plants outside, just kept on growing and growing and growing. Fang was delighted with all this mad progress.

The work was like a tonic and Fingal soon forgot about the ticks and the leeches currently chowing down on Scottish beef marinated in goon. A mug of mulled goon, from a big bowl, heated in the microwave (a superb Fang innovation), also helped calm the nerves, as did four, chain-smoked rollies.

At last, work on the third draft of the book could begin.

"Burn your good trees, brave island brothers," Fingal said while filling a second mug of goon, donkey-rooting a fifth smoke, and reaching for his writing equipment with his clawhand. "Mother's mood grows more fickle every stone," he hissed like the python. "Religion has turned sour across our land."

***

That was one of weirder days in the jungle. When, for example, Fingal moved outside to write, the moment he slumped into the lazy-boy something small and sharp jabbed into his sore back. "What continental deception is this?" he said on retrieving a plastic bag containing a postcard, a letter, and, infuriatingly, a Jesus Pamphlet.

The postcard was bizarre. On the front was a photograph, taken in the late 1980s, of four topless women with red lipstick, gold, hooped earrings, and huge, frizzy hairstyles. Each one wore a different coloured luminous G-string – pink, orange, lime-green and yellow. The two blondes, with small tits, were sipping on ridiculous cocktails while the two buxom brunettes were playing beach volleyball on a beach somewhere in in New Caledonia, apparently.

It came from Decent Old Col and his dead wife, and read:

Dear Fergus,

Me and Mary are having a lovely time on the cruise. Real film star treatment. Never seen so much food in all me life! It never stops, that and the music and the free grog. But I don't like the champagne. Too rich, and always comes back on me. Well, mate, we'd better get down to the pool. New Caledonia isn't very nice, by the way. Not like in the pictures. Haven't seen any nudey women playing volleyball yet. Hope Henry found his dinner, and the forest is looking after you. See you blokes next week!
All the best,

Col and Mary Jarvis.

"That man gets more decent by the day," said Fingal, genuinely touched by the gesture. Somewhere, out there on the ocean, Decent Old Col had been tottering around the bowels of an enormous cruise ship stuffed with food, grog and people, marvelling at every arcane detail, introducing confused people to his invisible wife until, at one point, he'd thought, "I really must send my neighbour a postcard of some women's tits."

"Bloody legend," said Fingal, looking up to the saucer where the king parrots had fed that morning. He still hadn't actually seen Henry or any of his pals. They ate early, or swooped in when he was napping at the desk or working on the Mad Posters that now covered the windows of the cottage/factory. Seed husks, feathers and little pile of birdshit were the only evidence the king parrots had visited. "But Henry keeps flying away, Col," said Fingal with some sadness. Maybe the birds just sensed a big, hairy ogre inside the blue cave, a source of dark matter?

The second item in the plastic bag made Fingal angry and sad at the same time. White and immaculate – virginal, you might say – the envelope had no stamp or address, just the words *Mr F. McKay, Esquire*, written in a neat but flowery script. It was from Andrew, and read:

Dear Fingal,

This crude postcard from Col arrived in my mailbox. At first, I could not figure out how such vulgar, naked imagery had come to me. However, God – though you have made your feelings on Him quite clear – does indeed move in the most mysterious of ways. Clearly, the postcard was a sign from God, a message telling me to reflect and, once more, reach out. As you do not appear to have a mailbox, Merv the postie delivered it to me.

Since your breakdown a week ago, I have fasted and prayed. At last, Praise Him, God showed me the error of my ways. Fingal, I am truly sorry for all the noise. I didn't realise that me going about my daily business caused you so much pain, especially when trying to overcome your "problem" with drugs. Although I most certainly did not appreciate your violent outburst, I now know that I was at fault, not you.

Jesus taught the higher love, Fingal. He did so because it was something for meek humans to aspire to. Please understand that all I have ever done is try to help you, to make you feel welcome, and to love you, as Jesus did. This, I now realise, was also wrong. Ugly scenes may have ensued but at least I'm now aware that you fiercely value your peace and privacy. I will now limit my music, and the use of my power tools.

If you are, I'm willing to let this matter rest. It's not good for neighbours to fight. Forgive me, but a familiar passage gives me hope and strength: "*Thou shalt love thy neighbour as thyself. There is none other commandment greater than these*" (Mark 12:31). Know this, neighbour: I forgive you, I love you, and remember that, should you ever need to talk, my door is always open.

The devil comes to us all at some point, but so does the
Lord, if you open your heart (see enclosed pamphlet). We
all have bad days, mate. We're only human.
God be with you,
Andrew McKenzie, Esq. (Elder, Robina Pentecostal
Church)

P.S. You'll find most of the money you offered me in the
envelope. It totals $485 dollars. As you advised, I bought
a broom.

At first, Fingal didn't know what to make of Andrew's letter. It was as if
the little Christian was firing out arrows with ropes attached to them from
John Donne's continent. As each one landed on Fingal's island, strange,
violent emotions stirred – anger that Andrew *still* insisted on invading his
private property even after he had been physically abused (how else had the
plastic bag got there?); shame, at the memory of smashing his neighbour's
leaf blower off a cement floor; relief, that someone still cared about him;
doubt, that The Experiment, the book, Mother and, ergo, his mind and
island were collapsing in upon themselves; and, worst of all, guilt. Guilt
that he, a bloody pacifist, had brutally abused – tortured would be a better
word – a smaller, older man who was just trying to be a good neighbour, all
be it a noisy, preachy and intrusive one.

A tear, of what origin he couldn't be sure, rolled down Fingal's hollow
cheek as he removed the $485 – which had been ironed – and inspected the
third item in the plastic bag, the Jesus Pamphlet Andrew had enclosed. It
was entitled *Drug and Alcohol Prayers. Every Wednesday, 7 p.m. with Pastor
Jimmy Davidson.* This too had a photograph on the front, of the pastor, a
young, rough-as-guts looking bloke wearing a cassock, dog collar, tattoos
and a friendly grin – a former junkie that had found God if ever Fingal had
seen one.

"It's all lies," the hermit snapped, imagining the prospect of sitting in
a room full of other loser nutjobs while some former smackhead talked to

them about the "Jesus", the "truth", the "light", and the moment "he had found God" (like, actually found him, or her, or whatever; like, under a stone or something?). The image of the pastor, King of Failures, repulsed him. "All lies. Just dreams and fucking images."

At last, the determination of men who choose to live on islands returned. The postcard, letter and pamphlet, the hermit realised, were but human, continental devices, kind on the surface but infused with tricks and ruses. They had nothing to do with who he was, why he was here, and, most importantly, what purpose his life currently held – finish that fucking book, force a way back into the temple and, armed with Col's lovely white rope, strike for the world-famous Cathedral Falls.

"Remember the mission, mate," he said. "The Experiment must proceed."

That's it, Cob. Keep it simple – eyes-on-the-fuckin'-prize, MATE.

Fingal stared through the rain at Andrew's drab, green cottage, took a deep, rattling breath and threw the letter, money and Jesus Pamphlet off the verandah, out into the mud and rain. He was surprised how much it hurt, and a little more of the human died within. "So be it," he said grimly.

He moved to the forest to cut bonds, not make them.

Fool.

Again, She came at him.

Pain, this time. He needed more pain.

Mother instructed one of her tiny, translucent ticks to make its move. The parasite had spent the last three hours climbing up a damp, white rock face studded with flat, black trees – Fingal's leg – toward a source of great heat – Fingal's testicles – which it now reached. Knowing *its* purpose in life the tick then sunk its barbed cheliceral digit into Fingal's scrotum and began hacking, eating and burrowing into his balls.

"Mother fucker!!" Fingal rocketed to his feet, not caring that he scattered five-dozen empty, dusty beer bottles full of cigarette-butts. In the madness of the day, he'd entirely forgotten that Mother Super-Bitch was eating him, bit by bit, and cell by cell.

A quick inspection of head and body and Fingal discovered sixteen tiny tick bites he'd picked up while trying to capture Mr Snake. Cursing like a Dundee shipyard worker, the recluse dashed inside to fetch the island's rudimentary surgical equipment – more goon, more tobacco and a Swiss army knife. The Chief Surgeon then tore his clothes and boots off, returned to his dilapidated throne, and got to work, furious at the distraction from the book.

He started with the scrotal ticks, scraping the blade across his sack until it flicked the parasite's abdomen. Suitably located, he then dug the tick from his balls with the tip of the knife. Then he moved onto the *gouch*, working by feel, not caring about the blood soaking the lazy-boy. Two more ticks had been excavated when Fingal realised there was something terribly wrong with his ankles. Four, small patches of tar had colonised the outside of each ankle, where the blue veins ran closest to the blue skin.

"Is that tar?" he asked.

"They're mair leeches, ya fuckin' dick."

"*More* ravenous beasts devour me!?!"

"Aye."

Four, big, black leeches were gorging on his meek goon-blood. Hidden by his socks until now, the parasites had grown to ten times their initial size. "You slag, Mother!" said the hermit, picking of one fat, bloated leech with his long, dirty fingernails and flicking it off the verandah. "Why the hell didn't I feel you bite?" he asked while removing another.

If the experimentalist hadn't executed the internet, it would have told him "*why, it's because the leech smears a magical, numbing saliva on its victim before it scissors into your flesh.*"

"And," he asked when all the leeches were gone, when four streams of blood ran freely down his ankles, "why am I bleeding so much?"

"*Because, dear ape,*" the wise computer would've told Fingal, "*of the ingenious anti-coagulant in leech saliva which causes the victim's blood to flow freely for anything from six to twelve hours (longer if you include the later bleeding from scratching the incredibly itchy wounds).*"

"I don't fucking get this," the hermit complained to an overgrown grevillea in the garden. "Why is Mother eating me?"

The God of the forest answered with a wet, distant shriek of a cockatoo.

Then the indomitable Mr Fang interjected.

"You know pain good fo' book," the boss said from inside Fingal's head. "Brudd good. Brudd make good wo'ds."

"Is blood good, Mr Fang? Does agony produce ecstasy?"

"Arways."

The labourer pointed to his two bloody socks. "Is the book worth this?"

"Of co' it is!"

"Forgive me, Mr Fang, but what does the book have to do with The Experiment? With running away from humanity?" Fingal wrung his thin hands. "Shouldn't I be happy by now?"

"You ah happee. You arone, no?"

"Yes, but—"

"So, shut up! And lite book."

"But—"

Fang screamed "LITE … FUCKING … BOOK!"

"But I want to go—"

"Pain good!"

"…home."

"NEVER!"

"Yes, Mr Fang."

"Now, lemove that tick flom back of knee."

"Right away, Mr Fang."

"And reech flom side of neck."

"Of course, Mr Fang."

"Then—"

"Yes?" Blood dripped onto the wet floorboards. "Then can I go home?"

Fang screamed so loud Fingal thought his head might explode. "THEN YOU LITE FUCKING BOOK!"

"Sorry, Mr Fang."

"SHUT UP! WORK!! THAT ALL YOU HUMAN DO! THAT ALL YOU GOOD FOR! WORK! WORK! WORK!"

"Yes, Mr Fang. Three bags full, Mr Fang."

Work would begin, of course, but in time. Ticks and surgery just – just – outranked labour, fame, and a blue highland castle where The One slept forever in the tallest tower. A bit of multi-tasking (surgery while thinking about the 17th strand story to be written by hand) would keep Fang at bay. Fingal got on with the grim task of removing insects from his skinny body. He sat on his damp throne for an hour or two, digging ticks out, drinking and smoking, mumbling dialogue from the novel, staring at Decent Old Col's lovely white rope, and dreaming of the deep forest and the world-famous Cathedral Falls, wanting more and more pain, beauty, insects, voices, and more torment.

All of which frustrated Mother immensely. The stupid ape didn't need anything. She was right here, literally on his doorstep! Yet, he wouldn't stop. The human just kept going; kept on evolving. Still, the stupid-ape didn't get it. Still, he hid behind that SHITE book in that SHITE factory, not understanding that greed, ego and work were the biggest ropes of all! Entirely continental in nature, they throttled and choked the poor bugger every stone of every bloody week, every time he put that stupid pen in his wrecked clawhand and began to write.

Still her son was blind.

Mother had sent the ticks and the leeches not because She was a cruel, bitter deity. She'd sent the creatures as further reminders to STOP, to LOOK AT ME!, to SEE ME! But, still, the ape remained blind to the simple truth. To be happy and content in life is quite simple: abandon all desires. Want for nothing. Stop working. Stop staring at those infernal phones! Leave your Factories and mortgages, turn off your televisions, turn down your music, and go outside. Stare at a tree – any tree – and you will see truth; you will drown in wild, natural philosophy, peace and beauty. You will find love, true love.

It saddened Her that hardly any of them looked at Her trees anymore. Most were lost causes, but This One was that little bit different. She would've given up altogether had he not known about, and sought with such determination, the higher love. The poor sod had just got lost along the way, blinded by that stupid fucking Book.

She would not give up, though. A strangler fig never did.

And a strangler fig never lost.

She would guide him. She would let Her blind son see.

***

"Bloody hell," said Fingal, looking up from his grim surgery to see a brilliant streak of colour whizzing straight toward the cottage through the silver raindrops. The bird had to crash into the French windows but, suddenly, gracefully, it flared its wings and came to a vertical, hovering stop. The king parrot hovered like an angel, then, comically, awkwardly, crash-landed onto the verandah, next to where the saucer of Decent Old Col's parrot seed was kept (to keep it dry). A rare smile erupted from behind Fingal's huge, damp beard. "G'day, Henry," he said. "You took your bloody time."

In stature, Henry the king parrot was roughly the size of a pigeon but with bright, tangerine feathers, emerald wings and two stunning eyes – one on either side of his oblong head. They reminded Fingal of a solar eclipse – of black suns rimmed with yellow halos. Compared to dear, sweet Jackie – a quiet, deep-thinking bird that preferred to sing alone – Henry was an absolute clown. He squawked, hopped, skipped, waddled and reeled as if drunk toward the seed, his oblong head bobbing comically from side to side. He then fussed around the seed until he found a dried kernel of corn, which he lifted with one claw and nibbled way on it, squeaking and chirping and softly squawking as he ate, looking up in sheer panic every two seconds at the smiling hairy-human-chair-thing ten foot away.

"He is absolutely gorgeous," Fingal said, fighting hard to extinguish a pilot light of love suddenly flaring on his island. It was too soon to love another bird. Love would distract him from the book, from Scotland. Henry also belonged to another man, to a lovely, Decent Old Man Called Col, who was currently enjoying a luxury cruise around New Caledonia with his invisible wife.

266

Parrot and ape stared at each other then, as if reading Fingal's thoughts, Henry shrieked and took off, whizzing past Fingal's head and vanishing into the forest.

The hermit flicked his beard and returned to surgery, looking up every few seconds and searching the bushes for young Henry. Mother was pleased with this progress. Looking for parrots, staring at white ropes and digging ticks out his body with a blunt knife was better than working on that mad, stupid book.

***

The last tick died an hour or so later. Stiff, sore and bleeding, Fingal hobbled to the verandah railing to inspect the drumming rain and the young forest encroaching on his Writing Factory. It was a beautiful, wondrous sight. Rivers of tall, stiff grasses meandered between large bushes and fat clumps of ferns. The weeds had turned into saplings which, in the rain, had turned into small, skinny trees. Some were already covered in creepers intent on hitching a free ride, all the way to the top. The hermit counted twenty-seven green pillars on the lawn. More vines spiralled around the verandah posts and out along the gutters. They were living curtains dripping with cool, silver rainwater.

"Hey, 277."

"No, please."

"Yes."

"NO!"

"It time."

It was as if Fingal was tethered to each world by an elastic rope. He hobbled toward the desk, then back to the verandah. Back and forth he tottered until the big ropes, Fang's ropes of greed, stupidity, ignorance, blindness and fear (at failing for a third time) tugged him harder toward the factory.

Fang always bloody won.

Fingal McKay knew he was drowning, slipping under and into a green sea of words, work and madness. Hunger compounded his myopia. Having not eaten for the past two stones, the labourer's stomach emitted a low, protracted growl. Tired, damp and bleeding, he decided against a sandwich – mainly because there was no more jam left in the cottage. In fact, food supplies were critically low. He hadn't gone to Gail's shop for weeks now, using the rain as an excuse.

The lack of food didn't bother him. Deep down, Fingal knew that The Experiment was drawing to an end. There was enough food for what he intended to do.

Naked, bleeding and sobbing, the writer shuffled toward Henry's bag of seed. His stomach growled so he grabbed a handful of seed, brought up to his mouth and started eating it, muttering, as he ate, some madness about a man called Fang, a book and some waterfalls named after a cathedral.

Chapter Twenty-Five
Drowning

It had been raining in Binjari national park for thirty-nine stones straight. The rain was different each day. Sometimes it pelted down in violent bursts, or lashed against the tin roof in great, squally sheets. On other days, it fell in a mist so fine it was hard to tell if it was raining at all. Today, the rain fell from the low, black clouds in stair-rods – heavy and straight down.

Twenty-three stones had passed since Fingal McKay had last spoken to a real human being (Andrew, and terrorising a Christian while executing his gardening equipment could hardly be classified as "speaking"). He had been working on the book for twenty-two hours per stone for the past twenty-one stones, somehow getting by on dwindling supplies of tinned beans, frozen bread, and parrot food, all of which were now rationed. Totally blind, he had stopped looking outside. Totally exhausted, he had even stopped walking outside. Still angry about the ticks and the leeches, he hadn't even bothered to go and see the Mother-Tree, for three whole weeks. Nothing outside the factory mattered now, not the rain, or the neighbours, or the cruel God in the forest.

The Scotsman didn't give a toss. Why? Because he was a genius and, as such, certain that agony would produce ecstasy. At last, at fucking long last, the book was *finally* coming together. While Mr Fang might be a slave-driving-Thai-bastard, he was also an industrial guru that knew how to eek every last atom of effort out his knackered workforce. "See! See! I to'd you, razeee Scotman," the irate Asian voice never failed to remind Fingal, "stland app'oach wo-king … unrike you! We awmost finish. Fasta! Ha'da! Bigga! Madda! WO'K!"

To be fair, the Strand Approach was pure genius. As you know, the trouble with the previous drafts of the book was its "jerkiness". Everything jumped – plot, history, the twenty-seven characters' stories, et cetera. This, Mr Fang brilliantly reasoned, was because his retarded workforce had so far worked on the novel as a whole, page by page, or scene by scene, if you prefer. They'd write a bit of Hazelrigg, then work on Lady Phoebe's "bit" and then Heracles before returning to Hazelrigg only to totally forget what the man and his story was all about.

That was why the first two drafts of *The Epic Novel of Sport* jerked. The factory workers hadn't been able to stay focused on one character. Therefore, weeks ago now, just before war, Fang had ordered that the book be ripped apart. Each character's story – or strand, or "stland" – was to be re-written from start to finish. Individually. By hand. Work, in other words, on twenty-seven stories instead of one big one … then weave the strands back together again into a magnificent, award-winning tapestry.

Genius.

And by Jove, it worked! Over the past weeks, Fingal's mighty pen sped across page after page, conquering the vast, blank, white tundra of paper with ease. Within the cold, damp walls of the oppressive, twenty-six-storey Victorian sweatshop inside his mind – which was, in fact, now real – the labourer's hammered out thousands and thousands of crisp, sharp, words by the day. 277, for example, had carved out the letters a, g and o, from the word agon! He was almost there. Draft three was almost finished.

Some of the strands, such as those of the main 'A' characters, were eighty and ninety pages long, while the lesser character's stories numbered around forty or fifty. Size didn't matter, however. Liberated from the idea of writing one, big, confusing story, the workforce adored the newer, simpler process.

Now, every character's history, personality and narrative began to flow effortlessly. After twenty-one consecutive shifts at the factory, twenty-one of the twenty-seven strands were complete. "Wo'ds frow rike brud flom reetal reech bite," as Mr Fang often said of the remarkable output of words.

Mr Fang also came up with many other innovations, all of which saved precious seconds in the factory. Moving from the desk to fetch goon or rollies, for example, not only wasted minutes but interrupted thought processes. So the boss ordered 277 to bring the fags and goon from the dusty kitchen over to his ashen, cluttered desk.

Coffee was totally banned because it took too long to brew, and what little water he drank was abolished for similar reasons: fucking time. From now on, Fang said, water was to be absorbed through osmosis.

Deep sleep in the mouse-infested bedroom was banned, however Churchill-style naps at the desk were permitted.

It took twenty-one steps for the labourer to walk to the bathroom to pee so the boss instructed Fingal – via a lot of screaming – to pee off the edge of the verandah instead.

And, lastly, getting up to clear his throat of baccy-grot and spit in the dirty kitchen sink was forbidden. Thus, 277 was ordered to spit into a vile, red bucket the boss placed next to his desk. This quickly filled with blobs of turgid phlegm. A vile measurement of sorts but firm proof that Mr Fang's ingenious, new time-saving systems worked.

"Ha! Rook at you!" the Thai prick always taunted Fingal when he staggered, outside, sometimes into a cloud of parrots he hadn't even noticed were there, "you no' pee rike monkeee. You pee rike dawg!"

These industrial innovations exacted a terrible physical cost, not that 277 noticed or cared anymore. His posture had collapsed and, so, when he did scurry outside to go pee-pee it was in the style of a cave-troll. His awful diet of goon, fags, frozen bread and bird-seed (tinned beans had just run out) saw twenty kilograms of weight drip from his wet bones. Sometimes, when Mr Fang was out crucifying puppy dogs, 277 touched his face, amazed at how prominent his cheekbones now felt. Due to the all the shit wine, his teeth had turned red. He had lost three teeth, one molar, one pre-molar and one canine tooth. Twitchy eye, caused by an over-stimulation of the nerves, had spread to both eyes, as well as, oddly, his left testicle, foot and hand. 277's clawhand, the mainstay of the writing industry, was now locked in permanent rictus. His hair and beard, which now fell onto his chest, had turned grey and silver. A rattling cough got into his sore, fragile lungs and never left. He probably had dry rot, or lung cancer, or both.

Didn't matter. It wasn't like 277 could light a fire and dry out as a normal person would. The islanders had burned all the good wood from the Nissen hut months ago.

Nothing mattered. "Onree wo'ds matta. Ruvree, ruvree wo'ds."

The mental cost was far greater. As anyone that has ventured deep into the creative cave will tell you, the mind becomes a lunatic asylum. Focus is impossible as hundreds of ideas compete for attention at the same time. To quote the Buddha, the mind becomes "like a runaway coach, and the driver never stops whipping the horses". Except 277 had thousands of coaches. Hundreds of old, dusty ones came from drafts one or two, and thousands of sparkling, new ones were born all the time while handwriting draft three.

The line between reality and fantasy disappeared. Sometimes, when Fingal looked at his writing claw for too long it turned into a machine, complete with pumps, pullies, pistons, wires and metal "bones". On other occasions, 277, or Fingal, or Fang, whoever was in charge, wasn't sure if The Experiment was real or some hideous nightmare he couldn't wake up from. Most of the time, Fingal had no idea where he really was – in a dark factory? Stranded on an island? In Australia? On planet Earth?

There was one bonus relating to the collapse of reality, however. Fingal developed the ability to visit home, to actually travel to Scotland. Very late at night, when Mr Fang was sreeping (rucky sod), 277 paced the floorboards until he felt faint and his vision failed. Then, amazingly, he didn't reel, hobble and stagger in a squalid cottage taken hostage by the rain, but strode across the cool, soft moss of a Scottish mountain, or on the cobbled streets of Edinburgh, or above the vast, red gravel driveway out the front of Sir Randolph Hazelrigg's stunning, gothic castle. One or two characters from the novel usually walked by his side, sharing a titbit of gossip, or a gin, or a pipe, Hazelrigg always guffawing at Fingal when he sprang to a Mad Poster to scribble more tiny words in the gaps between other tiny words. A madman's wallpaper, the cuneiform Posters now covered *every* wall of the kitchen, dining and living rooms of the blue cottage.

***

The loneliness was the worst, however. When Fingal McKay swore to prove John Donne was wrong, eons ago now, he knew it would come. Back then, he coveted solitude but now that it was here, now that it bred within him, loneliness had turned his island into a bleak, joyless wasteland totally and utterly dominated by industrial labour.

Sometimes the bent, emaciated hermit thought about Penny from the pink house, and what she might make of his current life choice? Perhaps she did impressions of him at night, and that was why her kids laughed so much? Maybe she talked about "the freak" next door at lively, al fresco dinner parties? Or, most likely, maybe the beautiful woman never thought about Fingal at all, which hurt the most.

Invisibility, Fingal soon came to realise, was overrated.

For the most part the pink house lay dark and still. The three little girls no longer played fashion shows indoors or splashed in puddles in the garden. They must've been staying at their father's place – Jonah, Jebediah, or whatever he was called. Occasionally, some random Binjarian mate stopped in to feed Pippa, but even Satan's Bitch had stopped barking as much. Heavily pregnant, Pippa sheltered underneath Penny's verandah, whimpering softly at the rain and the madness to come. Once or twice a week, however, a light did spring on in the cottage next door and Fingal could smell sweet, sweet marijuana and hear voices mumbling through the rain – an Aussie bloke pushing words through his nose, and a beautiful woman laughing.

Sadly, beautifully, Penny from the pink house had found herself a new man.

It hurt so bad.

The rain, heavier each day – combined with Fingal's violent "breakdown", which seemed so long ago, if, indeed, it ever happened – had even forced Andrew McKenzie, esquire's army of noise into retreat. No longer did the chirpy little Christian work on his crapped out old Bedford van, play awful fifties music, or torment Fingal with ABC News-for-the-deaf. The little man from the drab, green house rarely used power tools and, sadly, Fingal remembered thinking at the time, had even stopped his infernal, neighbourly pop-rounds.

Maybe Andrew was waiting for Fingal to reply to his kind letter?

Fat chance – all words on the island belonged to Mr Fang.

The hermit only saw Andrew twice during those wet, industrial weeks. Late at night, he saw a little face floating in the little turret, two little eyes peering at the dark man in his dark, damp throne. The two men stared and stared at one another but never waved. Metres separated the neighbours but they might as well have been looking at each other through telescopes on different planets.

Fingal also had no idea where Decent Old Col and his invisible wife had got to. They should've been back weeks ago, but Col's brown cottage also sat dark, empty and dripping wet. Perhaps Col and Mary had been shipwrecked on a real desert island?

Fingal hoped so.

For company the hermit took to reading Decent Old Col's nudey postcard out loud, the rarely used talking muscles in his hollow cheeks quickly tiring from the effort. He never looked at the four, hot, oiled topless women with their frizzy hair, suntans and luminous g-bangers, for that got him hard, and Fang fucking hated that.

Sometimes Fingal pretended he was on the luxury cruise with his friend Col, strolling arm in arm around the buffet, the two men stuffing their faces with steak, vegetables, and ice-cream, all washed down by a robust, 2010 Penfolds Grange. Sometimes, Fingal's vision would fade and flicker, and he could actually feel the human food in his mouth, taste the delicious wine.

These visions never lasted long, however.

Mr Fang, who now lived in the spare bedroom of the blue cottage, always charged out to grab Fingal by his dirty ear and drag him back to the ghastly desk in the ghastly Writing Factory. As further punishment, Mr Fang totally banned all non-related Book-thoughts, as well as all religion across the island. In political parlance, the island had become a religious dictatorship devoted to one god: work.

The latter prohibition suited Fingal just fine. He couldn't be bothered going out outside anymore. His love for Mother was passing. There was nothing more to learn or love about pouring rain, ticks, leeches and an angry snake that – now – spoke like a Glaswegian nightclub bouncer? Besides, Fingal could barely walk. His once strong legs felt weak, the muscles like wobbly packets of stringy ropes. Sitting at a desk for twenty-one stones straight, seeing nothing but goddamned, **FUCKING** words, will do that to an ape's legs.

***

Sometimes, above the water, great explosions of colour, living fireworks in the green, grey sky, distracted him.

He may have been intent on ignoring Her, but Mother would not let him go. She kept coming at the blind, starving fool, creeping closer and closer and closer to the blue cottage, and the rotting, dying man within. She kept trying to remind him of the real beauty in life.

Every grey dawn, for example, She sent new emissaries, turning his squalid verandah into an aviary for a time. Not that he knew why – loyalty to some Old Man, he supposed – but Fingal still absentmindedly laid out breakfast for the birds. Henry was the first to arrive, gobbling down as much seed as quickly as he could. Speed mattered because a minute later another king parrot descended to feast. A great deal of shrieking, flapping, and bickering then ensued, the cue for a third, fourth and fifth bird to appear and launch an attack on the food. Galahs, rainbow coloured lorikeets, a squadron of crimson rosellas – red, lilac and black birds with bitter tempers – then joined the melee, as well as a scattering of cheeky mynah birds. At the height of the feeding frenzy, thirty or so birds screeched, shat, fought and ate on the verandah.

But, still the blind man didn't look up from his evil labour. All he saw were smudges of colour at the periphery of his vision. All he heard were dull, faint screams, high above the surface of the water.

Inside the cottage, fifty or sixty mice had chewed through the bedroom door, escaped, and quickly established sovereignty over the cottage. The tired ape was no threat to them at all, so they moved around freely, shitting all over the floorboards, the kitchen work surfaces and, fittingly, all over the completed strands of the book. If Fingal dosed off at his desk they scurried across his damp, bare feet, and when he ate – bread or seed – they quarrelled like addicts over the pittance that fell from above.

He did not care, or see, or feel.

She sent more interlocutors.

In the afternoons, seven big, mean, rust-coloured hornets worked outside the French windows, tirelessly ferrying mud back and forth all day long, building large, intricate brown cocoons against the glass. Once completed, the hornets then buzzed around the verandah, stabbing ants, beetles and spiders, which were then crammed in the cocoon. After all this labour, a single larva was gently laid inside, and the cosy hamper sealed over.

Of course, the drowning hermit missed this crucial sign. The seasons were changing, and the rain would soon break.

At night, possums with mangy auburn coats corkscrewed tails and huge, pale eyes came mooching around the birdseed, sniffing everything with their long, pink noses, peering at the crooked man trapped behind the glass, thanking Mother they'd been born a marsupial and not a great ape.

But, again, Fingal rarely heard a peep or looked up from his desk or lazy-boy, and if he did it was to ponder yet another demented, brilliant strand of the book. All he could see were words. They flapped around outside the windows. They dripped from the clouds, bushes and silver-green curtains of creepers. They scurried around the floor, dozens of them at a time, some scurrying up his skinny legs, up and over his ladder of a ribcage, and into his big, hairy ear, into his mind. This tickled a fair bit until, like a kid with water in its ears, he'd thump the mice out, only for them to scramble up his leg again!

It started to rain under the ocean. The rain started to creep into his eyes, and his vision became damp and clouded; dreamlike. He knew he was drowning, sinking deeper and deeper and deeper and deeper into the ocean of words, and not giving a mouse's cock about it. Life, for him, was no longer about the island, The Experiment or Mother. Only the Writing Factory, Fang, and the third and final draft of the book mattered. Well aware that his mind and body were totally fucked, all the Fingal-277 knew was that he had to work harder, and harder, and harder, even if it destroyed him; even if it killed him.

Why, you may ask?

Because he had to. Because he breathed the same air as Sisyphus, George Mallory, and every other mortal ape that had walked the planet since Mitochondrial Eve. He had to finish The Fucking Book "because it was there", because the endless labour of rolling the rock up and down the hill every day somehow set him free; because it allowed him to hide in the darkness, to ignore life, and the world outside; because, he told himself, there was *meaning* to be found in the pain and squalor of factory work.

Although he would never admit it, for to do so would be to accept the absolute failure of all he had achieved in the forest, Fingal kept slaving away at the pointless, thankless hobby because he was only human. Finishing the book no longer meant writing a bestseller, owning a real Scottish castle with a paddock full of real haggis, or unequivocally proving to The One that *she* had missed out. It meant finishing a job he had started, however long ago. That was all that mattered now – getting to the top of the proverbial mountain, no matter what the cost.

A strong man, he could not stop.

A brave man, he would rather die than fail.

***

What a lot of utter, human shit.

She, and she alone, knew the real reason why Fingal laboured so hard, why he kept on going with a project doomed to fail?

Like most humans, Fingal McKay wasn't scared of the failure, pain or darkness.

Her son was scared of the light.

Chapter Twenty-Six
The End

It had been raining in Binjari for forty-nine stones straight. During this time, the sun hadn't appeared once and, as many Binjari locals commented, they "might not bloody well ever see the bastard again". Today was no different. Rain drummed off blue cottage's tin roof, battered off the huge plants in wild garden, and thumped into the sodden ground. Hard as it was to believe, the rain was getting heavier.

A king without a crown, Fingal McKay, mountaineer, author and merchant and master of fine pain, sat slumped in his lazy-boy – a dais attended by a court of hundreds of dirty beer and wine bottles. His great, shaggy head lay on his skeletal chest, and one hand – his bad writing hand – was frozen in a writing claw. The only signs of life were the wrinkled crow's feet around his twitching, bloodshot eyes, which alluded to a smile beneath his massive silver and black beard.

"Finished," the near dead labourer whispered. "*The* bloody end."

"Oh, rearree?"

"Yes, fucking rearree. Get stuffed, Mr Fang."

All food was finished. The book was finished. The man was finished.

That morning or night, 277 couldn't be sure, he had finished handwriting the thirty-nine-page story of Beau "The Hammer" Faloon, a washed-up darts player from Kirkcaldy, Fife, one of the "C" characters in *The Most Epic Novel of Sport* ever written. Beau's ripper yarn – a cheeky rollicking, rags to riches to rags to riches story – was the last of the twenty-seven "strands" (or stlands) that now constituted the third version of the book. This story flowed beautifully, just like the other twenty-six. Indeed, all might be considered as short stories, novellas, or, at a stretch, books in their own right.

Thirty-three stones had passed since Fingal had abused Andrew, the last time he had "interacted" with another human being. Human food ran out two days ago, and the factory workers now survived on strict rations of parrot seed, goon and fags, all of which were running perilously low. None of this mattered. Often handwriting for twenty hours straight, the book was finally completed.

"Hey! Hey, you! Ha-rroooooow!?" Fang persisted.

"Get fucked, Fang."

"But you no' finished!"

"Yes, I fucking am!" groaned Fingal, trying to revel in the satisfaction of mastering a very difficult hobby and surviving to tell the tale.

Bar the rain, the real world out there lay quiet, still and peaceful. Having drunk their fill, the horrible water trucks no longer swooshed and growled past the front of the factory. Henry the parrot's saucer lay empty, and not a peep sallied forth from the neighbours on either side of the blue cottage. It was so, so quiet, the quietest it had ever been in the jungle. 277 closed his eyes, fearing but not caring that if he did sleep he might never open them again, such was the toll draft three had exacted.

A squeak came from the front gate and with extreme effort one of Fingal's purple eyelids fluttered open. His black, twitching eye watched a large, bright, yellow plastic-bag-thing drifting through the young forest that used to be his lawn. A second eyelid peeled back upon realising the plastic-bag-thing now shaking itself off on the verandah was in fact a human, a very little man, a little Christian man trying but failing to conceal his worry over the dismal verandah and the broken man slumped in the lazy-boy. However, having learned the hard way about poking his nose into Fingal's affairs, Andrew McKenzie, Esquire, held his little tongue, steeled his formidable resolve, and approached the outskirts of Bottle City to deliver the bad news.

"Good morning, Fingal," he said politely.

"Harrow." 277 offered the rare continental visitor a wide, goon-stained smile. "Take a pew, King An-drew."

"Erm," said the church elder, realising there was no seat. "Thank you. But I'd prefer to stand. Fingal, there is no easy way to convey bad news, so—"

"Take a seat, manny." The hermit pointed his writing claw at the magnificent golden throne he saw five metres away. "Just shoo Sir Randolph off. He won't mind. I made him after all."

"Very amusing." Andrew removed his yellow rain hat, smoothed out his greying combover and tried again. "Fingal," he said. "I know you two were close."

"Wait a minute," said Fingal. "I'm not supposed to like you? Aren't we at feud, or something? Or, or, was that from the book?" In the rubble of his ruined mind, a faint memory of an angry, blue man smashing a leaf blower stirred. So, he whacked his head, calmly lit a smoke and said, "No, no, that was definitely from the book. Forgive me. Please, Excellency. Plo-ceed."

"Col is dead."

"Who?"

"Colin Jarvis, from the brown cottage."

"Shaky sort of chap?" said Fingal, as reality bit … a little. "Decent bloke that went on a cruise with an invisible woman and never came back? Left his rope and a parrot?"

"Col was a good man, Fingal."

"Was?" the labourer heaved himself forward, coughed and spat. "What the deuce happened to him?"

Andrew looked to the heavens. "He died, Fingal."

Fingal stared at the blurry yellow-thing. "I see."

"His daughter just called me. The family had great difficulty getting the body out of New Caledonia."

Fingal rubbed his sore eyes. His vision was clearing, somewhat. "The place where naked women volleyballers frolic?"

"Paperwork was hideous, apparently."

"Ah, yes." The labourer looked at the Mad Posters covering his kitchen window. "Paperwork can be a terrible nuisance, Andy, can't it? Blocks out all the ruddy light."

"A terrible tragedy…"

"The paperwork?"

With some difficulty, Andrew ignored the blithering idiot. "*Tragically*, our neighbour passed away on the cruise ship. The last night, while he was attending the gala ball." The little man pronounced the word *gay-la*. "Sharine, his daughter, told me that one minute Col was dancing away quite happily, then," Andrew gulped, "a massive cardiac arrest stole a good man away from these sodden earthly plains."

"Do you happen to know which song was playing?"

"Fingal, now is not the time for—"

"Was it Glenn Miller? Was it *In The Mood*?"

"The song is not important."

"Yes, yes, yes. You're right. Dreadful song. Dreadful."

"It was a rather ignominious departure, to say the least," Andrew continued, bravely. "As Colin fell, the poor soul defecated himself. I've thought long and hard about the manner of his passing and all I can say is that the Good Lord's will is unfathomable."

"And that is important?"

"What?"

"The defecation bit? The shat-attack? Why did you say that?"

"I am merely conveying a message," Andrew replied curtly. "That is what Sharine, his daughter, told me on the telephone."

Fingal giggled. "Did she actually say shat-attack?"

"No. She did not. You made that up."

"Why do you people do that, King Andrew?" Fingal demanded. "Why do you humans do that? Why do you always go into such grainy, gory details? Farmer John had both has arms *ripped* off by a combine harvester. Cancer *riddled* Aunty Jean's thorax until she could no longer breathe. Or, or, or, the car went right under the semi-trailer," Fingal drew his good hand across his beard, "and *sliced* the poor bugger's head clean off. Don't you find that strange, Sir Andrew? Why the specifics? Why the pathos? Is it because we, ha, sorry, you continentals like pain?"

""I will let you know when the funeral is. Sharine is flying from

London today, and gladly accepted my offer to hold the funeral at Robina Pentecostal Church, my church."

"WHAT!" Fingal shouted.

"Sharine is flying in from…"

"No, no, no." Fingal tried and failed to stand up. "Tell me, Christian. Is it a bury, bury funeral or a burny, burny one."

"Colin, as per his last will and testament, is to be cremated." Andrew gestured to the trees. "His ashes are to be scattered in the forest. Sharine is to do that."

Fingal tried to protest but he was too tired. "Old man wanted to be buried, mate," was the only resistance he could manage, "in the jungle."

Andrew smiled piously. "I can give you a lift, should you wish to pay your respects."

"To the forest?"

"To the funeral. To Col's funeral. Colin, your friend?"

"No. Absolutely not."

Fingal's mind lurched. Though he didn't know what, he had something to do; something about a white rope, and some waterfalls that were so world famous that some fool had gone and lost them. "Very well, Mr Blower of Leaves. We islanders grieve in different ways from you mainlanders. We will say goodbye to this Col fellow according to our own customs, deep in the temple. To the jungle, Robin! I don't care if Mother hates me, or if She wants to eat me." He beamed as if crazy. "We will honour this Colin's passing by striking for the lost falls."

This outburst was too much for the Christian. Determination washed across Andrew's tiny face, he muttered "this is ridiculous" and replaced his tiny yellow rain hat, for courage. "Fingal, I know it's really none of my business – really, trust me – but, by God's grace, are you all right?"

"Of course! Never been better! I'm finished, Andy, don't you see. The book, that is." With a great deal of grunting and swearing, he managed to stand up. "Well, actually no. No, no, no, no. I'm not. Shut up, Fang!"

"Fingal…"

"Shhh, Your Highness. Of course, you are worried. That is what you

282

charming Christian folk do."

"The Good Lord gave me eyes so that I may see." The Drab, Green King shook his wee head. "I'm not spying on you, please understand. But I can't help but look, Fingal. I see you – morning, noon or night – bent over that desk for hours on end. What on earth are you doing?"

"Labouring."

"At what?"

"At the factory, of course."

"What do you mean, of course? What factory?" Andrew said desperately. "I've barely seen you leave this … this, den."

"Awwwww," said Fingal, hobbling straight through Bottle City and embracing his neighbour, hard. "Don't you worry about the island, little-Cob. All is well. I've finished. No, no. Shut up!" The hermit shuddered then tapped his temple. "Ha, they're partying like crazy in there. We're all as happy as stink on a bat." Fingal held Andrew by his puny shoulders and grinned. "Rearree."

"Is it the heroin?"

"What?"

"Are you," Andrew closed his paper-thin eyelids, "using again?"

"No, your God, no." Fingal wobbled to the verandah railing for support. "I'm finished, Andrew. Don't you see? The words have gone. Shit, there were millions of them, *millions* of them, but now," he made a little smoke bomb with his good hand. "Poof. Gone! Twenty-seven strands are now complete. Twenty-seven lovely, fresh original stories. *Ils sont beau, mon ami! C'est finis!*"

"Are you drunk?"

"Totally." Fingal sculled an imaginary flagon of goon and his mind calmed. "By the way, now that you're here, on my island, with us, let me, let us, all of us on my island, take, no *seize*, this opportunity to say that we are all really, really sorry that Heracles destroyed the golf buggy outside your castle. I'm very sorry. Man. Very, very sorry for we I, we … he … did. Do you understand me? Can you hear me? WE'RE SORRY!"

That was definitely from the book but Andrew didn't seem to mind. All the try-hard bible-basher heard was the word sorry. "You do not need to apologise for the leaf blower incident," he said with a little smile. "It takes two to tango."

"Aye, ye'r a good man, Sir Andrew." Fingal moved closer so he could feed of the Christian's life-energy. "The islanders also greatly appreciate what you did with your fucking noise. Zank ooo. Maybe your God does exist after all? Blessed is the meek children so that God gave his one and truly Son; Jebus. Ahh, isn't religion just brilliant, mate. Sorry. Did we say that already? We're so, so sorry."

"I appreciate the apology, Fingal." The Christian's wide, rheumy eyes glassed over. The word was something for God to work with. Fingal's smackhead soul might yet be saved. "Oh, oh, oh," the jabbering skeleton with the huge beard continued, nodding to where Jackie sat perched on the verandah railing, "is there any chance of me and the Jackiebird could trouble you for some more of the sweet, delicious honey your drab, green island is renowned for? Energy supplies are running at very low. Very, very low."

"When was the last time you ate?"

"Squawk."

"You're skin and bones, laddie." Andrew frowned. "You need to eat and, guess what, you're in luck. Last night, I made a barley, liver and bacon stew, and some fresh bread." Fingal began to drool. God only knew when the last time he ate real, human food. "I'll be back."

The Drab, Green King made to leave, but Fingal took him gently by his arm. "Andy. Pandy. My Love. Not now. Later. Please. We ... we ... we must first deal with the shocking, bitter tragedy of the loss of our friend. Col, the Decent Man, and I were close. Very close." Fingal fought off a sudden urge to run to the forest. "We will need time to grieve, but – BUT – know that I shall visit your warm, island home in but a matter of stones."

"I'll bring round some stew, at least."

"Nay. Nay. Later, my dear." Now. Something, or someone, or some force, was calling him; pulling his body toward the trees. "Thank ooo. You're an amazing little man, Anderoo. May the peace of God, the Magnificent One, be upon you. Praise Him, yay."

"Yay, indeed," Andrew replied, suddenly excited by the prospect of charity, as well as all Fingal's God allusions, however awful they were. "You are welcome in my house anytime, Fingal. A Robina Pentecostal Church Elder's door is always open." The little man pumped Fingal's claw hand – something the hermit witnessed but never felt – and, deciding enough miracles had occurred for the day, turned and glided down Fingal's filthy verandah. Before he stepped out into the wild weather, however, he stopped and turned. "Tell you what, neighbour, the weather is building. A cyclone, so they're saying on the ABC," Andrew said while zipping up his yellow raincoat. "You know what that means, don't you?"

"Yes," said Fingal. "No."

Andrew donned a plastic yellow hat and pointed up at the heavens. "The Boss is angry about something. We'd better be on our best behaviour."

And with that, the kind, invasive little tosser was gone, mincing through the forest, humming church music, and thanking the good Lord above for a fresh soul to playeth with; a nice, fresh one gone all juicy and mad.

Whether it was Andrew's visit, the news that Col, however shitty his death might have been, was now actually with Mary, or the euphoria of finishing the book, Fingal felt a little surge of energy. "Time for another funeral," he said with some lucidity. "I really must go and bury my friend."

***

Terrified mice fled the coughing, cursing giant, as Fingal scampered around the blue cottage, throwing crumpled lasagne packets, empty boxes of goon and bits of paper everywhere. "Ah," he cried at last. "Our ticket!" This V.I.P. – or was it D.I.Y. – pass would surely grant entry into the temple. Fingal smiled down at Decent Old Col's nudey postcard, which had been buried halfway up Paper Mountain – the remnants of *The ENOS Ver. 2.0*, which was still piled behind the front door, which still had never been opened. "Mwah, mwah, mwah, mwah," said Fingal, giving each of the four gorgeous, nudey women on the postcard a big smacker of a kiss.

"It will be a glorious funeral!"

"Rike herr it wirr."

"Fucking wirr be, Fang."

"But you no' finish."

"I am. And so are you."

"Ha," it was the evilest laugh Fingal had ever heard. "Hahahahaha."

Outside, in the rain, a gang of kookaburras joined in. "Ooooo, ooooo, aaaaaa, aaaaaa," they said, and for the first time in many stones Fingal thought of Mother. "Ticks can be dug out," he supposed with growing confidence. "Leeches plucked off." Fingal didn't really mind if She ate him, so long as She let him get safely down to the Falls where he could pay his respects to Decent Old Col in the proper island fashion: not in a half-empty church full of strangers badly singing hymns at a wooden box with a grey corpse inside, but by tying Col's rope to a tree and jumping off a cliff.

Today would be the day. Of that, he was absolutely certain.

The rejuvenated explorer stuffed Col's postcard in the pocket of the shorts he'd been wearing for the last sixty-eight days, drunk a precious mug of goon, smoked a precious skinny rollie, and scoffed down a precious handful of bird food, wincing when the sharp seed jabbed into his swollen, bleeding gums. "No pain, no gain," the hermit said with a laugh, pulling on his walking boots, and hobbling down the verandah out into the rain. Obsessed by the quest, and, if the truth be told, keen to see Mother, the explorer walked straight past Col's lovely white rope.

***

Lucidity – of a sort – returned with every step away from the Writing Factory, as did a skerrick of faith in Mother. Silver rain poured in torrents from the heavens. She stunk of perfume, a dank rotting aroma of mud and water and decomposing leaf-litter. Not a soul stirred in the woods. Fingal McKay, rope-forgetteror, was the only human being alive on planet earth.

He did stop once, and quickly, for a sneaky, long overdue peak at Penny's cottage. No one was about but he did hear puppies whining. Satan's Bitch had just given birth but rather than leap the fence and stomp the devil-spawn to pulp, a crooked smile appeared behind his dripping beard. The excitable squeals of the girls as they drowned in puppies, Penny's beautiful voice, and even the droning, nasal comments of approval coming from some Aussie-bloke melted Fingal's once black heart.

"May peace be upon the pink-house-clan," the hermit said. "In Col's death, She gives life."

"Hey! Hey, Fingar! Risten to me!"

"Get fucked, Fang. We're finished." Fingal beat at his shaggy head with his writing claw. "LEAVE ME ARONE!"

"NE-VA."

The fire trail was treacherous. Forty-nine days of rain had washed away the topsoil and left a layer of slippery, red clay. This, combined with his awful posture and wasted leg muscles, saw the explorer slipping and falling on his arse every hundred metres or so. But he soldiered on, keeping the spirits up by thinking about the strange, disgusting, anarchic manner of Decent Old Col's passing – a heart attack, followed by a shit attack. In his mind's eye, Fingal could see it all: a cruise ship ploughing through the sea, rocking and rolling to Glenn Miller's *In The Mood*. Inside, at the height of the gay-la ball, an old man waltzed around the busy dance floor. Alone but not alone, he was dancing with his dead, invisible wife. Dressed in an ill-fitting tuxedo, drunk on two beers, and wearing a rubbery smile, Ol' Col was just dying to go, dying to be with the real Mary. When he – not the world – was ready, Col let go of all his ropes, let the massive heart attack come on, and, as a final salute to a bizarre life, shat his pants.

Take that, you bastards!

"What a man!" said Fingal when he eventually reached Python Gate, some two hours later. "Death by shit," the bent explorer added, as he slipped into the dark forest and tip-toed past the huge, hollowed out log where *Mister* Snake lived. Another auspicious sign, the giant serpent was nowhere to be seen.

"Oi! Fingar! Why you no wo'k? Chlyst!"

Fingal punched his face, hard. "I told you to leave me alone! The god damned book is finished!"

"No, it broddy not!"

"Hey! Hey, you! I got something rearree impo'tant to terr you!"

"Ok, fine. Sod this." Fingal decided to hear Fang out, to be done with the nagging matter so he could focus giving Decent Old Col a decent old send-off. "Plo-ceed, Mr Fang. Say your piece, and be done with it."

"It shit," Fang said. "Totar shit."

"What you talking about Fang?"

"It shit."

"Yes, you've said that already, Mr Fang. Three times," Fingal sighed. "Why might it be shit?"

"You got no book."

"Ha! The book is stunning."

"Seliousree, you no' finished. You stir got dlaft foah to do."

"You're mad," the labourer said. "The twenty-seven stories, hand-written, I might add, by me, not you, have never been better!"

"But, you no' finished. You got twenty-seven stolies now. Not one! You so stupid; you so brind."

"Shut up!" Fingal shouted, and charged into the temple to try and escape the high-pitched voice and the truth it spoke. As usual, he completely ignored the YOU WILL CERTAINLY DIE National Park sign.

"You can't lun."

"Yes, I can!"

"Don't you see, you gotta put arr the stlands back togetha again!"

"LEAVE ME ALONE!"

"DLAFT FOAH! DLAFT FOAH! DLAFT FOAH!"

At last the penny dropped. Fingal stopped and turned white. "Oh no, please no." Fang was bloody right. There was no book. Instead of one *Epic Novel of Sport*, the factory had only gone and produced twenty-seven epic *novellas* about sport, very few of which now related to one another. Weaving these "strands" back together into a single, stunning best-seller could take twice, maybe even three times as long if, indeed, it was even possible at all.

"Fuck! FUCK!" the egoist roared as the same gang of kookaburras wound up to piss itself laughing at another brilliant human stuff-up.

"Tord you it shit."

"You came up with the stland approach!" Fingal tore at his hair and ripped at his beard while staggering down the wild, private trail. "You! You evil little Thai cocksucker!"

"You make me, Fingar."

"Oh yeah, is that right?"

"Yeah, sirree monkee. That light."

"Oh yeah?"

"I, you, and you, me."

"If I make you, then I can fucking unmake you."

"Ha! You want to kirr me? Good ruck."

The starving labourer tripped and stumbled, his deluded mind anywhere but on the dangerous, slippery track. In fact, Fingal wasn't even in Binjari rainforest. He was on the island, executing someone, or something, he should've killed months ago.

277 was part of an angry mob of skinny workers. They carried a wriggling, squirming leech of a man: a real soul-sucker, their boss, Mr Fang. The daemon kept shouting "I boss, I make you" but no one listened, not anymore. Mob and tyrant reached the lip of a giant bucket of turgid, green phlegm, the essence of the factory, the book. In fact, the contents of the bucket stood more change of winning the Mann Booker than *The Jerkiest Novel Ever Written*.

277 started the chant. "Fang, die, Fang, die, Fang die," he shouted as the flung the Evil Cunt into a bucket full of phlegm, a bucket that he made. "I'rr be back," was the last thing the corrupt Thai policeman said before slipping under the thick, pasty surface, his shit-coloured hat the only reminder of his evil reign.

"The Fang is dead," the Jackiebirds wailed in the forest. "Long live The Fang!"

"Yay!" cried Fingal, now running down the dangerous track. "Fang is dead!"

"No I not."

Mother had had enough of this nonsense.

He had to let that shit book go.

At once, She commanded six leeches to slither down the tiny gap in Fingal's socks and begin to feed.

"Woah," said Fingal, slowing his pace. "Woah, there, mate. Don't throw babies out with bathwater. Maybe you just need a break, a week off or something. No, a day off." The explorer somehow negotiated a rock the size of a caravan without even seeing it. "Don't be so quick to throw away all that work, 277. Settle. The book can't be *that* bad? Maybe dlaft foah wouldn't take *that* long? Maybe I could expand the three main characters' stories and," Fingal grinned, "I'd then have three – THREE – books! Three books would mean three films! Three Oscars! Three castles!"

Blind fool, thought Mother, realising Fingal did not feel Her leeches bite and drink his blood because of their ingenious numbing agent. So, the Mighty Fig sent forth seven ticks, one of which began to saw into the lunatic's upper eyelid.

"Glass half-full, Cob. You have to focus on the positives." He ignored the tick burrowing into his eyelid. For a man used to swimming in pain, it was nothing. "Yes, yes, yes! Think about it, mate. You've still got a writing retreat in a rainforest and, and, and, a pen and lots of paper. And," he stabbed a finger at his temple, "you've still got this … this fucking mad, beautiful thing! It's not over, Fingal. Don't you see!"

"Harrow."

"Mr Fang! Welcome back!"

Totally fed up, She ordered a root to grow out the track five metres in front of Fingal McKay, Her stupid, blind son who had suddenly realised he had forgotten the…

"Rope! NO! How could I forget the bloody rope!" Not for the first time that day, Fingal's mad, starving mind lurched. "You fucking arsehole, McKay! How exactly did you expect to climb down a fuckin' cliff without a fuckin' rope! You are some piece of work, man. Col will be furious! Wait, wait. WAIT. Maybe I don't need it. Maybe I can climb down. Yes, fuck it. Maybe I can fly!"

Enough was enough.

Fingal's boot caught and jammed in the root but the rest of his body kept moving. A split second later, the tendon and ligaments supporting his ankle ruptured, the POP audible even above the pissing rain.

Fingal did not scream because there was no breath in his lungs. Somehow, he managed to pull his boot from the root. White pain seared in his ankle, and he tried to stand up and walk on. He fell and began rolling down the steep, muddy trail, powerless to stop the ticks, leeches, and the kookaburra's laughter booming throughout the woods. Twenty metres later, he slid off the track and would've fallen down a steep hundred-foot slope had it not been for the base of a giant rosewood, which he battered into.

Enough *was* enough.

Rather than thank Mother for the help, or the teaching, Fingal threw a huge Scottish tantrum. "You want to hurt me, eh, Mother!?" Anger roused the hermit, and he managed to clamber and crawl back to the trail. "Fucking good. 'M'oan then, ya Stupid Cunt-Tree! I'm no' scared of you! Eat me! Break me! I don't care anymore. I DON'T FUCKIN' CARE!" Rage dragged him to his feet. "Ya great, big, dirty, lyin' whore! All I tried to do was love and respect you! All I wanted to do was say cheerio to an old man that shat himself to death! All I wanted was to see you! And this is how you reward me? THIS! NOW!? THIS IS WHAT YOU DO TO ME! Well, fuck you, Mother! FUCK YOU!" He gobbed a massive pile of spit where he knew the colossal strangler fig brooded, some four kilometres away. "Know what quid pro quo is, eh, you Giant Mysterious Cunt?" Fingal tore a limb from one of Her young trees, and fashioned it into a crude crutch. "You like that, eh? How's that for fucking balance? Know what, Mother? You can shove your forest and your world-famous Falls right up your arse. We're done. We're totally fuckin' finished. I'm never, ever looking at you again! IT'S OVER." With his good hand, Fingal cast a magical spell-thing. "Poof," he said. "You're gone. You're so fucking dead to me. YOU DO NOT EXIST!"

***

With a breaking heart, an empty soul and a starving stomach, and with great physical difficulty, the now irreligious Scotsman began the long, long climb back up to the blue cottage – a prison of no love stuffed only with paper, words, mice and empty goon bags. Without his God-Tree, the ascent was appalling. The adrenalin soon wore off, and every step up the slippery track felt like a labour of Heracles. In addition to the pouring rain, a keen wind started through the wanker of a forest, pushing the hobbling hermit this way and that, slapping him around almost (not that he believed in such shite anymore).

A bitter hatred of Mother drove the broken man up the hill. With every step his face contorted further into an atheist's mask of hatred. Again, his mind lurched.

He couldn't quite believe the Mother-Tree was dead, for he never *knew* her religion. Rather, and it was difficult to explain in mere human words, he had *felt* it.

But still, *Law of the Jungle* (Kipling), *Super-Bitch. You just went and hurt me too many times. You tried to eat me!*

"Acht," he said, employing that great Scottish word, that onomatopoeic word, which simply meant fuck it, but in a sad, Gaelic way. "God is not a giant tree in a sub-tropical forest. It's over, man. Time to go home."

Further loathing, of wind and rain, air and space, somehow got Fingal to Python Gate, where he stopped, balanced on his good leg, and unleashed a torrent of rust-coloured urine down the barrel of the snake's den, begging it to come out. This time, he'd totally kick its snake cunt in or, gladly, die trying. The huge python wasn't even in the log. Knowing the cyclone to come, he'd retreated to his storm shelter, a dry cave under some huge rocks in the deep forest.

Darkness fell like an anvil, and without self-flagellation it is doubtful that Fingal McKay would have ever made it home. Too tired to hobble, the failed scientist had to crawl along the muddy fire trail, mentally whipping himself for the full three kilometres. "You are a fuckin' classic, McKay," he groaned on the trail, burying his good hand in the mud and pulling himself along. "One shite book isn't good enough for you, man. Oh no, no, no, no. Let's write another book, and another, each one more **SHITE** than the last! YOU FUCKING IDIOT!"

As he crawled, his mind flooded with hundreds of memories of fake genius. He didn't get this either. The memories felt so real, so believable. He actually *felt* like a writer. All those Mad Posters, all those drafts, and all those drunk, wide, red nicotine-stained smiles at just how brilliant his book *really* was. *Rearree, rearree was!*

"Oh no, I'm Fingal McKay! I'm George Mallory! I'm fuckin' Sisyphus!" the tirade continued as the broken man slithered toward the end of the fire trail. "I'm different. I'm an island of a man. I'm an islander. We islanders are different! We're brilliant! We're clever!" He spat blood into the mud. "Different? Brilliant? You fuckin' ballbag, McKay. Clever? Building islands with Writing Factories in your mind? You're a fucking lunatic, man. YOU'RE INSANE! YOU'RE CERTIFIABLE! YOU SHOULD'VE DONE NOTHING, MAN! NOTHING!"

It was only addiction, to goon and nicotine, as well as the knowledge that he was almost home, that pushed the furious hermit to his feet and got him hopping down the path toward the four stupid coloured cottages. In the time he'd been out communing with nature, Penny's pink cottage had been transformed. The windows were warm, orange, glowing rectangles, a sign of a good fire within. Many strings of bright, flashing lights had appeared, as well as a tree with a star on top of it. The chatter of three little girls talking about presents, and the sheer joy of living with lots of little puppy-dogs sallied across the black night. Incredibly, *incredulously*, the battered Scotsman could hear Christmas music. "It's Christmas?" he demanded of the darkness. "How long have I been in this interminable forest?"

All of a sudden, Fingal was in the living room of an old, homely Scottish farmhouse. It was Christmas there too. A good fire blazed in the hearth, the smell of smoke mingling with a rich aroma of gravy, Brussels sprouts, and turkey. Standing by the fire, Fingal rocked arm-in-arm with his father, Cameron, who was singing a local folk song after both of them had drunk far too much whisky. His mother, Mhairi, was trying to play the harmonica, which was virtually impossible considering that the woman with the aura of a rose garden was crying with laughter.

Then Fingal was in the Crown Tavern, Lanark, drinking cool pints of Tennant's Lager with his old Lanark Grammar school pals. Snow fell heavily outside, Primal Scream's *Loaded* played over the tinny pub speakers. The pals were standing round the pool table, pissing themselves laughing as Wee Dougie Boag brilliantly recounted the story about the night him and Fingal finally snogged the elusive McBray sister frae Carstairs Village before Mr McBray, who had done time in Barlinnie Jail, chased them "doon the road wi' a fuckin' nine iron!"

Then, sadly, beautifully, he was in a lonely chalet high in the Haute-Savoie, France. Fingal and The One had gone skiing for a week, only to get snowed in for three days. The only way to pass the time had been to indulge in the human love – that is, turn the heating up, lie in bed, sup on a full-bodied 1991 Saint-Émilion Grand Cru Classe A, eat Pringles, good steak and foie gras, and fuck like rabbits.

***

Just as quickly, Fingal was back in the sodden, sub-tropical rainforest that would most likely kill him. "What the fuck are you doing in Australia, man!" Fingal shouted at the wild, black night, stamping his bad ankle hard into the ground, the only way to stop more painful memories from blooming in his damp mind. "*Mate*, you couldn't get any further away from real love if you tried!"

At last, Fingal made it back to his soiled verandah. Livid, he hobbled straight past the marvellous gift that Andrew had left: an esky stuffed with liver, bacon and barely stew, fresh tomato soup, homemade bread, eggs, butter, tea, honey, two apples, three bananas and five Jesus Pamphlets. Nor did the blind prick notice that the wind had doubled in strength, or that the parrot seed in the saucer, the last in the blue cottage, hadn't been touched. Like Mr Snake, knowing a monster cyclone was coming, Henry and Co. had fled to an old secret spot in the woods to hide.

Fingal did not see the esky, or the seed, because he couldn't. His eyes hurt. His head hurt. His body, especially his ankle, ached. There was no juice left in the tank. Everything was coming to an end. The Experiment, religion, Mother, the book and – gulp – he, himself, had all failed. A bucket with a hole in it, he could feel his essence, his soul, draining away.

Fingal McKay, he knew, would soon die.

"Fuckin' good," he said while shouldering open the French windows.

In fact, all the exhausted, devastated man could do once inside the blue cottage was snatch up the half-empty goon bag, stagger down the corridor and, soaking wet, fully clad, and laden with ticks and leeches, collapse on a bed he once bought from the Salvos for a hundred bucks.

Even though he was dead tired, sleep refused to come. A modern-day Robert The Bruce, Fingal lay on his side for hours, staring and searching for meaning amidst the madness swirling around his worn-out brain. It was such a mess, in there. He could string four or five logical thoughts together before the same thing happened, over and over again. A vision always derailed his flickering train of thought. It was the sight of Ivy Mike, the world's first fifty-seven megaton hydrogen bomb whistling toward the little green island in his mind. The island, his, then disappeared behind a bright, white light, and a million little Fingal's cried out in pain as they were consumed by a fire mankind had no business fucking around with in the first place.

These sounds and images played in his ruined mind as if on loop.

Not only was Mother gone, the island was gone. Once a place of relief and sanctuary, it had turned into a morbid cesspit, a giant, industrial shithole dominated by a Writing Factory ran by a devil, a place of pain and torture, built on greed, ego, madness and gross stupidity.

The Island of Fingal McKay had failed, as had the John Donne Experiment.

He had nothing.

NOTHING.

What was the point?

***

Not that Fingal McKay believed anymore, but the ferocious weather building above the Binjari plateau alluded to the final chapter in his story. Mother was about to go ballistic. She intended to put on a ripper last show for Her lost, blind son – a great, furious spectacle of raw nature. It would be a celebration of brilliant silver and gold.

She would be heard and, at last, seen. Her son had done well. He had come far. She only hoped that She hadn't hurt him too much. She only hoped he would come a few steps further, for She was now ready to reveal herself.

A little more pain, just a cut or two, and they could be together.

Forever.

***

At least Fingal was not alone in his dark, damp bedroom with holes in the wall.

On his dusty bedside cabinet, a little grey mouse nibbled on a bit of plaster. It did not, however, make its customary and very fucking annoying tic-tic-tic-tic noise. Instead, the mouse kept opening its mouth and howling at the broken hermit.

"Wooooo," it said. "Woooo! WooOOO!"

The wind outside, a mere sixty kilometres per hour at that stage, gusted through the areshole-forest. The big show was about to begin.

In truth, Mother was absolutely thrilled with the boy's growth.

She was delighted that Fingal McKay was about to die.

After all, in order to rebuild, the human first has to tear down.

PART V
The Deep Forest

Day I

When a cyclone almost swept Binjari off the plateau, it had been raining for fifty days straight. As usual, the pea-brained, continental meteorologists named the tempest something silly, playful and utterly disrespectful – the pricks called the beast Cyclone Barry.

By the time Barry was two hundred kilometres east of the coast, which had recently recorded wind speeds of up to 120 kilometres per hour, he had swollen to a category 5 cyclone. A stunning weather system, he was the pinnacle of nature.

Good ol' Bazza would get the message through.

The four, brightly coloured Binjarian cottages woke to a bleak, grey light seeping through a forest ravaged by wind. With possibly the worst goonover in the history of mankind – ever – it was not a good environment to wake up in. Six leeches, engorged and stupefied from drinking too much booze-blood yesterday, lay beside Fingal's bleeding ankles. And, overnight, twelve ticks had burrowed deeper and deeper into his damp, white skin. A dozen hot, red welts stood out on the Scotsman's naked, scrawny body. Each of the red mounds was a little monument to failure.

The broken man slowly opened his eyes and looked at the bedside cabinet. There was no sign of the howling mouse. "Moused-off somewhere, eh?" Fingal noticed then ignored the terrible weather outside. "Another shitty day in a shitty, Godless rainforest on the shittiest planet in the shittiest galaxy in an entire universe of shit." To the atheist, the violent wind and the rain slinging off the tin roof, walls and windows of the shuddering cottage were just that: wind and rain. Besides, the Scotsman had never experienced a cyclone before, and with no radio, television or convivial relationships with neighbours, had no idea what was coming.

Coughing, Fingal struggled out of bed. He put weight on his bad ankle, sucked the word "Christ" through his teeth, and managed to hobble through the dark cottage toward the mouldy kitchen sink where he hacked and spat, liberally. For support, the hermit snatched up his silver goon bag and realised with horror that it was the last of its kind in the blue cottage. The bag contained but two litres of delicious, rancid wine. "Acht," he added on noting the twenty rollies worth of tobacco left, "fuckin' Experiment's over anyways." Days could pass before he was fit enough to make a long overdue trip up to Gail's for supplies if, indeed, he could make it that far.

"Need to ration the rations," the recluse said, bitterly.

Desperate for light, any light, Fingal looked at the windows but they were blocked by several layers of Mad Posters from the disastrous writing hobby. He stared at them for a while.

"Fucking words," he said, at last, "so many fucking words." Millions of them had come to dominate his life. He reckoned the three drafts of *The Failed Epic Novel of Total and Utter SHITE* totalled around 950,000 words. At least a million more words – tiny, scribbled, pathetic things – hung on the eight or nine hundred Mad Posters covering every inch of every wall. To produce these, millions more words had been read, in the dozens of books strewn throughout the fetid cottage, in the mountains of crumpled printouts stacked in every corner of every room, and on the internet, when that proselytiser of gross wankery had dominated the factory, when that bloody Writer's Room website insisted that he, and he alone, could actually write a best-seller in ten easy steps.

"Ten easy steps?" Fingal laughed, darkly. "That *is* insane. More like two or three million painful, bloody steps that go any which way but forward." They – whoever the hell they are – do say that everyone has a novel inside of them but what they forget to mention is that it's probably shite.[*]

"Fucking words," said Fingal.

Millions and millions and millions of words, a mad brain, a broken hand, a bulging portfolio of dead characters and failed dreams, and an ex-bird he was still in love with that was probably getting pumped from

---

[*]   Fingal McKay's Advice to Aspiring Writers™.

behind by Fraser-the-Cunt at that precise moment in time. Thousands of hours and hundreds of days spent busting his balls, and for what?

Nothing.

NO-THING.

"Bet J.K.-fucking-Rowling never felt like this," Fingal noted. "How could she? She got published." He regarded the Mad Posters. "I should've written about prepubescent wizards, gay villains, and non-threatening hobgoblins. I should've just copied someone else's homework. That's how you get castles, man."

Angry as a bag of cut snakes, and in no mood for further debate or soul-searching – by their God he was sick of that nonsense – Fingal acted intuitively for once. It was a small step but a significant one. With his clawhand, he reached up, peeled a Mad Poster from the kitchen window, crumpled it up, and tossed it into his dirty sink. "Ooooh," he said as a column of pale light oozed into the dark, blue cottage, "that actually felt quite nice."

He removed another poster, and another, until the rancid kitchen was bathed in a dull silver light. His dark eyes twinkling, the failed experimentalist then pulled off the *Scotland's For Me!* t-shirt he'd been wearing for the past three months. It felt like removing a layer of skin. The human then ripped, sliced and cut the t-shirt to shreds, employing the longest piece as strapping for his injured ankle.

It too felt better.

Emboldened by this devil-may-care attitude, and a ration of wine, and a precious, super-skinny rollie, Fingal then tottered around the cottage, ripping all the Mad Posters from the walls, windows and cupboard doors, crumpling them up, and mustering them in the living room, where a giant mountain of paper and a cunning plan soon formed.

"A very warm, toasty plan," said Fingal, seconds before thrashing his wooden bread bin to pieces; for kindling. Similarly, he pulled off two cupboard doors and smashed and thrashed them to bits against the work surface. In the pain of failure, he'd forgotten that he liked destroying things; hurting things; executing things.

Whistling an old Scottish ditty, Fingal collected the fuel, and limped over to the neglected fireplace in the abandoned living room. Minutes later a warm, fire crackled against the inclement weather, and a friendly orange light danced in the cottage for the first time in months. "Magical," said Fingal, rubbing his damp, sore hands above the hearty little blaze, a smile flickering beneath his giant beard.

This, however, disappeared as a dormant tick chose that moment to bury deeper into his gouch. "Surgery," he said, surprised by the positivity in his tone, which he ascribed entirely to the little warm fire. Working by touch and experience, Fingal flicked opened the Swiss army knife, pulled his ball sack to one side, and quickly dug out the first of twelve Binjari ticks that had called his body home since the tragic walk yesterday, healing a little as each of the parasites was scraped from its bloody abode and incinerated. Each tick-death was celebrated by tossing more and more balls of crumpled paper onto the blaze. Sometimes the balled up Mad Posters unfurled to reveal their tiny, cuntish detail before fire consumed them. As the letters, words, lines, maps, sketches of fake castles and such, vanished, Fingal's sore hand, body, and mind healed a little more.

Soon all the ticks were dead and burned but the mound of crumbled-up paper remained. "It'll take forever to burn them, man," the naked, bleeding man noted. Although hearty, the fire was small and there were thousands of sheets of paper to be burned. "I could stuff them in the bushes," Fingal supposed, thinking the paper would eventually decompose. "Or..." He looked outside the French windows and, at last, Fingal McKay met Cyclone Barry.

The world had gone mental. Curtains of silver water poured from the gutters and the air was full of swirling debris. Strips of bark, old crisp packets, newspapers, palm fronds, twigs, and leaves battled with an infinitesimal number of raindrops pouring from the low, black clouds. All, in turn, was whipped up by a wind that had already flattened half the young trees on the lawn outside. Closer, bushes scraped and pawed at the Fingal's windows, crying – if they could speak, which of course they fucking couldn't – "let us in! Let us in!'

"Aye, that might work," said Fingal, realising that the tempestuous wind could serve a very useful purpose. It took a good hour of hobbling back and forth, tossing arms of paper up and out to the crazed wind, but soon the living room and the cottage was rid of every single Mad Poster. They now belonged to the wind.

That gave the failed writer an even better idea. Without thinking, he grabbed all twenty-seven hand-written strands, of the disastrous *Epic Novel of Sport, Ver. 3.0* from his desk and stepped back out into the bedlam, this time, taking the time to enjoy the storm, to savour its wrath, to appreciate and relish the impending execution of a very, very bad hobby.

Most of Bottle City had been blown away. What buildings were left rolled violently on the soaking floorboards, clinking and clanking and breaking in the wind. Picking his way through the ruins, and careful to avoid the broken glass, Fingal felt bird shit, seed husks and fag buts on his bare feet.

"That's definitely a storm," he said on reaching the end of the squalid verandah. "A very, very big storm!" He stepped out into the weather but felt no doubt, or fear. Just certainty.

He remembered something his father once said to him – "Dinnae fash yersel' wi difficult shite, son. Life's hard enough. Aiways follow the path of least resistance, ye hear?"

"Aye, Dad." He cried to the north. "I hear ye, man!"

The tremendous wind played with his beard, tugging it this way and that, casting his long, greasy hair out in long, spectral tendrils. Cold rainwater washed over his bare skin, massaging his aching muscles, and cleansing and soothing the fresh tick bites. A small, random and very cool stream rushed over his bad, swollen ankle and washed away the pain, as well as the six gelatinous blobs of black blood where the leeches had recently gorged.

"Now, you epic pile of egotistical shite," he said to the twenty-seven short stories clutched to his chest. "Are you ready to fly?"

Fingal then did what he should've done ages ago. He gave up. He let go of the dreadful, confusing book, holding each and every page up to Barry until his vicious breath snapped it from his claw hand and blew it far out of sight. "See ya later, Sir Randolph Hazelrigg of Clyde Valley Castle!" he shouted as the last page of the baddy's short story vanished into the maelstrom. "Won't miss you, Heracles-wanker-face!" he screamed like a banshee as, five minutes later, another of the novellas disappeared. "Get fucked, Lady Phoebe Redgrave, you cantankerous old boot!"

No one would ever read his work, no one would ever tell him how brilliant he was, no agent would kiss his arse, and no publisher would jerk his ego off. There would be no appearances on Parky, and no blue castle in the Scottish Highlands, and, no, he'd never get to tell J.K. Rowling that she was not a real writer of literary fiction but a commercial dirtbag, a seller of market wares; a writer of – gulp – books that sell very well in airports. At least, J.K. would be pleased to know that Fingal didn't blame her. Had *The Epic Novel of Shite* been become a bestseller, he would've done exactly the same. Who wouldn't?

Well, him.

Not now.

"Let it go, man," Fingal said when Barry had claimed the last of the 1473 pages of shite. "The wise man let's go," he added, not sure where he'd heard that expression before.

It was incredible how little Fingal missed the book, the hobby he'd lived with, in the end, for 24 hours per day, seven days per week. Back then, he wouldn't have said boo to it. Back then, the book was him, and he was the book. And, now, one mere day after thinking he would win the Mann Booker, here he was standing in a storm killing the mother fucking hobby. He felt no regret whatsoever. Weirdly, he felt liberated now that the book was gone. He'd woken up from the nightmare.

A better idea for incendiary material then came to him, and he limped to the Nissen hut to fetch the axe he once used to murder a television, and returned to the healing cottage. He spotted the victim straight away: his slave-ship, the factory issue desk. It had to die.

Fingal lifted the axe and was about to strike when he saw a most wonderful sight, possibly the greatest thing he had ever seen in the rainforest. Outside the French windows, he at last noticed the esky that

Andrew, his neighbour, had left on the verandah while he'd been out trying to beat God yesterday. For a man that had existed on bad wine, bad rollies and sandwiches of diminishing merit for many, many months, it was an incredible, cornucopian vision.

Fingal dropped the axe, rushed toward the esky and tore it open. "STEW!" he cried on removing a three-litre Tupperware full of liver, barley, bacon, and tatties, soaked in gravy. "BREAD! No way! AND BUTTER! Sweet, salty butter! TEA! FRUIT! EGGS!" Fingal's eyes glassed over. "Andrew McKenzie, Esquire," he said. "You are a fucking saint."

The starving hermit virtually inhaled a banana and two slices of bread and butter. He wanted to eat more but thanks to the mad writer's diet his stomach had shrunk to the size of pea. Besides, for what he intended to do, once his ankle was strong enough, Fingal would need the food, for both strength and sacrifice.

Old Col deserved nothing less.

To celebrate this remarkable gift of food, the healing Scotsman then murdered his horrible, factory issue writing desk with gusto, smashing the sturdy bastard to pieces with the blunt axe. At last, it produced something useful: a large, hot fire which burned and crackled long into the wild, dark night.

That evening, Fingal ate a little more, some stew, washed down with several cups of warm, sweet tea. It was the best meal he had ever had. Sadly, though, Andrew, that gorgeous little man, hadn't bothered to include goon and tobacco, so, mindful of the rations, the addict in him only drunk two mugs of goon, accompanied by two of the skinniest rollies ever seen on the bizarre planet humans call earth.

More than once, the valuable goon was raised in the direction of the drab, green cottage next door, and the kind, little man with the little head who'd been hated, insulted and physically abused yet still had the heart to leave an esky stuffed with food for a man who'd clearly lost his marbles, for a man in trouble, and for a neighbour. "Aye, McKenzie," said Fingal, massaging blood and life back into his writing claw, staring into the fire as if it were a hypnotist's fob watch. "Ye'r no' a bad wee prick. But, I still hate leaf blowers. They machines'll be the end of us."

That night, the human thought nothing more of food, or Andrew McKenzie, God, leaf blowers, Scotland, or the beastly cyclone shredding the world outside the tiny blue cottage. Only the roaring fire, his distended belly, and the clear, amber walls of his cottage meant anything to Fingal. A well-read man, if you recall, he thought for a moment of Plato, Socrates, their cave and the one bright spark who had somehow escaped to experience reality. The Homo sapiens also thought of his distant ancestors. Twenty, fifty, a hundred thousand years ago, they too must have laid by their fires, cut, bruised and exhausted yet safe and warm, extremely satisfied at a job well done; a day and a life well lived.

They hadn't been afraid to die, so why should he be? Death, for a man who had tried, for a man who had loved and laughed, for a man who had travelled, and seen the Himalaya at dawn, and heard the sound of total silence on top of Khongoryn Els, surely the end was not the end. Those that feared death only feared unconsciousness, or another form of consciousness. For a good working life, a life well spent, death was a blessing. Death was peace.

It was only the beginning.

"The wise man lets go. So, let it go, man. Let it go. Let it go," Fingal muttered happily until he fell asleep in front of the warm fire, the shadows of a burning desk and his shattered but healing body dancing on the bare walls.

Outside the little blue cottage, Cyclone Barry huffed and puffed, and blew and spewed, and wrecked and ruined, but Fingal woke only once. This was on account of a vivid dream about the rainforest. One of its creepers had sneaked in through the French windows, wrapped itself around his swollen ankle, and dragged him out into the storm. Like a bit of paper from a really shit novel, the creeper then flung him up into the belly of the storm, and he was battered around a bit, well, a lot, so much that he thought he was dead. But, in the end, the storm spat him down – down, not up – into a beautiful golden world, a subterranean realm of huge trees, and silver oceans dotted with stunning little islands, all of which were populated exclusively by Jackie-birds, king parrots and huge, golden strangler figs.

It was one of the most beautiful universes he had ever conceived of.

Fingal McKay, dreamer, knew – no, he *felt* – that he was looking at heaven.

When he woke, however, Fingal was none too happy. In fact, the failed hermit, explorer, bird-fancier, and writer was once more tired, scared, and more than a little angry. Considering The Experiment was over, that Mother was just a tree, and that his island with its vile factory had recently been obliterated by a fifty-seven megaton hydrogen bomb, he knew the dream was just a dream. "Don't be a fucking dickhead, McKay. There's been too much madness. Let it go. Mother wasn't real. It's just a tree," he whispered until he fell asleep. "It's just a tree."

Day 11

Cyclone Barry battered into the coast around noon the following day. Wind speeds of up to 150 kilometres per hour were recorded, as well as cataclysmic lightning strikes, one every sixty seconds. Torrential rain, power cuts and a king tide wreaked havoc on the continent. Rivers, creeks and canals burst their banks and drowned civilisation, and, suddenly, there were no millionaires, middle classes and bogans anymore, just 650,000 people cowering in darkness, water, wind and awe. Just like their troglodyte ancestors, nothing had changed on the world of man. Equality at last, in the face of nature's grandeur.

Some fifty kilometres to the southwest, Fingal McKay could not hear the fury of the approaching cyclone because he was enjoying a long, hot, and very soapy shower. "Soooo gooooood," he groaned, wondering why he'd ever shunned this marvellous continental invention for a cold bathtub in a forest that hated him; why, he no longer cared, quite frankly.

The swelling on his ankle had gone down, eighty per cent movement had returned to his claw hand, and sleeping all night on a hard, wooden floor had done wonders for his crooked factory-issue spine. Every bone in his body still cricked and cracked, and every muscle ached, but the former experimentalist was recovering, and quickly. This was very positive news. Soon, Fingal McKay would be ready for his last journey.

"Maybe their world isn't so bad," said Fingal, stepping out from the amazing shower, feeling spotless for the first time in months. Ignoring Cyclone Barry, he dressed in the only clean, warm clothes he could find – a pair of tracky daks, a VB t-shirt, and a hoody – then limped to the kitchen, revelling in both the cleanliness and emptiness of the former Writing Factory.

"The first to forget is the happiest," the human said before wolfing down a breakfast of fried eggs, bread and butter, washed down with yet another magnificent cup of tea. Sated and happy, his spirit once more flared at the journey which now lay ahead.

It was time.

"Weel, laddie," he said in an increasingly thick, Scottish accent. "Ye'd best git packin'." Fingal went to the bedroom and began stuffing things – he didn't care what – into his trusty backpack. "Aye," he said solemnly, "you've been runnin' for too long, pal."

Time, indeed, not to return to the coast but farther afield, to whisky, heather, proper cold rain, bagpipes, love, deep fried Atlantic cod, people that used the word fuck a lot, and, most importantly, family. Time to go back, to give up and retreat to the wild, mystical nation of Scotland. The trip was over. It was time to shake his father by the hand, time to watch is mother working in her rose garden, and time to go home.

"Aye, laddie," said Fingal, stuffing his sporran into his bag, playfully mimicking his soon-to-be embraced father. "Ye gied thon travellin' shite a guid turn. Come hame, Son. I'll fetch a guid bottle of whisky. Git ye a dram."

"Aye, I suppose it is faither."

"Good boy. Oh, an 'dae ye ken that Claire Coleman's no' married yet?"

A square peg in a round hole, Fingal McKay just didn't belong in the Lucky Country. No one really got his accent and, still, everyone called him mate or buddy when they barely knew him. Strangers were friends here, and friends, strangers, which was still weird for Fingal. The weather was absolutely mental. It was always far too hot, far too wet or far too windy. Equally, the sky was far too big and far too empty, so big and empty Fingal it dwarfed and terrified him. Old Shaky Dead Men, or little men with little faces and huge hearts tormented him then left incredible gifts, and beautiful women in pink cottages worked with, rescued and bred psychotic dogs. The *sub-tropical* rainforest, once his forest, was just like the people: passive-aggressive yet loving. Both charming and abusive, the rain forest would be trying to eat him one minute then trying to love him the next, showing him sights and sounds more beautiful than anything he'd ever seen on his travels. And, best and worst of all, little black and white butcherbirds made his heart ache with a love and pity he felt would never leave him. Australia, Fingal had finally realised, was just too hard, too weird and, if he admitted, far too beautiful for a man from a tiny, wind-battered lump of rock in the north Atlantic. He didn't deserve Australia. He wasn't good enough, or strong enough, or mad enough to survive here. Australia, he accepted, was best watched on a TV screen, with David Attenborough providing the commentary.

"Aye," Fingal admitted with a melancholy sigh, zipping up his bag and dragging it to the front door, "ye can keep yer dagwood dogs, yer fuckin' poisonous snakes and spiders and jellyfish, and yer figs that strangler other trees. I'll tak' eight months of winter, oak and haggis any day of the week. We're done, Australia." A tear rolled down his cheek and he was furious at this sudden weakness. "AYE," he said, in a stronger accent. "It's time tae let ye go."

But, still it felt weird, as if someone was inside his head, pulling strings to make his legs and arms move, pushing buttons to make his mouth flap open and shut and say bizarre things. The decision to go back to Scotland made *logical* sense so why did his heart ache? A huge branch clanged off the tin roof.

"Fuck's sake. What now?"

Fingal stepped onto the verandah. Night or day, it was impossible to tell, such was the blackness in the belly of a massive cloud hanging and swirling two hundred metres above the tiny blue cottage. It looked like, no, it *was* an upside-down brain, blackish-blue in colour. Rain seethed from the leviathan, worlds of thunder rolled across its lobes and poured through its canals, twenty, thirty shards and neurons of blue lightning flashed at once, and a wind, a wind like nothing Fingal had ever experienced, screamed at the forest beneath the bizarre looking cloud.

Giant trees bent like fishing rods.

His heart began to beat, faster and faster.

It ... *She* ... no, She was beautiful!

His mind began to unravel.

Flickering, the boundary between reality and fantasy started to wobble and fade.

The lazy-boy, his dais, now lay at the foot of the stairs leading to the lawn. She had blown it away. Big, silver waterfalls poured from the tin roof, tearing away the lovely green drapes, the creepers, ripping them from the verandah posts, the gutters, and the awning overhead. On the lawn, the young forest now lay flat, as if sleeping, and five, maybe six, young creeks ran freely down the slope, pooling into a brown, muddy lake forming at the bottom of the garden.

"It is absolutely beautiful," Fingal said as the blue-black brain above the cottage grumbled and sparked, as if it were the epicentre of the world, the universe, the Kosmos. "Woooo," he screamed, momentarily forgetting himself, his new mission, and the fact he was Celtic, not convict. "Woooooo! WOOOOOO!!! GO FOR IT, MOTHER! TURN IT UP! TURN IT UP!"

In the corner of his vision, he saw his backpack.

"No!" Fingal's mood swung. "No, Fin. Forget aboot aw that shite. Fuckin' magical trees, fairies and wood nymphs are *not* real. *She* does not exist. That cloud is not the universe's brain. God is not a gigantic strangler fig, ya fuckin' lunatic. Ye ken where that path led ye afore!" Not fifty metres away a huge bolt of lightning connected with a giant rosewood, which exploded. "Inside wi' ye, laddie," he said, scared all of a sudden. "Shoo! Ye shouldnae be oot here."

However, as Fingal hobbled back inside, he again doubted the so-called truth. Granted, six conclusions about the John Donne Experiment were immutable: aye, ok, fair enough, he had to go home. Fifteen or so years on the road were enough. Second, if, indeed, everyone did have a book inside of them, then they should keep it there (this is true – Fingal once met an agent, from a small literary agency, that told him they received 26,000 manuscripts per year. Of those, they'd take eight – eight! – and, of those, maybe two would get published. People, don't bother. Go and stare at a tree instead. Uncle Fingal has done the research for you.) Third, all machines –

smarts phones in particular – are absolute cunts and deserve to die, horribly and bizarrely if possible. Fourth, butcherbirds are just birds, giant carpet pythons do not speak Glaswegian, and there's no such thing as a good tick. Fifth, goon and fags are amazing. And, sixth, and in sum, men are not fucking islands.

No man is an island, John.

"You're right," said Fingal, almost retching at the taste of defeat. "I think."

But other conclusions – well, one in particular – were almost impossible to accept. Mother? Really? That was all rubbish? Despite all the pain She'd caused him, Fingal could still not forsake Her, even now; at the end of things. It's worth repeating, on the day Fingal discovered Little Girl Clearing, he did not *know* he had fallen in love with a rainforest. He *felt* it. He felt it every time he saw an invisible bird, every time he walked into the temple, every time She revealed a bizarre creature or a weird plant to him, Her only worshipper. He felt it in every drop of rain, every breath of wind, every ray of sunshine, and every passing cloud. He felt it now, in every huge boom of thunder, every tremendous flash of lightning from Her upside-down blue-black brain, in every branch that clattered off the roof or the window.

She *was* calling to him.

"Damn you, soul," Fingal seethed.

All of this was fake, meaningless and downright stupid? After all the blood, tears and suffering, after all the joy, divinity, and ecstasy, he was supposed to just walk away and accept there was no animistic spirit in the woods, no Mother that loved him?

***

Hours later, Fingal was in the clean kitchen, pouring the third last mug of disgusting goon, his mind still plagued by doubt. "Mother *was* irrational," he said, shaking his great, shaggy head, pacing the old trails on the clean floorboards, and working the life and the blood back into his wrecked hand. "She wasn't real, mate. Accept it. Let it go, and move the fuck on!"

Such doubt, the continental in him was beginning to realise, was just normal. It was nothing but a remnant of the recent lunacy, or some sort of toxic psychosis caused by too much goon, fags and solitude.

Given time, the doubt would pass. Normalcy would return.

He had to stick to the plan.

He had to go home, and the sooner the better.

As darkness engulfed the chaotic world outside, Fingal smashed then burned his factory issue chair, enjoying the distraction. He then made a large, hearty bowl of Saint Andrew's tomato soup which was consumed in the company and heat of a magnificent fire. The traveller then smoked one of the last rollies, and savoured the penultimate ration of goon. But still, the question "was She real?" would not leave him alone.

"SHE HAS TO BE REAL!" Fingal decided after an hour of staring into the fire while conducting archival research, that is, playing more memories from their obvious, higher, relationship in theatre of his mind: the serendipitous music of the forest – gold frogs chiming, orchestras of crickets sawing their violins legs, or wompoo fruit pigeons calling to one another through the silver rain, their call like a heartbeat – "wooooom-pooo, woooooom-pooo, woooo-pooo"; the feel of the cold water on his skin the first time he plunged into The Enchanting Bathtub; the comical ferocity of a spiny crayfish from Harlem that was addicted to crack; or, truest of all, the palpable, divine ecstasy that blossomed in his soul the day he first found Mother at the end of a secret trail in a secret temple deep in a secret forest. His trail, his temple. His tree. Without a shadow of doubt, Mother had been most beautiful tree Fingal had ever seen. She was a living, breathing creature, with a mood, a family, a spirit, and a mother-fucking soul.

"She just had to be real," Fingal repeated, softer this time.

In the end, there was only one way to settle the real/unreal debate, to rid his mind of all this … this shite.

He needed to go and have a chat with the boss, the real boss.

Fingal grimaced, got to his feet and, unable to let go, walked toward the bathroom. He stopped for a moment outside, took a deep breath and said, "I just need to know, then I'll go."

Only one man could end the doubt.

His self.

***

Fingal stood in front of the mirror with his eyes closed, terrified of what he might see. It had been two years, at least, since he'd last seen his reflection. He breathed for some time, sucking in long, deep draughts of the mad, electrical air. Then, in a small voice, he said "Fuck it, it's time."

He opened his eyes and a mad, hirsute stranger looked back at him.

"Awright," the image said.

"No, mate. No," Fingal replied and burst into tears.

"It's fine, mate. Breathe. Just breathe."

At first, Fingal did not recognise not the gaunt, shaggy-haired man in the mirror. Their eyes were vaguely similar – wide-set, fierce, and blue as the Saltire – however, in the two years spent in the forest, they had grown deeper and, amazingly, wiser. His jaw and face, square and flat, hadn't changed so much but the pronounced cheekbones were new, as were the toothy grin, the pulsing, throbbing veins on each temple, and, of course, the huge, bushy beard and the long hair. More silver than black his hair and beard fell to his diaphragm, where his soul lay, dry, warm and intact. The man in the mirror both was and wasn't him but, if he was being honest, Fingal was quite pleased with the transformation. The image was strong and true. It was real. It was him, and, for what he intended, it would do.

"Who are you?" asked Fingal.

"I am you."

"No," said Fingal, "Really."

The reflection smiled. "I am reality."

"Oh."

"Stop trembling, my love."

"Sorry."

314

"Everything is ok," the image said. "I am here now."

Fingal frowned. "Why did you take so long to show up?"

"Because you did not want to see me, Brother. You had many paths to walk."

"Which I did."

"Yes, with courage."

Fingal frowned deeper. He had so many questions. "And what of The Experiment?"

"What of it?"

"What did it actually prove?"

The reflection smiled. "That it's easiest to be the wisest man on an island built for one."

"Or the maddest."

"The real challenge for a human is—"

"...is to fit in. To get along, or try to get along, with all the madness; out there."

"That is correct," the mirror said in a smooth, mellifluous voice. "The challenge for every human is to accept, not to escape."

Real Fingal nodded his head. "The wise accept humanity for what it is, warts 'n' all. They fit in, somehow. They eventually find their place as a tiny cog in the great industrial machine of society, even if they hate the fucking machine."

"Now, we're getting somewhere."

But, again, the doubt, the tears suddenly returned; tears of frustration. "The book!" Fingal cried. "All that work. All those dreams! Hours, stones, sorry days, weeks and months, wasted, man. Totally wasted. Fuck!" Fingal screamed then calmed his breathing. "So, tell me, now we're at the end, what the *fuck* was that shit book all about, eh?"

"An excuse." The reflection picked its nose. "Just an excuse for a grown man to sit on his arse, drink, and smoke to his heart's content"

"It was an excuse to hide, wasn't it?"

"Yes, my dear." The image's deep, wise eyes danced with mirth. "An excuse to pretend to be anyone but yourself."

"Fang?"

"He was you, my love. They were all you. They are all you."

Both men peed in the sink.

"Oh," Fingal said, after a while, trying to be casual, and still trying to lie to himself. "Meant to ask. I still love The One, don't I?"

"No," the reflection said with absolute certainty. "You do not."

"But I think about her all the time. I dream about her! I wrote about her. In the book!"

"Which was an epic concoction of utter shite."

"But The One was Miss Lucy Pendergrass, she was the heroine, she was—"

"Mate," the mirror wisely interrupted. "It is impossible to love a cunt."

"You're right, by jingo"

"By jingo?"

"It's from the book."

"Of shite."

The rope was straining, desperate to snap, but the pain still hurt, and again, he thought of Fraser The Cunt banging The One in their plush, four-bedroom granite house in Aberdeen. "But they have everything." Fingal began to sob. "Flash cars, good jobs, nice flats, plush sofas. Each other! In fact, I bet you Fraser does her on a Chesterfield."

"Probably."

Fingal ignored the jibe. It was too obvious. He went back to being a selfish, petulant idiot. "And what do I have?" he wailed. "Nothing. NOTHING!!!"

"Like Dr Usui, Cob."

Fingal dried his eyes. "What?"

"Mate," the mirror smiled. "You have nothing, don't you see? You're the richest man on the planet."

He did not. The rope held firm. "But I wanted her. Her! THE ONE! THE ONE!"

The man in the mirror waited for the moaning and groaning to stop, then held up two long, white and skinny hands. "Listen, mate. Forget about that stupid slut. If she had really loved you she wouldn't have hurt you. She would've taken you back."

"Given me a second chance."

"All you need to know now is that The One was – and remains – a total, utter, consummate CUNT. Aristophanes was right, Fingal. Weak people's souls are like his Androgyne; they're always looking for their other half. Crutches are for cripples, pal." The mirror smiled like Buddha. "You see, my dear friend, The One was a Crippled Cunt who found another Crippled Cunt. You're far mightier, far better, than two cunts."

And that was it. That was all it took for the second last big rope to go SNAP.

"I'm no cripple," Fingal said with pride.

"You are a mighty brush box, immovable in a storm."

"Man," Fingal snorted a laugh, "I could've married a CUNT."

"You dodged a bullet, man."

"Thank you, Mirror Fingal. You are so wise."

The image flicked its chin. "I know."

Again, they stared at each other for a while, staring deeply into each other's souls, laughing and smiling, shouting sudden things like AAARRGGGH at each other, picking stubborn bits of parrot seed from their ruined teeth, stroking their beards, squeezing their blackheads, and kissing each other.

After some time, Fingal popped the big question. "Mr Image," he said politely. "Sixty-four-million-dollar question. I have to ask. Was *she* real? Mother, I mean?"

"That is up to us to decide."

"But, I need to know."

"I know."

"So," Fingal said after a while, "what do we do now? Go and visit Andrew McKenzie, Esquire, to say thanks? Go home? Kill ourselves?"

"See your arms, my friend. Don't look them. *See* them." Fingal did. They were white and skinny and covered in lots and lots of dark, purple spots, like track marks from a man that has used too much heroin. "What do you *see*?"

"I see scars from tick bites."

"Ha." The reflection laughed. "You're still so negative, man. They're not *scars*. What do you *see*?"

"I see love bites." The men's wild blue eyes, like their hearts, surged open. "I see trophies! I see badges of honour! I see gifts! I see stripes, not suffering!"

"That's right, *Mister* explorer."

Both men grinned like crazed daemons.

"I don't believe it!" said the real Fingal.

"Believe it," the man in the mirror said, his voice smooth as honey. "You have read Her all wrong. What has She done to you, really? A bit – well, a lot – of rain, one snake attack (which was our own fault), half a dozen plagues of mice, ticks and leeches, and, well, that's about the sum of things."

"Yes, yes," babbled the real Fingal with a sense of rising excitement. "That's nothing compared to the higher lover Mother has shown our lost Tribe of Mad Scotsmen."

"She loves us, man; like, really, really loves us."

"Does She? Really?

"Abso-fuckin'-lutely, Brother."

Real Fingal thought for a while. His right eye began to twitch, he spluttered a laugh, and said "The Experiment's not over, is it?"

"Far from it, Sage Hermit. She is waiting for you."

"I know." Fingal stamped his bad ankle a few times. It was still painful but would hold. It would do. He would do. The two men looked at each other.

"So what do I do?"

"You know what to do. You've always known what to do."

"Cut the rope."

"*Your* rope, my love."

The Final Day

"Burn," said Fingal the following morning, as he tossed the last of the vile factory issue desk and chair into the fireplace. "Burn, you bastard."

"Are you ready to cut, my love?"

"Almost."

"Good, Precious One," he continued, talking to himself. "We need to be able to see the light, no?"

"Yes, we do," Fingal agreed.

He really wasn't sure about this cutting thing. Did he really need to cut his *self,* his *rope,* or was it *ropes?* They were vital to him. They *were* him, surely?

"When have we been sure about anything?" he pondered aloud.

This much was true. "You have to be able to see, mate. Look at the fucking state of you, man. You're a mess! You can't go and meet Her like this!" Also, true. "Cut your ropes, man. How else you supposed to see Her?" *Very* true.

"Very true," said Fingal.

He picked up the Swiss Army knife, and turned it over in his hand, approving of its razor-sharp blade glimmering in the orange firelight.

"Go on. Do it."

"Don't chicken out now."

"Do it. Cut them! You know you want to."

Sick of yet another debate, Fingal grabbed a bunch of his long silver and black hair and began to slice it off, working the blade close to his scalp but careful not to draw more blood. Mother only knew he'd suffered and bled enough.

It took a good hour of careful slicing, hacking and shaving, but soon the hermit's temple was as bald as bandicoot. To celebrate, Bald Fingal lobbed his hair on the fire and recoiled at the acrid smoke. It stunk of greed, ego and desire. It reeked of the book. His big, bushy beard went next, sliced and shaved, sizzling like soiled pubic hair on top of the burning remains of a chair that near broke his back.

Fingal ran his thin, strong hands over his bare skull and jaw, feeling that much lighter in terms of weight, burden and mood, vindicated that what he was about to do made absolute sense.

Scotland could wait for a day.

He had to know.

***

Most continentals would think the experimentalist mad for going for a nice, long walk in a category 5 cyclone called Barry, but (all together now) what the fuck did those crippled, materialistic arseholes know? Nada. Rien. Sweet fuck all.

Fingal now realised that going for a nice walk in a cyclone was the only way The Experiment would ever finish, the only way he could return to Scotland with a clear conscience, the only way of knowing that, in fifteen years of travelling and searching for meaning, the end of the road had been well and truly reached. "I need to know," the mad ape repeated in front of the small but magnificent fire, ignoring the cyclone for now, rocking back and forth, and drawing strength from the heat washing over his clear, bald head, face and jaw.

Events on the island were also drawing to a close. Hours ago now, the last of the goon and the final amazing, disgusting cigarette had been respectively drunk and smoked. Andrew's food was almost done too. Crutches, distractions and sedatives, none of this was required for the last and final phase of the John Donne Experiment.

Where Fingal McKay was going, drugs and food were not necessary.

At last, the fire died, and the last pilgrim rose to packed his last bag. Carefully, reverentially, he placed four items inside: one boiled egg, one banana, a lovely white rope left to him by a man called Decent Old Col, and, finally, and most importantly, the ticket: the nudey postcard Col had sent Fingal from his last cruise.

This, Fingal wrapped in cellophane, to keep it dry.

"Sacrifices," Fingal said when all was done, not sure if he meant the food, or the ticket, or himself. It didn't matter. He needed to know.

"Let us walk, brothers," the bald man said as the wind howled outside and, again, another massive branch clattered off the tin roof above him. The little blue cottage shuddered. The man did not. "Hold your horses, Mother," he said with a roll of his eyes. She was always like this. "I'm coming. We're coming. We're all coming."

Fingal McKay, explorer, lover, and sole parishioner of the Church of the Mighty Strangler Fig, gritted his remaining teeth, kicked open the French windows, and stepped outside into a cyclone called Barry.

***

The world lay in tatters. It was impossible to know where the earth finished and heaven began. The clouds were the land, and the land, the clouds. In addition to the 690 millimetres of rain that fell over the last two days, 280 mm fell that morning alone. No wonder the Old People used to call the national park Warrie. In the old tongue, the word meant "rushing water". But, to Fingal, the silver water was a good sign. It washed away the leeches.

Ten minutes later, the explorer stood at the head of the fire trail. Visibility – rain, debris, and more rain – were poor, very poor; no more than ten metres, at best. Cyclone Barry was totally peaking out. Winds gusts of 170 kilometres whored in from the ocean, tugging and bending and straining the trees on either side of the fire trail. Just to remind them who was really in charge, the wind flattened the young, pompous trees, and ripped limbs from the humbler ones. But, thought Fingal as he stepped gingerly onto the trail, at least the wind blew away all the ticks.

Amidst the elemental anarchy, the tiny figure limped down the fire trail, taking his time, enjoying it all, drinking it all in; comforting the trees that had lost limbs or loved ones; strolling almost, as if he and Col were out for walk on a pleasant summer evening.

His bald head was held high, and his wild blue eyes were wider than ever as they overdosed on the cataclysmic beauty of an extreme Australian weather event – nature at its truest; the world laid bare. The peak of a cyclone, like the crescendo of Rachmaninoff #3.

Fingal McKay had never felt more alive.

His plan "to know" was simple if somewhat typically impractical, lovely, and quite unusual. Armed with Decent Old Col's magical rope, Fingal would try to reach the world-famous Cathedral Falls with all his heart and spirit and might. If Mother let him in, or down, rather, then She was real and the past two years of his life hadn't been a monumental, drunken waste of time. On the other hand, if the Almighty Strangler Fig refused him entry, or if She hurt him, or worse, killed him, then She was indeed a myth, a figment of his mad imagination. At last, Fingal McKay would know if she was real or not. He would also know that, if he died, at least he died trying.

He didn't want to die like most men, in a pub or brothel, or on a golf course, or behind the wheel of car, or in a hospital, or boardroom. Continental deaths were so boring. He wanted to go out in style, riding on the edge of madness. *Cunt Rode on the Edge of Madness*. Yes, he decided, that would be his epitaph. In fact, this last wish of Fingal McKay was written into his last will and testament which he'd stuffed into Andrew's letter box not twenty minutes' prior.

This desire for a heroic death wasn't the main force driving the explorer into the storm, however. It was a much simpler desire that pushed the man on. Fingal just wanted to see his Mother, one last time.

***

"The world has no skin," he said, bracing against the ferocious wind.

This was also true. The fire trail had turned into a wide, silver river, three inches deep and four metres wide. The footing, the grip, however, was excellent. Barry's pissing rain and new river had eroded the layer of slippery, red clay from a trail he'd recently crawled home on. Remarkably, Fingal's magnificent Scarpa walking boots strode across a riverbed of clean, white gravel.

To the sole parishioner, it was a miracle.

The trail also ran close to the edge of Binjari plateau. One or two hundred metres to the left, the land fell sharply away. The ridge acted like the spoiler on a car, funnelling the worst of the furious easterly up and over the only worshiper in the temple on that wild, stunning day. "Sing, Mother!" Fingal shouted and laughed. "I hear you! The islanders hear you. We're coming."

Step by step, the loner picked his way through the devastation of Cyclone Barry and, after an hour or two – time really no longer mattered – made it to Python Gate, wet, soaking wet, but safe and sound. "Can you *see* us, Mother? May we come in?" Fingal kissed the top of the barrel of the snake's den, peered inside, and, as a peace offering, lobbed in the banana and egg. "Mr Snake, once more, I apologise profusely for trying to kidnap you, and for peeing in your house, but I was writing a book, you see. I was mad, back then, blinded by ego and hair and a man called Fang. Love and respect," Fingal added and plunged into the forest, swearing that the rain was easing.

The descent was challenging, to say the least. Walking into the tail end of a cyclone, into the wind, as it were, and with a dodgy ankle, Fingal often had to lean forward in the manner of a ski-jumper, or hobble under new waterfalls, or scramble and crawl across fresh orange landslips, or squirm through the canopies of fallen trees. If all got too intense, when the flurries of leaves, bark, rain and earth blinded him, he closed his eyes, muttered the Explorer's Motto – "Love and respect" – and groped and *felt* his way toward Mother, working by intuition, by faith in a track that was as familiar as breath.

"I swear that wind *is* dying," said Fingal, two hours later when the land began to flatten out. This much was also true. The wind had dropped. It was no longer a stupendous fart blown out Barry's backside, but a steady, howling gale.

Mother, he swore, had seized ownership of the wind.

Not everything was all fine and dandy. When, for instance, the pilgrim reached Crack Addict's Crossing, it was no longer a sweet, little creek. It had transformed into a big, wide river that was easily ten metres wide and running fast.

Fingal had to know. So strong was his commitment the final phase of The Experiment, as well as his renewed sense of faith, he refused to let any doubt enter his smooth, calm mind. "Onwards," he cried and boldly waded, staggered, fell, sank, and swam to the other side, emerging a good two hundred metres downstream.

"Pilgrims must be clean before meeting their Goddess," he said with a shake and a wild, crazy smile. "You know how picky She can be." While clambering back up to the track, Fingal's spirits began to soar. On a good day, the massive tree he reckoned was God grew but half an hour away. Lover and lover would soon be reunited. As further good portent, he looked up and saw that the clouds overhead were no longer static, black and cerebral. They were high, silver and moving fast.

"Onwards, you magnificent mad-bastard. Ya, ape. YA!"

Fingal hobbled on through the pillars of the old growth plateau, the giant columns which supported the ceiling of his vast rainforest temple. A strong wind ripped at their crowns but the enormous, antique trees barely moved. The stoics didn't bend, thrash or tremble like the younger gums. Instead, the mighty brush box, black booyongs, and tall, slender ghost gums laughed, honked and, in true Australian passive-aggressive fashion, taunted Barry:

"Call yourself a bloody cyclone!"

"Don't you blokes worry, the real one will be here soon."

"It'll pass. All things must pass."

"Is it just me, or is it a little bit windy today?"

"Powder room's open soon, Bazza."

Thousands of years old, and having lived and prospered through hundreds of storms, the massive trees rode out Cyclone Barry with irreverence, wisdom and an iron will.

They'd seen worse. They weren't for budging, *mate.*

"I swear the weather is breaking up," said Fingal a second before he tripped and fell. Thankfully, because – whoooooomp! – an epiphyte, a staghorn the size of a tinnie, crashed onto the trail but five metres in front.

Again, he smiled. "She knows I'm here."

Fingal got to his feet and barrelled on, staggering as fast as his bad ankle would allow, half-hobbling, half-running toward Her. "Children," he said on recognising a young, grey limpet tree attacking a pink rosewood, the first and youngest evidence of Mother's thuggish brood. He began to cry. "I'm coming! I'm coming, Mother!" So desperate to behold Her, to hold her, poor, mad, bald Fingal tripped once more. When he looked up She was there.

Of course, She was there. Where else would She have gone?

Mother towered above the prostrate worshipper. Her crown sheltered her friend from the rain. A huge buttress, three metres in height, protected him from the dying wind. Her massive, twisting, black-green trunk stood firm, and only the ferns, bromeliads and orchids that cloaked Her arms showed any form of duress, rattling like party streamers in a wind tunnel. Fingal stood, burst into tears, and embraced the massive fig tree, his tree. The world stopped turning, and life was no longer a riddle to be solved but a great mystery to behold.

"Mother," he said with great drama. "It is heavenly to see you."

After a while, Fingal dried his eyes and removed Col's nudey postcard from his pack. This, he placed in a hollow in her trunk, and stepped back so he could gaze up into Her enigmatic crown. "Mother," he said, very seriously. "I know we've had our ups and downs. I know I didn't see you for a while but that was Fang's fault. My fault. But, I need to know." The tree said nothing. "Please, Mother. I need to go home but, before I leave you, before I leave Australia, could you please just let me have a little look at your world-famous Cathedral Falls? Just a wee sticky beak?"

Mother said and did nothing but, Barry – good ol' Bazza – eased his wind back to 100 kilometres per hour and, incredibly, turned his shower down a bit. Taking this as an obvious sign, Fingal then calmly removed Decent Old Col's white rope, and stilled his breathing by remembering that what he was about to do simply had to be done.

A simple man, a man with only one desire left, Fingal gave Mother a big kiss and strode past the Goddess he hoped, no, he felt, spoke to him and him alone.

**

The Scotsman soon stood next to the broken YOU WILL PROBABLY DIE!! national park sign on top of the cliff where the trail ended. He ignored the stupid, paranoid sign, and got to work, tying, cursing, and re-tying one end of the rope around a sturdy Myrtle Beech. The knot was pathetic, a sort of triple-shoe-lace-thing.

"Aye," Fingal joked, "you never did get that knot-tying badge at the Scouts, but, fuck it, it'll hold. You'll hold." The rock climber then tested the rope, stroked his phantom-beard, and flung the remainder over the white coil out over the edge of the cliff.

Fingal didn't dare stop to admire the chaos ravaging the deep forest in the abyss below. Doing so would have stirred all the continental shite he'd worked so hard to abandoned over the past few years – doubt, panic, laziness, and good old-fashioned fear. "She'll be right," said Fingal, lifting Col's lovely white rope, taking the strain and, without a thought, backing out over the edge of the cliff.

As he descended, grip wasn't the problem. Due to all the typing, writing and rolling of cigarettes, his hands, particularly his right clawhand, griped the rope in the manner of a vice. Nor was doubt an issue. For once, Fingal's mind was entirely focussed on the job at hand. To him, this precise moment in time was why he had been put on earth. The spirit of the man who built Heroin Castle ran through his veins, as did a clausewitzian sense of decisiveness, a feeling that a great battle was hurtling toward its inevitable conclusion.

Barry was running out of puff, anger and energy.

He lumbered westward, and his fickle breath eased back to seventy-five kilometres per hour.

Logic also prevailed in Fingal's mind. Even though maths had never been his strong point, from previous dreams, explorations and calculations, Fingal knew that the drop to the little staircase leading the Falls had to be no more than eighty foot. Col's rope was one-hundred-foot-long, ten of which had been used for the triple-shoelace-knot-thing, and he stood exactly six foot tall. The numbers added up, in other words. The math made sense.

Then, at last, at bloody long last, the rain stopped falling in Binjari national park for the first time in fifty days.

Fingal didn't notice. The real danger was strength. A couple of days of good tucker, fires, rest, and an epic shave and haircut could hardly vanquish two years of sitting at a desk, eating bread, smoking fags and drinking goon. The experimentalist realised this about forty feet down Col's rope when the muscles in his shoulders began to ache and quiver. Stupidly, he looked down and rivers of doubt began pouring through the corridors of his fragile mind. The drop was much bigger than he thought! He was shit at maths; totally shit! It *was* a cyclone! What was he doing in the bush! He was Scottish, not Australian!

"Fuck," he hissed and tried to climb back up but there was no fuel left in the tank. Suddenly his knees collapsed and the wind ripped him from the cliff and sent him spinning in the air. Clutching the rope for dear life, his legs flailed until, at last, his trusty boots found purchase on the disintegrating cliff face. "It's all right, mate," he said through clenched teeth, trying to keep the spirits up. "Love and respect. Love and respect. Love and respect."

Stupidly, again, Fingal looked down but all he could see was rain, clouds, mud, rock, and, far below, the canopy of the deep forest waving its pompoms up at the great ape dangling on the rope. The top of the trees could be ten, twenty, fifty foot below. It was impossible to tell. "I hate maths," Fingal said. There was no sense of earth or rock below, no mass, only air and water, and wind and space. "Where's the fucking ground!?"

Suddenly the hermit's grip faltered, he fell and the rope whizzed through his hands, badly scorching his thenar (the web of skin between thumb and forefinger). *No, Mother, no*, thought Fingal, his hands desperately feeling for and clasping at the rope, blessing the knot Decent Old Col had tied in the end when he eventually stopped falling. Somehow, he clung on but, again, his body swung out then battered into a muddy waterfall full of sticks and leaves and rocks.

The hermit was totally fucked. There was no way up.

Down was the only choice, a proverbial leap – or drop – of faith, in a tree, in a rainforest. One choice. One rope. One man.

This precise moment made total sense to Fingal McKay. Perilously close to death or, at least, serious fucking injury, the hermit did not feel any fear. Delusional, perhaps, weak and exhausted, yes, but his faith burned strong. Dangling and spinning at the end of Col's rope, he knew in his heart of hearts that Mother would look after him.

He was fed up with darkness anyway.

It was time to see the light.

Expending the last of his energy, eyes squeezed shut with exertion, Fingal pulled himself up into a sort of inverted plank position and was about to let go but incredibly – amazingly, un-fuckin'-believably – the sun, the mother-fucking sun, erupted from behind the tail of Barry's furious cape.

The brilliant dying star made a typical, dramatic entrance to Fingal's story, bathing the damp, grey world in warm, bright sunshine. Her light found Col's lovely rope. It poured down the rope and covered the Scotsman's straining hands, arms and muddy and bleeding face in a mask of golden triumph. All of a sudden, Fingal McKay was King Agamemnon.

His eyes flared open and, at last, he let go of the last rope. A smile spread across his golden mask as he fell backwards to the forest, and a fate Mother would soon decree.

***

They say a lot can happen after death. A human brain, for example, can keep doing its thing for a good five or six minutes after the heart has stopped beating. This is why some people brought back from death speak of miraculous visions full of bizarre lights.

Lifetimes can also be lived, won or lost in but a microsecond of time, just ask anyone who's fallen asleep behind the wheel of a speeding motor vehicle, king-hit a bloke, or fell over the lip of a huge wave knowing that the Ocean Gods will most certainly fuck them up.

Seconds matter in the great game of life.

A man's life can flash before his eyes, and all that sort of continental jazz.

Not quite for our protagonist. As Fingal fell toward the canopy, no Hollywood reel flickered in the cinema of his mad, tripping brain. Three stark, noteworthy events, however, bear fleeting mention.

First, the flying Scotsman saw his island. It had not been nuked by a fifty-seven megaton hydrogen bomb called Ivy Mike, just obfuscated by the final days of pain, and the apparent failure of the John Donne Experiment. Fingal's island sanctuary, his retreat – a place Aurelius, writing in 273 A.D., noted should "wash away all your pain and send you back free of resentment at what you must rejoin" – still existed. What's more, Fingal had never seen the old girl looking more beautiful; more complete.

All the commodious factory buildings were there – the Industries for Science, Defence and Writing. They were part of him now, fresh and bright as the day they were initially conceived.

His beloved, little, blue castle nestled in the forest by the beach, which was full of little Fingals born in the two years spent dreaming in the rainforest (mainly, there were two types: soldiers dancing to hard-core, Dutch techno pulsing from *Fanni's Vulgar Discotheque*, and labourers sucking on huge, silver sacks of goon and smoking enormous rollies, partying like there was no tomorrow, because, at this rate, there wouldn't be).

The Professor was there! That dear, old radge clinked a flagon of goon with 277 before he returned to his latest experiment: drowning John Donne in a giant, red bucket of phlegm. Fingal's penis was there too, jumping around the place, trying to shag everything and anything. And, by Mother, Fang was there too, shouting at and whipping a rock to death for, well, not rocking enough.

Offshore, whales, turtles and dolphins frolicked in the turquoise waters, and, in the huge, green forests dense swarms of Jackiebirds feasted on clouds of toxin-free VAGFs. The butcherbirds flew in great clouds that soon formed a massive arrow pointing to the summit of Mt Fingal, a lone peak whose rock twisted like the trunk of an ancient strangler fig. On the summit stood a monstrous golden statue of Mother and a small, hairy man staring up in awe.

Amazingly, there were no more fucking ropes. Having just let go of the last, and biggest one – desire – the Island of Fingal McKay was finally free of the continent of man. Unfettered, it rode high on a vast, silver ocean.

Damn it, the architect thought while falling to his certain death, John-fucking-Donne *was* wrong. Fingal McKay was an island after all.

Second, the doomed experimentalist realised something amazing. Although present circumstances were less than ideal he was finally alone, totally and utterly alone. No one knew what he was up to or where he was, albeit falling toward a deep forest where no humans had ever visited.

His life, he now knew, was as gloriously insignificant as a lone cicada flying up from the deep forest.

At last, Fingal saw himself for what he truly was – not a human, nor a hermit, but a speck of insignificant matter falling through an ever-expanding universe, a cold, black and beautifully silent realm.

Third, reality bit, or, more accurately slapped, kicked and punched. Fingal was suddenly in a car wash, a large and violent one with jade pompoms, very cold water, and the odd iron bar that thumped into his thighs, shoulders and arse, slowing his fall as he crashed through the ceiling of Mother's gracious if brutal canopy.

Then, he felt air, clean, golden air – for a second – before the fall was finally arrested by a mound of leaf-litter fifteen foot in height. The brush turkey's nest absorbed all the physics of the hermit's first and last rainforest flight.

Fingal McKay lay perfectly still.

For a while.

The explorer wiggled his toes, then his fingers, and blinked his eyes wide open. Fingal assumed he was in heaven. Shards of sunlight pierced the canopy, drops of golden water plipped and plopped from the exhausted trees, and wave after wave of bizarre, honeyed birdsong drifted between the ancient pillars of Her divine temple.

Heaven on Earth.

'Straya.

"Fuckin' hell," said the island-builder extraordinaire when Mother had yanked him upright.

Thinking his legs had to be broken, the Scotstralian (a term suddenly popular on the island) was amazed that, despite trembling with adrenalin, after such a fall both columns held fine. Pelvis, spine, arms, neck, balls, and other vital shit? Intact.

"Mother be praised," the rainforest zealot said in awe.

In fact, the only serious injury from the epic fall was to his writing hand. Middle, ring and pinky finger were bent, twisted things, a mangled claw, Ver. 2.0. Oh, and half his left ear was missing, but the misophonic hermit would most certainly not that miss dreadful device. "Passport to the big boys' club," he said, thinking of van Gogh and what beautiful islands that mad bastard must have seen.

Fingal looked up to see a passage back to Donne's continent, an escape. A tall flooded gum felled by the cyclone leaned casually against the cliff at a forty-five-degree angle. Decent Old Col's lovely white rope was snagged in its crown.

Higher still, Mother peered down at her only worshipper. She was no longer green but pure gold. "I KNEW IT!" shouted Fingal, his heart bursting with ecstasy at the love of a strangler fig, at the madness and beauty of a life lived on a little, blue planet. "I KNEW YOU WERE REAL! I LOVE YOU, MOTHER! IN THE HIGHER FASHION!"

***

Fingal McKay, guru, understood what the crazy journey meant, for him anyway (you can find your own strangler fig, thank you very much). He had not found the higher love in Scotland or, as he and his all-conquering penis

331

had once thought, in the arms of some fine lassie. Like Ian Fairweather, the mad, lovely Scottish-Australian artist, or Alexander Selkirk (the Scot that the Robinson Crusoe character was based off), Fingal McKay had found true love in a wild, brutal and gorgeous sub-tropical Australian rainforest 16,000 miles south and east from the country of his birth. It was a bizarre realisation for a man who thought his skin had once been woven from tartan.

There was no time to celebrate any of this, however.

A deep roar seized the sole parishioner's attention. Far louder than a hundred continental jet engines, the awesome roar came from deep in the woods, two, maybe three kilometres away. It was the roar of millions of litres of white, pure water coursing off the Binjari plateau. It was the roar of Mother's world-famous Cathedral Falls.

The ascent to the blue cottage could wait. Home could wait. The world could wait. Getting back up wouldn't be a problem anyway, because the lost man who had just fallen deeply in love with Australia now knew that he could fly. In addition, turning back would be such a continental thing to do, such a cowardly, European manner of behaviour.

More importantly, Fingal McKay was not alone. Two metres to the left, an invisible bird had materialised on a branch. It was a humble brush turkey, and he was absolutely livid.

No wonder. The turkey had spent the last year diligently raking dead leaves into the biggest, sexiest mound in the deep forest. Then, after enduring fifty days of rain, and a bloody cyclone, some great ape had chosen that precise moment to fall from the sky and destroy his life's work. The turkey's black, cosmic eyes were incredulous.

"Mate," the bird said, "you wrecked me bleedin' nest!"

"What's your name?" Fingal asked, smiling like Buddha.

"Me name? Fuck's that got to do with anything?"

"It's Barry, isn't it?"

"Bazza, *actually*."

"Of course, it is. I love you, Bazza."

"Rack off, poof!"

Fingal laughed, spat blood, and gazed around the deep forest.

He knew he'd see them, two of them, waltzing in and out the huge trees, appearing then disappearing. Flickering, they were moving in the general direction of the Falls. Two of them, two friends – Colin Jarvis, a handsome young bloke with his shirt off, and, on his arm, a beautiful woman in a red dress smoking a cigarette, his soon-to-be wife, Mary.

Fingal almost called out but decided to follow the loving couple at a respectful distance.

Besides, the scrub chook was irate. "Where do you think you're going, *mate*?"

"To Her world-famous Cathedral Falls, of course," Fingal called out over a bruised and bleeding shoulder. "There is work to be done. Don't you see, my dear Bazza? The Experiment's only just begun."

"Bloody typical," the turkey noted. His obscene yellow wattle trembled with passive aggression. "That's what you apes do best, isn't it? Go on, then! Run away, *mate*!"

Fingal McKay, man, stopped and turned. "Mate, I've never ran away from anything in my life." His smile was wide, golden and completely sunburnt. "I walk, and only towards beauty."

Lightning Source UK Ltd.
Milton Keynes UK
UKHW04f0614231018
331030UK00001B/240/P